Praise for Michael Connelly

'*Two Kinds of Truth* is vintage Connelly'   *USA Today*

'It is testament to Connelly's skill as a storyteller that the twentieth novel in this bestselling series still feels fresh and relevant. The world-weary yet tough Bosch has been given a new lease of life in retirement – 5*'   *Express*

'Harry Bosch is a one-of-a-kind hero'   *New York Times*

'*Two Kinds of Truth* is a well-written and interesting crime thriller that exposes the all-too-real crime of pill mills and illegal prescription drug addiction'   *Washington Post*

'A master of the genre'   Stephen King

'Harry Bosch is one of American crime fiction's great detect-ives'   *Irish Times*

'Crime thriller writing of the highest order'   *Guardian*

'*Two Kinds of Truth* is as brilliant as anything Connelly has written'   *Evening Standard*

'Connelly is a crime writing genius' *Independent on Sunday*

Also by Michael Connelly

A former police reporter for the *Los Angeles Times*, Michael Connelly is the internationally bestselling author of the Harry Bosch thriller series. The TV tie-in series – *Bosch* – is one of the most watched original series on Amazon Prime and is now in its fourth season. He is also the author of several bestsellers, including the highly acclaimed legal thriller, *The Lincoln Lawyer*, which was selected for the Richard & Judy Book Club in 2006, and has been President of the Mystery Writers of America. His books have been translated into thirty-nine languages and have won awards all over the world, including the Edgar and Anthony Awards. He spends his time in California and Florida.

To find out more, visit Michael's website or follow him on Twitter or Facebook.

www.michaelconnelly.com
@Connellybooks
/MichaelConnellyBooks

MICHAEL CONNELLY

TWO KINDS OF TRUTH

ORION

An Orion paperback

First published in Great Britain in 2017
by Orion Books
This paperback edition published in 2018
by Orion Books,
an imprint of The Orion Publishing Group Ltd,
Carmelite House, 50 Victoria Embankment
London EC4Y 0DZ

An Hachette UK company

5 7 9 10 8 6 4

A CIP catalogue record for this book
is available from the British Library.

ISBN 978 1 4091 4759 6

Typeset by Input Data Services Ltd, Somerset

Printed in Great Britain by Clays Ltd, Elcograf S.p.A.

MIX
Paper from
responsible sources
FSC® C104740

www.orionbooks.co.uk

For Heather Rizzo.
Thanks for the title and everything else.

PART ONE
Cappers

1

Bosch was in cell 3 of the old San Fernando jail, looking through files from one of the Esme Tavares boxes, when a heads-up text came in from Bella Lourdes over in the detective bureau.

> LAPD and DA heading your way. Trevino told them where you are.

Bosch was where he was at the start of most weeks: sitting at his makeshift desk, a wooden door he had borrowed from the Public Works yard and placed across two stacks of file boxes. After sending Lourdes a thank-you text, he opened the memo app on his phone and turned on the recorder. He put the phone screen-down on the desk and partially covered it with a file from the Tavares box. It was a just-in-case move. He had no idea why people from the District Attorney's Office and his old police department were coming to see him first thing on a Monday morning. He had not received a call alerting him to the visit, though to be fair, cellular connection within the steel bars of the cell was virtually nonexistent. Still, he knew that the surprise visit was often a tactical move. Bosch's relationship with the LAPD since his forced retirement three years earlier had been strained at best and his attorney had urged him to protect himself by documenting all interactions with the department.

While he waited for them, he went back to the file at hand. He was looking through statements taken in the weeks after Tavares had disappeared. He had read them before but he believed that the case files often contained the secret to cracking a cold case. It was all there if you could find it. A logic discrepancy, a hidden clue, a contradictory statement, an investigator's handwritten note in the margin of a report – all of these things had helped Bosch clear cases in a career four decades long and counting.

There were three file boxes on the Tavares case. Officially it was a missing-persons case but it had gathered three feet of stacked files over fifteen years because it was classified as such only because a body had never been found.

When Bosch came to the San Fernando Police Department to volunteer his skills looking at cold case files, he had asked Chief Anthony Valdez where to start. The chief, who had been with the department twenty-five years, told him to start with Esmerelda Tavares. It was the case that had haunted Valdez as an investigator, but as police chief he could not give adequate time to it.

In two years working in San Fernando part-time, Bosch had reopened several cases and closed nearly a dozen – multiple rapes and murders among them. But he came back to Esme Tavares whenever he had an hour here and there to look through the file boxes. She was beginning to haunt him too. A young mother who vanished, leaving a sleeping baby in a crib. It might be classified as a missing-persons case but Bosch didn't have to read through even the first box to know what the chief and every investigator before him knew. Foul play was most likely involved. Esme Tavares was more than missing. She was dead.

Bosch heard the metal door to the jail wing open and then footsteps on the concrete floor that ran in front of the three group cells. He looked up through the iron bars and was surprised by who he saw.

'Hello, Harry.'

It was his former partner, Lucia Soto, along with two men in suits whom Bosch didn't recognize. The fact that Soto had apparently not let him know they were coming put Bosch on alert. It was a forty-minute drive from both the LAPD's headquarters and the D.A.'s Office downtown to San Fernando. That left plenty of time to type out a text and say, 'Harry, we are heading your way.' But that hadn't happened, so he assumed that the two men whom he didn't know had put the clamps on Soto.

'Lucia, long time,' Bosch said. 'How are you, partner?'

It looked like none of the three were interested in entering Bosch's cell, even if it had been repurposed. He stood up, deftly grabbing his phone from beneath the files on the desk and transferring it to his shirt pocket, placing the screen against his chest. He walked to the bars and stuck his hand through. Though he had talked to Soto intermittently by phone and text over the past couple of years he had not seen her. Her appearance had changed. She had lost weight and she looked drawn and tired, her dark eyes worried. Rather than shaking his hand, she squeezed it. Her grip was tight and he took that as a message: Be careful here.

5

It was easy for Bosch to figure out who was who between the two men. Both were in their early forties and dressed in suits that most likely came off the rack at Men's Wearhouse. But the man on the left's pinstripes were showing wear from the inside out. Bosch knew that meant he was wearing a shoulder rig beneath the jacket, and the hard edge of his weapon's slide was wearing through the fabric. Bosch guessed that the silk lining had already been chewed up. In six months the suit would be toast.

'Bob Tapscott,' he said. 'Lucky Lucy's partner now.'

Tapscott was black and Bosch wondered if he was related to Horace Tapscott, the late South L.A. musician who had been vital in preserving the community's jazz identity.

'And I'm Alex Kennedy, deputy district attorney,' said the second man. 'We'd like to talk to you if you have a few minutes.'

'Uh, sure,' Bosch said. 'Step into my office.'

He gestured toward the confines of the former cell now fitted with steel shelves containing case files. There was a long communal bench left over from the cell's previous existence as a drunk tank. Bosch had files from different cases lined up to review on the bench. He started stacking them to make room for his visitors to sit, even though he was pretty sure they wouldn't.

'Actually, we talked to your Captain Trevino, and he says we can use the war room over in the detective bureau,' Tapscott said. 'It will be more comfortable. Do you mind?'

'I don't mind if the captain doesn't mind,' Bosch said. 'What's this about anyway?'

6

'Preston Borders,' Soto said.

Bosch was walking toward the open door of the cell. The name put a slight pause in his step.

'Let's wait until we're in the war room,' Kennedy said quickly. 'Then we can talk.'

Soto gave Bosch a look that seemed to impart the message that she was under the D.A.'s thumb on this case. He grabbed his keys and the padlock off the desk, stepped out of the cell, and then slid the metal door closed with a heavy clang. The key to the cell had disappeared long ago and Bosch wrapped a bicycle chain around the bars and secured the door with the padlock.

They left the old jail and walked through the Public Works equipment yard out to First Street. While waiting for traffic to pass, Bosch casually pulled his phone out of his pocket and checked for messages. He had received nothing from Soto or anyone else prior to the arrival of the party from downtown. He kept the recording going and put the phone back in his pocket.

Soto spoke, but not about the case that had brought her up to San Fernando.

'Is that really your office, Harry?' she asked. 'I mean, they put you in a jail cell?'

'Yep,' Bosch said. 'That was the drunk tank and sometimes I think I can still smell the puke when I open it up in the morning. Supposedly five or six guys hung themselves in there over the years. Supposed to be haunted. But it's where they keep the cold case files, so it's where I do my work. They store old evidence boxes in the other two cells, so easy access all around. And usually nobody to bother me.'

7

He hoped the implication of the last line was clear to his visitors.

'So they have no jail?' Soto asked. 'They have to run bodies down to Van Nuys?'

Bosch pointed across the street to the police station they were heading toward.

'Only the women go down to Van Nuys,' Bosch said. 'We have a jail here for the men. In the station. State-of-the-art single cells. I've even stayed over a few times. Beats the bunk room at the PAB, with everybody snoring.'

She threw him a look as if to say he had changed if he was willing to sleep in a jail cell. He winked at her.

'I can work anywhere,' he said. 'I can sleep anywhere.'

When the traffic cleared, they crossed over to the police station and entered through the main lobby. The detective bureau had a direct entrance on the right. Bosch opened it with a key card and held the door as the others stepped in.

The bureau was no bigger than a single-car garage. At its center were three workstations tightly positioned in a single module. These belonged to the unit's three full-time detectives, Danny Sisto, a recently promoted detective named Oscar Luzon, and Bella Lourdes, just two months back from a lengthy injured-on-duty leave. The walls of the unit were lined with file cabinets, radio chargers, a coffee setup, and a printing station below bulletin boards covered in work schedules and departmental announcements. There were also numerous Wanted and Missing posters, including a variety showing photos of Esme Tavares that had been issued over a period of fifteen years.

Up high on one wall was a poster depicting the iconic Disney ducks Huey, Dewey, and Louie, which were the proud nicknames of the three detectives who worked in the module below. Captain Trevino's office was to the right and the war room was on the left. A third room was subleased to the Medical Examiner's Office and used by two coroner's investigators, who covered the entire San Fernando Valley and points north.

All three of the detectives were at their respective workstations. They had recently cracked a major car-theft ring operating out of the city, and an attorney for one of the suspects had derisively referred to them as Huey, Dewey, and Louie. They took the group nick-name as a badge of honor.

Bosch saw Lourdes peeking over a partition from her desk. He gave her a nod of thanks for the heads-up. It was also a sign that so far things were okay.

Bosch led the visitors into the war room. It was a soundproof room with walls lined with whiteboards and flat-screen monitors. At center was a boardroom-style table with eight leather chairs around it. The room was designed to be the command post for major crime investigations, task force operations, and coordinating responses to public emergencies such as earthquakes and riots. The reality was that such incidents were rare and the room was used primarily as a lunchroom, the broad table and comfortable chairs perfect for group lunches. The room carried the distinct odor of Mexican food. The owner of Magaly's Tamales up on Maclay Avenue routinely dropped off free food for the troops and it was usually devoured in the war room.

'Have a seat,' Bosch said.

Tapscott and Soto sat on one side of the table, while Kennedy went around and sat across from them. Bosch took a chair at one end of the table so he would have angles on all three visitors.

'So, what's going on?' he said.

'Well, let's properly introduce ourselves,' Kennedy began. 'You, of course, know Detective Soto from your work together in the Open-Unsolved Unit. And now you've met Detective Tapscott. They have been working with me on a review of a homicide case you handled almost thirty years ago.'

'Preston Borders,' Bosch said. 'How is Preston? Still on death row at the Q last time I checked.'

'He's still there.'

'So why are you looking at the case?'

Kennedy had pulled his chair close and had his arms folded and his elbows on the table. He drumrolled the fingers of his left hand as if deciding how to answer Bosch's question, even though it was clear that everything about this surprise visit was rehearsed.

'I am assigned to the Conviction Integrity Unit,' Kennedy said. 'I'm sure you've heard of it. I have used Detectives Tapscott and Soto on some of the cases I've handled because of their skill in working cold cases.'

Bosch knew that the CIU was new and had been put into place after he left the LAPD. Its formation was the fulfillment of a promise made during a heated election campaign in which the policing of the police was a hot-ticket debate issue. The newly elected D.A. – Tak Kobayashi – had promised to create a unit that would respond to the seeming groundswell of cases where new forensic technologies had led to hundreds of exonerations of people imprisoned across the country. Not only was new science leading the way, but old science once thought to be unassailable as evidence was being debunked and swinging open prison doors for the innocent.

As soon as Kennedy mentioned his assignment, Bosch put everything together and knew what was going on. Borders, the man thought to have killed three women but convicted of only one murder, was making a final grab at freedom after nearly thirty years on death row.

'You've gotta be kidding me, right?' Bosch said. 'Borders? Really? You are seriously looking at that case?'

He looked from Kennedy to his old partner Soto.

He felt totally betrayed.

'Lucia?' he said

'Harry,' she said. 'You need to listen.'

2

Bosch felt like the walls of the war room were closing in on him. In his mind and in reality, he had put Borders away for good. He didn't count on the sadistic sex murderer ever getting the needle, but death row was still its own particular hell, one that was harsher than any sentence that put a man in general population. The isolation of it was what Borders deserved. He went up to San Quentin as a twenty-six-year-old man. To Bosch that meant fifty-plus years of solitary confinement. Less only if he got lucky. More inmates died of suicide than the needle on death row in California.

'It's not as simple as you think,' Kennedy said.

'Really?' Bosch said. 'Tell me why.'

'The obligation of the Conviction Integrity Unit is to consider all legitimate petitions that come to it. Our review process is the first stage, and that happens in-house before the cases go to the LAPD or other law enforcement. When a case meets a certain threshold of concern, we go to the next step and call in law enforcement to carry out a due diligence investigation.'

'And of course everyone is sworn to secrecy at that point.'

Bosch looked at Soto as he said it. She looked away.

'Absolutely,' Kennedy said.

'I don't know what evidence Borders or his lawyer

brought to you, but it's bullshit,' Bosch said. 'He murdered Danielle Skyler and everything else is a scam.'

Kennedy didn't respond, but from his look Bosch could tell he was surprised he still remembered the victim's name.

'Yeah, thirty years later I remember her name,' Bosch said. 'I also remember Donna Timmons and Vicki Novotney, the two victims your office claimed we didn't have enough evidence to file on. Were they part of this due diligence you conducted?'

'Harry,' Soto said, trying to calm him.

'Borders didn't bring any new evidence,' Kennedy said. 'It was already there.'

That hit Bosch like a punch. He knew Kennedy was talking about the physical evidence from the case. The implication was that there was evidence from the crime scene or elsewhere that cleared Borders of the crime. The greater implication was incompetence or, worse, malfeasance – that Bosch had missed the evidence or intentionally withheld it.

'What are we talking about here?' he asked.

'DNA,' Kennedy said. 'It wasn't part of the original case in 'eighty-eight. The case was prosecuted before DNA was allowed into use in criminal cases in California. It wasn't introduced and accepted by a court up in Ventura for another year. In L.A. County it was a year after that.'

'We didn't need DNA,' Bosch said. 'We found the victim's property hidden in Borders's apartment.'

Kennedy nodded to Soto.

'We went to property and pulled the box,' she said. 'You know the routine. We took clothing collected from the victim to the lab and they put it through the serology protocol.'

'They did a protocol thirty years ago,' Bosch said. 'But back then, they looked for ABO genetic markers instead of DNA. And they found nothing. You're going to tell me that—'

'They found semen,' Kennedy said. 'It was a minute amount, but this time they found it. The process has obviously gotten more sophisticated since this killing. And what they found didn't come from Borders.'

Bosch shook his head.

'Okay, I'll bite,' he said. 'Whose was it?'

'A rapist named Lucas John Olmer,' Soto said.

Bosch had never heard of Olmer. His mind went to work, looking for the scam, the fix, but not considering that he had been wrong when he closed the cuffs around Borders's wrists.

'Olmer's in San Quentin, right?' he said. 'This whole thing is a—'

'No, he's not,' Tapscott said. 'He's dead.'

'Give us a little credit, Harry,' Soto added. 'It's not like we went looking for it to be this way. Olmer was never in San Quentin. He died in Corcoran back in twenty fifteen and he never knew Borders.'

'We've checked it six ways from Sunday,' Tapscott said. 'The prisons are three hundred miles apart and they did not know or communicate with each other. It's not there.'

There was a certain *gotcha* smugness in the way Tapscott spoke. It gave Bosch the urge to backhand him across the mouth. Soto knew her old partner's triggers and reached over to put a hand on Bosch's arm.

'Harry, this is not your fault,' she said. 'This is on the lab. The reports are all there. You're right – they found nothing. They missed it back then.'

Bosch looked at her and pulled his arm back.

'You really believe that?' he said. 'Because I don't. This is Borders. He's behind this – somehow. I know it.'

'How, Harry? We've looked for the fix in this.'

'Who's been in the box since the trial?'

'No one. In fact, the last one in that box was you. The original seals were intact with your signature and the date right across the top. Show him the video.'

She nodded to Tapscott, who pulled his phone and opened up a video. He turned the screen to Bosch.

'This is at Piper Tech,' he said.

Piper Tech was a massive complex in downtown where the LAPD's Property Control Unit was located, along with the fingerprint unit and the aero squadron-using the football field-size roof as a heliport. Bosch knew that the integrity protocol in the archival unit was high. Sworn officers had to provide departmental ID and fingerprints to pull evidence from any case. The boxes were opened in an examination area under twenty-four-hour video surveillance. But this was Tapscott's own video, recorded on his phone.

'This was not our first go-round with CIU, so we have our own protocol,' Tapscott said. 'One of us opens the box, the other person records the whole thing. Doesn't matter that they have their own cameras down there. And as you can see, no seal is broken, no tampering.'

The video showed Soto displaying the box to the camera, turning it over so that all sides and seams could be seen as intact. The seams had been sealed with the old labels used back in the eighties. For at least the past couple of decades, the department had been using red evidence tape that cracked and peeled if tampered with. Back in 1988, white rectangular stickers with LAPD ANALYZED EVIDENCE printed on them along with a signature and date line were used to seal evidence boxes. Soto manipulated the box in a bored manner and Bosch read that as her thinking they were wasting their time on this one. At least up until that point, Bosch still had her in his court.

Tapscott came in close on the seals used on the top seam of the box. Bosch could see his signature on the top center sticker along with the date September 9, 1988. He knew the date would have placed the sealing of the box at the end of the trial. Bosch had returned the evidence, sealed the box, and then stored it in property control in case an appeal overturned the verdict and they had to go to trial again. That never happened with Borders, and the box had presumably stayed on a shelf in property control, avoiding any intermittent clear-outs of old evidence, because he had also clearly marked on the box '187' – the California penal code for murder – which in the evidence room meant 'Don't throw away.'

As Tapscott moved the camera, Bosch recognized his own routine of using evidence seals on all seams of the box, including the bottom. He had always done it that way, till they moved on to the red evidence tape.

'Go back,' Bosch said. 'Let me just look at the signature again.'

Tapscott pulled the phone back, manipulated the video, and then froze the image on the close-up of the seal Bosch had signed. He held the screen out to Bosch, who leaned in to study it. The signature was faded and hard to read but it looked legit.

'Okay,' Bosch said.

Tapscott restarted the video. On the screen Soto used a box cutter attached by a wire to an examination table to slice through the labels and open the box. As she started removing items from the box, including the victim's clothing and an envelope containing her fingernail clippings, she called each piece of property out so it would be duly recorded. Among the items she mentioned was a sea-horse pendant, which had been the key piece of evidence against Borders.

Before the video was over, Tapscott impatiently pulled the phone back and killed the playback. He then put the phone away.

'On and on like that,' he said. 'Nobody fucked with the box, Harry. What was in it had been there since the day you sealed it after the trial.'

Bosch was annoyed that he didn't get a chance to watch the video in its entirety. Something about Tapscott – a stranger – using his first name also bothered Bosch. He put that annoyance aside and was silent for a long moment as he considered for the first time that his thirty-year belief that he had put a sadistic killer away for good was bogus.

'Where'd they find it?' he finally asked.

'Find what?' Kennedy asked.

'The DNA,' Bosch said.

'One microdot on the victim's pajama bottoms,' Kennedy said.

'Easy to have missed back in 'eighty-seven,' Soto said. 'They were probably just using black lights then.'

Bosch nodded.

'So what happens now?' he asked.

Soto looked at Kennedy. The question was his to answer.

'There's a hearing on a habeas motion scheduled in Department one-oh-seven a week from Wednesday,' the prosecutor said. 'We'll be joining Borders's attorneys and asking Judge Houghton to vacate the sentence and release him from death row.'

'Jesus Christ,' Bosch said.

'His lawyer has also notified the city that he'll be filing a claim,' Kennedy continued. 'We've been in contact with the City Attorney's Office and they hope to negotiate a settlement. We're probably talking well into seven figures.'

Bosch looked down at the table. He couldn't hold anyone's eyes.

'And I have to warn you,' Kennedy said. 'If a settlement is not reached and he files a claim in federal court, he can go after you personally.'

Bosch nodded. He knew that already. A civil rights claim filed by Borders would leave Bosch personally responsible for damages if the city chose not to cover him. Since two years ago Bosch had sued the city to reinstate his full pension, it was unlikely that he would find a single soul in the City Attorney's Office interested in indemnifying him against damages collected by Borders. The one thought that pushed through this reality was of his daughter. He could be left with nothing but an insurance policy going to her after he was gone.

'I'm sorry,' Soto said. 'If there were any other . . .'

She didn't finish and he slowly brought his eyes up to hers.

'Nine days,' he said.

'What do you mean?' she said.

'The hearing's in nine days. I have until then to figure out how he did it.'

'Harry, we've been working this for five weeks. There's nothing. This was before Olmer was on anybody's radar. All we know is he wasn't in jail at the time and he was in L.A. – we found work records. But the DNA is the DNA. On her night clothes, DNA from a man later convicted of multiple abduction-rapes. All cases home intrusions – very similar to Skyler's. But without the death. I mean, look at the facts. No D.A. in the world would touch this or go any other way with it.'

Kennedy cleared his throat.

'We came here today out of respect for you, Detective, and all the cases you've cleared over time. We don't want to get into an adversarial position on this. That would not be good for you.'

'And you don't think every one of those cases I cleared is affected by this?' Bosch said. 'You open the door to this guy and you might as well open it for every one of the people I sent away. If you put it on the lab – same thing. It taints everything.'

Bosch leaned back and stared at his old partner. He had at one time been her mentor. She had to know what this was doing to him.

'It is what it is,' Kennedy said. 'We have an obligation. "Better that one hundred guilty men go free than one innocent man be imprisoned."'

'Spare me your bastardized Ben Franklin bullshit,'

Bosch said. 'We found evidence connecting Borders to all three of those women's disappearances, and your office passed on two of them, some snot-nosed prosecutor saying there was not enough. This doesn't fucking make sense. I want the nine days to do my own investigation and I want access to everything you have and everything you've done.'

He looked at Soto as he said it but Kennedy responded.

'Not going to happen, Detective,' he said. 'As I said, we're here as a courtesy. But you're not on this case anymore.'

Before Bosch could counter, there was a sharp knock on the door, and it was cracked open. Bella Lourdes stood there. She waved him out.

'Harry,' she said. 'We need to talk right now.'

There was an urgency in her voice that Bosch could not ignore. He looked back at the others seated at the table and started to get up.

'Hold on a second,' he said. 'We're not done.'

He stood up and went to the door. Lourdes signaled him all the way out with her fingers. She closed the door behind him. He noticed that the squad room was now empty – no one in the module, the captain's door open, and his desk chair empty.

And Lourdes was clearly agitated. She used both hands to hook her short dark hair behind her ears, an anxiety habit Bosch had noticed the petite, compact detective had been exhibiting since coming back to work.

'What's up?'

'We've got two down in a robbery at a *farmacia* on the mall.'

'Two what? Officers?'

'No, people there. Behind the counter. Two one-eighty-sevens. The chief wants all hands on this. Are you ready? You want to ride with me?'

Bosch looked back at the closed door of the war room and thought about what had been said in there. What was he going to do about it? How was he going to handle it?

'Harry, come on, I gotta go. You in or out?'

Bosch looked at her.

'Okay, let's go.'

They moved quickly toward the exit that took them directly into the side lot, where detectives and command staff parked. He pulled his phone out of his shirt pocket and turned off the recording app.

'What about them?' Lourdes said.

'Fuck them,' Bosch said. 'They'll figure it out.'

3

San Fernando was a municipality barely two and a half square miles and surrounded on all sides by the city of Los Angeles. To Harry Bosch it was the proverbial needle in the haystack, the tiny place and job he had found when his time with the LAPD ended with him still believing he had more to give and a mission unfulfilled, but seemingly no place to go. Racked by budgetary shortfalls in the years that followed the 2008 recession, and having laid off a quarter of its forty officers, the police department actively pursued the creation of a voluntary corps of retired law officers to work in every section of the department, from patrol to communications to detectives.

When Chief Valdez reached out to Bosch and said he had an old jail cell full of cold cases and no one to work them, it was like a lifeline had been thrown to a drowning man. Bosch was alone and certainly adrift, having unceremoniously left the department he had served for almost forty years, at the same time that his daughter left home for college. Most of all, the offer came at a time when he felt unfinished. After all the years he had put in, he never expected to walk out the door one day at the LAPD and not be allowed back in.

At a period in life when most men took up golf or bought a boat, Bosch felt resolutely incomplete. He was a closer. He needed to work cases, and setting up shop as a private eye or a defense investigator wasn't going to suit him in the long run. He took the offer from the chief and soon was proving he was a closer at the SFPD. And he quickly went from part-time hours working cold cases to mentoring the entire detective bureau. Huey, Dewey, and Louie were dedicated and good investigators but together they had a total of less than ten years' experience as detectives. Captain Trevino was only part-time in the unit himself, as he was also responsible for supervising both the communications unit and the jail. It fell to Bosch to teach Lourdes, Sisto, and Luzon the mission.

The mall was a two-block stretch of San Fernando Road that went through the middle of town and was lined with small shops, businesses, bars, and restaurants. It was in a historic part of the city and was anchored on one end by a large department store that had been closed and vacant for several years, the JC Penney sign still on the front facade. Most of the other signs were in Spanish and the businesses catered to the city's Latino majority, mostly bridal and *quinceañra* salons, secondhand shops, and stores that sold products from Mexico.

It was a three-minute drive from the police station to the scene of the shooting. Lourdes drove her unmarked city car. Bosch tried his best to put the Borders case and what had been discussed in the war room behind him so that he could concentrate on the task at hand.

'So what do we know?' he asked.

'Two dead at La Farmacia Familia,' Lourdes said. 'Called in by a customer who went in and saw one of the victims. Patrol found the second in the back. Both employees. Looks like a father and son.'

'The son an adult?'

'Yes.'

'Gang affiliation?'

'No word.'

'What else?'

'That's it. Gooden and Sanders headed out when we got the call. Sheriff's forensics have been called.'

Gooden and Sanders were the two coroner's investigators who worked out of the subleased office in the detective bureau. It was a lucky break having them so close. Bosch remembered sometimes waiting for an hour or longer for coroner's investigators when he worked cases for the LAPD.

While Bosch had solved three cold case murders since coming to work for San Fernando, this would be the first live murder investigation, so to speak, since his arrival. It meant there would be an active crime scene, with victims on the floor, not just photos from a file to observe. The protocol and pace would be quite different, and it invigorated him despite the upset from the meeting he had just escaped from.

As Lourdes turned in to the mall, Bosch looked ahead and saw that the investigation was already starting off wrong. Three patrol cars were parked directly in front of the *farmacia*, and that was too close. Traffic through the two-lane mall had not been stopped and drivers were going slowly by the business, hoping to catch a glimpse of whatever had caused the police activity.

'Pull in here,' he said. 'Those cars are too close and I'm going to move them back and shut down the street.'

Lourdes did as he instructed and parked the car in front of a bar called the Tres Reyes and well behind a growing crowd of onlookers gathering near the drugstore.

Bosch and Lourdes were soon out of the car and weaving through the crowd. Yellow crime scene tape had been strung between the patrol cars, and two officers stood conferring by the trunk of one car while another stood with his hands on his belt buckle, a common patrol officer pose, watching the front door of the *farmacia*.

Bosch saw that the front door of the store containing the crime scene was propped open with a sandbag, which had probably come from the trunk of a patrol car. There was no sign of Chief Valdez or any of the other investigators, and Bosch knew that meant they were all inside.

'Shit,' he said as he approached the door.

'What?' Lourdes asked.

'Too many cooks . . .' Bosch said. 'Wait out here for a minute.'

Bosch entered the pharmacy, leaving Lourdes outside. It was a small business with just a few retail aisles leading back to a rear counter, where the actual pharmacy was located. He saw Valdez standing with Sisto and Luzon behind the counter. They were looking down at what Bosch guessed was one of the bodies. There was no sign of Trevino.

Bosch gave a short, low whistle that drew their attention and then signaled them to come to the front of the store. He then turned around and walked back out the door.

Outside, he waited by the door with Lourdes, and when the three men stepped out, he pushed the sandbag out of the way with his foot and let the door close.

'Chief, can I start us off?' he asked.

Bosch looked at Valdez and waited for the chief to give him the nod. He was asking to take charge of the investigation and he wanted it clear to all parties.

'Take it, Harry,' Valdez said.

Bosch got the attention of the patrol officers huddled together and signaled them over as well.

'Okay, listen up everybody,' Bosch said. 'Our number one priority here is to protect the crime scene, and we're not doing that. Patrol, I want you guys to move your cars out and shut down this block on both ends. Tape it up. Nobody comes in without authorization. I then want clipboards on both ends, and you write down the name of every cop or lab rat that comes into the crime scene. You write down the license-plate number of every car you let out too.'

Nobody moved.

'You heard him,' Valdez said. 'Let's move it, people. We've got two citizens on the floor in there. We need to do this right by them and the department.'

The patrol officers quickly returned to their cars to carry out Bosch's orders. Bosch and the other detectives then split up and started moving the gathered onlookers back up the street. Some shouted questions in Spanish but Bosch did not reply. He scanned the faces of those he was pushing back. He knew the killer could be among them. It wouldn't be the first time.

After a two-zone crime scene had been established, Bosch and the chief and the three detectives reconvened by the door of the pharmacy. Bosch once more looked at Valdez for confirmation of his authority, because he didn't expect his next moves to go over well.

'I still have this, Chief?' he asked.

'All yours, Harry,' Valdez said. 'How do you want to do it?'

'Okay, we want to limit people inside the crime scene,' Bosch said. 'We get this thing into court and a defense lawyer sees all of us crammed in there, wandering around, and it just gives him more targets to potshot, more confusion to throw at a jury. So there's only going to be two people inside and that's going to be Lourdes and me. Sisto and Luzon, you've got the exterior crime scene. I want you going down the street in both directions. We're looking for witnesses *and* cameras. We—'

'We got here first,' Luzon said, pointing to himself and Sisto. 'It should be our case and us inside.'

At about forty, Luzon was the oldest of the three full-time investigators, but he had the least experience as a detective. He was moved into the unit six months earlier after spending twelve years in patrol. He had gotten the promotion to fill the void left by Lourdes's leave of absence and then Valdez found the money in the budget to keep him on board at a time when there was a spike in property crimes attributed to a local gang called the SanFers. Bosch had observed him since he'd gotten the promotion and concluded he was a good and earnest detective – a good choice by Valdez. But Bosch had not yet worked with him on a case and he had had that experience with Lourdes. He wanted her to take the lead on this.

'That's not how it works,' Bosch said. 'Lourdes is

going to be lead. I need you and Sisto to go two blocks in both directions. We're looking for the getaway vehicle. We're also looking for video and I need you guys to go find it. It's important.'

Bosch could see Luzon fighting back the urge to again argue Bosch's orders. But he looked at the chief, who stood with his arms folded in front of his chest, and saw no indication that the man ultimately in charge disagreed with Bosch.

'You got it,' he said.

He went in one direction, while Sisto headed off in the other. Sisto did not bother to complain about the assignment but had a hangdog look on his face.

'Hey, guys?' Bosch said.

Luzon and Sisto looked back. Bosch gestured to Lourdes and the chief to include them.

'Look, I'm not trying to be an arrogant ass,' he said. 'My experience comes with a lot of fuckups. We learn from our mistakes, and in over thirty years of working homicides, I've made many. I'm just trying to use what I've learned the hard way. Okay?'

Reluctant nods came from Luzon and Sisto and they headed off to their assignments.

'Take down plates and phone numbers,' Bosch called after them, immediately realizing it was an unneeded directive.

Once they were gone, the chief stepped away from the huddle.

'Harry,' Valdez said. 'Let's talk for a second.'

Bosch followed him, awkwardly leaving Lourdes alone on the sidewalk. The chief spoke quietly.

'Look, I get what you're doing with those two and

what you said about learning the hard way. But I want you on lead. Bella's good but she's just back and getting her feet wet. This – homicide – is what you've been doing for thirty years. This is why you're here.'

'I get that, Chief. But you don't want me on lead. We have to think about when this gets into court. Everything's about building a case for trial, and you don't want a part-timer on lead. You want Bella. They try character assassination on her, and she'll eat their lunch after what happened last year, what she went through and then her coming back to the job. She's a hero and that's who you want on the witness stand. On top of that, she's good and she's ready for this. And besides, I may have some problems coming up soon from downtown. Problems that could be a big distraction. You don't want me on lead.'

Valdez looked at him. He knew that 'downtown' meant from outside the SFPD, from Bosch's past.

'I heard you had visitors this morning,' he said. 'We'll talk about that later. Where do you want me?'

'Media relations,' Bosch said. 'They'll get wind of this soon enough and will start showing up. "Two Dead on Main Street" will be a story. You need to set up a command post and corral them when they start coming in. We want to control what information gets out there.'

'Understood. What else? You need more bodies for the canvass. I can pull people in from patrol, take one officer out of every car and run solo patrols till we get a handle on this.'

'That would be good. There were people in all of these shops. Somebody saw something.'

'You got it. What if I can get the old Penney's open

and we use that as the CP? I know the guy who owns the building.'

Bosch looked across the street and down half a block at the facade of the long-closed department store.

'We're going to be out here late. If you can get lights on in there, go for it. What about Captain Trevino? Is he around?'

'I have him covering the shop while I am here. You need him?'

'No, I can fill him in on things later.'

'Then I'll leave you to it. We really need a quick conclusion to this, Harry. If there is one.'

'Roger that.'

The chief headed off and Lourdes came up to Bosch.

'Let me guess, he didn't want me as lead,' she said.

'He wanted me,' Bosch said. 'But it was no reflection on you. I said no. I said it was your case.'

'Does that have something to do with the three visitors you had this morning?'

'Maybe. And it has to do with you being able to handle it. Why don't you go in and watch over Gooden and Sanders? I'll call the sheriff's lab and get an ETA. First thing we want are photos. Don't let those guys move the bodies around until we get the full photo spread.'

'Roger that.'

'The bodies belong to the coroner. But the crime scene is ours. Remember that.'

Lourdes headed toward the door of the *farmacia* and Bosch pulled his phone. The SFPD was so small, it did not have its own forensics team. It relied on the sheriff's department crime scene unit and that often put it in second position for services. Bosch called the liaison at the lab and was told a team was on the road to San Fernando as they spoke. Bosch reminded the liaison that they were working a double murder and asked for a second team, but he was denied and told there wasn't a second team to spare. They were getting two techs and a photographer/videographer, and that was it.

As he hung up, Bosch noticed one of the patrol officers he had given orders to earlier was standing at the new crime scene perimeter at the end of the block. Yellow tape had been strung completely across, closing the road through the mall. The patrol officer had his hands on his belt buckle and was watching Bosch.

Bosch put his phone away and walked up the street to the yellow tape and the officer manning it.

'Don't look in,' Bosch said. 'Look out.'

'What?' the officer asked.

'You're watching the detectives. You should be watching the street.'

Bosch put his hand on the officer's shoulder and turned him toward the tape.

'Look outward from a crime scene. Look for people watching, people who don't fit. You'd be surprised how many times the doer comes back to watch the investigation. Anyway, you're protecting the crime scene, not watching it.'

'Got it.'

'Good.'

The sheriff's forensics team arrived shortly after that and Bosch ordered everyone out of the pharmacy so the photographer could go in and take a preliminary photo-and-video sweep of the crime scene with only the bodies in view.

While waiting outside, Bosch pulled on gloves and a pair of paper booties. Once the all clear came from the photographer, the whole team entered the *farmacia*, passing through a plastic crime scene containment curtain that had been hung by the techs over the door.

Gooden and Sanders separated and continued to process the bodies. Lourdes and Bosch first went behind the pharmacy counter, where Gooden and one of the crime scene techs were examining the first body. Lourdes had a notebook out and was writing down a description of what she was seeing. Bosch leaned close to his partner's ear and whispered.

'Take the time to just observe. Notes are good but clear visuals are good to keep in your mind.'

'Okay. I will.'

When Bosch was a young homicide detective, he worked with a partner named Frankie Sheehan, who always kept an old milk crate in the trunk of their unmarked car. He'd carry it into every scene, find a good vantage point, and put the crate down. Then he'd sit on it and just observe the scene, studying its nuances and trying to take the measure and motive of the violence that had occurred there. Sheehan had worked the Danielle Skyler case with Bosch and had sat on his crate in the corner of the room where the body was left nude and viciously violated on the floor. But Sheehan was long dead now and would not be taking the free fall that was awaiting Bosch on the case.

4

La Farmacia Familia was a small operation that appeared to Bosch to rely mostly on the business of filling prescriptions. In the front section of the store, there were three short aisles of shelved retail items relating to home remedies and care, almost all of them in Spanish-language boxes imported from Mexico. There were no racks of greeting cards, point-of-purchase candy displays, or cold cases stocked with sodas and water. The business was nothing like the chain pharmacies scattered across the city.

The entire back wall of the store was the actual pharmacy, where there was a counter that fronted the storage area of medicines and a work area for filling prescriptions. The front section of the store seemed completely untouched by the crime that had occurred here.

Bosch moved down the aisle to the left, which brought him to a half door leading to the rear of the pharmacy counter. He saw Gooden squatting down behind the counter next to the first body, that of a man who appeared to be in his early fifties. He was lying on his back just behind the counter, his hands up and palms out by his shoulders. He was wearing a white pharmacist's jacket with a name embroidered on it.

'Harry, meet José,' Gooden said. 'At least he's José

until we confirm it with fingerprints. Through-and-through gunshot to the chest.'

He formed a gun with his thumb and finger as he gave the report and pointed the barrel against his chest.

'Point-blank?' Bosch asked.

'Almost,' Gooden said. 'Six to twelve inches. Guy probably had his hands up and they still shot him.'

Bosch didn't say anything. He was in observation mode. He would form his own impressions about the scene and determine if the victim's hands were up or down when he was shot. He didn't need that information from Gooden.

Bosch squatted and looked across the floor around the body and bent down further to look under the counter.

'What is it?' Lourdes asked.

'No brass,' Bosch said.

No ejected bullet casings indicated one of two things to Bosch. Either the killer had taken the time to pick up the casings or he had used a revolver – which did not eject bullet casings. Either way, it was notable to Bosch. Picking up critical evidence showed a cool calculation to the crime. Using a revolver could indicate the same – a weapon chosen because it would not leave critical evidence behind.

He and Lourdes moved into the hallway to the left of the pharmacy counter. The twenty-foot passageway led to the work and storage areas and a restroom. There was a door at the end of the hall with double locks and an exit sign as well as a peephole. It presumably led to the back alley from which deliveries would come.

Just short of the door, Sanders, the second coroner's

tech, was on his knees next to the other body, also a male wearing a pharmacist's coat. The body was chest down, one arm reaching out toward the door. There was a trail of blood smears on the floor, leading to the body. Lourdes walked down the side edge of the hallway, careful not to step in the blood.

'And here we have José Jr.,' Sanders said. 'We have three points of impact: the back, the rectum, the head – most likely in that order.'

Bosch stepped away from Lourdes and crossed over the blood smears to the other side of the hallway so he could get an unobstructed view of the body. José Jr. was lying with his right cheek against the floor, eyes partially open. He looked like he was in his early twenties, a meager growth of whiskers on his chin.

The blood and bullet wounds told the tale. At the first sign of trouble, José Jr. had made a break for the rear door, running for his life down the hallway. He was knocked down with the first shot to the upper back. On the floor, he turned to look behind him, spilling his blood on the tiles. He saw the shooter coming and turned to try to crawl toward the door, his knees slipping on and smearing the blood. The shooter had come up and shot him again, this time in the rectum, then stepped up and ended it with the shot to the back of the head.

Bosch had seen the rectum shot in prior cases, and it drew his attention.

'The shot up the pipe – how close?' he asked.

Sanders reached over and used one gloved hand to pull the seat of the victim's pants out taut so the bullet entry could be clearly seen. With the other hand he pointed to where the cloth had been burned.

'He got up in there,' Sanders said. 'Point-blank.'

Bosch nodded. His eyes tracked up to the wounds on the back and head. It appeared to him that the two entrance wounds he could see were neater and smaller than the one shot to José Sr.'s chest.

'You thinking two different weapons?' he asked.

Sanders nodded.

'If I were betting,' he said.

'And no brass?'

'None evident. We'll see when we roll the body but that would be a miracle if three shells ended up underneath.'

Bosch nodded in reply.

'Okay, do what you have to do,' he said.

He carefully stepped back down the hallway and moved into the pharmacy's work- and drug-storage area. He started by looking up and immediately saw the camera mounted in the corner of the ceiling over the door.

Lourdes entered the room behind him. He pointed up and she saw the camera.

'Need the feed,' he said. 'Hopefully off-site or to a website.'

'I can check that,' she said.

Bosch surveyed the room. Several of the plastic drawers where stores of pills were kept were pulled out and dropped to the floor, and loose pills were scattered across it. He knew a difficult task of inventorying what had been in the pharmacy and what had been taken lay ahead. Some of the drawers on the floor were larger than others and he guessed that they had contained more commonly prescribed drugs.

On the worktable, there was a computer. There were also tools for measuring out and bottling pills in plastic vials as well as a label printer.

'Can you go out and talk to the photographer?' he asked Lourdes. 'Make sure he got all of this stuff in here before we start stepping on pills and crunching them. Tell him he can start videoing the crime scene processing now, too.'

'On it,' Lourdes said.

After Lourdes went out, Bosch moved into the hallway again. He knew they would need to collect and document every pill and piece of evidence in the place. A homicide case always moved slowly from the center out.

In the old days, he would have stepped out at this point to smoke a cigarette and contemplate things. This time, he went out through the plastic curtain to just think. Almost immediately his phone vibrated in his pocket. The caller ID was blocked.

'That wasn't cool, Harry,' Lucia Soto said when he answered.

'Sorry, we had an emergency,' he said. 'Had to go.'

'You could have told us. I'm not your enemy on this. I'm trying to run interference for you, keep it below the radar. If you play this right, the blame will go on the lab or your former partner – the one who's dead.'

'Are Kennedy and Tapscott with you right now?'

'No, of course not. This is just you and me.'

'Can you get me a copy of the report you turned in to Kennedy?'

'Harry . . .'

'I thought so. Lucia, don't say you're on my side,

running interference for me, if you're not. You know what I mean?'

'I can't just share active files with—'

'Look, I'm in the middle of things here. Give me a call back if you change your mind. I remember there was a case that meant a lot to you once. We were partners and I was right there for you. I guess things are different now.'

'That's not fair and you know it.'

'And one other thing? I'd never sell out a partner. Even a dead one.'

He disconnected. He felt a pang of guilt. He was being heavy-handed with Soto but felt he needed to push her toward giving him what he needed.

Since he had finished his career with the LAPD working cold cases, it had been many years since he had worked a live murder scene. With the return of crime scene instincts came the tug of old habits. He felt a deep need for a cigarette. He looked around to see if there was anyone he could borrow a smoke from and saw Lourdes approaching from the short end of the block. She had a troubled look on her face.

'What's wrong?'

'I came out to talk to the photographer, and got signaled up to the tape. Mrs. Esquivel, the wife and mother of our victims, was stopped at the tape and she was hysterical. I just put her in a car and they're taking her to the station.'

Bosch nodded. Keeping her away from the crime scene was the right move.

'You up for talking with her?' he asked. 'We can't leave her over there too long.'

'I don't know,' Lourdes said. 'I just ruined her life. Everything that's important to her is suddenly gone. Husband and her only child.'

'I know, but you have to establish rapport. You never know, this case could go on for years. She's going to need to trust the person carrying it. You've got Spanish and a lot of years ahead of you here. I don't.'

'Okay, I can do it.'

'Focus on the son. His friends, what he did when he wasn't working, enemies, all of that stuff. Find out where he lived, whether he had a girlfriend. And ask the mother if José Sr. was having any problems with him at work. The son is going to be the key to this.'

'You get all that from a shot up the ass?'

Bosch nodded.

'I've seen it before. On a case where we talked to a profiler. It's an angry shot. It has payback written all over it.'

'He knew the shooters?'

'No doubt. Either he knew them or they knew him. Or both.'

5

Bosch didn't get to his home until after midnight. He was beat from a long day working the crime scene and coordinating the efforts of the other detectives as well as the patrol division. He had also been drawn into briefing Chief Valdez on where the investigation stood before the chief faced the cameras and reporters that had gathered on the mall. The update was concise: no suspects, no arrests.

The assessment for the media was accurate but the investigators of the *farmacia* murders were not without leads. The murders and subsequent looting of the store's supplies of prescription drugs had indeed been captured on three cameras inside the drugstore, and the full-color videos gave insight into the cold calculation of the crime. There had been two gunmen wearing black ski masks and carrying revolvers. They cut down José Esquivel Sr. and his son with a coldness that implied planning, precision, and intention. Bosch's first thought after seeing the videos was that they were hit men there to do a job. Stealing pills was simply a cover for the true motive for the crime. Sadly, initial viewings of the video revealed few usable identifiers of either shooter. When one of the men extended his arm to shoot José Sr., his sleeve pulled back to reveal white skin. But nothing else stood out.

After parking in the carport, Bosch skipped the side-door entrance to the house and walked out front so he could check his mailbox. He saw that the top of the box attached to the house was held open by a thick manila envelope. He pulled it out and held it under the porch light to see where it had come from.

There was no return address and no postage on the envelope. Even his own address was missing. The envelope had only his name written on it. Bosch unlocked the door and carried it inside. He put the envelope and the mail he had received down on the kitchen counter while he opened the refrigerator to grab a beer.

After his first draw on the amber bottle, he tore open the envelope. He slid out a one-inch-thick sheaf of documents. He recognized the top report right away. It was a copy of the initial incident report relating to Danielle Skyler's murder in 1987. Bosch riffled through the stack of documents and quickly determined that he had a copy of the current investigative file.

Lucia Soto had come through.

Bosch was dead tired but he knew that he would not be going to sleep anytime soon. He dumped the rest of the beer down the drain, then brewed a cup of coffee on the Keurig his daughter had given him for Christmas. He grabbed the stack of documents and went to work.

After his daughter had left for college, and family dinners became a rare occurrence, Bosch turned the dining room of the small house into a workspace. The table became a desk wide enough to spread investigative reports across – reports from cases he was pulling out of the jail cell at San Fernando or that he had taken on privately. He had also installed shelving on the two walls of the alcove and these were lined with more files and books on legal procedure and the California penal code as well as stacks of CDs and a Bose player for use when his vinyl collection and phonograph didn't cover his musical needs.

Bosch slotted a disc called *Chemistry* in the Bose and put the volume at midrange. It was an album of duets between Houston Person on tenor sax and Ron Carter on double bass. It was part of an ongoing musical conversation, their fifth and most recent collaboration, and Bosch had the earlier recordings on vinyl. It was perfect for midnight work. He took his usual spot at the table, with his back to the shelves and the music, and started going through the cache of documents.

Initially he divided the documents along lines of old and new. Reports from the original investigation of Danielle Skyler's murder – many of which he had written himself thirty years before-went into one pile, while the newer reports, prepared during the current reinvestigation, went into a second stack.

While he clearly remembered the original investigation, he knew that many of the small details of the case had receded in his memory and that it was prudent for him to start with the old before reviewing the new. He was first drawn to the chronological record, which was always the starting point for reviewing a case. It was essentially a case diary – a string of brief dated and timed entries describing the investigative moves made by Bosch and his partner, Frankie Sheehan. Many of the entries would be expanded upon in summary reports but the chrono was the place to start for a step-by-step overview of the investigation.

There was not a single computer in the Robbery-Homicide Division in 1987. Reports were either handwritten or typed out on IBM Selectrics. Most of the time chronos were handwritten. They were on lined paper in section 1 of the murder book. Each investigator, including those filling in or handling ancillary case tasks, would follow their own entries in the log with their initials, even though the different handwriting styles made the identity of the author obvious in most cases.

Bosch was looking at photocopies of the original case chrono and recognized his handwriting as well as Sheehan's. He also recognized the two different report-writing styles he and Sheehan employed. Sheehan, who was the more experienced of their team, used fewer words and often wrote in incomplete sentences. Bosch was more verbose, a characteristic of his report writing that would change over time as he learned what Sheehan already knew: less is more, meaning the less time you spent on paperwork, the more time you had to follow the leads of the case. And fewer words on the page also meant fewer words for a defense attorney to twist into his own interpretation in court.

Bosch had gotten his detective's badge in 1977 and spent five years working in various divisions and crime units before he was promoted to homicide detective and posted first at Hollywood Division and then eventually the elite Robbery-Homicide Division working out of Parker Center, downtown. At RHD he was paired with Sheehan, and the Skyler case was one of the first murders they handled as lead investigators.

Danielle Skyler's story was the universal story of Los

Angeles, with an added irony of origin. Raised by a single mother who worked as a motel maid in Hollywood, Florida, she filled the holes in her life with applause that came with success in beauty pageants and on the high school stage. Armed with her beauty and fragile confidence, she crossed the three thousand miles from Hollywood to Hollywood at age twenty. She found, as most do, that there was one of her from every small town in America. The paying jobs were few and she was often taken advantage of by the leeches who were part of the entertainment industry. But she persevered. She waited on tables, took acting classes, and went to an endless string of auditions for parts that usually didn't have character names or many lines.

She also built a community – young men and women engaged in the same struggle for success and fame. She saw many of them at the same auditions and casting offices. They traded tips on jobs both in entertainment and hospitality – meaning the restaurant business. By the time she was five years into the struggle, she had managed to amass a handful of movie and TV credits where she was primarily cast as eye candy. She had also given numerous showcase performances in small playhouses across the Valley and had finally transitioned out of restaurant work to a part-time job as a receptionist for a freelance casting agent.

The five years in Los Angeles were also marked by several apartment moves, several roommate changes, and several relationships with different men ranging in age from five years younger than her to twenty-two years older. When she was found raped and strangled in the empty second bedroom of her Toluca Lake apartment,

44

Bosch and Sheehan were faced with filling out a victim history that would take several weeks to complete.

As Bosch read through the case chronology, several details about Skyler and the moves he and Sheehan had made came back to him, and the case seemed as fresh to him as the killings in La Farmacia Familia that morning. He remembered the faces of the friends and associates interviewed and listed in the chrono. He remembered how sure he and his partner were when they zeroed in on Preston Borders.

Borders was also an actor who was struggling for a foothold in Hollywood. But he wasn't doing it without a net. Unlike Danielle Skyler and thousands of other would-be artists who roll into L.A. each year with the certainty of the tide on Venice Beach, Borders didn't have to work in hospitality or in phone sales or anywhere else. Borders was from a suburb of Boston and was staked by his parents in his efforts to become a movie star. His rent and car were paid for and his credit-card bills were sent to Boston. This allowed him to fill his days auditioning for film and TV roles and his nights moving through a seemingly endless rotation of clubs, where there were always numerous women like Skyler hoping for someone to clear their bar tab in exchange for a smile and conversation and maybe something more intimate if the feeling was right.

According to the chrono, Bosch and Sheehan connected Borders to Skyler on November 1, 1987, the ninth day of the investigation. That was when they knocked on the door of a Skyler acquaintance named Amanda Margot. At the time, Margot was another ingenue actress. Thirty years later she could count herself among the lucky ones. She'd had a solid career in the film and television arenas, appearing in small roles in several films and as a lead in a long-running show where she played a no-holds-barred homicide detective. Bosch had read interviews with her in which she said that she drew her TV character's sympathy for victims from the real-life murder of a close friend.

Bosch remembered the initial interview with Margot like it was yesterday. At the time, the young actress had none of the trappings of success in her small Studio City apartment. Bosch and Sheehan sat on a threadbare couch from a secondhand store, and Margot sat on a chair she pulled into the living room from the kitchen.

The two detectives had been interviewing four or five friends and associates of the victim a day and Margot was high on their list, but she had secured a week's work at an auto show in Detroit presenting cars and had left town shortly after the murder. The appointment was set up for when she returned.

Margot proved to be a font of information about Skyler. The two had been close, though they had never lived together. At the time of the murder, Skyler's roommate had just moved out and given up on the dream of stardom. She had returned home to Texas, and Skyler was looking for a new roommate. Margot was in the last months of a lease and planned to move in with her friend right after the new year. Skyler was living by herself until then, though her family had told the investigators that her younger sister, traveling while on a gap year after high school, was planning on arriving for Thanksgiving and using the spare bedroom until both sisters went back to Florida for the Christmas holidays.

Margot and Danielle had met three years previously in the waiting room of a casting agency where they were auditioning for the same part. Rather than becoming competitors, they had hit it off. Neither of them got the part but they got coffee afterward and a friendship was born. They moved in similar circles both professionally and socially. They tried to look out for each other, tipping one another off to potential jobs and about which casting directors or acting coaches were lecherous.

Over time, they even dated some of the same men, and this was the point the detectives zeroed in on. Evidence and autopsy results indicated that Danielle Skyler had been brutally abused during the course of the night. She had been raped vaginally and anally and choked repeatedly. There were multiple thin furrow lines around her neck, some cutting through the skin, indicating that her killer had most likely choked her to unconsciousness and then brought her back for more abuse at least six times. It was possible that the garrote had been a necklace worn by the victim.

The body was also mutilated with a knife that matched others from the kitchen, but at autopsy it was determined that the slashes were postmortem.

It also appeared that the apartment had been tricked out to look like there had been an intruder. A sliding door on the second-floor balcony off the empty bedroom was left ajar, but there were no indications outside that anyone had climbed up and onto the balcony to pop the door and enter. The balcony's metal railing had a thick layer of smog dust on it that had not been disturbed at any point on its entire length. This meant an intruder would have had to vault the railing without touching it to get to the sliding door. It was an improbable scenario, which led the investigators to consider the opposite – that Skyler's killer had entered through the front door and without a struggle. It meant that he had known her on some level and wanted to disguise that fact from investigators.

Amanda Margot revealed during her interview that one night two weeks before Skyler's death, the two young women had gotten together in Margot's apartment to drink cheap wine and order takeout. They were joined by a third actress, named Jamie Henderson, whom they also knew from the audition circuit. At some point during the evening, they started talking about men and learned that they had dated several of the same men, having met them through acting schools, casting agencies, and talent showcases. The women started making a 'one-and-done' list of men they agreed should never be dated again.

High on the list of reasons was that each man mentioned had been demanding and in some cases physically threatening when it came to wanting sex. Margot explained that many of the men they dated expected to have sex after one or two dates. It was the men who didn't handle rejection well who were put on the one-and-done list.

Here was where Bosch and Sheehan's pursuit of this angle paid off. Though the one-and-done list might have come out of an alcohol-fueled girls'-night gossip session, Margot still had the piece of paper torn from a notebook and attached by a bottle-opener magnet to her refrigerator door. She provided it to the detectives and was able to point out the four names that Danielle Skyler had contributed to the list. They weren't full names, and some, like 'Bad Breath Bob,' were just nicknames.

But number one on her list was the single name Preston. Margot said it was the name of a man only Skyler had dated and she couldn't remember if it was a first or last name but she did recall the story that went with it. Danielle had said that Preston was a scholarship actor, meaning he had some kind of financial support and didn't have to work a side job, and that he felt entitled to sex after a first date in which he had paid for dinner and drinks. Danielle said that he had grown very angry upon her rejection when she was being dropped off at her apartment and that he later came back to knock on her door and demand to be let in. She refused to open the door but he would not leave until she threatened to call the police.

Margot reported that the date with Preston had occurred two weeks before the night the three women got together, which made it about four weeks before Skyler's murder. When pressed for more details about Preston and where he and Skyler may have first met, Margot said it could only have been through some kind of industry nexus, since both Danielle and Preston were actors.

The chronology revealed that finding Preston became a priority in the investigation. Bosch and Sheehan reworked ground already trodden, going back to those previously interviewed and asking about a man named Preston. They had no luck until they requested the audition logs from the prior three months of casting sessions conducted by the company Skyler had worked for as a receptionist. In the weeks leading up to the gossip session, the company had been casting secondary roles for a television show about people working in a hospital emergency room.

On the sign-in list for auditions held on September 14, 1987, was the name Preston Borders. That list had been kept on a clipboard at the desk of the agency's receptionist, Danielle Skyler.

Bosch and Sheehan had found their one-and-done man.

6

The detectives carried out their due diligence and interviewed Jamie Henderson, the third woman involved in drawing up the one-and-done list. She confirmed Amanda Margot's account of the evening and Danielle Skyler's contributions to the list. They then identified and interviewed all the men Skyler had discussed, even Bad Breath Bob. But Bosch and Sheehan saved Preston Borders for last, because their instincts told them he could rise from the level of a person of interest to a suspect. A guy who would go back to the apartment of a woman who had rejected him, pound on the door, and demand to be allowed in for sex struck both detectives as behavior indicating the kind of psychosis found in sexual predators.

A week after interviewing Amanda Margot, the detectives positioned themselves on a surveillance of Borders's apartment in Sherman Oaks and waited for him to exit for the day. They wanted to approach him away from the apartment in case he revealed something in the interview that would serve as probable cause to search his home. They didn't want to knock on the door and give him the chance to hide or destroy incriminating evidence.

They were also working a hunch. With the help of Danielle Skyler's mother and friends, they had inventoried her apartment and found only one piece of personal property missing. It was a blue sea-horse pendant that had been attached to a necklace made of braided twine. Her mother had given it to her on the day she left home for California. Danielle had gone to a high school that had the sea horse as a mascot, and the pendant was a reminder of the Hollywood Danielle had come from and that her mother didn't want her to forget. Her mother had attached it to a necklace she had made herself. The piece of jewelry, though not outwardly valuable, was said to be the young woman's most prized possession.

Despite three different searches of Skyler's apartment, Bosch and Sheehan did not find the sea horse or necklace. They were certain Skyler had not lost it, as it was prominently shown in a new set of head shots taken a few weeks before her death. The detectives believed that the killer had taken the necklace and pendant as a souvenir after the murder. If they were found in a suspect's possession, any blood residue on the twine could be type-matched to Danielle and would be a valuable piece of evidence.

Late in the morning of the surveillance, Borders emerged from his apartment on Vesper and walked a block south to Ventura Boulevard. Bosch and Sheehan gave him a lead and then followed on foot. Borders first entered the Tower Records store at the corner of Cedros and Ventura and browsed in the video section for more than a half hour. The detectives observing him debated whether they should approach and ask for an interview but decided to hang back and intercept him only if he started back to his apartment.

After leaving the record store, Borders walked back across Ventura and went into a restaurant called Le Café, where he had lunch by himself at the bar while chatting familiarly to the bartender. Bosch had been in Le Café several times because above the restaurant and bar was a jazz club called the Room Upstairs that was open late and featured world-class performers. He had seen Houston Person and Ron Carter perform there just a few months before.

When lunch was finished, Borders left a twenty on the counter and left. Bosch and Sheehan quickly approached the three-sided bar and Bosch drew the bartender over to one side with a question about what bourbons he had available, while Sheehan went to the other side and placed the empty beer glass Borders had drunk from into a paper bag. He headed out and waited for Bosch on the sidewalk. Borders was nowhere to be seen at first when Bosch joined him but they checked a drugstore two businesses down and found him inside shopping with a plastic basket.

Borders bought a box of condoms and other toiletry items at the drugstore before heading back to his apartment. As he was unlocking the security gate, Bosch and Sheehan approached him from different sides. They had a plan for talking him into agreeing to a voluntary interview. His reported behavior with Skyler suggested a narcissistic personality, two hallmark traits of which were an inflated sense of self-importance and feelings of superiority. The detectives played to those traits by identifying themselves to Borders and saying they needed his help solving the murder of Danielle Skyler. Sheehan said they were grasping at straws and hoped, since Borders had dated her, he could give insight into her personality and lifestyle. Borders agreed to the interview without hesitation. Bosch and Sheehan read that as Borders believing that if he went with the detectives that he would learn more from them than they would from him. It was similar to the psychology that often led a murderer to volunteer to join the search for the missing person they had actually killed and buried. They had to get close to the investigation to learn what was going on, while hiding in plain sight also brought them psychological fulfillment.

They drove Borders over to the nearby Van Nuys station, where they had previously reserved an interview room with the detective commander. The room was wired for sound, and the interview was taped.

Bosch dropped off his reading of the chrono log and changed the CD as *Chemistry* came to an end. This time he put in Frank Morgan's *Mood Indigo* and soon he was hearing 'Lullaby,' one of his favorite recordings. He then looked back through the stack of old reports for the transcript of the interview conducted thirty years earlier with Borders. It was the thickest report in the stack, weighing in at forty-six pages. He quickly leafed through it to find the moment when Borders was caught in the lie that ultimately led to his arrest and conviction. It was two-thirds through the thirty-minute conversation and during a segment where Bosch was asking the questions. It was also after Borders had signed a consent form acknowledging his Miranda rights and agreeing to talk to the detectives.

HB: So you and Danielle didn't have sex? You just

dropped her at her place and took off?

PB: That's right.

HB: Well, were you a gentleman? Did you walk her to her door?

PB: No, it was like she jumped out and was gone before I could even be a gentleman.

HB: You mean like she was mad at you?

PB: Sort of. She didn't like what I'd had to say.

HB: Which was what?

PB: That there wasn't any chemistry. You know, nice try but it wasn't right. I thought she understood and thought the same thing but then she jumped out of the car and was gone without so much as a good-bye. It was rude but I guess she was disappointed. She liked me better than I liked her. Nobody likes getting rejected.

HB: And you said you had not picked her up at her place earlier?

PB: Yeah, she took a cab and we met at the restaurant, because she was coming from the Westside and for me to go all the way over the hill to get her would be a slog, man. I liked the girl, or at least I thought I did, but not that much, you know what I mean?

HB: Yeah, I get it.

PB: I mean, I'm not running a taxi service. Some of these girls think you are their chauffeur or [unintelligible]. Not me.

HB: Okay, so what you're saying is that you didn't pick her up and then you just dropped her at the curb and took off.

55

PB: That's it. Not even a good-night kiss.

HB: And you were never in her apartment?

PB: Nope.

HB: Not even to her door?

PB: Never.

HB: What about after that night? You knew where she lived now. Did you ever come back?

PB: No, man, I'm telling you. I wasn't interested.

HB: Well, then, we have a problem that we need to work out here.

PB: What problem?

HB: Why do you think we approached you today, Preston?

PB: I don't know. You said you needed my help. I thought maybe one of her friends told you Skyler and I had dated.

HB: Actually, it was because we found your fingerprints on the front door of her apartment. The problem is, you just told me you'd never been to the door.

PB: I don't understand. How'd you get my fingerprints?

HB: You know, that's sort of funny. I tell you that your fingerprints were found at a murder scene and you ask how I got your fingerprints. I think most guys would've said something else, especially if they had previously said they were never, ever at that scene. Is there something you want to tell us, Preston?

PB: Yeah, I want to say this is all bullshit.

HB: You're sticking with the story that you were never there?

PB: That's right, everything else is bullshit. You don't have any prints.

HB: What if I told you that she told two different friends about you trying to break down her door after she rejected your sexual advances on the night of the date?

PB: Oh, man, I see it now. I get it. Those bitches are lining up against me. Let me tell you, she didn't reject me. Nobody rejects me. I rejected her.

HB: Answer my question, did you go to her door on the night of your date with Danielle? Yes or no?

PB: No, I did not, and there are no fucking fingerprints, and I'm done talking to you. Get me a lawyer if you want to ask any more questions.

HB: Fine, who do you want?

PB: I don't know. I don't know any lawyers.

HB: Then I'll get you the yellow pages.

Bosch had lied about the fingerprints. Multiple prints had been found on the door and in the apartment, but they had found no prints for Borders on file. Prints subsequently taken from the collected beer glass would not match any from Skyler's apartment. But Bosch was on steady legal ground. Courts across the country had long approved the use of deception and trickery by police in an interview setting with a suspect, holding that an innocent person would see through the deception and not falsely confess to the crime.

The interview with Borders was the only time he ever spoke to anyone in law enforcement. Based on the contradiction between what Margot and Henderson had reported about Skyler's account of the ill-fated date and Borders's denying that he had returned to the apartment, he was arrested in the interview room on suspicion of murder and booked two floors up, in the Van Nuys jail. The case at that point was beyond weak and Bosch and Sheehan knew it. Catching Borders in the lie about not coming to the victim's door supported their belief that he was the killer, but it was based on hearsay. It relied on the memories of two friends of the victim, and Danielle's story had been told while all three women were drinking. The bottom line was that it would be their word against the suspect's. Defense attorneys thrived and reasonable doubt lived in the gray areas in between.

The detectives knew that they needed to find corroborating evidence or kick Borders loose at the end of the forty-eight-hour arrest hold. Using the witness statements from Margot and Henderson connecting victim and suspect, they got a friendly judge to issue a search warrant based upon probable cause. It gave them twenty-four hours to search Preston Borders's car and home.

They got lucky. Three hours into the search of the Vesper apartment, Bosch noticed that a set of wooden shelves had been put together without two screws that held the bottom shelf in place on the unit's base. Bosch figured that if someone was going to cut corners on assembling a set of shelves, they would do it at the top, not the base.

Once he removed the books and other items from the shelf, he was able to easily lift up the laminated board, revealing a hiding space within the base of the shelving unit. He found the sea-horse pendant there wrapped in a tissue. The braided twine necklace was gone. He found several other pieces of women's jewelry as well and a collection of pornographic magazines specializing in sadomasochism and bondage.

With the discovery of the sea-horse pendant, the case against Borders went from weak to strong. Skyler's mother was still in town, having made arrangements for her daughter's body to be returned to Florida for burial. Bosch and Sheehan met her at her hotel and she identified the pendant as the one she had given her daughter.

The detectives were overjoyed and felt they had snatched victory from the jaws of defeat. That night after filing the case with the District Attorney's Office, they would go out and click martini glasses at the Short Stop in Echo Park.

Thirty years later, Bosch remembered the thrill of finding the key evidence. He savored the moment across time as he stacked the loose pages of the interview transcript. He remained unshaken in his confidence in the case he and Sheehan had built, and in his belief that Borders had murdered Danielle Skyler.

In the run-up to the trial, Bosch and Sheehan attempted to link the other pieces of jewelry found in the hiding place to other cases. They pulled all unsolved murders and disappearances of young women during the four years Borders had lived in Los Angeles. They believed he was good for at least two other sex slayings. Both victims were women who had tangential connections to the entertainment industry and who moved in the same Ventura Boulevard bar circuit as Borders.

They found photos of the women wearing jewelry that they believed matched pieces from the hiding place in his apartment, but expert analysis could not confirm the connections and the D.A.'s Office decided to try Borders only for the Skyler murder. Bosch and Sheehan objected to the decision but the prosecutor always got final call.

At trial Borders and his lawyer had to scramble to explain the sea-horse pendant. But the effort seemed desperate. Defense attorney David Siegel, known in courthouse circles as Legal Siegel because of his shrewd understanding and use of the law, attempted to challenge the authentication of the piece of jewelry as Skyler's.

The prosecution had presented the victim's mother, who identified the piece and tearfully told the story behind it, as well as the photos of Skyler taken just a few weeks before the murder in which the pendant could be seen hanging around her neck. Siegel presented a representative of the jewelry piece's manufacturer, who testified that several thousand sea-horse pendants in the exact color and style were made and distributed across the country, including hundreds in Los Angeles-area retail stores.

Borders testified in his own defense and claimed he had bought the pendant found in his apartment at a store on the Santa Monica pier. He explained that he had remembered seeing a similar pendant on Skyler during their date and liking it. He bought his own to give at some point as a gift and that was why he had hidden the piece as well as other women's jewelry in the shelving unit. He kept the jewelry as potential gifts for women he dated and he didn't want the cache stolen should there be a break-in at his apartment.

Siegel backed his client's testimony with the introduction of burglary statistics for the Van Nuys Division, but the strained explanation for possession of the sea-horse pendant did not impress the jury, particularly when juxtaposed with a playback of the audiotape from the interview with Borders. The jury deliberated for six hours before delivering a guilty verdict. After a separate hearing, the same jurors took only two hours deliberating on the horrors to which Skyler was subjected to recommend the death penalty. The judge followed through and imposed the ultimate sanction on Borders.

Bosch completed his review of the initial investigation at four a.m. The music had stopped without his noticing. He was tired and he knew he had an all-hands meeting at seven thirty in the war room at SFPD to discuss where the *farmacia* murder investigation stood. He decided to grab a couple hours' sleep and get to the new investigation conducted by Soto and Tapscott as soon as the next break came up in the current case.

He headed down the hallway to his bedroom, remembering the moment when he had found the sea horse and knew in the deep folds of his heart that Borders was the murderer and that he was going to pay for his crime.

7

Bosch was on the road at seven, gulping home-brewed coffee as he drove down the ramp at Barham Boulevard onto the northbound 101 freeway. It was a cool, crisp morning and the mountains that ringed the Valley and usually trapped smog under the crosscurrents were clear across the northern horizon. After transitioning onto the 170, the second of three freeways that would take him to San Fernando, he pulled his phone and called the number he had for the Investigative Services Unit at San Quentin State Prison.

The call was answered by a human voice and Bosch asked for an investigator named Gabe Menendez. The prison had its own squad of investigators who handled inmate-on-inmate crimes and also gathered intel on the activities of the criminals housed within the prison. Bosch had worked with Menendez in years past and knew him as a straight shooter.

After a short delay, a new voice came on the line.

'This is Lieutenant Menendez. How can I help you?'

He had gotten a promotion since the last time Bosch had spoken to him.

'This is Harry Bosch down in L.A. Sounds like you've been moving up in the world.'

Bosch was careful not to say he was calling from

the LAPD. He was skirting the reality of his situation because he believed he would get better cooperation if Menendez believed he was dealing with the LAPD than with the tiny SFPD.

'That's been a while, Detective Bosch,' Menendez said. 'What can I do for you?'

'One of your guys on death row,' Bosch said. 'Name's Preston Borders. I put him there.'

'I know him. Been here longer than me.'

'Yeah, well, then you may have heard. He's trying to change that.'

'I may have heard something about it, yeah. We just got travel orders for him. He's heading your way next week. I thought a guy like him being here so long, his appeals would have run out.'

'They did, but this is a new angle he's playing. What I need to know is his visitor history and who is on his list.'

'I don't think that will be a problem. How far back you want to go?'

Bosch thought about when Lucas John Olmer had died.

'How about going back two years?' he asked.

'Not a problem,' Menendez said. 'I'll put someone on it and get back to you. Anything else?'

'Yeah, I was wondering, does Borders have phone and computer access on death row?'

'Not directly, no. No phone and no computer but he has access to regular mail. There are a number of websites out there that facilitate communication between death row inmates and pen pals, things like that. He connects to them through mail.'

Bosch thought about that for a moment before continuing.

'Is that monitored?' he asked. 'The mail, I mean.'

'Yes, it all goes through readers,' Menendez said. 'Somebody in this unit. It's on a rotation. Nobody can stand doing it for too long.'

'Any record of it kept?'

'Only if follow-up action is required. If there's nothing suspicious about the letter, it's passed on.'

'Do you know if Borders gets much mail?'

'They all do. Remember Scott Peterson? His mail is off the charts. There are a lot of fucked-up women out there, Bosch. They fall in love with the bad guys. Only this is safe for them, because these bad guys aren't getting out. Usually.'

'Right. What about letters going out?'

'Same thing. It goes through vetting before it's sent. If there's an issue with it, we turn it back to the inmate. Usually when we do that, it's because the guy's spinning some sick sex fantasy or something. Like what he'd do to the girl if they ever met up, shit like that. We don't allow that out.'

'Got it.'

'Anyway, I've got your number on my Rolodex. I'm the last guy around here who still uses one. Let me find somebody to put on this and we'll get back to you.'

'Then let me give you my cell. I'm out and about on another case – a double murder yesterday – and the cell is best. You can put it in your Rolodex.'

Bosch gave him the number and thanked him before disconnecting. He realized after the call that the information he was seeking might already be in the reports

Soto had slipped to him. The new investigation should have covered who Borders was meeting with or communicating with, but Menendez gave no indication that he had received a similar request already. It left Bosch thinking that either Soto and Tapscott had dropped the ball or Menendez had just been playing him.

Either way Bosch would find out soon enough.

Bosch next called his lawyer, Mickey Haller, who also happened to be his half brother. Haller had handled the legal issues that had come up when Bosch left the LAPD, ultimately suing the department for a full pension payout. The department folded and Bosch received an additional $180,000 that went into the kitty he hoped one day to leave to his daughter.

Haller answered with what Bosch would describe as a reluctant grunt.

'It's Bosch. I wake you?'

'No, man, I'm awake. I usually don't answer blocked calls this early. It's usually one of my clients saying, "Mick, the cops are knocking on my door with a warrant, what do I do?" Stuff like that.'

'Well, I got a problem, but a little different.'

'My brutha from another mutha, what's wrong? DUI?'

Haller was fond of the line and said it every time, always employing a half-assed impression of the Texas-bred Matthew McConaughey, the actor who had played him in a movie six years earlier.

'No, no DUI. Worse.'

Bosch proceeded to tell Haller about the visit the day before from Soto, Tapscott, and Kennedy. 'So my question is, should I be putting my pension and my house and everything else in Maddie's name right now? I mean, all of this is for her, not Borders.'

'First of all, fuck that. You won't pay a dime to that guy. Let me ask a couple of questions. Did these people who came to see you say or imply that there was any malfeasance on your part? Like you planted evidence or you withheld exculpatory evidence from the defense during the trial? Anything like that?'

'Not so far. They acted like it was a lab fuckup, if there even was one. Back then they didn't have the same techniques they use today. No DNA or any of that.'

'That's what I mean. So if something was missed during the due diligence and you were just carrying out your job in good faith, then the city has to cover you in any action Borders might take against you. Simple as that, and we'll sue the city if it doesn't. Wait till the union gets ahold of that and realizes the city isn't covering guys just doing their jobs.'

Bosch thought about what Soto had said about casting blame on Sheehan. It had not come up in the meeting with Kennedy. Was she trying to tip him off to another issue raised in the reinvestigation? He decided not to bring it up until he had been able to review the entire file.

'Okay,' he said.

He felt some relief from talking to Haller. He might soon face a career-ending humiliation but it appeared that at least his finances and his daughter's inheritance would be protected.

'What's the name of the DA from CIU who came to see you?' Haller said. 'I've dealt with those people a few times.'

'Kennedy,' Bosch said. 'I can't remember his first name.'

'Alex Kennedy. He's a real D-bag. He may have played the respect card with you but that guy's going to come up with the knife behind your back and try to take your scalp.'

So much for the relief Bosch felt. He was now on the 5 freeway and approaching the exit for San Fernando.

'The good news is, fuck him,' Haller said. 'If this is all based on new evidence and not malfeasance of duty, then, like I said, the city will have to cover you. You want me to get involved with this?'

'Not yet,' Bosch said. 'I'm looking into it. I reviewed my own investigation and I don't think I was wrong back then. Borders did this and I'm going to find the fix. But the hearing is scheduled for next Wednesday. What are my options there?'

'Depending on what you find out between now and then, I could always file a motion challenging the whole shooting match and asking to be heard on the matter. It might stay the ruling, give the judge something to think about for a week or so. But we'll eventually have to put up or shut up.'

Bosch thought about that. If he needed more time to investigate the case, that might be an option.

'That would be weird, though,' Haller said.

'What would?' Bosch asked.

'Me going into court to ask a judge *not* to release a prisoner on death row. That would be a first, as a matter of fact. I might have to farm it out to an associate. Being on the wrong side of this could be bad for business, bro. Just saying.'

'You wouldn't be on the wrong side.'

'All I'm saying is, DNA is the great equalizer. How often do you think the cops get it wrong and send innocent people to prison?'

'Not very often.'

'One percent of the time? I mean, nobody's perfect, right?'

'I don't know, maybe.'

'In this country, there are two million people in prison. Two million. If the system gets it wrong one percent of the time, that is twenty thousand innocent people in jail. Lower it to a half of a percentage point and you're still at ten thousand people. This is what keeps me awake at night. Why I always say, the scariest client is the innocent man. Because there is so much at stake.'

'Maybe you *are* the wrong guy for this, then.'

'Look, I'm just saying that the system is imperfect. There are innocent people in prison, innocent people on death row, innocent people executed. These are facts, and you have to think about that before you go whole hog on this. No matter what, you are personally protected. Just remember that.'

'I will. But I gotta go now. I have a meeting.'

'All right, bro. Call me when you need me.'

Bosch disconnected the call, now feeling worse about his situation than when he had started out from the house that morning.

8

Bosch entered the war room shortly before seven thirty, but Lourdes was already putting up case details and task lists on one of the whiteboards.

'Morning, Bella.'

'Hey, Harry. There's a fresh pot in the squad.'

'I'm all right for now. You get some sleep?'

'A little. Hard to sleep with the first live murder case we've had around here in four years.'

Bosch pulled out a chair at the head of the table and sat down so he could study what she was putting up. To the left she had started two columns with a vertical line between them. One was marked 'José' and the other 'Junior.' Basic facts about each of the victims were listed below their names. He knew that she had spent most of the afternoon after the murders with the wife and mother of the two victims and she had gathered good intel on the family dynamic. Fresh out of pharmacy school, José Jr. was living at home but he was at odds with his parents over the living and working arrangements.

Lourdes was now writing on a second board and listing investigative leads and tasks that needed to be assigned and performed. Some she wrote in black ink and some in red. There were the autopsies and ballistics to cover. Video from the *farmacia*'s cameras going back thirty days prior to the murders was available and would take several hours to review. There were other pharmacy robberies in Los Angeles in recent years that needed to be reviewed for similarities.

'Why the red?' Bosch asked.

'High priority,' Lourdes said.

'What is MBC?'

She had written and underlined the letters in red, then drawn an arrow to her own initials. It was a lead she was going to handle.

'Medical Board of California,' Lourdes said. 'I was in Junior's room yesterday and found a letter from the MBC saying they were in receipt of his complaint and would be in contact after an investigator had reviewed it.'

'Okay,' Bosch said. 'What makes it a priority?'

'A couple things. One is that he had the letter in his room in a drawer, like he was hiding it.'

'From who? His parents?'

'I don't know yet. The other is that the mother gave up that Junior and his father had been fighting lately. She didn't know what it was about but it was something to do with work. They weren't talking at home. My hunch is it has something to do with the complaint he made to the medical board. It seems like it's worth checking out.'

'I agree. Let me know what you get.'

The door opened and Sisto and Luzon entered, followed by Captain Trevino. They all had steaming mugs of coffee.

Trevino was midfifties, with a salt-and-pepper mustache and a shaved head. He was in uniform, which was his routine but always seemed odd to Bosch because he was in charge of the detective bureau, where no one wore uniforms. It was known within the department that he was the heir apparent to the chief, but there was no sign that the chief, a lifelong resident of the town, was going anywhere. Bosch's perception was that this left Trevino frustrated and he channeled it into being a stickler for rules and discipline.

'I'm going to sit in and update the chief after,' Trevino said. 'He's got a Business Leaders breakfast and needs to be there.'

In a small town like San Fernando, the chief had to be equal parts police administrator, politician, and community cheerleader. A double murder on one of the main business and community-gathering streets would be a hot topic, and Valdez would need to calm nerves and promote confidence in the investigation. In some ways that was as important as the investigation itself.

'No problem,' Bosch said.

He and Trevino had gotten off to a rough start when Bosch first came to the department. Based on Bosch's history with the LAPD, the captain viewed Bosch as a loose cannon who had to be closely monitored. That didn't work for Bosch, but things smoothed out some a year later when an investigation by Bosch and Lourdes identified and led to the arrest of a serial rapist who had been targeting women in the small city for over four years. The subsequent publicity created a groundswell of community support for the department, with Trevino receiving the lion's share of credit as the man in charge of the detective squad. Since then, Trevino had been content to give Bosch free rein as he worked through the cold case files and evidence boxes in the city's old jail. But Bosch sensed that suspicion remained and he knew that as soon as Trevino found out about the Borders situation, he would start whispering in the chief's ear that Bosch had to go.

'Why don't we start by looking at the video from the pharmacy?' Bosch said. 'Not all of us have seen it. Then we can go around the room and summarize yesterday's work so Captain Trevino can keep the chief up to speed. Bella?'

Lourdes picked up a remote and turned on one of the screens on the wall opposite the whiteboards. The video from the *farmacia* was already cued up because Bosch and Lourdes had watched it several times the night before, their last work before heading home.

There were three cameras in the *farmacia*, and the ceiling camera over the prescription counter offered the most complete recording of the murders. The five people in the war room watched silently as the video advanced in slow motion.

On the screen both José Esquivel and his son were behind the counter in the pharmacy section. They were setting up for the day, as the *farmacia* opened at ten o'clock each day except Sunday. José Sr. was at the counter, going through a plastic basket with several small white bags in it – packaged prescriptions waiting for pickup. José Jr. was standing at a computer at the end of the counter, apparently checking for new prescriptions sent by medical offices. There were no other employees in the store. It had been determined through interviews the day before that the father and son were the only full-time employees. There was a part-time employee who worked on the busiest days of the week or when one of the Esquivels was off, but she was not a pharmacist and she functioned primarily as a cashier.

At 10:14, according to the timer on the video, the front door of the pharmacy opened and two men entered, already with ski masks pulled down and holding their weapons with gloved hands at their sides. They didn't run but walked quickly as they separated into two of the retail aisles and moved toward the counter at the rear of the store.

José Sr. looked up first and saw the man in an aisle leading directly toward his position. It could not be known from the camera angle if he realized there were two men. But he immediately moved to his right and pushed a forearm into his son's side, shoving him away from the computer and alerting him to the approaching danger.

Though the video was silent, it was clear that José Sr. yelled something to his son. José Jr. then turned to his right toward the half door that led to the hallway and the rear exit. It appeared that he did not realize that this put him in the path of the man moving down the other aisle. José Jr. started to run into the hallway. The gunman emerged from the aisle and followed, both of them disappearing off camera into the rear of the pharmacy.

The other gunman continued without hesitation toward the counter and raised his weapon. José Sr. raised his hands palms out in surrender. The gunman extended the gun between Esquivel's raised hands and shot him nearly point-blank in the chest, a through-and-through shot that tore into the cabinets behind him.

José Sr. took a step back and bumped into the cabinets, then collapsed to the floor, his arms still extended up by his shoulders.

'Holy shit, that's cold,' said Sisto, who had not seen the video previously.

No one responded. They watched in stunned silence.

Moments after Esquivel went down, the second gunman appeared in the doorway, coming from the rear hallway, presumably after shooting and killing José Jr. He moved to the counter and reached underneath to a white plastic trash can. He dumped its contents on the floor and then started moving among the drug cabinets, opening drawers and dumping the stores of pills and capsules into the trash can. The other gunman kept his eyes trained on the front door, two hands on his weapon and ready to use it. Bosch again realized how lucky it was that there had not been more victims – customers wandering into the store, not knowing the danger awaiting them. These killers were clearly not going to leave witnesses.

It could have been a massacre.

Ninety seconds after the gunmen had entered through the front door, they moved into the back hallway and disappeared for good, having gone out the rear exit.

'We think they must've had a car and driver in the alley,' Lourdes said. 'Anybody want to see it again?'

'No, thanks,' Trevino said. 'Any video from where the son got hit?'

'No, the rear hallway wasn't covered by camera,' Lourdes said.

'What about the street?' Trevino pressed. 'We have anything that shows those two bastards without masks on?'

'Nothing,' Luzon said. 'There are cameras on both ends of the mall but they didn't pick up shit.'

'We think they were dropped off in the alley and went in the back door of the Three Kings,' said Sisto, using the English name for the bar located two doors down from the pharmacy.

'They walked through the bar and out the front door,' Luzon said. 'Then down to La Familia and pulled down their masks before going in.'

'They knew what they were doing,' Sisto added. 'And where the cameras were.'

'We get descriptions out of the Kings?' Trevino asked.

'Not a very cooperative group in there, Captain,' Luzon said. 'We got nothing other than the bartender saying he saw two guys walk through real quick. He said they were white and that's about it.'

Trevino frowned. He knew full well that the Tres Reyes was the source of frequent patrol calls because of fighting, gambling, drunk and disorderly conduct, code violations, and other disruptive issues. The establishment was a sore spot on the mall, and the department had for years been under community pressure to do something about it. Chief Valdez routinely visited roll calls at the station and singled out the establishment for proactive enforcement, meaning he wanted patrol officers to walk through the bar several times a shift – a practice not welcomed by anyone on either side of the bar. Subsequently, the relations between the police and the bar's management and clientele were not good. There would not be much help coming from the Tres Reyes on this case.

'Okay, what else?' Trevino asked. 'This match up with any recent cases in the city?'

He meant Los Angeles. Most residents of San Fernando referred to it as the town and Los Angeles as the city.

'We have two similars,' Sisto said. 'Both in the city. I'm getting details and video today. But the basics are the same – two white men in ski masks, driver waits outside. Only difference is, nobody got hurt in those. They were straight robberies – one in Encino and the other in West Hills.'

Bosch involuntarily shook his head and Trevino noticed.

'Not our suspects?' the captain asked.

'I don't think so,' Bosch said. 'I think our suspects wanted us to think that. But this was a hit.'

'Okay,' Trevino said. 'Then where's our focus?'

'On the son,' Lourdes said.

'How so?' the captain asked.

'Well, as far as we can tell, the kid was a straight shooter. He graduated last year from the pharmacy school at Cal State-Northridge. No arrest record, no known gang affiliation. "Most likely to succeed" in his high school class. But Mrs. Esquivel said he was going through a rough patch relating to the family business and his living at home.'

'Do we know any more than that and how it might connect?'

'Not at the moment but we're working on it. I need

to take another run at Mrs. Esquivel. Last night was not the right time.'

'Then why do we think it's about the kid?'

Bosch pointed to the screen where the image was frozen on a shot that showed José Sr. sprawled dead on the floor of his business.

'The video,' he said. 'It looks like the father recognized what was about to happen and tried to get his son out of there. Then you have the overkill – the father shot once, the kid shot three times.'

'Plus nothing says it's personal like a shot up the ass,' added Sisto.

Trevino computed all of this and nodded.

'Okay, what about next moves?' he asked.

The caseload was then chopped up, with Luzon assigned the autopsies and ballistics, with a rush order to find out what weapons were used in the killings and if they matched other cases in the databases containing ballistic profiles. Sisto got video duty, with instructions to go back through video from the *farmacia* to look for indications that the two gunmen had cased the place earlier in the month as well as to study the relationship between father and son. Sisto would also check in with the LAPD about the two similar pharmacy robberies and see if he could look at video from those crimes.

Lourdes said she would follow up on backgrounding the son and checking out the complaint he had made to the state's medical board. Bosch would serve as case coordinator and back Lourdes when her inquiries took her out of the station.

Picking up on that, Trevino gave the final instruction to all.

'This is a murder investigation, so the stakes are higher,' he said. 'That goes for everybody, including our shooters. I know we are a small department, but nobody should go out on the street on this case without a partner. You never know what you might walk into. Roger that?'

He received a chorus of confirmations back.

'Okay,' he said. 'Let's find these guys.'

9

After the war room meeting, Bosch left the station, while Lourdes attempted to get hold of someone in the investigations unit of the state medical board. He walked two blocks to a shopping plaza on Truman and into a bodega that sold throwaway phones to new immigrants who could not establish addresses and the credit histories required by the big service providers. He bought a throwaway with texting capability and a full charge. He then stepped out of the store and sent a two-word text to Lucia Soto.

Thank you.

Less than a minute later he got a response.

Who is this?

He typed in,

Go to a private spot. 5 minutes.

He checked his watch and started walking back to the station. Five minutes later he was standing in the side parking lot and made the call. Soto took the call but said nothing.

'Lucia, it's me.'

'Harry? What are you doing? Where's your phone?'

'This is a burner. I thought you wouldn't want to have any record of talking to me.'

'Don't be silly. What is going on? What are you thanking me for?'

'For the file.'

'What file?'

'Okay, if that's how you want to play it, fine. I get it. I have to tell you, I got through the old case – my part in it – and it's all there, Lucia. It was a solid case. Circumstantial, yes, but solid down the line to the verdict. You need to stop this whole thing and not put this guy back on the street.'

'Harry . . .'

She didn't finish.

'What, Lucia? Look, don't you understand? I'm trying to save you from getting caught in the middle of a big problem here. Somehow, some way, this is a scam. Can you get me a copy of that video Tapscott showed me of you two opening the box?'

There was another long pause before Soto responded.

'I think the only one with a big problem here is you, Harry.'

Bosch had nothing to say to that. He sensed that something had changed in her view of him. He had fallen in her eyes, and she had sympathy for him but not the respect she'd once had. He was missing something here. He had to get back to the investigative file he knew she had stuffed into his mailbox, whether she acknowledged it or not. He now had to consider that she had done so not to help him but to warn him about what lay ahead.

80

'Listen to me,' Soto said. 'I'm putting my neck out here for you because . . . because we were partners. You need to let this play out without setting a fire. If you don't, you are going to get hurt in a big way.'

'You don't think it's going to hurt in a big way to see that guy – that killer – walk out of San Quentin a free man?'

'I need to go now. I suggest you read the whole file.'

She disconnected and Bosch was left holding a phone that he'd just spent forty dollars for and would probably never use again.

He headed toward his car. He had brought the Skyler file with him from the house and left it on the rear floorboard. Soto had clearly just directed him back to the file. There was something in the new investigation that she was pushing him toward and that, at least in Alex Kennedy's mind, invalidated the old investigation. Bosch suspected it was more than DNA.

Before he made it to the car, the side door of the station opened and Lourdes stepped out.

'Harry, I was coming to get you. Where are you going?'

'Just getting something from my car. What's up?'

'Let's take a ride. I talked to an investigator for the state medical board.'

Bosch shoved the burner into his pocket and followed her to her city ride. He got in the passenger side and she started backing out. He saw that she had put a piece of scratch paper down on the center console that said 'S.F. and Terra Bella,' which he knew was an intersection in the nearby Pacoima neighborhood of Los Angeles. It was to the immediate south of San Fernando.

'Pacoima?' he asked.

'José Jr. sent an e-mail to the medical board, complaining that a clinic down in Pacoima was over-prescribing oxycodone,' she said. 'I just want to do a drive-by, check the place out.'

'Got it. When did Junior send the e-mail?'

'Two months ago. He sent it to the Central Complaint Unit in Sacramento, where it sat for a while before being sent down to the enforcement unit in L.A. I tracked down the guy who caught it there. He said he was early stages with it. Never talked to José Jr. and was gathering data before making any sort of enforcement move.'

'Gathering data? You mean like how much the clinic was prescribing?'

'Yes, identifying the clinic, what doctors were in there, licensing, prescription counts, all of that kind of stuff. Early stages, which I think was his way of saying nothing had happened yet. He did say that this clinic was not on their radar and that it sounded like a fly-by-night pill mill. Here today, gone as soon as authorities take notice. The thing is, he said, most of the time they don't use legit pharmacies. Usually the pharmacies are in cahoots, or at least willing to look the other way and fill the prescriptions.'

'So, let's say José Sr. was looking the other way. The son graduates from pharmacy school all wide-eyed and naive and thinks he's doing a good thing, pointing his finger at a shady clinic.'

Lourdes nodded.

'Exactly,' she said. 'I told you he was a straight shooter. He saw what was going on and made the complaint to the board.'

'So this is what the father and son were having issues with – why they were fighting,' Bosch added. 'Either José Sr. liked the money the bogus prescriptions brought in, or he was afraid of the danger the complaint might bring in.'

'Not only that, Junior said in his e-mail that he was going to stop filling prescriptions from the clinic. That could have been the most dangerous move of all.'

Bosch felt a dull pain in his chest. It was guilt and embarrassment. He had underestimated José Esquivel Jr. He had first asked about gang affiliation and jumped to the conclusion that Junior's activities and associations would be the motivating factor in the murders. He was probably correct in one sense, but he was far off the mark about the young man. The truth revealed that he was an idealist who saw something wrong and was blindly trying to do the right thing. And it cost him his life.

'Damn,' he said. 'He didn't know what he was doing if he stopped filling scrips.'

'Which makes it so sad,' added Lourdes.

Bosch was silent after that as he thought about his mistake. It bothered him deeply because a relationship was always established between a victim and the detective charged with solving the crime. Bosch had doubted the goodness of his victim and let him down. In doing so he had let himself down as well. It made him want to double-down on his efforts to find the two men who had moved so swiftly and lethally through the pharmacy the morning before.

Bosch thought about the terror José Jr. must have felt as he tried to make it down the hallway to the exit door.

The horror of knowing he had left his father behind.

Bosch couldn't be sure, because there was no sound on the video and the shooting of José Jr. was off camera, but he guessed that the father had been shot first, and in the hallway his son had heard it as he tried to escape. Just before he too was shot and his killer came up on him to commit a final indignity and finish the job.

They took Truman south to where it merged with San Fernando Road and soon they crossed the city limits and into Pacoima. There was no 'Welcome to Los Angeles' sign and the difference between the two communities was stark. The streets here were trash-strewn, the walls marked with graffiti. The medians were brown and weed-filled. Plastic bags were snagged on the fence line that guarded the Metro tracks that paralleled the road. To Bosch it was depressing. Though Pacoima had the same ethnic makeup as San Fernando, there was a visible disparity in the economic levels of the side-by-side communities.

Soon they were driving along the south perimeter of Whiteman Airport, a small general-aviation field ironically named, considering that it was surrounded by a community that was overwhelmingly brown and black. Lourdes slowed the car as they approached Terra Bella. Bosch could see a white one-story building on the corner. It stood out because its paint was fresh and shining in the sun and because there was no door or any signage announcing it as a clinic or anything else.

Lourdes made the turn on Terra Bella so they could check the side of the building. They spotted the double-door entrance on the side but there was no indication that the clinic was in operation. The new paint and lack of signage made it appear to be a clinic not quite open for business.

Lourdes kept driving south.

'What do you think?' she asked.

'I don't know,' Bosch said. 'You want to watch for a while, see if we can tell if it's even open for business? Or you could just pull over and I could go try that door.'

Lourdes pondered what to do, while the car continued down the street.

'I don't like barging in there when we don't know what we've got,' she finally said.

She turned into the entrance drive of a company that manufactured fire sprinkler systems, then backed out to turn the car around.

'Let's watch for a while,' she said. 'See what happens.'

'Sounds like a plan,' Bosch said.

She drove a half block back up Terra Bella and then parked at the curb behind a sedan. It gave them a blind but still allowed them to keep eyes on the clinic's door. They sat in comfortable silence for almost fifteen minutes before Lourdes spoke.

'You still tight with Lucy Soto?' she asked.

Bosch had forgotten that Lourdes and Soto knew each other at least casually through a Latina law enforcement organization.

'We talk now and then but I think yesterday was the first time I'd seen her in a couple years,' Bosch said.

He knew that Lourdes was angling to find out what the visit from downtown the day before was all about, but he wasn't interested in talking about it. He changed the subject.

'Your son excited about the Dodgers this year?' he asked.

'Oh, yeah,' Lourdes said. 'He picked his games and I need to get the tickets. He thinks they are going to win it all this year.'

'About time.'

'Yeah.'

'You know that Soto's never been to a Dodgers game? Her grandparents and her father were kicked out of Chavez Ravine back in the fifties and she'll never set foot in that place. She doesn't even like going to the academy.'

Bosch was talking about the forced relocation of an entire Latino neighborhood to make way for the baseball stadium near downtown. The bitterness of the move – including many tearful and violent evictions recorded on news cameras – still blemished the history of the much-loved team. The LAPD academy was on the edge of one of the stadium's vast parking lots.

'I guess I understand all of that,' Lourdes said. 'But it was a long time ago. Baseball is baseball. Like I'm going to deny a little boy his love of baseball because of something that happened before his mother was even born?'

'His mother's love of baseball too,' Bosch said.

He smiled. Before Lourdes could formulate a comeback, they both saw a van turn the corner from San Fernando onto Terra Bella. Bosch at first thought it was heading to the sprinkler manufacturer, but it stopped directly in front of the door to the clinic. Bosch and Lourdes watched silently as the side door of the van slid open and people started climbing out and heading to the door of the clinic.

Bosch counted eleven people, not including the driver, who remained in the van. They disappeared into the clinic.

'So what was that?' Lourdes asked.

'Got me,' Bosch said. 'Maybe they picked people up at an old folks home or something.'

'They weren't all old.'

'Mostly old.'

'And they looked more like they were homeless than from a home.'

Bosch nodded and they dropped back into silence as they continued to watch. The van's driver remained in place behind the wheel and the side door remained open.

About twenty minutes after they disembarked from the van, the passengers started coming out of the clinic and getting in line to get back in the van. Bosch looked more closely this time. They were diverse in gender and race but consistent in the scruffy clothing that hung loose on their bony frames. To Bosch it looked like a line for a soup kitchen on 5th Street in downtown.

'What do you think?' Lourdes asked.

'I don't know,' Bosch said. 'What kind of clinic doesn't have a sign out front?'

'The illegitimate kind.'

'And those are patients?'

'Maybe pill shills. Jerry, the medical board investigator, called them that. They go to the so-called clinic, get a prescription, and then go collect the pills at the pharmacy. They're paid a dollar a pill. I guess it's not bad if you're picking up sixty pills a pop.'

'But then what do the pills sell for on the street?'

'He said that depends on dosage and what you're buying. Generally, a dollar a milligram. Oxycodone scrips usually come in thirty-milligram pills. But he said the holy grail of hillbilly heroin these days is the eighty-meg dose. Also something called oxymorphone. It's the next big thing. The high is supposedly ten times as powerful as you get with oxycodone.'

Bosch took out his phone and opened up the camera app. Steadying the phone on the dashboard, he started taking photos of the clinic and the van. He used the zoom to get a closer look at the people waiting to climb in but their features blurred.

'You think the van's going to start taking them around to pharmacies now?' he asked.

'Maybe,' Lourdes said. 'Jerry said old people make the best shills. They're prized.'

'Why's that?'

'Because they want people who look old enough to be on Medicare. They give them counterfeit Medicare D cards – they buy the names of legit cardholders – and then they don't have to pay full price for the prescriptions they fill.'

Bosch shook his head in disbelief.

'So Medicare pays the pharmacy back for the drugs,' he said. 'In other words, the federal government finances the operation.'

'A lot of it,' Lourdes said. 'According to Jerry.'

One last man came out of the clinic's door and headed toward the van. By Bosch's count, twelve men and women were now crammed into the back. They were white, black, and brown, the one unifying factor being that they all looked like they had been down rough roads. They had gaunt faces and a shabbiness about them that unmistakably came from the hard life. The driver, wearing sunglasses and a black golf shirt, got out and went around the front of the van to slide the door closed. By the time Bosch had zoomed in his camera, it was too late to get the shot. The driver was in the van and hidden behind reflections on the windshield.

The van pulled away from the clinic and headed down Terra Bella in the direction of the two detectives. Bosch pulled his phone down below the dashboard.

'Shit,' Lourdes said.

There was no disguising that Bosch and Lourdes were in an unmarked police car. It was black and had government hubs and flashers mounted behind the front grille.

But the van went by without slowing, the driver preoccupied with a call on his cell phone. Bosch noticed he had a goatee and a gold ring on the hand that held his phone.

Lourdes watched in her side-view mirror until the van went two blocks down to El Dorado and turned right.

'Should we?' she asked.

'Might as well,' Bosch said.

She pulled the car away from the curb and made a three-point turn. She punched it to get down to El Dorado and made the same turn the van did. They caught up to the van as it made another right at Pierce and then drove north, crossing San Fernando and the Metro tracks before entering Whiteman Airport.

'Didn't expect this,' Lourdes said.

'Yeah, weird,' Bosch added.

The van pulled up to a gate across from an entrance to the private hangar area, and the driver's window came down. An arm extended from the window and held a key card to a reader. The gate lifted and the van went through. Lourdes and Bosch couldn't go through but there was a perimeter road that ran parallel to the internal road and allowed them to follow the van from outside the restricted area. They watched it pull into an open hangar and then lost sight of it from their angle.

They parked on the side of the perimeter road and waited.

'What are you thinking?' Lourdes asked.

'No idea,' Bosch said. 'Let's just see what happens.'

They watched in silence after that, and a few minutes later a single-engine plane, its prop a spinning blur, emerged from the hangar and started moving toward the runway. After it cleared the hangar, the van pulled out and headed back toward the gate.

'The van or plane?' Lourdes asked.

'Let's stay here with the plane,' Bosch said. 'I have the plate off the van.'

Bosch counted seven windows running down the side of the plane behind the cockpit. Shades were pulled down inside each window. He pulled a pen and note-book out of his pocket and wrote down the tail number of the plane. He also noted down the time. Then, raising his phone again, he started taking photos of the plane as it taxied to the runway.

'What the hell are we looking at here?' Lourdes asked.

'I don't know,' Bosch said. 'But I got the tail number. If they filed a flight plan, we can get it.'

Bosch checked the hangar and saw the big, wide door slowly coming down. There was an advertisement in faded paint on the corrugated metal.

TAKE THE PLUNGE!
SFV SKYDIVING CLUB
CALL TODAY! JUMP TODAY!

Bosch turned his attention back to the runway and watched silently as the plane moved down the tarmac. It was white with a burnt-orange stripe running down its side. It had an overhead wing and a jump deck below the outline of a wide passenger door.

Bosch switched the camera to video and filmed as the plane picked up speed and then lifted into the air. It flew off to the east and then banked south below the sun.

Bosch and Lourdes watched until it disappeared.

10

The air traffic control tower at Whiteman was up a staircase from a small general administration building. There was one receptionist between the public and the stairs and she folded at the sight of the police badges. Bosch and Lourdes went up the stairs and knocked on a door with a sign on it that said A.T.C. – NO ADMITTANCE.

A man answered the door and started raising his hand to point to the words 'No Admittance,' when he too saw the badges.

'Officers,' he said. 'Is this about the drag racers?'

Bosch and Lourdes looked at each other, not expecting the question.

'No,' Lourdes said. 'We want to ask about that plane that just took off.'

The man turned and looked back into the room behind him and out the window to the airfield as if to confirm he was at an airport and that a plane had just taken off. He then looked back at Lourdes.

'You're talking about the Cessna?' he asked.

'The jump plane,' Bosch said.

'Yeah, the Grand Caravan. Also known as the mini-van. Not much else I can tell you beyond that.'

'Is there room in there for us to come in and talk? This is a homicide investigation.'

'Uh, sure. Be my guests.'

He held his arm out for them to enter. Bosch pegged him as late sixties with a military background – something about his bearing and the way he held out his hand like he was snapping off a salute.

The tower was a small space with the requisite windows offering a full view of the airfield. There were two seats in front of a radar-and-communications console. Bosch signaled Lourdes to take one of the seats and he leaned against a four-drawer filing cabinet next to the door.

'Can we start with your name, sir?' Lourdes said.

The man took the remaining seat after turning it to face the two detectives.

'Ted O'Connor,' he said.

'How long have you worked here, Mr. O'Connor?' she asked.

'Oh, let's see, about twenty years now over two different stints. Came here after the Air Force – put in twenty-five there, dropping napalm and shit on foreign lands. Then I came here for ten, retired, then decided I didn't like being retired and came back after a year. That was twelve years ago. You might think sitting up here all day is boring but you try spending a summer in a double-wide with a single-wide AC unit, you want hot *and* boring. Anyway, who gives a shit, really? You want to know about that Cessna.'

'Do you know how long it has been here?'

'Offhand, I can tell you it's been hangared here longer than I have and it's changed hands quite a few times over the years. The owner for the past couple years is a company from down in Calexico. At least that's where

Betty downstairs tells me the hangar and fuel invoices go.'

'What's the name of the company?'

'Betty will have to get you that. She told me but I don't remember. Cielo something or other. It's a Spanish name and I don't have much Spanish.'

'Is it still used for skydiving?'

'I hope not. The people I see getting on that plane wouldn't make it to the ground alive.'

Bosch leaned forward and looked out through the windows. He saw that O'Connor had a direct line of vision into the hangar. The binoculars on the console would give him a close-up view inside when the big door was open.

'So, what do you see going on in that hangar, Mr. O'Connor?' Bosch asked.

'I see a lot of people coming in and out,' O'Connor said. 'A lot of people as old as . . . well, me.'

'Every day?'

'Just about. I'm only here four days a week, but every day that I am, I see that plane either landing or taking off and sometimes both.'

'Do you know if that plane is still configured inside for skydiving?'

'As far as I know.'

'Long jump benches on both sides?'

'That's right.'

'So, how many people can they put in there at once?'

'That plane's a stretch model with the big tail section. You can get fifteen, maybe twenty, in there if you have to.'

Bosch nodded.

'Did you ever report what you saw to anyone?' Lourdes asked.

'Report what?' O'Connor said. 'What's the crime in getting on a plane?'

'Did they file a flight plan today?'

'They never file a flight plan. They don't have to. They don't even need to check in with the tower as long they're flying VFR.'

'VFR, what's that?'

'Visual flight rules. See, I'm here to provide radar to those who request it and to guide instrument fliers in or out if they need it. Trouble is, you mighta noticed we're in California, and if it's sunny out, you're gonna go VFR, and there is no FAA rule requiring a pilot to make contact with the tower on a general aviation airfield. The guy flying the Caravan today? He said one thing to me, and that was it.'

'What was it he said?'

'That he was positioning for an easterly takeoff. And I told him the field was his.'

'That's it?'

'That's it, except he said it with a Russian accent. I think because we have a westerly wind today, he was letting me know he was going down to the other end in case I had somebody coming in.'

'How do you know it was a Russian accent?'

'Because I just do.'

'Okay, so no flight plan means there's no documentation of where he's going or when he's due back?'

'Not required at an airfield like this and for a plane like that.'

O'Connor pointed out the window as though the

plane in question were hovering out there. Lourdes looked at Bosch. She was clearly surprised by the lack of security and control of who came in and out of the airport.

'If you think the days are wide open here, you should check this place out at night,' O'Connor said. 'We close the tower at eight. It's an uncontrolled field after that. People can come in and out as they please – and they do.'

'You just leave the runway lights on?' Bosch asked.

'No, the lights are radio controlled. Anybody in a plane can toggle them on and off. The only thing you have to worry about are the drag racers.'

'Drag racers?'

'They sneak out onto the tarmac at night and have their races. We had a guy coming in here about a month ago, flicked on the lights and almost put it down on top of one of those hot rods.'

They were interrupted by a call on the radio, and O'Connor turned to the console to handle it. It sounded to Bosch like a plane was coming in from the west. O'Connor told the pilot the airfield was his. Harry looked at Lourdes. She raised her eyebrows and Bosch nodded. The message between them was clear. They didn't know if what they were asking about had any-thing to do with their investigation, but what they had just seen – -several men and women transported from the clinic directly to a plane and then flown away with-out so much as a head count – was highly unusual, and the ease with which it was done was surprising.

O'Connor stood and leaned over the console to look through the windows. He picked up the binoculars and held them to his eyes as he looked out.

'We've got one coming in,' he said.

Bosch and Lourdes remained silent. Bosch was unsure if he should interrupt O'Connor's observation and handling of the landing. Soon a small single-engine plane came gliding over the airfield from the west and safely landed. O'Connor wrote the plane's tail number down on a log page on a clipboard and then hung it on a hook on the wall to his right. He then turned back to the detectives.

'What else can I tell you?' he asked.

Bosch pointed to the clipboard.

'You document every takeoff and landing that occurs during business hours?' he asked.

'We don't have to,' O'Connor said. 'But we do, yes. If we're here.'

'Mind if I take a look?'

'No, I don't mind.'

O'Connor took the clipboard back off the wall and handed it to Bosch. There were several pages documenting the comings and goings at the airport. The single aircraft that made the most takeoffs and landings had the tail number Bosch had written down earlier – the jump plane.

He handed the clipboard back. His plan was to officially reclaim it with a search warrant.

'Are there cameras on the runways and in the hangars?' he asked.

'Yes, we have cameras,' O'Connor said.

'How long is the video archived?'

'Not sure. I think a month. The LAPD was out here to look at video of the drag racing, and they went back a few weeks, I heard.'

Bosch nodded. It was good to know they could come back to look at video if needed.

'So, in summary,' Lourdes said. 'This airport essentially has unrestricted access in and out. No flight plans required, no passenger or cargo manifests required, nothing like that.'

'That's about right,' O'Connor said.

'And there's no way to tell where that plane – the Grand Caravan – is heading?'

'Well, that depends. You're supposed to fly with your transponder on. If he's following the rules, then he's got the transponder on and that will register as that plane moves through airspace from one ATC region to the other.'

'Can you get that in real time? Like right now?'

'No, we would need to get the unique transponder code from the plane and put out the request. Might take a day. Maybe longer.'

Lourdes looked at Bosch. He nodded. He had nothing more to ask.

'Thank you, Mr. O'Connor,' she said. 'We appreciate your cooperation. We would also appreciate it if you would keep this conversation to yourself.'

'Not a problem,' O'Connor said.

Bosch and Lourdes waited until they were back in the car before discussing what they had learned in the last hour.

'Holy shit, Harry,' Lourdes said. 'I mean, where the fuck's TSA when you need them? Somebody could just get in a plane here, load it up with whatever they want, and fly it downtown or to a water reservoir or wherever and do who knows what.'

'Scary,' Bosch said.

'No matter what, we need to tell somebody about this. Leak it to the media or something.'

'Let's see how it figures into our thing before we get the media crawling all over this.'

'Got it. But speaking of our thing, where to next?'

Bosch thought for a moment.

'Downtown to the Reagan. Let's go talk to your medical board guy.'

Lourdes nodded and started the engine.

'Jerry Edgar. He told me he was LAPD back in the day.'

Bosch shook his head once in surprise.

'What, you know him?' Lourdes asked.

'Yeah, I know him,' Bosch said. 'We worked together in Hollywood. Back in the day. I knew he retired but I thought he was selling houses in Las Vegas.'

'Well, he's back here now,' Lourdes said.

11

The Medical Board of California had offices inside the Ronald Reagan State Office Building on Spring Street three blocks from the LAPD headquarters. It was a forty-five-minute slog in heavy traffic down from Pacoima. Along the way, Lourdes had called Jerry Edgar and said that she and her partner were on their way to see him. When Edgar balked, saying he had a meeting to attend and wanted to set up an appointment, she identified her partner as Harry Bosch, and Edgar couldn't refuse. He said he would clear space in his schedule.

They parked in a pay lot and Edgar was waiting for them in the lobby of the state building. He greeted Bosch warmly but with an awkward embrace. It had been several years since they had been in each other's company, professionally or otherwise. The last message Bosch could remember coming from Edgar was one of condolence about Bosch's ex-wife several years before. Bosch had heard that his old partner had retired after that, but he had not gotten an invite to a retirement party, though he did not know if there had actually been one. Still, they had cleared several cases together while assigned to the homicide table at Hollywood Division. Now there wasn't even a homicide unit in Hollywood. All murders were handled out of West Bureau detectives or RHD. Things change.

It was said among cops that a true test of a partnership came when there was an officer-needs-help call. The response is to drop everything and go, pinning the accelerator to the floor and blowing through traffic lights with the siren blaring to get to the officer in need. True partners each take one side of every intersection as they speed through. The driver takes the left, the passenger takes the right, each calling out 'Clear!' as the car screams through red lights and intersections. It takes an inordinate amount of trust not to cheat and check the other side, even as your partner calls it clear. With a true partner, you don't need to check the other side. You know. You believe. When Bosch and Edgar were partners, Bosch always found himself checking the other side of the street. An outsider might view it as a distance forged in the racial divide between them. Edgar was black and Bosch was white. But for each man it was something else, something well below the skin. It was the gap between how each man viewed the job. It was the difference between how a cop works a case and a case works a cop.

But none of that surfaced as the two men smiled at each other and tentatively hugged. Edgar's head was shaved now and Bosch wondered if he would even have recognized him if he hadn't known it was his old partner.

'Last I heard, you pulled the pin, moved to Vegas, and were selling real estate,' Bosch said.

'Nah,' Edgar said. 'That lasted about two years and I came back here. But look at you. I knew you'd never be able to give it up, but I thought you'd end up with the D.A.'s Office or something. S-F-P-D. They call themselves the Mission City, right? That's perfect for Harry Bosch.'

Lourdes smiled and Edgar pointed at her.

'You know what I'm talkin' about,' he said, smiling. 'Harry's always the man on the mission.'

Edgar dropped the smile and the subject when he read Bosch's frozen look as a hint he was pushing the main difference between them too far. He signaled them to follow him into the elevator alcove and they moved into a crowded box. Edgar pushed the button for the fourth floor.

'Anyway, how's your daughter doin'?' he asked.

'She's in college,' Bosch said. 'Second year.'

'Wow,' Edgar said. 'Crazy.'

Bosch just nodded. He hated carrying on conversations in crowded elevators. Besides, Edgar had never met Maddie, so it was clear that they were now down to idle banter. He said nothing else as they rode up. They got off on the fourth floor, and Edgar used a key card to enter a suite of offices with a large government seal on the wall that showed a seven-pointed star surrounded by the words California Department of Consumer Affairs.

'My crib's back here,' Edgar said.

'Are you Consumer Affairs?' Lourdes asked.

'That's right, Health Quality Investigation Unit. We handle enforcement for the medical board.'

He led them to a small private office with a crowded desk and chairs for two visitors. Once they were sitting, they got down to business.

'So this case you're working,' Edgar said. 'You think it's linked to the complaint one of your victims sent to us?'

Edgar looked at Lourdes as he spoke, but Bosch and Lourdes had agreed on the ride down that Harry would take lead in the meeting, even though Bella had first made contact with Edgar. Bosch had the history with Edgar and would know best how to work the conversation to their advantage.

'We're not a hundred percent on that yet,' Bosch said. 'But it's getting there. The whole thing was on video, and our read on it is that this was a hit disguised as a robbery. Two shooters, masks, gloves, in and out, no brass left behind. We're looking at the kid as the target and that brings us to the complaint he sent. He was a good kid – no record, no gangs, most-likely-to-succeed sort of kid just out of pharmacy school. He and his father were at issue about something and it might have been filling prescriptions from that clinic.'

'The sad irony here is that the kid probably went to pharmacy school on money the old man banked filling shady scrips,' Edgar said.

'That is sad,' Bosch said. 'So what happened with the kid's complaint?'

'Okay,' Edgar said. 'Well, like I told Detective Lourdes, the complaint landed on my desk but I had not acted on it yet. I pulled it up when we spoke, and judging by the date it was sent and received, this thing was gathering dust in Sacramento for about five or six weeks before they took a look at it and sent it down here to me. Bureaucracy – you know about that, right, Harry?'

'Right.'

'The statute of limitations on these offenses is three years. I would have gotten to it sooner rather than later, but the harsh reality is, it would have been a couple months before I'd have acted on it. I've got more open files than I can handle.'

He gestured to the stacks of files on his desk and a shelf to his right.

'Like everybody else in this building, we are critically understaffed. We are supposed to have six investigators and two clerical support slots in this unit to cover the whole county but we have four and one and they added half of Orange County to our territory last year. Just driving down and back to the OC on a case takes half a day.'

Edgar seemed to be going out of his way to explain why the complaint hadn't yet been followed up on and Bosch realized that it was because of their prior history. Bosch had been so demanding as a partner that Edgar always felt under pressure to perform, and after all these years, he was still making excuses and trying to justify himself to Bosch. It made Bosch regretful and impatient at the same time.

'We understand all of that,' Bosch said. 'Nobody's got enough bullets – that's the system. We're just sort of trying to jump-start some stuff here because we've got a double murder. What can you tell us about this clinic over in Pacoima that the pharmacist was complaining about?'

Edgar nodded and opened a thin file on his desk. It had a single page of notes in it, and Bosch got the feeling that Edgar hadn't done much with it until Lourdes called and mentioned Bosch and that they were on their way downtown.

'I checked it out,' Edgar said. 'The clinic is licensed and doing business as Pacoima Pain and Urgent Care.

The doctor who owns it is listed as Efram Herrera, but then I checked his DEA number and he—'

'What's a DEA number?' Bosch asked.

'Every physician needs a DEA number to write prescriptions. Every pharmacy is supposed to check that on the scrip before putting pills in the bottle. There is a lot of abuse with phony numbers and stolen numbers. I checked Dr. Herrera's number and he wrote no prescriptions at all for two years and then came back with a vengeance last year and has been writing them like a madman. I'm talking hundreds a week.'

'Hundreds of pills, or hundreds of prescriptions?'

'Prescriptions. Scrips. As far as pills go, you're talking thousands.'

'So what's that tell you?'

'It confirms that the place is a pill mill and no doubt the kid pharmacist's complaint was on target.'

'I know you told Bella some of this already, but can you school me a little bit? How does a pill mill – how does all of this work?'

Edgar nodded vigorously as Bosch asked the question, jumping at the opportunity to show some expertise to the man who had always doubted him.

'They call the people involved in the mills "cappers",' he said. 'They run the show and you need unscrupulous doctors and pharmacies in the mix to make it all work.'

'The cappers are not the doctors or pharmacists?' Bosch asked.

'No, they're the bosses. It starts with them either opening a clinic or going into an existing clinic in a marginal neighborhood. They go to a dirtbag doctor, somebody just this side of having their license revoked.

A lot of docs that worked in the medical marijuana joints are perfect candidates. The capper goes in and says, "Doc, how'd you like to make five grand a week for a couple mornings in my clinic?" That's good money for somebody like that and they sign up.'

'And they start writing prescriptions.'

'Exactly, the cappers line up the shills in the morning, and they get their scrips from the doctor – no good-faith physical exam, nothing legit about it-and then they go out and get in a van and the capper drives them to the pharmacies to get the pills. Usually, it's more than one pharmacy in cahoots so they can spread it out and try to fly under the radar for as long as possible. A lot of them have multiple IDs, so they hit two, three, places a day and it doesn't come up on the computer. Doesn't matter that the phony IDs are for shit, because the pharmacist is in on it. He doesn't look too close at anything.'

'And then the pills go to the capper?'

'Exactly right. Most of these shills, they're addicts themselves. That capper is the straw boss and he reports to somebody down the line, and he's gotta make sure nobody guzzles those pills. So he keeps everybody in the van and they hit the pharmacies, maybe two going in at a time, and they turn those pills over right away when they get back to the van. The capper will front them what they need out of the day's haul to maintain their addiction and keep them working. He keeps them high and keeps them moving. It's a trap. They get in and they can't get out.'

Bosch thought about the man in the sunglasses with the goatee who was driving the van of old people that he and Lourdes had tailed.

'What happens next?' Bosch asked.

'The pills get distributed,' Edgar said. 'They hit the streets, go to the addicts. Fifty-five thousand dead and counting since this all started. Almost as many as we lost in the Vietnam War. That is sadly quantifiable, but the money, forget it. It's off the charts. So many people are making money off this crisis – it's the growth industry of this country. Remember what they used to say about the banks and Wall Street being too big to fail? It's like that. But too big to shut down.'

'David and Goliath,' Bosch said.

'Worse than that,' Edgar said. 'Let me tell you one story that to me says it all. Opiate addiction, in case you don't know, clogs the pipes. It stunts the gastrointestinal tract. Bottom line is, you can't shit. So one of the big pharmaceutical companies comes up with a prescription laxative that does the job and costs about twenty times what your over-the-counter laxative runs. The next thing you know the pharma's stock goes through the roof. They're selling so much of this that they're advertising on national television. Of course, they don't say dick about addiction or anything like that. They just show some guy mowing the lawn and, oh, he can't shit, so get your doctor to give you this. So now you've got Wall Street invested and the national media selling ads. Everybody is making bank, Harry, and when that happens it can't be stopped.'

'I thought they were trying to change things in Washington,' Lourdes offered. 'You know, new laws, putting a big focus on this.'

'Not likely,' Edgar said. 'The pharmas are major

campaign contributors. Nobody's going to bite the hand that feeds them.'

Edgar seemed to be using the national picture to justify his own local inertia. Bosch wanted to keep the focus small for the moment. You always start small and go big.

'So going back to this particular case in Pacoima, the capper got to Dr. Herrera. He went from signing no prescriptions to doing hundreds.'

'That's right and these are big prescriptions. Sixty pills, sometimes ninety. There's nothing subtle about it. I pulled his records and he's seventy-three years old. It looks like he retired and they brought him back, reopened the clinic, and put a prescription pad in front of him. For all we know, the guy might be senile. We've seen that. They drag some schnook out of retirement because he's still got that DEA number and a license to practice. "You want to make an extra twenty K a month?" and so on.'

Bosch was quiet as he tried to digest all of the information. Edgar went on unprompted.

'Another thing they do with these old doctors is they go through all their old records and pull legit names to phony up IDs and Medicare cards. They use real people who have no idea their names are being used in all of this. The government thinks the subsistence requests are legit.'

'That's crazy,' Lourdes said.

'So then what do you guys do about it?' Bosch asked.

'When we can identify it, we can shut the doctor down,' Edgar said. 'We work with the DEA to get the number revoked and then we yank the license to practice. But it is a long administrative process and most of the time these cappers have moved on to the next guy. A guy like Efram Herrera is left holding the bag. Not that I have any sympathy for the doctors, but the real villains here are elusive. I don't have to tell you how frustrating that is.'

'I can see that. The pill shills, have you heard of them being moved around by plane?'

Bosch asked the question casually, but it came out of the blue and gave Edgar pause. Bosch read in the hesitation that they might be onto something out of the routine with the Esquivel case.

'Is that what you have up there?' Edgar asked.

'It looks like it,' Bosch said. 'We followed a van from the clinic to Whiteman Airport and several people were loaded onto an old jump plane. It took off and headed south. They didn't file a flight plan. We checked with the tower. A guy said the plane comes in and goes out every day. The clinic is right across the street from the airport.'

'The fuel bills from Whiteman go to a company down in Calexico,' Lourdes added.

Bosch could see a change come over Edgar, an added level of concern working its way into his eyes and the deep set of his brow. He leaned forward and put his elbows on the desk.

'Things make a little more sense now,' he said.

'How so?' Bosch asked.

'I mean as far as killing the kid. One of the biggest operators in the pill-mill business in the country is a Russian-Armenian syndicate. Most of the pills that come out of these small operations go to them, and they feed Chicago, Las Vegas, all the hot spots.'

Bosch threw a sideways glance at Lourdes. O'Connor at the Whiteman tower had said the pilot spoke with a Russian accent. Lourdes exchanged eye contact and then returned attention to Edgar, who was still talking.

'Supposedly they use planes to keep people in motion, hitting multiple clinics and pharmacies a day,' he said. 'The planes help keep the shills in circulation, cashing out scrips for pills. Like I said before, they have multiple IDs and they're moved through three, four, pharmacies a day. We are talking big money and with big money comes big danger. This kid had no idea what he was bringing on when he decided to stand tall.'

'They would hit him just to send a message?' Bosch asked.

'Entirely possible. "If you ain't filling my scrips, you ain't filling nobody's scrips." Like that.'

'Where is this syndicate based? Here?'

'You need to be talking to the DEA, Harry. This is a whole different level of—'

'I'm talking to you, Jerry. Tell me what you know.'

'Not a lot, Harry. We handle enforcement for the medical board, man. This isn't an organized crime unit. What I heard through my contact at Drug Enforcement is that they're out there in the desert.'

'Which desert? Las Vegas?'

'No, down toward the border and Calexico. Out near Slab City, Bombay Beach – that no-man's-land they call the south side of nowhere. There's all kinds of airstrips down there abandoned by cartels, even the U.S. military, and that's what they use when they're flying people around. Out in the middle of nowhere it's like a gypsy caravan or something. They stay mobile. They sense trouble, they move like fucking nomads.'

'What about names? Who runs the syndicate?'

'Some Armenian guy who uses Russian enforcers and pilots. He calls himself Santos because he looks Mexican, but he isn't. And that's all I've got on that.'

'If they know where these people are and what they're doing, why don't they move in and take them down?'

'That's a DEA question, man. I wonder the same thing. I think it's Santos. They want him and he's like smoke.'

'Give me a name at DEA.'

'Charlie Hovan. He's their expert on Armenian drug dealers. He told me his family Americanized the name from Hovanian or something like that.'

'Charlie Hovan. Thanks, Jerry.'

Bosch looked at Lourdes to see if she had anything else to ask. She shook her head. She was ready to go. Bosch looked back at his old partner.

'So we'll leave you to it,' he said. 'Thanks for the cooperation.'

Bosch stood up and Lourdes followed.

'Harry, there's a story about Santos,' Edgar said. 'I don't know if it's true but you should know.'

'Go.'

'The DEA flipped one of his shills. Guy was an oxy addict and they leveraged him. He was supposed to keep working the game and feed intel back to the narcs.'

'What happened?'

'Somehow Santos figured it out or got wind of it. One day the informant got on the plane with a bunch of other shills and took off for a day's work. But when the plane landed, he wasn't on it anymore.'

'He got tossed.'

Edgar nodded.

'They've got the Salton Sea down there,' he said. 'Supposedly the high salt content of the water chews a body up pretty quick.'

Bosch nodded.

'Good to know who we're dealing with,' he said.

'Yeah, you two watch yourselves out there,' Edgar added.

12

After leaving the meeting in the Reagan Building, Bosch and Lourdes walked over to the Nickel Diner on Main Street for a late lunch. Bosch was a regular at the restaurant when he had worked downtown for the LAPD but had not been back since he'd left the department. Monica, one of the owners, welcomed him warmly and still remembered his routine order of a BLT sandwich.

Bosch and Lourdes discussed the information they had gotten from Edgar and debated whether to reach out to the DEA agent they had gotten a line on. Ultimately, they decided to wait until they had a better handle on their case and knew more about the activities surrounding La Farmacia Familia and the clinic in Pacoima. They still had nothing connecting the two things other than José Esquivel Jr.'s complaint about the clinic.

On the drive back up to the Valley, Lourdes took a call from Sisto, who said he had found a few things during his review of video from the pharmacy cameras that he wanted everybody on the team to see. Lourdes told him to set it up in the war room and they'd be back by four.

Exhaustion started to settle over Bosch as the car moved slowly in early rush-hour traffic. He made the mistake of leaning his head against the passenger-door window and soon he was out. It was the buzzing of his phone in his pocket that woke him up a half hour later.

'Shit,' he said as he dug the phone out. 'Was I snoring?'

'A little bit,' Lourdes said.

He answered the call before it went to message. He was still disoriented from sleep when he mumbled his name into the device.

'Yes, sir, this is Officer Jericho with San Quentin ISU. Did you say you are Detective Bosch?'

'Yes, Bosch. That's me.'

'Lieutenant Menendez asked me to handle an inmate research request and get back to you. The inmate is Preston Ulrich Borders.'

'Yes, what've you got?'

Bosch reached in his pocket for a notebook and pen. He tilted his head to hold the phone between his ear and shoulder and got ready to write.

'Not a lot, sir,' Jericho said. 'He only has one approved visitor and that is his attorney. His name is Lance Cronyn.'

'Okay,' Bosch said. 'Do you have any cross-outs? People who used to be approved?'

'This is off a computer, sir. We don't have cross-outs.'

'Okay, do you have a visitation history with the lawyer?'

'Yes, sir. It shows he received approved-visitor status in January last year. He has made regular visits on the first Thursday of every month ever since. Except he missed December last year.'

'That's a lot of visits, isn't it? I mean that's like fourteen or fifteen visits so far.'

'I wouldn't know what would constitute a lot of visits, sir. These guys on death row get a lot of legal attention.'

'Okay, what about mail? Did the lieutenant ask you to see what was going on with mail that goes to Borders?'

'Yes, he did. I reviewed that, sir, and Inmate Borders receives about three pieces of mail per day and it goes through a review process. He has had mail rejected because the letters were pornographic in nature or contained pornography. Nothing else unusual.'

'Do you keep any sort of entry log for knowing who is sending the mail to him?'

'No, sir, we don't do that.'

Bosch thought for a moment. The results of his request to Menendez were coming up dry. He looked out the windshield at a freeway sign and realized that he had slept through almost the entire drive back to San Fernando. They would be on Maclay in five minutes.

He took a long shot on one last tack with Jericho.

'You said you're on a computer, right?' he asked.

'Yes, sir,' Jericho said.

'Can you look up inmates anywhere in the DOC system or just San Quentin?'

'This is the system-wide database.'

'Good. Can you look up another inmate for me? His name is—'

'Lieutenant Menendez didn't ask me to check multiple inmates.'

'That's okay, I can hold while you ask him.'

There was a pause while Jericho decided whether he really wanted to ask his lieutenant if it was okay to look up another name.

'What is the name?' he finally asked.

'Lucas John Olmer. He's probably listed as deceased.'

Jericho asked Bosch to spell the full name and he heard typing.

'Yes, deceased,' Jericho said. 'D-O-D November ninth, twenty fifteen.'

'Okay,' Bosch said. 'Is there still an approved-visitor list on the file?'

'Uh, hold one.'

Bosch waited.

'Yes,' Jericho finally said. 'He had five visitors approved.'

'Give them to me,' Bosch said.

He wrote the names Jericho recited in his notebook.

Carolyn Olmer

Peyton Fornier

Wilma Lombard

Lance Cronyn

Victoria Remple

Bosch stared at the list. One was obviously a family member, and the other women were probably prison groupies, women attracted to a man of danger as long as the danger is incarcerated. Only Cronyn's name was important. The lawyer currently representing Preston Borders had previously represented the now dead inmate who supposedly committed the murder that Borders was held on death row for.

'How did you know?' Jericho asked.

'Know what?' Bosch said.

'That the lawyer was on both visitor lists.'

'I didn't until now.'

But it was an obvious thing to check, and Bosch knew Soto and Tapscott had to have made the connection as well. And yet it had not hindered the conclusion that

Borders was innocent in the killing of Danielle Skyler.

Bosch knew he needed to get to the file and review the second half – the recent investigation. He thanked Jericho for his time and asked him to pass on his appreciation to Lieutenant Menendez. He then put both his phone and notebook away.

'Harry, what's going on?' Lourdes asked.

'It's a personal matter,' Bosch said. 'It's not related to our case.'

'It is if it's keeping you up at night and then you're falling asleep in my car.'

'I'm an old man. Old men take naps.'

'I'm not kidding. You need to be on your game for this.'

'Don't worry. It won't happen again. I'm on my game.'

They drove in silence the rest of the way to the SFPD station. They entered the detective bureau through the side door and immediately went to the war room, where Sisto, Luzon, and Trevino were waiting.

'Whatcha got?' Lourdes asked.

'Take a look,' Sisto said.

He was holding the remote for one of the screens. There was a frozen image from the camera over the prescription counter at La Farmacia Familia. Sisto hit the play button. Bosch first noted the time-and-date stamp. The video was recorded thirteen days before the murders.

Everyone stood in front of the screen in a semicircle to watch. On the screen José Esquivel Sr. was standing behind the counter, his fingers on the computer keyboard. A customer stood on the other side of the counter, a young woman holding a baby. There was a white prescription bag on the counter.

While the customer transaction was taking place, a man entered the store through the front door. He was wearing a black golf shirt and sunglasses and had a goatee. Bosch immediately recognized him as the man he and Lourdes had seen driving the van from the clinic to Whiteman Airport that morning. The capper. He went along two of the aisles and idly perused the shelves as if he were looking for something.

But it was clear he was waiting.

Esquivel finished his computer work and handed what appeared to be an insurance card back to the woman holding the baby. He then handed her the prescription bag and nodded as the interaction was completed. The woman turned and left the store and then the man in the black shirt stepped up to the counter.

There was no sign of José Jr. in the store. The playback was without sound, but it was clear from the body language and hand gestures that the man in black was angry and began to confront Esquivel. The pharmacist took a step back from the counter to put some space between himself and the angry visitor. The visitor first held a finger up like he was saying *one more thing* or *one last time*. He then pointed it at Esquivel's chest and leaned across the counter to drive home the point.

That was when Esquivel apparently made a mistake. He gestured with his own hands in defense and started to say something. It appeared that he was engaging in the argument, verbally pushing back. Suddenly the visitor's arm shot out and he grabbed Esquivel by the lapel of his lab coat. He jerked the pharmacist forward and half over the counter. He then got right in his face, their noses inches apart. Esquivel went up on his toes, his thighs braced against the edge of the counter. He instinctively raised his hands to show contrition and that he was not resisting. The visitor held him in the awkward position and continued to talk, his head jerking in a paroxysm of anger.

And then came the moment Sisto wanted everybody to see. The visitor raised his left hand and formed a gun, forefinger pointing and thumb up. He put the finger against Esquivel's temple and pantomimed shooting him in the head, his hand even jerking back to show the recoil. He then pushed the pharmacist back over the counter and released his hold. Without another word he turned and walked through the pharmacy and out the front door. José was left disheveled and trying to pull himself together.

Sisto raised the remote to stop the playback.

'Wait,' Bosch said. 'Let's watch him.'

On the screen the pharmacist paced for a moment behind the counter. He rubbed his face with both hands and then looked up as if asking the heavens for guidance. His face was clear on the overhead camera angle, and José Esquivel Sr. seemed like a man carrying a tremendous burden. He then put his hands on the edge of the counter and leaned down.

Everything about his face and body language said *What am I going to do?*

Finally straightening up, he opened a drawer in the counter. He took out a pack of cigarettes and a throwaway lighter. He pushed through the half door to the back hallway and out of sight, presumably going to the back alley to smoke and calm his nerves.

'Okay,' Sisto said. 'Then there's this.'

He fast-forwarded the video playback for twenty seconds and then returned to normal play. Bosch checked the time counter as Sisto narrated.

'This is two hours later on the same day,' the young detective said. 'Watch when the son comes in.'

On the screen José Sr. was standing behind the pharmacy counter, looking at the computer's screen. His son entered the business through the front door and walked behind the pharmacy counter. As he pulled his pharmacist's coat from a hook, José Sr. looked up from the screen and waited for his son to turn around.

An argument ensued between the father and son, with the father making pleading gestures – hands clasped together as if in prayer – and the son looking away, even shaking his head. It ended with the son removing the coat he had just put on – and days later would be murdered in – and throwing it into the air as he stormed out of the store. Once again the father was left leaning against the counter, supporting himself by both hands and shaking his head in dismay.

'He saw it coming,' Luzon said.

They all took seats at the big table to talk about what they had seen and what it meant. Lourdes looked at Harry and they exchanged nods, a silent communication that they were on the same page.

'We think we know who the guy in the black shirt and shades is,' she began.

'Who?' Trevino asked.

'He's what they call a capper. He works for a clinic operating as a pill mill. We saw him today driving people around. People who take illegitimate prescriptions to pharmacies like the Esquivel family's. We think the father was neck-deep in the whole thing and the son was probably trying to get them out of it.'

Trevino made a low whistling sound and told Lourdes to fill in the story. With Bosch pitching in here and there, she proceeded to bring the team up-to-date on their activities during the day, including the Whiteman angle and the visit with Edgar downtown at the Reagan Building. Trevino, Sisto, and Luzon asked few questions and seemed duly impressed by the progress Lourdes and Bosch had made on the case.

Halfway through the session, Chief Valdez entered the war room, pulled out a chair, and sat down at the end of the table. Trevino asked if he wanted Bosch and Lourdes to start at the top and Valdez demurred, saying he was just trying to catch some of the update.

When Lourdes concluded her report, Bosch asked Sisto if he could put a freeze-frame of the capper on the screen next to a freeze-frame of the killers in the pharmacy. It took Sisto a few minutes to accomplish this and then everyone stood in front of the screens to compare the man who had threatened José Esquivel Sr. to the men who had killed him and his son. The conclusion based on body size was unanimous: neither of the killers was the man who had threatened José Sr. Additionally, Lourdes noted, the capper had used his left hand to pantomime shooting José Sr., while the two shooters had held their weapons in their right hands.

'So,' Trevino said. 'Next moves?'

Bosch held back, letting Lourdes take the lead, but she hesitated.

'Search warrant,' Bosch said.

'For what?' Trevino asked.

Bosch pointed to the man in black on the video screen.

'My read is that he threatened to kill Esquivel and then those two guys were brought in to actually do the job,' he said, pointing to the second screen. 'What we're hearing is that this organization is operating south of here and uses planes to move people around. We get a search warrant to look at video at Whiteman going back maybe twenty-four hours from our shooting. We see if they flew the shooters in.'

The police chief nodded and that made Trevino follow suit.

'I'll write the warrant,' Lourdes said. 'We can take it over there tonight before O'Connor leaves.'

'Okay,' Bosch said. 'Meantime, I'll try to make contact with Edgar's guy at the DEA. Maybe they already have a line on our shooters.'

'Can we trust the DEA with this?' Valdez asked.

'The medical board guy happens to be my old partner,' Bosch said. 'He vouched for the guy, so I think we're good.'

'Good,' the chief said. 'Then let's do it.'

After the meeting ended, Bosch walked out to the parking lot before heading over to his desk in the old jail. He grabbed the copy of the Skyler case file out of his car and carried it with him across the street. It was time to go back to work on it.

13

As expected, Bosch's call to DEA agent Charlie Hovan was not accepted. It had been Bosch's experience over many years that DEA agents were a different breed of federal law officers. Because of the nature of their work, they were often treated with suspicion by others in law enforcement – as had been exhibited earlier by Chief Valdez. It was odd and unwarranted; all law officers deal with criminals. But there was a stigma attached to drug agents, as though the scourge of the particular crime they fought could rub off on them. Lie down with dogs, get up with fleas. It was a phenomenon most likely rooted in the need for infiltration and undercover work in so many drug investigations. That stigma left agents paranoid, isolated, not interested in talking on the phone with strangers, even if they were law enforcement and it could be argued that they were all part of the same team protecting society.

Bosch suspected that he would not hear back from Hovan unless there was a pressing need on the agent's part. Harry tried to give him that with one sentence left on the agent's voice mail.

'This is Detective Bosch with the San Fernando Police Department and I'm looking for some intel on a guy who calls himself Santos and flies a plane in and out of an airstrip up here, where we just had a double murder in a pharmacy that was filling opioid scrips for him.'

Bosch left his phone number before disconnecting. He still believed that he might need to call Jerry Edgar in a day or two and ask him to vouch for him with Agent Hovan in order to prompt a simple conversation.

Bosch knew that it would probably take Lourdes a couple hours to write up a warrant for the Whiteman video archives and then get a telephonic approval from a Superior Court judge. It would take longer if she could not find a judge – the courthouses were closing now and most jurists would soon be in their cars, commuting home. Bosch's plan was to use whatever time he had to dig further into the Skyler investigation. Despite the double murder being the priority of the moment, Bosch could not stop thinking about the Skyler case and the threat it posed to his public reputation and private self-worth. In his career, he had chased down hundreds of killers and put them in prison. If he was wrong about one, then it would put the lie to everything else.

It would cast him adrift.

He first had to push the file boxes from the Esmerelda Tavares case to the side. When he lifted one box to put it on top of another, a photo dropped onto his makeshift desk. It had slipped through a separation in the bottom seam of the box and fallen out. Bosch picked it up and studied it. He realized he had not seen it before. The photo was of the baby daughter who had been left in the crib when her mother went missing. Bosch knew she would be fifteen or sixteen now. He'd have to get her exact birthday and check the math on that.

A year after her mother's disappearance, her father decided he could not raise her. He turned her over to the county's foster care program and she was raised by a family that adopted her and eventually moved from Los Angeles up to Morro Bay. The photo reminded him that he had long planned to go up there to find her and talk to her about her mother. He wondered if she had any distant memories of her natural mother and father. But it was a long shot and he had never made the trip. He put the photo on top of the contents of the box so it would serve as a reminder next time he checked into the case.

Bosch split the Skyler files in half and put the stack of copies from the original investigation to the side. He then started reviewing the chronological record that Soto and Tapscott had begun keeping once assigned to reinvestigate the case.

It quickly became clear that the new look at the Skyler case began with a letter sent seven months earlier to the Conviction Integrity Unit from the man who was the nexus between both sexual predators involved. Attorney Lance Cronyn. Bosch put the chrono aside and looked through the stack until he found the document. It was on Cronyn's letterhead, showing his office address on Victory Boulevard in Van Nuys. The letter was directed to Kennedy's boss and the head of the CIU, Assistant District Attorney Abel Kornbloom.

Mr. Kornbloom,

I write to you today in hopes that you will follow your sworn duty and right a terrible wrong and miscarriage of justice that has plagued our city and our state for three decades. It is a wrong that in some ways I helped propagate and extend. I now need your help fixing this.

I currently represent Preston Borders, who has resided on death row in San Quentin State Prison since 1988. I took on his representation only recently and quite frankly solicited him as a client. Attorney – client privilege in another case has prevented me from coming forward until this point. You see, until his death in 2015, I represented Lucas John Olmer, who was convicted of multiple counts of sexual assault and abduction in 2006 and sentenced to more than 100 years in prison. He served that sentence until his death from cancer at California State Prison, Corcoran.

On July 12, 2013, I had occasion to meet with Mr. Olmer at Corcoran to discuss potential grounds for a final appeal of his conviction. During the course of this privileged conversation, Mr. Olmer revealed to me that he was responsible for the murder of a young woman in 1987 and that another man had been falsely convicted of the crime and sentenced to death. He did not name the victim but said that the crime had occurred in her home in Toluca Lake.

As you will understand, this was a privileged conversation between attorney and client. I could not reveal this information because to do so would be to put my own client at risk of a conviction leading to the death penalty.

Attorney—client privilege survives after death. However, there are exceptions to the rule of privilege – if revealing protected communication will help right a continuing wrong or prevent serious *injury or death to an innocent person. And that is exactly what I am trying to do now. Charles Gaston, an investigator in my employ, took the facts as revealed to me by Olmer and investigated the matter. He determined that a young woman named Danielle Skyler was sexually assaulted and murdered in her home in Toluca Lake on October 22, 1987, and that Preston Borders was later convicted of the crime and sentenced to death after a trial in Los Angeles Superior Court.*

I subsequently went to San Quentin to interview Borders and he retained me as his attorney. In that capacity I sincerely request that the murder of Danielle Skyler be reviewed by the Conviction Integrity Unit and that the District Attorney's Office right this wrong. Preston Borders is factually innocent and has spent more than half his life in prison under the threat of state-sanctioned death. This miscarriage of justice must be remedied.

This request is the first of many options available to Mr. Borders. I intend to explore all avenues of amelioration, but I am starting with you. I look forward to your expedited reply.

Sincerely yours,
Lance Cronyn, Esq.

Bosch read the letter a second time and then quickly scanned a letter of receipt from Kornbloom to Cronyn that told him his request would be given the utmost priority and urged him not to take any other action until the CIU had the opportunity to review and investigate the matter. It was clear that Kornbloom didn't want this case spilling into the media or referred to the Innocence Project, a privately funded legal group that had a national record of overturning wrongful convictions. It would be a political blunder if the work of an outside entity instead of the district attorney's much ballyhooed unit led to a revelation of innocence.

Bosch went back to the chrono. The letter from Cronyn clearly got the ball rolling. Soto and Tapscott pulled the files and went to property control, where the evidence box was found and opened on camera. While the forensics unit studied the contents for new or overlooked evidence, the two detectives went to work reviewing and reinvestigating the case – this time with another suspect as the leading person of interest.

Bosch knew it was not the right way to work a murder case. Rather than looking for a suspect, they started with the suspect already in hand. It narrowed the possibilities. Here they started with the name Lucas John Olmer and they stuck with it. Their efforts to confirm that he had been in Los Angeles at the time of the Skyler murder were less than conclusive. They found employment records at the billboard company where he worked as an installer that appeared to place him in L.A. but little else in terms of housing records or live witnesses who could attest to his whereabouts. It wasn't nearly enough to take the case further, but then the lab reported finding a minute amount of semen on the victim's clothing. The material had not been stored under today's DNA evidence protocols, but because the piece of clothing had been in a sealed paper bag, it was in remarkably good condition and could be tested against samples from both Olmer and Borders.

Olmer's DNA was already in the state's offender data bank. It had been used at trial to link him to the rapes of seven different women. But genetic material had never been collected from Borders because he had been convicted and sentenced to death row a year before DNA was approved for use in California in courts and by law enforcement. Tapscott flew up to San Francisco to go to San Quentin and collect a sample from Borders. It was then analyzed by an independent lab and comparisons were made between the evidence taken from Danielle Skyler's pajamas and the samples from Olmer and Borders.

After three weeks, the lab finally reported that the DNA on the victim's clothing had come from Olmer and not Borders.

Just reading it in the chronological record made Bosch break into a cold sweat. He had been as sure of Borders's guilt as that of any other killer he had taken to trial and put in prison. And now the science said he was wrong.

Then he remembered the sea horse. The sea horse put the lie to all of this. Danielle Skyler's favorite piece of jewelry had been found in the secret place in the apartment where Borders lived. DNA could not explain that away. It might be possible that Borders and Olmer knew each other and had committed the crime together, but possession of the sea horse made Borders culpable in a big way. At his trial Borders had testified that he'd bought an exact duplicate of Skyler's sea horse at the Santa Monica pier because he wanted one for himself.

The jury didn't buy it then, and Soto and Tapscott should not have bought it now.

Bosch switched back to the chrono and soon found out why they did. After the DNA matching came back, the investigators as a pair returned to San Quentin to interview Borders. The entire transcript of the interview was available in the documents but the chrono referenced the specific pages where discussion about the sea horse took place.

Tapscott: Tell us about the sea horse.

Borders: The sea horse was a big fucking mistake. I'm here because of that fucking sea horse.

Tapscott: What do you mean by 'mistake'?

Borders: I didn't have the greatest lawyer, okay? And he didn't like my explanation for the sea horse. He said it wouldn't sell to a jury. So we go into court and try to sell a bullshit story that nobody on the jury believed anyway.

Tapscott: So the story about you buying a matching sea-horse pendant on the Santa Monica pier because you liked it, that was a lie you told to the jury?

Borders: That's right, I lied to the jury. That's my crime. What are you going to do, send me to death row? [laughing]

Tapscott: What was the story your lawyer said he couldn't sell to the jury?

Borders: The truth. That the cops planted it when they searched my place.

Tapscott: You're saying the key piece of evidence against you was planted?

Borders: That's right. The guy's name was Bosch. The detective. He wanted to be judge and jury, so he planted the evidence. Him and his partner were completely bent. Bosch planted it and the other one went along with it.

Soto: Wait a second here. You're saying that weeks before you were even on his radar as a suspect, Bosch took the sea horse off the body or from the murder scene and carried it around with him so at just the right moment and with the right suspect he could plant it as evidence? You expect us to believe that?

Borders: The guy was really obsessed with the case. You can check it. I found out later that his mother had been murdered when he was a little kid, you know. There was a whole psychology to it, him being this obsessed avenging angel. But it was too late by then; I was here.

Soto: You had appeals, you had lawyers, how come in thirty years you've never once brought up that Bosch planted the sea horse?

Borders: I didn't think anybody cared or anybody'd believe me. The truth is, I still don't. Mr. Cronyn convinced me to tell what I know and that's what I'm doing.

Soto: Why did your lawyer back at the trial say that claiming the evidence was planted was the wrong move?

Borders: Remember, this was back in the eighties. Back then the cops had a free ride. They could do anything and get away with it. And what proof did I have? Bosch was like this hero cop who had solved big cases. I had no chance against that. All I know is that they supposedly found the sea horse and a bunch of jewelry hidden in my house and I was the only one who knew that I didn't have the sea horse. That's how I knew it was planted against me.

Bosch read the short section of the transcript again and then moved on to two amendments that were attached. One was an obituary from the *California Bar Journal* for Borders's original attorney, David Siegel, who had retired from the practice of law a decade after the Borders trial and passed away soon after. The second amendment was actually a timeline constructed by Soto that showed when it was during the investigation that Bosch wrote the initial report stating that Danielle Skyler's prized sea-horse necklace was missing. The timeline showed all the days that went by and the case developments that occurred during which he would have had to hold on to the sea horse before planting it in the hiding place in Borders's apartment. The report was clearly an attempt by Soto to delineate the tenuousness of the claim that Bosch planted evidence in the case.

Bosch appreciated Lucia's efforts on his behalf and believed it might have been the reason she got him a copy of the file on the down low. She wanted him to know that what was happening was not a betrayal on her part, that she was watching out for her former mentor but letting the chips – and the evidence – fall where they may.

That aside, the allegation that Bosch had planted evidence in the case thirty years ago was now part of the record of the case and it could blow up publicly at any moment. It was clearly the leverage that Kennedy, the prosecutor, hoped to use to quiet any protest from Bosch about the move to vacate the conviction. If Bosch objected, he would get smeared.

What Kennedy, Soto, and Tapscott could not know was what Bosch knew in the deepest, darkest part of his heart. That he had not planted evidence against Borders. That he had never planted evidence against any suspect or adversary in his life. And this knowledge gave Bosch an affirming jolt of adrenaline and purpose. He knew there were two kinds of truth in this world. The truth that was the unalterable bedrock of one's life and mission. And the other, malleable truth of politicians, charlatans, corrupt lawyers, and their clients, bent and molded to serve whatever purpose was at hand.

Borders, either with or without his attorney's knowledge, had lied to Soto and Tapscott at San Quentin. In doing so, he had corrupted their investigation from the start. It confirmed for Bosch that this was a scam and that it was up to him to root out those who plotted against him wherever they were. He was coming for them now. The weight and guilt of possibly having made a horrible mistake so long ago was lifted.

It was Bosch who felt like the man proven innocent and released from a cage.

14

The killers of José Esquivel and his son had acted in the pharmacy video with the assurance of men who had done this kind of work before. They used revolvers both to prevent their weapons jamming and to avoid leaving behind critical evidence. They showed no hesitation, no remorse. Bosch knew that in every large criminal enterprise, there was a need for such men, enforcers willing to do what had to be done to ensure the survival and success of the organization. In reality, such men were rare. This was what led to his suspicion that the killers were brought in from far outside San Fernando to deal with the problem created by the idealistic but naive José Esquivel Jr.

That suspicion seemed to be confirmed when Bosch, Lourdes, and Sisto returned to Whiteman Airport early that evening with a warrant to view surveillance footage from the airstrip's cameras. Beginning their review of video at noon Sunday, they fast-forwarded through the hours, slowing to real-time speed only when the occasional plane landed or took off, or when a vehicle approached the row of hangars that ran along the edge of the airfield. They were in the airport's cramped utility room beneath the tower. It also served as the security office. The space was so tight that Bosch could smell Sisto's nicotine gum.

At 9:10 a.m. on the video, their vigil paid off when the same van they had seen pick up the lineup of pill shills at the clinic drove up to the hangar, opened its two doors wide by remote control, and then waited, its driver getting out and going inside only briefly before returning.

Fourteen minutes later the jump plane landed and taxied to and then into the hangar. Only two men disembarked – white men in dark clothing that appeared very similar to that worn by the *farmacia* shooters. They walked directly to the van and climbed in through the side door. The van drove off before the plane's propeller had even stopped turning.

'It's them,' Sisto said. 'Fuckers now go to the mall and kill our victims.'

He said it with a tone of anger Bosch liked, but he knew that emotional belief and evidence were two different things.

'How do you know?' he asked.

'Oh, come on,' Sisto said. 'It's gotta be. The timing is perfect. They fly in, do the job, and you watch: they're going to fly them out again after it's over.'

Bosch nodded.

'I'm there with you, but what we know and what we can prove are two different things,' he said. 'The men in the pharmacy were masked.'

He pointed to the video monitor.

'Can we prove that's them?' he asked.

'We can ask the sheriff's lab to try to clean this up,' Lourdes said. 'Make it clearer.'

'Maybe,' Bosch said. 'Speed it up.'

Sisto was handling the remote. He boosted the

playback to 4× speed and they waited. Bosch watched the minutes go by on the video timer. At the 10:15 a.m. mark, he told Sisto to drop it back to real-time playback. The pharmacy video that had captured the murders placed the time of the killings at 10:14 a.m., and the drugstore was approximately two miles from Whiteman.

At 10:21 the van returned to the airport. It traveled within the speed limit, no hurry as it went through the gate and approached the hangar. Once it was there, the side door slid open and the two men exited and walked directly to the jump plane. Its prop was already turning and it taxied back out to the runway for takeoff.

'In and out, just like that, and two people are dead,' Lourdes said.

'We gotta get these guys,' Sisto said.

'We will,' Bosch said. 'But I want the guy who made the call. The man who put those two hitters on the plane.'

'Santos,' Lourdes said.

Bosch nodded. It was a moment of true resolve for the three detectives.

Sisto finally broke the silence.

'So, what's our next move, Harry?' he asked.

'The van,' Bosch said. 'Tomorrow we bring in the driver and see what he has to say.'

'We work our way up the ladder,' Sisto said. 'I like it.'

'Easier said than done,' Bosch said. 'We have to assume that anybody working for Santos is working for him because he's a trusted soldier. He won't be afraid of prison time and that will make him hard to crack.'

'Then, what do we do?'

'We put the fear of God in him. We make him afraid of Santos if he's not afraid of us.'

Before leaving the airport, Bosch sent Lourdes up the tower to talk to O'Connor and use the second warrant to collect the clipboard log that documented the comings and goings of the jump plane, in particular the landing on Monday morning before the pharmacy shooting. It would be marked as evidence with the video itself. The detectives then called it a day, agreeing to meet in the war room at eight the following morning to plan the takedown of the van driver. From there Sisto and Lourdes headed to Magaly's for a late dinner, while Bosch decided to head home. He wanted to put in some time on the Borders case file before sleep deprivation caught up and knocked him down.

There was a time when Bosch could easily go two days on a case without sleep. But that time was long gone.

It was late enough for the freeway to be clear and he moved easily into the slipstream of traffic. He called his daughter, whom he had not talked to in several days except through customary good-night texts. She surprised him by answering. Usually at night she was too busy to talk.

'Hey, Dad.'

'How are you, Mads?'

'Stressed. I've got midterms this week. I'm about to go to the library.'

This was a sore subject with Bosch. His daughter liked to study at the school library because the place helped her focus. But she often stayed until midnight or later and that left her walking by herself to her car, parked in an underground garage. They had discussed this repeatedly but she had dug in on it and was unwilling to accept the ten p.m. curfew Bosch had tried to impose.

When he didn't respond, his daughter did.

'Please don't add to my stress by lecturing me on the library. It's perfectly safe and I will be there with lots of kids.'

'I'm not worried about the library. I'm worried about the garage.'

'Dad, we've been over this. It's a safe campus. I'll be fine.'

There was a saying in police work, that places were safe until they weren't. It only took one moment, one bad actor, one chance crossing of predator and prey, to change things. But he had already shared all of this with her and didn't want to turn the call into an argument.

'If you have midterms, does that mean you'll be coming up to L.A. after?'

'No, sorry, Dad. Me and the roomies are going down to IB as soon as we're all free. I'll come up next time I can.'

Bosch knew that one of her three roommates was from Imperial Beach down by the border.

'Just don't go across, okay?'

'*Da-ad.*'

She drew the word out like it was a life sentence.

'Okay, okay. What about spring break? I thought we were going to go to Hawaii or something.'

'This is spring break. I'm going to IB for four days and then back up here, because spring break isn't really a break. I have two psych projects to work on.'

Bosch felt bad. He had fumbled the Hawaii idea, having mentioned it a few months earlier and then not followed through. Now she had plans. He knew his time with her and being part of her life was fleeting, and this was a reminder.

'Well, look, save one night for me, would you? You name the night and I'll come down and we can eat somewhere on the circle. I just want to see you.'

'Okay, I will. But actually there's a Mozza down here in Newport. Can we go there?'

It was her favorite pizza place in L.A.

'Wherever you want.'

'Great, Dad. But I gotta go.'

'Okay, love you. Be safe.'

'You, too.'

Then she was gone.

Bosch felt a wave of grief. His daughter's world was expanding. She was going places and it was the natural way of things. He loved seeing it and hated living it. She had only been a daily part of his life for a few years before it was time for her to go. Bosch regretted all the lost years before.

When he got to his house, there was a car parked out front with a figure slumped in the front seat. It was nine p.m. and Bosch was not expecting company. He parked in the carport and walked out to the street, coming up behind the car blocking the front walkway to his house. As he approached, he turned on the light on his phone and shined it through the driver's open window.

Jerry Edgar was asleep behind the wheel.

Bosch tapped lightly on his shoulder until Edgar startled and looked up at him. Because there was a streetlight above and behind him, Bosch was in silhouette.

'Harry?'

'Hey, partner.'

'Shit, I fell asleep. What time is it?'

'About nine.'

'Shit, man. I was out.'

'What's up?'

'I came by to talk to you. I checked the mail in the box and saw you're still in the same house.'

'Then let's go in.'

Bosch opened the car door for him. They went in the front door after Bosch gathered the mail Edgar had checked.

'Honey, I'm home,' Bosch called out.

Edgar gave him an are-you-kidding-me look. He'd always known Bosch to be a loner. Bosch smiled and shook his head.

'Just kidding,' he said. 'You want a drink? I'm out of beer. I've got a bottle of bourbon and that's about it.'

'Bourbon's good,' Edgar said. 'Maybe with a cube or two.'

Bosch signaled him into the living room, while he cut right into the kitchen. He got two glasses out of a cabinet and dropped some ice into them. He heard Edgar pull the broomstick out of the sliding door track and open the slider. Bosch grabbed the bottle of bourbon off the top of the refrigerator and went out to the deck. Edgar was standing at the railing, looking down into the Cahuenga Pass.

'Place still looks the same,' Edgar said.

'You mean the house or the canyon?' Bosch asked.

'I guess both.'

'Cheers.'

Bosch handed him both glasses so he could crack the seal on the bottle and pour.

'Wait a minute,' Edgar said when he saw the label. 'Are you kidding me?'

'About what?' Bosch asked.

'Harry, do you know what that stuff is?'

'This?'

Now Bosch looked at the label. Edgar turned and dumped the ice over the railing. He then held the empty glasses out to Bosch.

'You don't put ice in Pappy Van Winkle.'

'You don't?'

'That'd be like putting ketchup on a hot dog.'

Bosch shook his head. He didn't get the comparison Edgar was making.

'People put ketchup on hot dogs all the time,' he said.

Edgar held out the glasses, and Bosch started pouring.

'Easy now,' Edgar said. 'Where'd you get this?'

'It was a gift from somebody I did some work for,' Bosch said.

'He must be doing pretty good. You look this stuff up on eBay and you'll wish you never cracked the seal. You coulda bought your daughter a car.'

'It's a she. The one I did the work for.'

Bosch looked at the label on the bottle again. He held the opening to his nose and picked up a deep, smoky tang.

'A car, huh?' he said.

'Well, at least a down payment,' Edgar said.

'I almost regifted this and gave it to the chief up at San Fernando. I guess it would've made his Christmas.'

'More like his whole year.'

Bosch put the bottle down on the two-by-four railing cap, and Edgar immediately panicked. He grabbed the bottle before an earthquake or a Santa Ana wind could send it down into the dark arroyo below. He put it safely down on a table next to the lounge chair.

He came back and they leaned side by side on the rail and sipped and looked into the pass. At the bottom, the 101 freeway was still a ribbon of white light coming up through Hollywood and one of red light going south.

Bosch waited for Edgar to get down to the reason for his visit but nothing came. His old partner seemed content to sip rare bourbon and view the lights.

'So what made you drive up here tonight?' Bosch finally asked.

'Oh, I don't know,' Edgar said. 'Something about seeing you today. Seeing that you're still in the game made me think. I hate my job, Harry. We never get anything done. Sometimes I think the state wants to protect bad doctors, not get rid of them.'

'Well, you're still pulling down a paycheck. I'm not – unless you count the hundo they give me a month for equipment costs.'

Edgar laughed.

'That much, huh? You're rolling in the green.'

He held out his glass, and Bosch clicked his off of it.

'Oh, yeah,' he said. 'Making bank.'

'How about fucking Hollywood?' Edgar said. 'Don't even have a homicide table anymore.'

'Yeah. Things change.'

'Things change.'

They clicked glasses again and sipped for a few quiet

moments before Edgar finally got down to what he had come up the hill to say.

'So Charlie Hovan called me up today, wanted to know all about you.'

'What did you say?'

Edgar turned and looked directly at Bosch. It was so dark on the deck that Bosch could only see a glint of reflection in his eyes.

'I said you were good people. I said trust you and treat you right.'

'I appreciate that, J. Edgar.'

'Harry, whatever this is, I want in. I've been sitting on the sidelines too long, watching this shit go down. I'm asking you to include me.'

Bosch took a draw of smoky bourbon before responding.

'We could use all the help we can get. Today I thought you just wanted to get us out of the office.'

'Yeah, because you were a reminder of what I should be fucking doing.'

Bosch nodded. When he and Edgar were partners in Hollywood twenty-five years before, he had never had the sense that Edgar was all in. But he knew the need for redemption comes in all kinds of ways at all kinds of times.

'You know where San Fernando even is?' Bosch asked.

'Sure,' Edgar said. 'Went up to the courthouse in San Fernando a few times on cases.'

'Well, if you want in, be at San Fernando PD at eight tomorrow. We've got a strategy meeting. We're going to take down a capper and start fishing. We'll probably bring Dr. Herrera in at some point too. We could probably use your help with that.'

'Do you have to clear it first?'

'I think the chief will take all the help he can get on this. I'll talk to him.'

'I'll be there, Harry.'

He took down the last of his bourbon in one gulp, savored it, and then swallowed. He put the empty glass on the railing and pointed at the glass as he backed away.

'Smooth. Thanks for that, Harry.'

'Want another hit?'

'Would love it, but early start tomorrow. I should go home.'

'You got somebody there waiting, Jerry?'

'Matter of fact, I do. I got remarried when I was working in Vegas. Nice girl.'

'I got married in Vegas once.'

It was the first time Bosch had thought about Eleanor Wish in a long time. Edgar gave him a sad smile.

'Tomorrow,' he said.

He clapped Bosch on the upper arm and headed back into the house and toward the front door. Bosch remained on the deck, sipping his expensive bourbon and thinking about the past. He heard Edgar's car start up and pull away into the night.

15

In the morning Bosch ate breakfast at the counter at the Horseless Carriage, a diner located in the center of the vast Ford dealership in Van Nuys. It would only be a few miles from there to San Fernando and he had grown tired of eating the free breakfast burritos dropped off in the war room each morning. The Horseless had a fifties feel to it and was a lasting reminder of the population and expansion boom that swept the Valley after World War II. The car became king and Van Nuys was an auto-buying mecca, with dealerships lined up side by side and offering coffee shops and restaurants as draws to their customers.

Bosch ordered the French toast and watched the video he had been texted the night before on the burner phone he had bought to communicate with Lucia Soto. The video had come from a strange number, which he assumed belonged to a burner Soto was now using herself.

The video was Tapscott's recording of the opening of the evidence box in the Danielle Skyler case. Bosch had watched it repeatedly the night before until he was too tired to keep his eyes open, but no matter how many times he viewed it, he could not figure out how the evidence box had been tampered with. The old and yellowed evidence labels were clearly intact as the box was presented to the camera and then cut open by Soto.

This continually agitated Bosch, because he knew there was a kink in the line somewhere between property control and the lab table where Lucas John Olmer's DNA was found on Skyler's clothing. If he started with the bedrock knowledge that Olmer's DNA had been planted, then he had to figure out two things. One was how DNA from a man who died two years earlier had been procured in the first place, and the other was how it had been planted on the clothing contained in a sealed evidence box.

The first question had been answered – to Bosch's satisfaction, at least – the night before, after Edgar left and he finally got the chance to review the Borders investigative file for a second time. This time, he paid careful attention to the file within the file – the records from Olmer's prosecution and conviction on multiple rape charges in 1998. In his first swing through the records Bosch had paid closer attention to the investigative side of the case, exhibiting a detective's bias that a case was put together during the investigation and that the prosecution was only the strategic revelation of the accumulated facts and evidence to the jury. Therefore, he believed, anything in the prosecution files would already have been covered in the investigative files.

Bosch learned how wrong he had been about this mind-set when he read through a sheaf of motions and countermotions filed by both the prosecution and defense. Most were boilerplate legal arguments: motions to suppress evidence or testimony made by the prosecution or defense. Then Bosch came across a defense motion stating that it was Olmer's intention at trial to challenge the DNA evidence in the case. The motion asked the judge to order the state to provide the defense with a portion of the genetic evidence collected during the investigation so that independent analysis could take place. The motion was not challenged by the state, and Judge Richard Pittman ordered the District Attorney's Office to split the genetic material with the defense.

The defense motion had been written by Olmer's attorney, Lance Cronyn. It was a routine pretrial move, but what drew Bosch's attention was the witness list submitted by the defense at the start of the trial. There were only five witnesses on the list and after each name, there was a summary of who the person was and what they would testify to. None of the five were chemists or forensic specialists. This told Bosch that during the trial, Cronyn did not put forth alternate DNA findings, as the motion filed earlier had suggested. He had gone in another direction, which could have been anything from claiming the sex was consensual to hammering at the state's own DNA collection protocol and analysis. Whatever it was, it didn't work. Olmer went down on all charges and was shipped off to prison. And there was no record in the file of what happened to the genetic material signed over to his lawyer by the judge.

Bosch knew that the DA's Office should have requested the return of the material after the trial, but there was nothing in the records to indicate this had been done. Olmer was convicted and sent away on a sentence he couldn't possibly outlive. The reality, Bosch knew, was that institutional entropy probably took over. Prosecutors and investigators moved on to other cases and trials. The missing DNA was unaccounted for, and therefore it could have been the source of the genetic material found on Danielle Skyler's pajamas. Proving it, though, was another matter, especially when Bosch could not figure out how that microdot of DNA got there.

Still, for the moment, he had what was certainly a crack in the facade of a seemingly solid case for wrongful conviction. There was DNA unaccounted for and the defense lawyer who moved between the two cases in question may have had access to it.

He pushed his plate away and checked his watch. It was seven forty and time to get to the war room. He stood up, left a twenty on the counter, and headed out to his car. He stayed on surface streets, taking Roscoe over to Laurel Canyon and then heading up. Along the way he took a call from Mickey Haller.

'Funny, I was going to call you,' Bosch said.

'Oh, yeah?' Haller said. 'About what?'

'I've decided I definitely want to engage your services. I want to come in as a third party at the hearing next week and oppose the release of Preston Borders. Whatever that takes in legal terms.'

'All right. We can do that. You want any media on it? This is going to be an unusual hearing with a retired detective going up against the D.A. It's a good story.'

'Not yet. It's going to get ugly when it comes up that Borders claims I planted evidence and the D.A. apparently agrees.'

'What the fuck?'

'Yeah, I've been through the whole file. Borders claims that I planted the key evidence – the sea-horse pendant-in his apartment. Accusing me is the only way to sell this.'

'Did he offer any proof of this?'

'No, but he doesn't have to. If the DNA points to a convicted rapist, then the only plausible evidence for Borders being in possession of the pendant is that it was planted.'

'Okay, understood. You're right, this is going to get down and dirty, and I see why you want to keep the media out of it if possible. But now the big question: Whaddaya got that knocks down this house of cards?'

'I'm only halfway there. I know where and how they could've gotten Olmer's DNA. I just need to find out how they were then able to salt the evidence with it.'

'Sounds like you've done the easy part, if you ask me.'

'I'm working on the hard part. Is that why you called? To encourage me?'

'No, actually I've got a little gift for you.'

'What's that?'

Bosch was now off of Laurel Canyon and cruising up Brand Boulevard and passing the 'Welcome to San Fernando' sign.

'Well, when you first told me about this, the name Preston Borders rang a bell. I remembered it but I couldn't place it. I was in law school at Southwestern and of course I didn't know about you at the time. Anyway, I used to go to the Criminal Courts Building between classes and sit in courtrooms, watch defense lawyers work.'

'Never interested in how prosecutors worked?'

'Not really. Not with my father – our father – having been a defense attorney. The point is, I'm pretty sure I watched some of the Borders trial, and that would have put you and me in the same room without knowing each other thirty years ago. I thought that was sort of neat.'

'Yeah, neat. That's why you called? That's the gift?'

'No, the gift is this: Our father died young – in fact, I never saw him in a courtroom-but he had a young partner who carried on, and that's the guy I used to go watch at the CCB.'

'You're talking about David Siegel? He was the partner?'

'That's right. And he defended Preston Borders in that trial in nineteen eighty-eight. I grew up calling him Uncle David. He was a great lawyer and they called him Legal Siegel around the courthouse. He's the one who sent me to law school.'

'What happened to his practice? Do you think there are any records still around from the trial? They might be useful.'

'You see, that's my gift to you, my brother. You don't need records; you've got Legal Siegel.'

'What are you talking about? He's dead. There's an obit in the file – I read it last night.'

Bosch had to wait at the crossing a block from the station for a Metro train to go screaming through. Haller heard it over the phone and waited for silence before responding.

'Let me tell you a story,' he said. 'When he retired from the practice of law, Legal Siegel did not want to be found by any of the, let's say, unsavory clients he represented over the years, especially those who might not have been pleased with the outcome of their interaction.'

'He didn't want guys getting out of prison and looking him up,' Bosch said. 'Geez, I wonder why.'

'I've had the experience myself and it's not pleasant.

So Legal Siegel sold his practice and pulled a disappearing act. He even had one of his sons send an obituary of his own creation to the newsletter of the California bar. I remember reading it. It called him a legal genius.'

'That's what I read. Soto and Tapscott put it in the file because they said Siegel was dead. You're telling me he's still alive?'

'He's going on eighty-six years old and I try to visit him every few weeks or so.'

Bosch pulled into a parking space in the SFPD's side lot. He checked the dash clock and saw he was late. The personal cars of all the other detectives were already there.

'I need to talk to him,' he said. 'In the new files, Borders throws him under the bus. He's not going to like that.'

'I'm sure he won't,' Haller said. 'But that's a good break for you. If you impugn the reputation of a lawyer, he's allowed to fight back. I'll set up an interview and we'll record it. What's your availability going to be?'

'The sooner the better. You said he was pushing eighty-six. Is he all there?'

'Absolutely. Sharp as a stiletto mentally. Physically, not so much. He's bedridden. They move him around in a wheelchair. Bring him a sandwich from Langer's or Philippe's and he'll go on a nostalgic bender about old cases. That's what I do. I love to hear him talk cases.'

'All right, set it up and let me know.'

'I'm on it.'

Bosch killed the engine and opened the Jeep's door. He quickly tried to remember if there was anything else he needed to ask Haller.

'Oh, one other thing,' he said. 'You remember at Christmas when we got those bottles of bourbon from Vibiana at the Fruit Box Foundation?'

Vibiana Veracruz was an artist both Haller and Bosch had encountered on a private case they had worked the year before.

'Happy Pappy, yes, I do,' Haller said.

'I remember you offered me a hundred bucks for mine,' Bosch said. 'I almost took it.'

'Offer still stands. Unless you finished that sucker off.'

'No, I didn't even crack it open until last night. And that's when I found out I could've gotten about twenty times what you offered.'

'Really?'

'Yeah, really. You're a scoundrel, Haller. Just wanted you to know I'm onto you.'

Bosch could hear Haller chuckling at the other end of the line.

'Laugh it up,' Bosch said. 'But I'm keeping it.'

'Hey, there are no morals and no ethics when it comes to choice Kentucky bourbon,' Haller said. 'Especially Pappy Van Winkle.'

'I'm going to remember that.'

'You do that. Talk to you later.'

The call ended and Bosch went in the side door to the station. He walked through the empty detective bureau and opened the door to the war room. He was immediately hit with the fresh smell of breakfast burritos.

It was a full house. Sitting around the table and eating were Lourdes, Sisto, Luzon, Captain Trevino, and Chief Valdez. Jerry Edgar was also in attendance with a man

Bosch had never seen before. He was late thirties with dark hair and a deep tan. He wore a golf shirt with sleeves tight on his expanded biceps.

'Sorry I'm late,' Bosch said. 'I didn't know it was going to be all hands on deck.'

'We were eating while waiting,' Lourdes said. 'Harry, this is Agent Hovan from the DEA.'

16

The man with the tight sleeves stood up and reached across the table to shake Bosch's hand. As he did so, he assessed Bosch the way an art critic might look the first time at a sculpture, or a college football coach at a high school cornerback.

After freeing his hand from Hovan's grip, Bosch pulled out a chair at the end of the table and sat down. Lourdes picked up the tray of breakfast burritos and offered to pass it down but Bosch put up his hand and shook his head.

'So,' he said. 'Agent Hovan, what brings you here first thing this morning?'

'You called, I wanted to respond,' Hovan said. 'Since it was Jerry who referred me to you, I spoke with him yesterday about you and the case and thought it would be best if we all met in person.'

'To brief us all on Santos?' Bosch asked.

Before Hovan answered, the chief spoke up.

'Agent Hovan came in to see me first thing this morning,' he said. 'He's going to brief us all, but he also has a couple ideas about our investigation.'

'*Our* investigation,' Bosch said.

'Harry, don't get ruffled,' Valdez said. 'It's not what you think. Just hear the man out.'

'I think Harry's right,' Sisto said. 'When the feds

come in, they come in to take things over. This is our case.'

'Could we just give him a chance to talk?' the chief insisted.

Bosch made a gesture, giving Hovan the go-ahead, but he admired Sisto for standing up.

'Okay, I think I got the lay of the land from your chief and Jerry,' Hovan said. 'You got the two-bagger and you've zeroed in on the clinic over in Pacoima. Today you were probably going to come in here, put your heads together, and decide to go small to get big. Am I right?'

'What does that mean?' Lourdes asked.

'You were going to pick off a pill shill or a capper and start trading up, right?' Hovan said. 'It's how it usually works.'

'And that's a problem?' Lourdes asked. 'It's usually the way it works because it's what works.'

She glanced at Bosch to back her up.

'Yes, that was the plan,' Bosch said. 'But I suppose the DEA has an alternate suggestion.'

'Correct,' Hovan said. 'If you want to get the man who ordered the hit on that pharmacy, then you're talking about Santos, and there ain't nobody in the world who knows Santos and his operation like I do. And I can tell you, catching small fish to go after the big fish is not going to work.'

'Why is that?' Lourdes asked.

'Because the big fish is too insulated,' Hovan said. 'Based on what I've been told about this case, I would say you have it right. Those two hitters were sent by Santos, but you'll never make that connection. For all we know, those two are already dead and buried in the desert. Santos doesn't take chances.'

'So then how do we get him?' Lourdes asked.

The tone of her voice revealed her dislike of the idea of the big-shot fed dropping in to school them on their own case.

'You need somebody inside,' Hovan said.

'That's your idea?' Lourdes asked.

'That's it,' he said. 'You have an opportunity here. A way in.'

'Me,' Sisto said. 'I'll go undercover.'

Everyone turned to look at Sisto. His eagerness to assume a key role in the case was outweighing his inexperience and the danger of undercover work.

'No, not you,' Hovan said.

He pointed across the table at Bosch.

'Him,' he said.

'What are you talking about?' Lourdes asked.

'How old are you, Detective Bosch?' Hovan asked. 'Over sixty-five, I'm guessing?'

'Yes,' Bosch said.

Hovan gestured as if presenting Bosch to the others at the table.

'We take Detective Bosch, make him look a little older, a little more worn, and a little more hungry. We give him a new ID and Medicare card. We change his clothes, take away his razor and soap for a few days. What we do is follow the clinic's van and arrest a few of the shills at a pharmacy, make it look like a random enforcement operation. Jerry and I take care of that. Then, when the capper gets back to the clinic and is a few bodies short and looking at being a few thousand pills short by the end of the month, in walks the perfect recruit.'

Hovan used his hands again to offer Bosch to the group.

'The "perfect recruit"?' Luzon said.

'He's the right age and just what they'll be looking for,' Hovan said. 'You ever work undercover, Detective?'

All eyes went to Bosch.

'Not really,' he said. 'A few times here and there on cases. Nothing serious. Just how close would I be able to get to Santos if I'm being run around the state to pharmacies all day?'

'Put it this way: closer than anybody else in law enforcement,' Hovan said. 'Santos is a phantom. He's the Howard Hughes of hillbilly heroin. Nobody's seen him in nearly a year. Our intel photos of him are even older. But here's the thing.'

Hovan opened a thin manila file that had been on the table in front of him. It contained a two-page document stapled together. He held it up for all to see.

'This is a John Doe arrest warrant for Santos. It's a RICO case and it's solid, and this warrant was issued more than a year ago. We have not executed it because we can't identify or find the guy. But you might be able to. You get recruited and you might get close enough to signal us in. We'll set you up with all you need. You see Santos, you call us in and we take him down. You take down the man who ordered the hit on that pharmacy. Maybe we even get the shooters.'

Hovan had spun the plan with an urgent tone in his voice. It was met with a long silence as it was considered. Bosch held his hand out for the file containing the warrant, and Hovan passed it over. Harry took a quick glance at it to make sure it hadn't been a prop. It looked legit. John Doe AKA 'Santos' charged under the federal Racketeering Influenced and Corrupt Organizations Act. It was the catchall law used by the feds to go after mobsters for almost fifty years.

It was Lourdes who broke the silence.

'We heard your last inside man took a plane ride and never came back,' she said.

'Yeah, but he wasn't a cop,' Hovan said. 'He was an amateur and made an amateur mistake. That wouldn't happen with Bosch. He'd be prepped and pretty – that's what we call being totally ready to go under. I mean, this is a perfect opportunity here.'

Hovan looked directly at Bosch to make his final pitch.

'I gotta admit, when I checked you out with Jerry and heard you were an old guy, my mind started working overtime. We don't get guys your age doing UC work. I mean, none. You're the perfect way in.'

Bosch was beginning to bristle.

'Yeah, enough with the "old guy" stuff,' he said. 'I get your point.'

Chief Valdez cleared his throat and stepped into the conversation before anybody else could respond.

'If Harry gets on a plane, he could end up anywhere,' he said. 'I don't like that.'

'Most likely he'd be taken down to Slab City,' Hovan said.

'And what exactly is Slab City?'

'A retired military base down near the bottom of the Salton Sea. When they closed the base, they pulled everything out of there except the hard surfaces. That's the landing strips and the slabs they built the Quonsets on. Squatters came in and took over, built their own places. Then the Santos operation came in, uses the airstrips, and built a tent city for his operation.'

'Why don't you just go in and shut it all down?' Lourdes asked.

'Because we want Santos,' Hovan said. 'We don't care about the addicts he runs as shills. They're a dime a dozen. We want the head of the snake, and that's why we need somebody inside to send out the signal when he's there.'

'Okay, we need to think about this,' Valdez said. 'Detective Bosch also needs to decide if this is something he would even be willing to do. He is a reserve officer in the department and I'm not going to order him to do anything with a risk factor like you're talking about here. So give us a day or two and we'll get back to you with an answer.'

Hovan raised his palms in a hands-off manner.

'Hey, roger that,' Hovan said. 'I just wanted to come up here and make my pitch. I'll let you people get back to work. You call me with your decision.'

He stood up to leave but Bosch stopped him with three words.

'I'll do it,' he said.

Hovan looked at him, and a smile started to spread on his face.

'Harry, wait a minute,' Valdez said. 'I think we should take our time and consider other options.'

'Harry, are you sure?' Lourdes added. 'This is a dangerous—'

'Give me a couple days to get ready,' Bosch said. 'I'll give it a shot.'

'Okay, okay,' Hovan said. 'Don't shave and don't bathe. Body odor is a tell. If you don't stink, you ain't a user.'

'Good to know,' Bosch said.

'I can hook you up with a user if you want to research it,' the agent offered.

'No,' Bosch said. 'I think I know somebody I can talk to. When do we do this?'

Bosch looked at the faces surrounding the table. The looks of concern far outweighed the look of excitement on Hovan's face.

'How about we go Friday?' Hovan said. 'That'll give us time to work out logistics and request a shadow team. Maybe get you some time with our UC trainers.'

'I'll want full coverage on him,' Valdez said. 'I don't have the people to do it but I don't want Harry out there with his ass in the breeze.'

'He won't be,' Hovan said. 'We'll have him covered.'

'What about when he's on that plane?' Lourdes asked.

'We'll have air support,' Hovan said. 'We won't lose him. We'll be so high above that plane, they won't even know we're there.'

'And when he lands?' Edgar asked.

'I'm not going to candy-coat it. When he gets to Slab City, he's on his own. But we'll be nearby and ready for the signal.'

That ended the questions from Lourdes. Hovan looked at the chief.

'You have a photo of Bosch we can use to make a dummy DL?'

Valdez nodded.

'We have the shot we made his police ID with,' he said. 'Captain Trevino can take you into the op center to get that.'

Trevino got up to lead Hovan out. The DEA agent said he would be in touch and would come back Friday morning ready to go with the undercover operation.

After he was gone, all eyes returned to Bosch.

'What?' he said.

'I still want you to think about this,' Valdez said. 'Any second thoughts and we pull out.'

Bosch thought about José Jr. and his naive bravery.

'No,' he said. 'Let's do it.'

'Why, Harry?' Lourdes asked. 'You've done your part for years and years. Why are you doing this?'

Bosch shrugged. He didn't like all the attention on him.

'I think about that kid going to college to learn how to do what his father did,' he said. 'Then he graduates and gets into the business and finds the corruption of it. He goes through all of that and – big surprise – he does the right thing and it gets him killed. People can call him stupid or naive. I call him a hero and that's why I'm all in. I want Santos more than Agent Hovan does.'

He had their rapt attention now.

'What they did to José Esquivel shouldn't just go by,' Bosch added. 'If this is the best shot we have at Santos, then I want to take it.'

Valdez nodded.

'Okay, Harry, we get it,' he said. 'And we're with you one hundred percent.'

Bosch nodded his thanks and looked across the table at his old partner Edgar. He nodded too. He was on board.

17

Haller set up the Legal Siegel interview for that afternoon. The former defense attorney presumed dead by many, including Lance Cronyn and his client Preston Borders, was living in a nursing home in the Fairfax area. Bosch met Haller in the parking lot at two p.m. It was one of the rare occasions Bosch saw Haller emerge from the front seat of his Lincoln and the lawyer explained that he was between drivers at the moment. They proceeded inside. Haller held a briefcase that he told Bosch he was using to carry a video camera and to smuggle in a French dip sandwich from Cole's in downtown.

'This is a kosher joint,' Haller explained. 'No food allowed in from the outside.'

'What happens if they catch you?' Bosch asked.

'I don't know. Maybe I get banned for life.'

'So he's cool with doing the interview?'

'Said he was. Once he eats, he'll want to talk.'

In the lobby, they signed in as David Siegel's lawyer and investigator. They then took an elevator up to the third floor. Signing in as Haller's investigator reminded Bosch of something.

'How's Cisco doing?' he asked.

Dennis 'Cisco' Wojciechowski was Haller's longtime investigator. Two years earlier he and his Harley were taken down on Ventura Boulevard in an intentional hit-and-run. He went through three surgeries on his left knee and came out with a Vicodin addiction that took him six months to recognize before he treated it cold turkey.

'He's good,' Haller said. 'Real good. He's back and busy.'

'I need to talk to him.'

'Not a problem. Can I tell him what it's about?'

'Got a friend I think is addicted to hillbilly heroin. I want to ask him what to look for and what to do.'

'Then he's your man. I'll call him for you as soon as we get out of here.'

They exited the elevator on the third floor and Haller informed the woman posted at the nursing station that he was visiting his client David Siegel and should not be disturbed. They proceeded down the hallway to Siegel's private room. Haller pulled a doorknob hanger out of the inside pocket of his suit coat. It said 'Legal Conference: Do Not Disturb.' He winked at Bosch as he hung it on the knob and closed the door.

The wall-mounted TV was blaring a CNN report on a congressional investigation into Russia's meddling with the presidential election the year before. An old man propped up on a hospital bed was watching it. He looked like he didn't weigh more than a hundred pounds, and he had wispy white hair that surrounded his head on the pillow like a halo. He wore an old golf shirt with the Wilshire Country Club crest. His arms were skinny, the skin wrinkled and mottled with age spots. His hands looked lifeless and were folded on top of the blanket that was tucked up neatly under his arms and over his chest.

Haller moved around the bed and waved to get the bedridden man's attention.

'Uncle David,' Haller said loudly. 'Hi. I'm going to turn this down.'

Haller took the TV remote off a side table and killed the sound from the TV.

'Damn Russians,' Siegel muttered. 'I hope I live long enough to see that guy impeached.'

'Spoken like a true lefty,' Haller said. 'But I doubt that's gonna happen.'

He turned back to the man in the bed.

'So how are you?' Haller said. 'This is Harry Bosch, my half brother. I've told you about him.'

Siegel put his watery eyes on Bosch and studied him.

'You're the one,' he said. 'Mickey told me about you. He said you came to the house one time.'

Bosch knew he was talking about Michael Haller Sr., his father. Bosch had met him only the one time, in his Beverly Hills mansion. He was sick and soon to die. Bosch was fresh back from war in Southeast Asia. When he entered the house he saw a boy of about five or six standing with a housekeeper. He knew then that he had a half brother. A month later he stood on a hillside and watched as their father was put into the ground.

'Yes,' Bosch said. 'That was a long time ago.'

'Well,' Siegel said. 'For me everything was a long time ago. The longer you live, the more you can't believe how things change.'

He gestured weakly toward the silent TV screen.

'I brought you something that hasn't changed in a

hundred years,' Haller said. 'Dropped by Cole's on my way over and got you a French dip.'

'Cole's is good,' Siegel said. 'I didn't eat at lunch because I knew you were coming. Raise me up.'

Haller grabbed another remote off the table and tossed it to Bosch. While Haller opened his briefcase to get out the sandwich, Bosch raised the upper portion of the bed until Siegel was in an almost seated position.

'We've met before,' Bosch said. 'Sort of met. You cross-examined me on the stand in the case we are going to talk about today.'

'Of course,' Siegel said. 'I remember. You were very thorough. A good witness for the prosecution.'

Bosch nodded his thanks as Haller tucked a napkin into the open collar of the old man's shirt. He then slid the over-bed table across his lap and unwrapped the sandwich in front of him. He opened up a Styrofoam sidecar of *jus* and put it down on the table as well. Siegel immediately picked up one half of the sandwich, dipped the edge into the juice, and started eating it, taking small bites and savoring each one of them.

While Siegel ate his sandwich and thought about the old days, Haller took the mini-camcorder out of his briefcase and set it up on a mini-tripod on the over-bed table. He adjusted the table while looking at the framing of the shot, and then they were ready.

It took Legal Siegel thirty-five minutes to eat his French dip sandwich.

Bosch waited patiently while Haller asked the old man questions about days gone by, getting him ready for the interview. Finally, Siegel balled up the sandwich wrap and was done. He tossed it toward a trash can in the corner and came well short. Haller picked up the debris and put it back in his briefcase.

'You ready, Uncle Dave?' he asked.

'Been ready,' Siegel said.

Haller pulled the napkin out of the collar of Siegel's shirt and adjusted the camera once more before holding his finger on the record button.

'All right, here we go,' he said. 'Look at me, not at the camera.'

'Don't worry, they had video cameras back when I was practicing,' Siegel said. 'I'm not that much of a relic.'

'I just thought maybe you were out of practice.'

'Never.'

'Okay, then we'll start. Three, two, one, recording.'

Haller introduced Siegel and stated the date, time, and location of the interview. Though the camera was solely focused on Siegel, he identified himself and Bosch as well. Then he began.

'Mr. Siegel, how long did you practice law in Los Angeles County?'

'Almost fifty years.'

'You specialized in criminal defense?'

'Specialized? That was the entire practice, yes.'

'Did there come a time when you represented a man named Preston Borders?'

'Preston Borders engaged my services in his defense of a murder charge in late nineteen eighty-seven. The trial ensued the following year.'

Haller proceeded to walk him through the case, first the preliminary hearing to determine if the charge was valid, then on to the jury trial. Haller was careful to avoid any questions regarding the internal discussions of the case, as they were privileged attorney—client communications. Once the case was summarized to the point of a guilty verdict and the subsequent sentence of death, Haller moved on to contemporary times.

'Mr. Siegel, are you aware of a new legal effort being undertaken on your former client's behalf to vacate his conviction after almost thirty years?'

'I am aware of it. You made me aware of it.'

'And are you aware that in the legal filings, Mr. Borders makes the claim that you suborned his perjury during the trial by telling him to testify about things that you both knew were untrue?'

'I'm aware of it, yes. He threw me under the bus, to use today's terminology.'

Siegel's voice had drawn tight with contained anger.

'Specifically, Borders makes the claim that you furnished him with the sworn testimony regarding his purchase of a sea-horse pendant on the Santa Monica pier. Did you provide that testimony to Mr. Borders?'

'I certainly did not. If he lied, he did so on his own and at his own counsel. As a matter of fact, I did not want him to testify during the trial, but he insisted. I felt I had no choice, so I let him and he talked himself onto death row. The jury did not believe a word he said. I talked to several of the jurors after the verdict and they confirmed that.'

'Did you ever consider putting forth a defense that included the allegation that the lead detective on the case had planted the sea-horse pendant in your client's home in order to frame him?'

'No, I didn't. We had both of the detectives on the case checked out and challenging their integrity was not an option. We didn't try it.'

'Have you allowed me to interview you today freely and without outside pressure?'

'I volunteered. I'm an old man but you don't trash me and the integrity of a forty-nine-year career in law without a word from me about it. Fuck them.'

Haller leaned away from the camera, not expecting the off-color language. He tried not to put laughter on the sound track.

'One final question,' he managed to say. 'Do you understand that giving this interview today could result in an investigation and sanctions against you from the California bar?'

'They can come and get me if they want. I've never been afraid of a fight. They were stupid enough to believe and print the obit I sent them. Let them come at me.'

Haller reached over and turned off the recorder.

'That was good, Uncle David,' he said. 'I think it's going to help.'

'Thank you,' Bosch said. 'I know it will help.'

'Like I said, fuck them,' Siegel said. 'They want a fight, they got it.'

Haller started packing up the camera.

Siegel turned his head slightly and looked at Bosch.

'I remember you at that trial,' he said. 'I knew you spoke the truth and Borders was done for. You know, in forty-nine years, he was the only one of mine to end up on the row. And I never felt bad about it. He was where he was supposed to be.'

'Well,' Bosch said, 'with any luck he'll stay there.'

Twenty minutes later Bosch and Haller stood by their cars in the parking lot.

'So what do you think?' Bosch asked.

'I think they picked the wrong lawyer to mess with,' Haller said. 'I loved that "fuck them" line.'

'Yeah. But they thought he was dead.'

'They're going to be shitting bricks next Wednesday, that's for sure. Just need to keep this all under wraps if we can.'

'Why shouldn't we be able to?'

'It's about standing. I'll file for you as an intervening party. The D.A. will probably object, saying they represent you as the lead on the case. If I lose that battle, then I may have to file on Legal Siegel's behalf to get in the door. That's all we want, a foot in the door to make our case.'

'You think the judge will allow the interview in?'

'He'll look at some of it, at least. I started out with the basic stuff on purpose. To lull Cronyn and Kennedy into thinking it's fluff. Then – *boom* – I ask the question about perjury. It crosses the line into privilege, so we'll see. I'm hoping the judge will be a little bit pregnant by then and say he wants to watch the whole thing. I checked him out. We got lucky there. Judge Houghton's been on the bench twenty years and was practicing law for twenty before that. That means he was around when Legal was active. I'm hoping he'll cut the old guy a break and hear him out.'

'I've had a number of cases before Houghton over

the years. He likes to get the full story on things. I think he'll want to hear what Legal has to say. What about Borders? Will he testify at this thing?'

'I doubt it. That would be a mistake. But he'll be there and I want to see his face when we put Legal Siegel on the video screen.'

Bosch nodded. He thought about facing Borders again himself after so many years. He realized that he wasn't even sure what the man looked like. In his mind and memory Borders was a shadowy figure with piercing eyes. He had taken on the dimensions of a monster from imagination.

'You need to step things up now,' Haller said.

'How so?' Bosch asked.

'What we've got is good, but it's not good enough. We've got you, we've got Legal Siegel, and we've got the DNA in question being in Cronyn's possible possession. But we need more. We need the whole frame. That's what this is. They're framing you for hanging this on an innocent man.'

'I'm working on it.'

'Then work harder, my brother.'

Haller opened his car door, ready to go.

'I'll have Cisco give you a call,' he said.

'Appreciate it,' Bosch said. 'And, uh, you might not hear from me for a few days. I've got something I've gotta do on my San Fernando case. I probably won't be available.'

'What case, man? This should be your only case. Priority one.'

'I know, but this other thing can't wait. I've got it covered. I'll figure out the frame and then we're home free.'

'Famous last words, "home free". Don't stay away too long.'

Haller dropped into his car and closed the door. Bosch watched him back out and leave.

18

Bosch had made a deal with Bella Lourdes on the San Fernando case. He would go off to take care of some personal business and prep for his undercover assignment while she and the remaining members of the detective team continued to pursue all avenues of the investigation and prepare for Friday's operation. That left Bosch a solid day and a half to pursue the Borders frame, as Haller had termed it, as well as take a meeting set by Hovan with a DEA undercover training team.

Bosch had realized after talking with Haller that he might have had his focus on Borders wrong from the start. Because he knew Borders was guilty of the crime he was on death row for, Bosch had put him at the origin of the frame. He was the evildoer, the monster, and so this was all his cunning orchestration, his one last manipulation of the system and attempt to escape from prison through legal means.

But now he understood that this was wrong. The starting point was Lance Cronyn. The attorney was at the center of every stage of this case. While he had cast himself as a lawyer with a conscience just bringing a miscarriage of justice to the attention of the powers that be, it was clear now that he was the one pulling the strings of the D.A.'s Office, the LAPD, and most likely Borders himself.

Still sitting in his car outside Legal Siegel's nursing home, Bosch rested his wrist on the steering wheel and drummed his fingers on the dashboard as he thought about next moves. He had to be careful. If Cronyn picked up on any investigation directed by Bosch toward him, then he would go running to the judge and the D.A. and claim intimidation. Bosch wasn't sure yet what the first step was, but he had always employed a battering-ram philosophy when he found himself stuck on the logic of a case. He would step back and then move quickly forward, hoping the momentum of what he did know would carry him through the block.

He went back to the beginning of how Cronyn could have engineered the frame and then carried it out. He decided it had to have started with the death of Lucas John Olmer. From there Bosch started free-associating, using the knowns of the case as the waypoints between the unknowns.

He figured it began when Cronyn got the word that his client Olmer had died in prison. What did he do? Clear space in the files, send everything collected over the years on Olmer to archives? Did he take one last look for old time's sake? For whatever reason, Cronyn reviewed the files and was reminded of the strategy not taken: semen identified as Olmer's taken in evidence on the rape cases. The judge had ordered the police lab to share the genetic material with the private lab of Cronyn's choosing. It was sent there and either tested or not and that is the last record of the material's whereabouts.

Bosch kept rolling with it, putting pieces together. Upon his client's death, Cronyn could have reached out to the lab and requested that the material be returned.

The suspect was dead, the case was closed, and the attorney was tying up all loose ends. Cronyn ended up with the material and then needed to figure out a way to use it.

What was his goal? To make money? Bosch believed so. It was always about money. In the case at hand, Borders stood to make millions in a city payout for wrongful conviction. The attorney who brokered that deal would get as much as a third of it.

Going back to his evolving case theory, Bosch knew that Cronyn was Olmer's longtime attorney and therefore would have more knowledge of the rapist and his activities than anyone else. Cronyn goes back in time in Los Angeles, looking through newspaper archives for a case that will fit the bill. A case before the advent of DNA evidence. A case in which he could use DNA as an out.

He comes across Preston Borders. Convicted of murder in a largely circumstantial case, with the exception of the sea-horse pendant being the only hard evidence against him. Cronyn knows that dropping the DNA of a serial rapist into the case would be like setting off a bomb. Eliminate the sea-horse pendant and the DNA is like a golden key that unlocks the door to death row.

Bosch liked it. It worked so far. But Cronyn would not have taken a step further with it without first enlisting Borders as a willing component in the plan. Of course this would not have been a difficult sell. Borders was on death row, out of appeals, and running out of time, given the recent statewide vote in favor of a measure to speed up the culmination of death penalty cases.

Cronyn shows up and offers a potential get-out-of-jail card with a seven- or maybe eight-figure chaser: Walk out of prison and death row and have the City of Los Angeles pay you for your troubles. What was Borders going to say, 'I pass'?

Bosch realized he had a way to partially confirm his theory. He reached over the seat to where he had placed the Borders case files. He brought the rubber-banded top half of the stack forward and quickly went to the letter Cronyn had sent to the Conviction Integrity Unit. It was the official starting point of the frame. All Bosch was interested in was the date on it. It had been sent by Cronyn in August of the previous year. He realized that he'd had a small piece of evidence of the frame all along. Officer Jericho had said that Cronyn had visited Borders the first Thursday of every month since January of the previous year.

Cronyn had gone up to San Quentin and had several meetings with Borders before sending the letter to the D.A.'s Office. If that didn't show the making of a conspiracy and the plan to frame, then he didn't know what did.

Buzzed by having made a connection that could be documented at the hearing the following week, Bosch had the battering ram moving with high velocity. The block was still the application of the plan. He had Cronyn and Borders tied together. He had Olmer's DNA in Cronyn's possession. He just needed step three. The execution of the plan.

Bosch decided to break the possibilities into two pieces, with the separator between them being the video that Tapscott took of Lucia Soto opening the evidence box, presumably after many years of its sitting undisturbed on a shelf in LAPD property control.

If the planted evidence was already in place when Soto opened the box, then the fix came before – most likely in the window between Cronyn journeying to San Quentin to meet Borders in January, and August, when he sent the letter to the D.A.'s Office, having presumably reached some form of agreement with Borders on the plan. That was a lot of time and Bosch knew that realistically he would need Soto's help in identifying who might have had access to the box.

In a space the size of a football field, the archives were strictly monitored and access was documented on multiple levels. A fleet of bonded civilian employees comprised the staff and worked under the on-site supervision of a police captain. Access to evidence was restricted to law enforcement officers, who needed to provide proper identification and a thumbprint for all requests, and there were also cameras that kept the evidence viewing areas under surveillance 24/7.

If the genetic evidence was planted after Tapscott and Soto retrieved the box from property control, then there were a number of places along the chain of custody where that could have happened. The detectives would have hand delivered the contents of the evidence box to the lab at Cal State L.A. for examination and analysis in the serology unit. This brought into play several lab technicians who could have had access to the clothing being examined. But it was a lot of *could haves*. Bosch knew that these cases were randomly assigned to technicians and that there were several integrity checks built into the protocols and personnel of the DNA unit to guard against corruption, cross-contamination, and evidence tampering, intended or not. In the early days of DNA use in criminal proceedings, the science and protocols were challenged from every angle and with such frequency that over time a firewall of integrity had made the lab nearly impervious. Bosch knew this side of the equation was a long shot.

The more Bosch considered the two possibilities, the more he believed that it was unlikely that the frame had occurred in the lab. The random assignment of a technician to each case alone seemed to undercut the possibility. Even in the unlikely event that Cronyn had a corrupt technician in hand, there seemed to be no way for him to be sure that his tech would even get the case, let alone have access to plant DNA on Danielle Skyler's pajamas.

Bosch kept coming back to the evidence box and the possibility of it being tampered with before Soto cut through his seals and opened it under Tapscott's camera. He pulled out the burner phone he had the video on and once again watched the opening of the box. The evidence seals were intact as Soto cut through them and opened the flaps of the box. Bosch saw nothing wrong and again it confounded him.

He thought about texting Soto and asking if she had access to the archive's overhead cameras and whether she had asked to view them. But he knew such a question would likely make her suspicious of Bosch's activities. It would also make her angry. After all, Tapscott had filmed Soto opening the box because the two detectives wanted video confirmation that the box's seals were unbroken. They had filmed the process themselves as a means of avoiding having to request the footage from the overhead cameras. It was unlikely they would be interested in doing it for Bosch now. They were satisfied that there had been no tampering and that Olmer's DNA had been in the box on the pajamas since day one.

Bosch watched the video again, this time muting Tapscott's commentary so he could concentrate on the images as Soto used a box cutter to slice through the seals. Halfway through, his real phone buzzed in his pocket and he paused the playback and dropped the burner into a cup holder in the center console. He pulled his phone and saw a number he didn't recognize but he took the call anyway.

'Hello.'

'Harry Bosch?'

'Yes.'

'Cisco. Mickey said you wanted to talk to me.'

'Yes, how are you doing?'

'Doin' good. What's up?'

'I'd like to meet and talk to you about something. It's confidential. I'd rather do it in person.'

'What are you doing right now?'

'Uh, sitting in a parking lot near Fairfax High.'

'I'm not too far. The upstairs at Greenblatt's will be pretty quiet this time of day. Meet there?'

'Yeah, I can head there.'

'You don't want to give even a hint about what this is?'

Bosch had always felt a low-grade friction from Cisco during the few times they had been in each other's company. Bosch had chalked it up to the standard hostility between those who work for the defense and those who work for the prosecution. Added to this was the fact that since before Haller had hired him, Cisco had been associated with the Road Saints – a motorcycle gang in the police's estimation, a club in the membership's own view. And there was also a bit of jealousy thrown in. Bosch and Cisco's boss shared a blood connection, which gave them a unique closeness that Cisco could not have. Bosch thought Cisco might be worried that one day Bosch was going to replace him as Haller's defense investigator. In Harry's mind, that was improbable.

Bosch decided to give him more than a hint.

'I want you to help me go undercover as a functioning oxycodone addict,' he said.

There was a pause before Cisco responded.

'Yeah,' he finally said. 'I can do that.'

19

Fifteen minutes later, Bosch was sitting in a booth in the upstairs dining room of Greenblatt's on Sunset, nursing a cup of coffee and watching the muted video on his burner again. The place was empty except for one other table on the other side of the room.

Bosch heard the slow, methodical sound of heavy footsteps coming up the wooden stairs. He paused the video and soon Cisco emerged. He was a big man who worked out like a fiend and as usual was wearing a black Harley T-shirt stretched tight by his muscular chest and biceps. He had gray hair tied back in a ponytail and dark Wayfarer sunglasses. He was carrying a black cane with flames painted on it and what looked like a wrap-around knee brace.

'Hey, Bosch,' he said as he slid into the booth.

They bumped fists across the table.

'Cisco,' Bosch said. 'We could have met downstairs so you didn't have to make the climb.'

'Nah, it's quiet up here and stairs are good for the knee.'

'How's that going?'

'It's all good. Back on the bike, back on the job. Only time I complain is in the mornings when getting out of bed. That's when the knee still hurts like a motherfucker.'

Bosch nodded and gestured toward the items Cisco had brought.

'What's all of this?'

'These are your props. They're all you need.'

'Tell me.'

'You want to pharmacy-shop, right? Stack prescriptions? It's what addicts do.'

'Uh, yeah.'

'I did it for a year. I was never turned away once. You go in these places, they want to make money like everybody else. They aren't looking to turn you away, they're looking to be convinced. You put on the knee brace-be sure to wear it outside your pants – and use the cane, and you won't have any problems.'

'That's it?'

Cisco shrugged.

'Worked for me. I bought a prescription pad off a bent doctor in La Habra for five grand. Had him sign the line on every slip. I did the rest. Filled them out and went to every mom-and-pop *farmacia* in East L.A. In six weeks I accumulated over a thousand pills. That's when I made the deal with myself. When those pills ran out, I was going to rise up and beat it. And I did.'

'I'm glad you did, Cisco.'

'Fucking A. Me, too.'

'So no help from the V.A.?'

'Fuck them, the docs at the V.A. were the ones got me hooked in the first place after my surgeries. Then they cut me loose and I'm on the street, strung out, trying to keep a job, trying to keep my wife. Fuck the V.A. I'll never go back to them.'

The story was not surprising to Bosch. It was the

story of the epidemic. People start out hurt and just want to kill the pain and get better. Then they're hooked and need more than the prescriptions allow. People like Santos fill the space, and there is no turning back.

'When the pills ran out, what did you do?'

'I bought a can opener.'

'What?'

'A can opener and thirty days of rations. I then had a friend put me in a windowless room with a toilet and nail the door shut. He came back in thirty days and I was clean. I'll never take another pill again. I'll take a fucking root canal but I still won't take a pill.'

Bosch could only nod at the end of that story. A waitress came by and Cisco asked for an iced tea and one of their garlic pickles sliced into quarters.

'You want more than that?' Bosch asked. 'I'll buy you lunch.'

'Nah, I'm good. I like the pickles they have here. The garlic brine. One other thing is no eye contact. In the pharmacy. Keep your head down, hand them the piece of paper and your ID, and don't make eye contact.'

'Got it. The people I'm dealing with are giving me a Medicare card too.'

'Of course, saves you a ton of money. Sticks it on the government.'

Bosch nodded.

'You mind me asking why you're doing this?' Cisco asked.

'I'm working a case,' Bosch said. 'Two pharmacists murdered up in San Fernando. A father and son.'

'Yeah, I read about that. Looks like some dangerous people. You got backup? I'm free at the moment.'

'I do. But I appreciate the offer.'

'I've been in the black hole, man. I know what it's like. Anything I can do to help.'

Bosch nodded. He was aware that the Road Saints, Cisco's motorcycle 'club,' had once been suspected of being a primary manufacturer and mover of crystal meth, a drug with similarly devastating consequences for the addicted. The waitress arrived with iced tea and a sliced pickle, saving Bosch from bringing up the irony of Cisco's offer.

Cisco used his fingers to take a slice of pickle off the dish and slid it into his mouth in two bites. When the waitress had brought the plate, Bosch had moved his phone out of the way and accidentally activated its screen. Cisco pointed a wet finger at it.

'What's that?' he asked.

The screen was frozen on an image of Soto using the cutter on the evidence box. Bosch picked up the phone.

'It's nothing,' he said. 'It's another case. I was trying to figure something out while I was waiting for you.'

'Is that what you're working with Mickey on?' Cisco asked.

'Uh, yeah. But I have to figure the thing out before we can go into court.'

'Can I see?'

'Nah, it's kind of meant to be private. I can't show – well, you know, why not?'

Bosch realized he was grasping at straws when it came to the sealed box. Maybe fresh eyes would bring a fresh idea.

'It's a video of a detective cutting open an old evidence box, and they filmed it to prove it hadn't been tampered with. To prove nobody had gotten into it.'

Bosch started the playback from the beginning of the video and then put the phone down on the table and turned it toward Cisco. He took it off mute as well, hoping the couple eating on the other side of the room would not object.

Cisco leaned down and watched the screen while eating another slice of pickle. When it was over, he straightened back up.

'Looked legit to me,' he said.

'Like it hadn't been tampered with?' Bosch asked.

'Right.'

'Yeah, that's my take too.'

Bosch took the phone off the table and buried it in his pocket.

'Who's the guy?' Cisco asked.

'Her partner,' Bosch said. 'He took it on his phone and narrated. He talks too much.'

'No, the other guy. The one watching.'

'What guy watching?'

'Give me the phone.'

Bosch pulled the phone out again, set up the video playback, and handed it across the table. This time Cisco held it and poised one of his pickle fingers over the play button. Bosch waited. Cisco eventually stabbed at the screen several times.

'Come on, stop. Shit. I have to go back.'

He manipulated the phone's screen until it was playing again and once again hit the play/stop button.

'This guy.'

He handed the phone to Bosch, who quickly looked at the screen. It was nearly in the identical spot where he had paused the playback when Cisco had arrived. Soto was cutting through the seals down the lengthwise seam on the top of the box. Bosch was about to ask what Cisco was talking about, when he saw the face in the background. It startled him because he had not noticed it before. But someone had been watching Soto from outside the viewing room. Someone from the next room was leaning across the property counter and looking in.

During all his previous viewings of the video Bosch had been so consumed with checking the integrity of the seals on the evidence box that his eyes had not wandered to the borders of the frame. And now he saw it. A counterman who was interested enough in what Soto and Tapscott were doing to lean over to watch them.

Bosch recognized the man but couldn't immediately recall his name. Bosch had worked cold cases the last several years of his time with the LAPD and had gone to property control often to look at old evidence for new clues. The man on the screen had pulled the boxes for him on numerous occasions, but it was one of those quick bureaucratic relationships that never went much past the 'Howyadoin'?' phase. He thought his name was Barry or Gary or something along those lines.

Bosch looked up from the phone to Cisco.

'Cisco, you working on something right now for Haller?'

'Uh, no. Just sort of standing by till he needs me. Like I said, I'm free at the moment.'

'Good. I've got a job for you. It's the thing I'm doing with Haller, so it won't be a problem.'

'What do I do?'

Bosch held the phone up so Cisco could see the screen.

'You see this guy? I want to know everything there is to know about him.'

'He a cop?'

'No, a civilian employee called a property officer. He works in Property Control at Piper Tech downtown. He'll get off at five and come out past the guard shack on Vignes. If you set up under the freeway underpass, you should get a look at him when he puts his car window down and key-cards the exit gate. Tail him from there.'

'You paying or Mick?'

'Doesn't matter. I pay you or he pays you and charges me. It's part of the same case. I'm calling him as soon as we're done here.'

'When do you want me to start?'

'Right now. I'd do it myself but this guy knows me. If he saw me tailing him, the whole thing could blow up.'

'Okay, what's his name?'

'I can't remember. I meant that he knows me on sight – from when I was LAPD. If he's part of this and he saw me, the cat's out of the bag.'

'Got it. I'm on it.'

'Call me when you have him at his home. But you need to go. You're going to get caught in traffic going downtown.'

'Lane splitting – it's why I ride a Harley.'

'Oh, right.'

Cisco finished the last slice of pickle and then climbed out of the booth.

From the parking lot behind the deli, Cisco rode off on his Harley, and Bosch headed home to wait to hear from him. The first thing he did when he got there was text the video from his burner to his real phone. He then e-mailed it to himself and for the first time watched the video on the thirteen-inch screen of his laptop.

Though he studied the opening of the box once more, his eyes were drawn now to the figure who was momentarily caught watching Soto cut through the labels. On the larger screen Bosch saw a clearer expression on the man's face but could not read whether he was watching out of curiosity or something more. His excitement over Cisco's find began to give way to disappointment. They were chasing a dead end and Bosch was back to the question: How did Cronyn get the DNA into the evidence box?

He stepped away from the computer, taking the cane and knee brace Cisco had given him down the hall to his daughter's bedroom. The room seemed so still. She had not been up to L.A. in weeks. He sat on the bed and wrapped the brace around his left knee and over his pants, then secured it tightly with the buckles and straps. He then got up and walked stiff-legged to the center of the room, where he could see himself in the full-length mirror on the back of the door.

Holding the cane in his right hand, he walked toward the mirror, the brace minimizing the mobility of his knee. He pushed against the restraint and practiced walking. He didn't want to present himself as someone who was actually injured. Rather, he wanted to be a man using props to appear injured. There was a difference, and in that difference was the secret to being the perfect pill shill.

Soon he was moving about the house, working the brace and the cane into a rocking gait that he thought would be effective in his undercover capacity. At one point, he accidentally put the rubber tip of the cane into the sliding door track as he stepped onto the back deck. The cane momentarily became stuck and he twisted his wrist to pull it free. He felt the curved handle turn loose from the barrel of the cane. Thinking he might have broken it, he examined the handle and saw a seam just below its curve. He grasped the barrel and pulled, sliding the two pieces apart. The handle was attached to a four-inch blade with a dagger point.

Bosch smiled. It was what every undercover pill shill needed.

Satisfied with his physical prep work, Bosch went to the kitchen to make an early dinner. He was spreading peanut butter on a piece of whole wheat bread when his cell buzzed. It was Cisco. Bosch answered the call with a question.

'Hey, how come you didn't tell me the cane was a deadly weapon?'

There was a pause before Cisco answered.

'Holy shit, I forgot about that. The blade. Sorry, man, I hope that didn't get you in trouble. Don't try to go through TSA with that thing.'

'The kind of flying I'm expecting to do, there won't be any TSA. Actually, it's all good. I like having a little something up my sleeve if I need it in a jam. What's happening with our guy?'

'I've got him tucked in already at home. Not sure if that's for the night or what.'

'Where's he live?'

'Altadena. Has a house.'

'Were you able to get his name yet?'

'I got his whole package, man. This is what I do. His name is Terrence Spencer.'

'Terry, yeah, I knew it was something like that. Terry Spencer.'

Bosch ran the name through his memory to see if it came up in any other way besides the routine interactions at the property control counter. No other connections came to light.

'What's the whole package include?' he asked.

'Well, no criminal record, or I guess he wouldn't be working there,' Cisco said. 'I pulled his credit history. He's owned the house I'm sitting here looking at for eighteen years and is carrying a mortgage of five-sixty-five on it. I'd say that is a bit high for this neighborhood. He's probably maxed out on it. He's been spotty making his payments the past few years, a couple months late here and there, but about seven years ago he went through a real shaky period. The house went into fore-closure. He apparently fought it off somehow and got the refi he's on now. But that and his late-payment dings have pretty much tanked his credit score.'

Bosch wasn't really interested in Spencer's credit score.

'Okay, what else?'

'Drives a six-year-old Nissan, is married, his wife drives a newer Jaguar. Both cars were financed but paid off over time. Don't know about kids. This guy's fifty-four, so if he had them, they're probably out of the house. I can knock on doors in the neighborhood if you want me to go deeper.'

'No, nothing like that. I don't want to alert him.'

Bosch thought for a few moments about Cisco's

report. Nothing stood out in a big way. The mortgage trouble was of note, but since the financial crash a decade earlier, the middle class was squeezed, and missing payments and dodging foreclosure were not unusual. Spencer, however, was essentially a clerk, and the size of his mortgage would stand out if it were not for the fact that he had owned the house for eighteen years. In that length of time it was likely that the property's value had more than doubled. If he took equity out of it, then it might explain how he got stuck with a high-six-figure note.

'Any idea what his wife does?' Bosch asked.

'Lorna's still working on that,' Cisco said.

Bosch knew that Lorna Taylor was Mickey Haller's ex-wife and office manager, even though he didn't have an office. She was also currently married to Cisco, completing an incestuous circle in which everybody was somehow happy and worked together.

'You want me to stay on him?' Cisco asked.

Bosch thought about making a move that would bring clarity to the Spencer situation and allow Bosch to move on or focus in. He checked his watch. It was six fifteen.

'Tell you what,' he finally said. 'Sit tight for a few minutes. I gotta make a quick call and then I'll call you right back.'

'I'll be here,' Cisco said.

Bosch disconnected and went to his laptop in the dining room. He closed down the Tapscott video on the laptop and Googled the name Lance Cronyn. He got a website and the general number for a law firm called Cronyn & Cronyn.

He then pulled the burner phone out of his pocket and called the number. Most law offices were nine-to-five establishments but the call for defense attorneys could come at any hour, and most often those hours were at night. Most lawyers specializing in criminal defense had answering services or forwarding numbers so they could be reached quickly – especially by paying customers.

As expected, Bosch's call eventually reached a live human being.

'I need to speak to Lance Cronyn right away,' Bosch said. 'It's an emergency.'

'Mr. Cronyn has left for the day,' said the voice. 'But he will check soon for messages. Can I have your name?'

'Terry Spencer. I need to talk to him tonight.'

'I understand and will give him the message as soon as he checks in. What number should he call?'

Bosch gave the burner's number, repeated that it was an emergency situation, and disconnected. He knew that saying Cronyn would check in for messages was just a way of giving the lawyer an out if he didn't want to call back. Bosch was certain that the go-between would forward his message right away.

He got up and went to the kitchen to finish making his peanut-butter-and-jelly sandwich. Before he was done, he heard the burner's generic ringtone in the other room. He left the sandwich on the counter and went to the phone. He didn't recognize the number on the screen but assumed it was Cronyn's cell phone or home number. He answered with one word spoken into the palm of his hand in an attempt to disguise it.

'Yes.'

'Why are you calling me? I'm not your contact.'

Bosch stood frozen. There it was. Cronyn obviously knew who Spencer was. The annoyed tone and the intimacy of what was said showed without a doubt that the lawyer knew who he was talking to.

'Hello?'

Bosch said nothing. He just listened. It sounded as though Cronyn was in a car, driving.

'Hello?'

For Bosch, there was something absolutely energizing about the moment and listening silently to Cronyn's puzzled tone. Thanks to Cisco's one-look view of the video, Bosch had now made the jump to the next level. He was closer to the frame.

Cronyn disconnected on his end and the line went silent.

20

Bosch drove down out of the hills and was sitting dead still behind a long line of red lights on the Barham overpass when he took a call back from Cisco.

'Hey, he's on the move, and this time, I can tell, he's looking for a tail.'

Bosch immediately surmised that Cronyn had made contact with Spencer by other means and learned that it had not been Spencer who had left the emergency message. Now the question was whether they had decided to meet somewhere or whether Spencer was simply trying to determine if he was being surveilled.

'Can you stay with him? I'm not going to get there in time. Traffic.'

'I can try but what is more important to you – to see where he's going or to make sure I don't get made? Tailing on a Harley has its drawbacks when the target's on high alert. Namely, it's loud.'

That was confirmed by the background sound. Bosch could hear the wind whistling into Cisco's earpiece, as well as the baritone sounds of his bike's illegal muffler.

'Shit.'

'Yeah, if I knew I was going to be doing this, I would have been prepped and I could've tagged his car, you know? Hung back on him. But I went straight from

Greenblatt's to downtown to make sure I didn't miss him. Didn't have the equipment.'

'Yeah, yeah, I know, I'm not blaming you. I'm thinking you should let him go. I think I just spooked them with a call I made. It confirms this guy's part of this thing, so he might just be trying to see if he has a tail. Let him keep wondering.'

'He's done a couple pullovers and rectangle moves.'

Bosch knew a rectangle move was when you took four rights around a block and came back to where you were. It usually revealed all followers.

'Then maybe you've already been made.'

'Nah, I didn't fall for his bullshit. He's an amateur. Right now I got him four blocks ahead on Marengo. You sure you want me to let him go?'

Bosch thought for a moment and second-guessed his first instincts. He was torn. He might be passing up an opportunity to see Spencer and Cronyn together. One photograph of such a meeting would blow the whole case open. If he texted that to Soto, she would rethink everything and there probably would be no hearing on vacating Borders's sentence. But would Cronyn really be stupid enough to call for a meeting after getting the scam call from Bosch?

Harry didn't think so. Spencer was up to something else.

'I changed my mind; stay on him,' he finally said. 'Very loose. If you lose him, you lose him. Just don't get made.'

'Got it. Did you hear from Mick yet?'

'No. About what?'

'He's got more on this guy's mortgage. Some good

stuff and maybe an angle to play. At least that's what he said.'

'I'll call him. Let me know about Spencer. And thanks for jumping in on this, Cisco.'

'What I do.'

'Call me if you figure out what he's up to.'

They disconnected and Bosch called Haller next.

'I was just on with Cisco. He said you have some good stuff.'

'You bet. My girl Lorna has kicked some major ass on this. She was able to pull up the foreclosure record and I think crack this thing open.'

'Tell me.'

'I have to make a quick search on the computer first and then I'll have everything. You want to catch dinner in a bit and talk then?'

'Yeah. Where?'

'I feel like pot roast. You ever been to Jar?'

'Yeah, I like eating at the counter there.'

'Of course, you're a counter sort of guy. You're like the guy sitting by himself in that Hopper painting.'

'I'll see you at Jar. When?'

'Half an hour.'

Bosch disconnected. He wondered if there was some kind of psychic connection between himself and his half brother. He had often considered himself to be like that man at the counter in Hopper's *Nighthawks*.

He realized that he had not moved on the overpass in nearly ten minutes. Something was wrong up ahead on Barham. The cars were lined up all around the bend where it went down into Burbank and the Warner's lot. He reached over, opened his glove compartment, and looked at the mobile police light. Because he was only a reserve officer at SFPD, he was not given a city ride. In lieu of that, he had been given the blue strobe light he could throw on the roof of his personal car, but it came with the proviso that it not be used unless Bosch was inside the bounds of San Fernando.

'Fuck it,' he said.

He grabbed the light and put it out through the window and up onto the roof, a magnet on the bottom holding it in place. He plugged the juice line into the cigarette lighter and started seeing the flashing blue light reflecting off the rear window of the car in front of him. The car blocking his way inched forward enough for Bosch to make a U-turn and head back to Cahuenga Boulevard. Cars stopped at the intersection and he breezed through. He started heading south.

After he slipped by the Hollywood Bowl and onto Franklin, the traffic slackened off enough for Bosch to pull the plug out of the cigarette lighter. He got to Jar, down on Beverly, well ahead of Haller, and he took one of the stools at the counter. He was nursing his first martini when Haller came through the door fifteen minutes later. He asked for a table in the corner of the dining room for privacy. Bosch followed with his martini.

Haller matched Bosch's drink order and got down to business as soon as they were alone.

'I like the way you put my investigator to work without consulting me,' he said.

'Hey, I'm the client here,' Bosch retorted. 'You're working for me and that means he works for me too.'

'I'm not sure I agree with that logic, but it is what it is. You're going to love what we've got.'

'Cisco filled me in on some of it.'

'Not the really good stuff.'

'So tell me.'

Haller waited for his martini to be put down in front of him. The waiter was also about to hand out menus, when he was cut off with a wave of Haller's hand.

'Two orders of pot roast and a side of duck fried rice,' Haller said.

'Perfect,' said the waiter.

He went away.

'I like the way you order for me without consulting me first,' Bosch said.

'Must be something in our father's blood,' Haller said.

'I actually already ate a sandwich.'

'So eat again – this is the good stuff. Anyway, I don't know if you remember this but during the mortgage crisis, I shifted a lot of my business over to foreclosure defense. I made out, too. Remember, I hired Jennifer Aronson as an associate and we made some good money for a few years there.'

'I remember something about that, yeah.'

'Well, that's my way of telling you I know the ins and outs of that illustrious time in our nation's financial history. I wasn't the only one making bank and I know how others made out as well.'

'Okay, so what's it have to do with our man Spencer?'

'His foreclosure suit is public record. You just need to know how to find it, and lucky for us, Lorna does. So I've spent the past hour with it and, like I said, you're going to like it. Check that. Love it.'

'So get to it. What do you have?'

'Spencer got in over his head. He bought the house in two thousand, saw it go up in value, and pulled the value out in a home-equity loan six years later. I don't know what he did with the money but he didn't put enough aside to pay his now two mortgages. He then took the first step down the road of desperation. He combined those two loans into a single refi with one reasonable payment on an adjustable rate.'

'And let me guess, it didn't solve anything.'

'No, in many ways it made matters worse. He can't keep up and then the crash happens and he is circling the drain financially. He gets so far upside down on his mortgage he's breathing dirt. He stops making payments altogether and the bank starts foreclosure proceedings. He does a smart thing and hires a lawyer. The only thing is, he hired the wrong lawyer.'

'He should have hired you, is that what you're saying?'

'Well, it couldn't have hurt. The lawyer he does hire doesn't really know what she's doing, because she's like all the other lawyers in town and jumping into the fore-closure business with both feet.'

'Like you.'

'Like me. I mean, paid criminal defense work dried up. Nobody had any money. I was taking referrals from the public defender and working for chump change. I couldn't even make my child-support payments on time. So I went into foreclosure work. But I did my goddamn homework on it, and I hired a smart young associate out of the kind of law school that puts a chip on your shoulder and gives you something to prove.'

'Okay, I get it, you did it right and Spencer's lawyer did it wrong. What happened?'

'Well, the one thing she got right was the assessment that a legitimate bank wasn't going to touch Spencer's dumb ass. So she puts him into hard money.'

'What's hard money?'

'It doesn't come from a bank. It comes from investor pools, and because it's not a bank, they charge points up front and interest rates above market – sometimes damn close to the rates the mafia guys charge for money on the street.'

'And so Spencer's problems only got worse.'

'Oh, yeah. This poor guy's trying to hold on to his house and make his payments. Meantime, he's sitting on a big fat seven-year balloon. And guess what, that balloon is about to pop.'

'Back up and speak English. I paid off my house twelve years ago. I don't know what any of this means. What's the balloon?'

'Spencer made a deal with an investor pool called Rosebud Financial. I heard about them back then, that they had money to bail people out. Supposedly it came from a bunch of guys in Hollywood and it was run by another guy, named Ron Rogers, a real shark. He cut these deals and didn't care whether the taker could pay or not. If there was enough bottom-line equity in the property, he'd cut the deal, because he knew he'd get two shots at foreclosure: either when the poor slob homeowner couldn't make his monthly payments or at the end of the term, when there was a balloon payment for the balance.'

'So, the deal is, you pay these high monthlies, and then at the end you still have to pay off the whole note.'

'Exactly. These hard-money deals were short-term

mostly. Two years, five years. Spencer got a seven-year deal, which was pretty long, but the seven years is up in July and he'll owe all the money.'

'Can't he now go to a real bank and refinance again? The financial markets are pretty good now.'

'He could but he's fucked. His credit rating is shit and Rosebud Financial is putting the boots to him. They've dinged him every time he pays late by a week. You see? They want to put him in a corner. They know he's got no money to pay the balloon and he can't refinance the debt because of his record. In July they're going to take the house from him. And this is where it gets good. You know what Zillow is?'

'Zillow? No.'

'It's an online real-estate database. You can plug in a property address and get a ballpark valuation based on neighborhood comps and other factors. That was the thing I had to check before we talked, and sure enough, Spencer's property comes in at high six figures – almost a million bucks.'

'Then why doesn't he just sell it, pay off the balloon, and walk away with the profit?'

'Because he can't. That deal he cut with Rosebud requires company approval before a sale can be made. And that's where he hired the wrong lawyer. The fine print on the contract – she either didn't read it, didn't understand it, or didn't care. She just wanted to put him into that loan and move on, maybe even getting a kickback in the process.'

'Rosebud's not letting him sell.'

'That's correct.'

'So, they won't let him sell. He can't pay the balloon.

Rosebud's going to take the house, sell it, and split the profits among the Hollywood investors.'

'You're getting good at this, Bosch.'

Bosch sipped the last of his martini and thought about the scenario. Spencer was facing the loss of his house unless he could come up with more than a half million in cash to pay off the balloon. If that didn't make him vulnerable to corruption, nothing would.

Haller sipped his martini and nodded as he watched Bosch track it all. Then he smiled.

'I saved the kicker for last,' he said.

'What?' Bosch asked.

'Spencer's lawyer? The dumb one? Her name was Kathy Zelden. I knew her back in those days. She was a junior lawyer in a small firm, and her boss would send her to the courthouse the first Monday of every month, because that's when they published the foreclosures list. I was there, she was there, Roger Mills, a bunch of us – first Monday of every month. We'd buy a copy of the list and then the flyers would go out in the mail. "In foreclosure? Call the Lincoln Lawyer." Like that. Everybody on the list got flyers in the mail, phone calls, e-mails, the works. That's how I got most of my clients.'

'That's your kicker?'

'No, the kicker is that I'm talking seven, eight, years ago, when I knew her as Kathy Zelden. She was a real looker, and a year or two later her boss got his hand caught in her cookie jar. It was a mini-scandal. He ended up divorcing his wife of like twenty-five years and marrying Kathy. So the last five years, Kathy Zelden's been known as Kathy Cronyn.'

Haller held up his glass for a well-earned toast.

Bosch was empty but he took his glass and banged it hard enough to draw attention from nearby tables.

'Holy shit,' he said. 'We got 'em.'

'We fucking-A do,' Haller said. 'I am going to blow their shit right out of the water when we get to that hearing next week.'

He drained his glass just as the waiter brought their dishes of pot roast and duck fried rice.

'Gentlemen,' the waiter said. 'It looks like we are in need of more essential vitamins.'

Haller picked up his empty glass and offered it.

'We definitely are,' he said. 'We definitely are.'

21

After the pot roast and fried rice, Bosch and Haller tried to piece things together. They agreed that the whole scheme likely started when Spencer, facing the upcoming balloon payment with no money and no approval to sell his home, went to the lawyer who put him into the Rosebud deal: Kathy Cronyn née Zelden.

'She says, "Sorry, pal, but next year that balloon is going to pop and you're going to be fucked",' Haller said. "But let me introduce you to my husband and law partner. There might be a way for you to get the money you need before July." She makes the intro, and Lance tells him that all he has to do is figure out how to get something into one of the sealed boxes in that big warehouse where he works. Guys like Spencer probably sit around on their breaks talking about ways to defeat the system. Idle work gossip becomes a real thing and the way out of the mess he's in.'

'We still have to figure that out,' Bosch said.

'My guess is that when all of this hits the fan, Spencer's going to cut a deal and tell us exactly how he did it. If he hires the right lawyer this time, he can probably come out of this looking like a victim. Everybody likes the lawyer for the villain. The D.A. will trade Spencer for Cronyn and Cronyn in a heartbeat.'

'Spencer's no victim. He's part of the frame. He's trying to put me in the dirt.'

'I know that. I'm just giving you the reality of it. How it will play out. Spencer's a guy who got in over his head and was played by these people.'

'Then we should go at him now. Confront him, show him the video. Get him on our side before next week.'

'Might be worth a try, but if he doesn't crack, then we're giving Lance Cronyn a head start on Wednesday. I'd rather sandbag the whole bunch of them in the courtroom.'

Bosch nodded. It was probably the better plan. Just then, thoughts of confronting Spencer reminded him that the property officer was currently under surveillance. He pulled his phone.

'I forgot about Cisco,' he said. 'He's watching him right now.'

Bosch made the call and Cisco answered with a whisper.

'What's happening?' Bosch asked.

'He drove around for an hour until he was sure he had no tail,' Cisco said. 'Then he drove down into Pasadena and met somebody – a woman – in the parking lot of Vroman's.'

'What's Vroman's?'

'It's a big bookstore with a big parking lot at the edge of Old Town. They're parked window to window, you know, like cops do.'

'Who's the woman?'

'I don't know. She's got dealer blanks, so I can't run a plate.'

'Does it look like a new car?'

'No, it's a scratched-up Prius.'

'Can you get a photo of her without getting noticed? I'm here with Haller and he might know who she is.'

'I can try. I can do the old walk-by on a call and grab video. I'll text it to both of you.'

'Do it.'

Bosch disconnected. He knew the maneuver Cisco was undertaking. He'd start recording on his phone's video app, then hold the phone to his ear like he was on a call and walk by the front of the subject's car, hopefully focusing on the woman behind the wheel.

'Spencer is talking to a woman,' he reported to Haller. 'Cisco's going for some video.'

Haller nodded and they waited.

'At some point I should tell Soto,' Bosch said, mostly to himself.

'What do you mean?' Haller asked.

'She's my ex-partner. We sandbag Cronyn, we sandbag her.'

'Do I have to remind you that she's part of a machine that's trying to take everything you have away from you?'

'She's following a case where it goes.'

'Well, she took a wrong turn, didn't she?'

'It happens.'

'Do me a favor, don't talk to her. Not yet, at least. Wait till we're closer and we've confirmed some of these theories as facts. Don't give the LAPD the chance to flip this on us.'

'Fine. I can wait. But she wouldn't flip things. If we set her straight with facts, we wouldn't have to go after Cronyn or Spencer or Borders. She would.'

Before Haller could respond, their phones buzzed in unison as a text came to them both. It was the video from Cisco. They each watched on their phones. Bosch saw an unsteady frame as the camera moved down a line of cars in the bookstore parking lot. It was accompanied by the audio of Cisco's fake phone-call banter, which was designed to help document the time and place of the recording.

'Hi, I'm at Vroman's, the bookstore in Pasadena. It's eight o'clock Wednesday and I'll be here for a while. Hit me back . . .'

The camera moved across a row of parked cars as Cisco spoke until it came to one backed into a spot. The camera moved across the windshield and showed a woman behind the wheel. She was in profile because she was turned toward the open side window and was talking to someone in the car parked next to her. Cisco wisely stopped his faux message as he crossed in front of the car. It allowed the camera to pick up a snippet of dialogue as it was spoken by the woman and Spencer, who could not be seen in the other car.

'You're overreacting,' she said. 'Everything will be fine.'

'I'm telling you, it better be,' he said.

A few steps past the two cars, Cisco turned the phone's camera on his own face and identified himself.

'This is Dennis Wojciechowski, California private investigator license oh-two-sixty-two, ending this recording. Ciao.'

The video ended. Bosch looked expectantly at Haller.

'It's not a good view and I haven't seen Kathy Cronyn since she was Kathy Zelden,' he said.

He was replaying the video and froze the playback at one point and then used two fingers to enlarge the image. He paused for a long moment as he studied it.

'Well?' Bosch finally asked.

'Yes,' Haller said. 'I'm pretty sure it's her. Katherine Cronyn.'

Bosch immediately called Cisco back. He answered Bosch with a question.

'Did he ID her?'

'He did. Katherine Cronyn. You did good, Cisco. You're done for the night.'

'Just let him go?'

'Yeah, we got what we need and we don't want to risk them finding out we know.'

'You got it. Tell Mick I'll check in with him in the morning.'

'Will do.'

Bosch disconnected and looked at Haller. He was beaming.

'Can you run with it from here?' Bosch asked. 'Like I told you, I'm going to drop out for a few days. At least.'

'I can run with it, but are you sure you've got to drop out?' Haller said. 'You're a part-timer up there. Can't somebody else take the reins on that case?'

Bosch thought about it. His mind filled with the image of José Esquivel Jr. sprawled on the floor of the back hallway.

'No,' he finally said. 'Only me.'

PART TWO
The South Side of Nowhere

22

Bosch stood in front of the counter with his eyes down. A man sat there reading a newspaper printed in a foreign language. It was a different man than the goateed driver of the van. This man was older, his hair flecked with gray. He looked to Bosch like an aged enforcer who now relied on the younger generation to do the heavy lifting.

He didn't bother to look up when he spoke to Bosch with a thick Russian accent.

'Who sent you here?' he asked.

'Nobody,' Bosch said.

The man finally looked up at him and studied his face for a moment.

'You walk here?'

'Yes.'

'From where?'

'I just want to see the doctor.'

'From where?'

'The shelter over by the courthouse.'

'That is long walk. What do you want?'

'To see the doctor.'

'How do you know there is doctor?'

'At the shelter. Somebody told me. Okay?'

'What for you need doctor?'

'I need pain medication.'

'What pain?'

Bosch stepped back, raised his cane, and lifted his leg. The man leaned forward so he could see over the counter. He then sat back and eyed Bosch.

'The doctor is very busy,' he said.

Bosch looked behind him and around the room. There were eight plastic chairs in the waiting area and all of them were empty. There was only him and the Russian.

'I can wait.'

'ID.'

Bosch pulled the worn leather wallet out of the back pocket of his jeans. It was connected by a chain to a loop on his belt. He unsnapped the flap and pulled out the driver's license and the Medicare card and dropped them on the counter. The Russian reached up, took them both, and then leaned back in his chair as he looked them over. Bosch hoped that his distancing himself was a reaction to Bosch's body odor. He had actually made the long walk over from the shelter as part of his dropping into character. He was wearing three shirts and the walk had soaked the first layer in sweat and dampened the next two.

'Dominic H. Reilly?'

'That's right.'

'Where is this Oceanside place?'

'Down near San Diego.'

'Take off glasses.'

Bosch raised his sunglasses up over his brow and looked at the Russian. It was the first big test. He needed to show the eyes of a drug addict. Just before being dropped at the shelter, he had spread peppermint oil provided by his DEA handler on the skin below his eyes. Now the cornea of each was irritated and red.

The Russian looked for a long moment and then tossed the plastic cards back on the counter. Bosch dropped his sunglasses back into place.

'You can wait,' the Russian said. 'Maybe doctor have time.'

Bosch had passed. He tried not to show any relief.

'Okay,' he said. 'I'll wait.'

Bosch picked his backpack up off the floor and limped over to the waiting area. He picked a chair closest to the clinic's front door and sat down, using the backpack as a stool for his braced leg. He put the cane on the floor and slid it under the chair, then folded his arms, rested his head against the wall behind him, and closed his eyes. In the darkness behind his eyes he reviewed what had just transpired and wondered if he had given any sort of tell to the Russian. He felt he had handled his initial interaction as a UC well and knew the wallet-and-ID package put together by the DEA team was perfect.

He had spent several hours the day before with the DEA handler, being trained in the art of going under-cover. The first half of the all-day session dealt with the nuts and bolts of the operation: who would be watching and from where, what his cover was, what would be at his disposal in his wallet and backpack, how and when to call for an extraction. The second half was largely role-playing, with his handler teaching him the look of an oxycodone addict and putting him through different scenarios that could come up while he was under.

The interaction he had just had with the Russian behind the counter had been one of those scenarios, and Bosch had played it the way he had several times the previous day. The key point of the one-day UC school was to help Bosch conceal fear and anxiety and channel them into the persona he would be taking on.

The handler, who claimed his name was Joe Smith, also drilled Bosch on court credibility – being able to testify in court or privately before a judge that he had not committed crimes or moral transgressions while acting in an undercover capacity. This would be vital to winning over juries should a prosecution arise from the operation. The cornerstone of court credibility was to avoid taking the drug he was posing as being addicted to. Short of that, he carried two doses of Narcan secreted in the hem of one of his pant legs. Each yellow pill was a fast-acting opioid antagonist that would counteract the effect of the drug if he was forced physically or by circumstances to ingest it.

A few minutes went by and Bosch heard the Russian get up. He opened his eyes and tracked him as he disappeared into the hallway behind the counter. Soon afterward, he heard him speaking. It was a one-sided conversation and in Russian. A phone call, Bosch assumed. He picked up an urgent tone to the Russian's words. He guessed that word was coming in that some of their shills had been taken down by the DEA and the state medical board. This was part of the UC insertion plan. Thin the herd, so to speak, and increase the need to recruit replacements, Dominic H. Reilly among them.

Bosch checked the walls and ceiling. He saw no cameras. He knew it would be unlikely that members of a criminal operation would set up cameras that could document their transgressions. He slid the brace down over his knee so he could walk normally and moved quickly to the counter. While the Russian continued to talk in the rear area of the clinic, Bosch looked over the counter to see what was there. There were several Russian-language and English-language newspapers, including the *L.A. Times* and the *San Fernando Sun*, scattered haphazardly, most of them folded open to stories about the past election and the investigation of the Russian connection. The counterman seemed to be as captured by the story as Legal Siegel had been.

Bosch moved a stack of menus from food-delivery services and found a spiral notebook. Bosch quickly opened it and found several pages of notes in Russian. There were tables with dates and numbers but he could decipher none of it.

The Russian abruptly stopped talking and Bosch quickly closed and replaced the notebook and went back to his chair. He pulled the brace back into place and was just leaning back again when the Russian returned to his position behind the counter. Bosch watched him through squinted eyes. The Russian showed no sign that he had noticed anything out of place at the counter.

Forty minutes of inactivity went by before Bosch heard a vehicle come to a stop out front. Soon the door opened and several bedraggled men and women entered the clinic. Bosch recognized some of them from his surveillance of the van earlier in the week. They followed the Russian down the hallway and out of sight. The van's driver, the same one Bosch had seen before, stayed behind at the counter and soon approached Bosch, his hands on his hips.

'What do you want here?' he asked, his accent easily as thick as the counterman's.

'I want to see the doctor,' Bosch said.

He raised his leg off the backpack in case the knee brace had not been noticed. The driver proceeded to ask Bosch many of the same questions the counterman had. He kept his hands on his hips. After the last question was answered, there was a long moment of silence while the driver decided something.

'Okay, you come back,' he finally said.

He started walking toward the hallway. Bosch got up, grabbed his cane and backpack, and hobbled after him. The hallway was wide and led to an unused nursing station and then branched to the right and left. The driver took Bosch to the left into a hallway where there were four doors of what Bosch assumed were examination rooms from a time when there was a legitimate clinic operating here.

'In here,' the driver said.

He pushed open a door and held his arm out, gesturing for Bosch to go in. As Bosch stepped across the threshold, he saw that the room was furnished only with a single chair. He was suddenly and violently shoved forward and across the room. He dropped both backpack and cane so he could raise his hands and stop himself from crashing face-first into the opposite wall.

He immediately spun around.

'What the fuck was that, man?'

'Who are you? What do you want?'

'I told you and I told that other guy. You know what? Forget it, I'm out of here. I'll find another doctor.'

Bosch reached down to the backpack.

'Leave it there,' the driver ordered. 'You want pills, you leave it there.'

216

Bosch straightened up and the man came forward, put his hands on his chest, and pushed him back against the wall.

'You want pills, take your clothes off.'

'Where's the doctor?'

'The doctor will come. Take off clothes for examine.'

'No, fuck this. I know other places to go.'

He slid the brace down off his knee so he could bend it. He reached down for the cane, knowing it would be more useful than the backpack as a weapon. But the driver quickly took a step forward and put his foot on it. He then grabbed Bosch by the collar of his denim jacket. He pulled him up and shoved him back against the wall, bouncing his head hard off the drywall.

He leaned in close, his breath sour in Bosch's face.

'Take off clothes, old man. Now.'

Bosch raised his hands up until his knuckles were against the wall.

'Okay, okay. No problem.'

The driver stepped back. Bosch started by pulling off his jacket.

'And then I see the doctor, right?' he asked.

The driver ignored the question.

'Put clothes on the floor,' he said.

'No problem,' Bosch said. 'And then the doctor, right?'

'The doctor will come.'

Bosch sat on the chair to unstrap the brace and remove it. Then his work boots and dirty socks. He started peeling off the three layers of shirts. The DEA code name given to his UC personality and the whole operation was Dirty Denim and it fit. His DEA handler had at first objected to the knee brace and cane but eventually gave in to Bosch's wish to put a little bit of his own spin on the character. The handler of course wasn't aware of the weapon hidden in the cane.

Soon Bosch had peeled away the layers and was down to his boxer shorts and one dirty and sweat-stained T-shirt. He dropped his jeans on the pile of clothes after disconnecting the chain and keeping the wallet in his hand.

'No,' the driver said. 'Everything.'

'When I see the doctor,' Bosch said.

He stood his ground. The driver stepped closer. Bosch was expecting more words but instead the man's right fist shot out, and Bosch took a hard punch into his lower stomach. He immediately doubled over and brought his arms in for protection, expecting more. His wallet fell to the floor, its chain rattling on the dirty linoleum. Instead, the driver grabbed Bosch by the hair and leaned down to speak directly into his right ear.

'No, clothes off now. Or we kill you.'

'Okay, okay. I get it. Clothes off.'

Bosch tried to straighten up but needed to put a hand on the wall to steady himself. He pulled off the T-shirt and threw it onto the pile, then dropped the boxers and kicked them to the pile as well. He spread his arms, displaying himself.

'Okay?' he said.

The driver was looking at the tattoo on Bosch's upper arm. It was barely recognizable after nearly fifty years – a tunnel rat holding a pistol, a Latin slogan above it, 'Cu Chi' below it.

'What is Cu Chi?' he asked.

'A place,' Bosch said. 'Vietnam.'

'You were in the war?'

'That's right.'

Bosch felt bile rising in his throat from the punch.

'They shot you, the communists?' the driver asked.

He pointed to the scar from a gunshot wound on Bosch's shoulder. Bosch decided to stick to the script that he had been given for the character.

'No,' he said. 'The police did that. Back here.'

'Sit,' the driver said.

He pointed to the chair. Keeping one hand on the wall for balance, Bosch made his way over and sat down, the plastic cold against his skin.

The driver crouched down, grabbed the backpack and slung it over one shoulder. He then started gathering the pile of Bosch's clothes. He left the cane on the floor.

'You wait,' he said.

'What are you doing?' Bosch said. 'Don't take my—'

He didn't finish. The driver was heading for the door.

'You wait,' he said again.

He opened the door and was gone. Bosch sat naked on the chair. He leaned forward and gathered his arms in close. Not for modesty or warmth. The position eased the pain in his gut. He wondered if the punch from the driver had torn muscle tissue or damaged internal organs. It had been a long time since he had taken a punch unguarded like that. He chastised himself for not having been ready for it.

He knew, however, that except for the punch, things had gone exactly as planned. Bosch guessed that the driver and the other Russian were probably going through the clothes he had been wearing and the contents of the wallet and backpack.

In addition to the very valid-looking driver's license, the wallet had various pieces of identification with a variety of names on them, all exemplars of things a drifter addict might carry in order to help him scam the next hit and next prescription. There was also a worn photo of a woman long out of Dominic Reilly's life as well as cards and notes about other clinics scattered across Southern California.

The backpack had been completely designed to be searched and to help convince those who looked through its contents of Dominic Reilly's legitimacy as a drifter addict. They would find the paraphernalia of opiate addiction – over-the-counter laxatives and stool softeners – as well as a gun wrapped in a T-shirt and secreted at the bottom of one of the compartments. They would also find a burner cell complete with fake text files and call log.

It was all put together by careful design. Reilly carried the things a drifter would have. The gun was an old revolver missing one of its grips. It was loaded but the firing pin had been filed down so that it could not function as a firearm. It was anticipated that it would be confiscated as Bosch hopefully worked his way into the Santos operation, but the DEA did not want to be responsible for giving a functioning weapon to the enemy. There was no telling how that could come back at the agency later. The reputation of the ATF was still recovering from an undercover program that ended up putting weapons in the hands of Mexican drug cartels.

Most important, the backpack contained a plastic

pill vial with the name Dominic Reilly on the prescription label. It would have a West Valley pharmacy listed as the provider and the prescribing doctor as Kenneth Vincent of Woodland Hills. These would come back as legitimate if checked out. There would be only two pills in the vial, Reilly's last two eighty-milligram doses of generic oxycodone. They would help make clear why he had come to the clinic in Pacoima.

The backpack also contained a pill crusher made out of an old fountain pen, which could serve double-duty as a sniffer – place the pill inside, turn the barrel to grind it to dust, remove the top, and snort. Powdered oxycodone produced the best high, and crushing pills defeated the manufacturer's time-release additives.

It was all there in the backpack, the complete persona. The only thing Bosch had to worry about at the moment was the wallet and chain. The wallet contained a GPS transmitter secreted within one of its leather bifolds. The attached security chain was both an antenna and a rescue switch. If it was pulled loose from the wallet, it would add an emergency code to the GPS pulse and bring the DEA's ghost team crashing in.

Bosch hoped that wouldn't happen. He didn't want the ghost team to descend on the clinic and end his mission before it had actually even started.

Bosch sat patiently on the plastic chair, naked and waiting to find out.

23

By Bosch's estimate, more than an hour went by without anyone coming into the room. Several times he heard voices or movement from the hallway but no one opened the door. He reached to the floor and grabbed the cane, holding it across his thighs with the curved handle near his left hand.

The minutes went by like hours but still Bosch's mind raced. His attention was focused on his daughter and on his decision not to call her to say he would be out of contact for a while. He didn't want her to worry or ask him questions. He realized in choosing not to call and tell her, he had robbed himself of what might be a last conversation with the most important person in his world. Realizing his mistake, he vowed to himself that it wouldn't matter. That he would do everything possible to return to his life and make his first call one to her.

The door was suddenly flung open, startling Bosch. He almost turned the handle on the cane to pull out the blade but he held back. The counterman entered, carrying everything the driver had left with. He threw the clothes into Bosch's lap and dropped the backpack off his shoulder to the floor with a thud.

'You get dress,' he said. 'No gun, no phone.'

'What are you talking about?' Bosch said. 'I paid for those. They're mine. You can't just take them.'

Bosch stood up, letting his clothes drop to the floor. He held the cane halfway down the barrel like he was ready to start cracking heads with it, unashamed of being naked.

'Get dress,' the counterman repeated. 'No gun, no phone.'

'Fuck this,' Bosch said. 'Give me my gun and give me my phone and I'm out of here.'

The counterman smirked.

'The boss come back, talk to you,' he said.

'Yeah, he better,' Bosch said. 'I want to talk to him. This is bullshit.'

The Russian went back through the doorway and closed the door behind him. Bosch got dressed but took a fresh but still dirty T-shirt out of the backpack to put on as his first layer. He found the wallet in the backpack, chain still attached, and checked through it. He was able to determine that the seams in the partition where the GPS tracker was located had not been tampered with. He found his driver's license and Medicare card missing, however.

Before he finished dressing, the door opened again, and this time both Russians entered. Bosch was on the chair lacing up one of his work boots. The counterman went to the far wall and leaned back in the corner with his arms folded as the driver stood front and center.

'We have work for you,' the driver said.

'You mean a job?' Bosch asked. 'What can I tell you – I don't work.'

The driver took a step toward him and Bosch braced himself this time. But the driver only held out a folded slip of paper. Bosch hesitated and then took it. He opened it to find it was a prescription slip. Dr. Efram Herrera's name was printed at the top along with his required state and federal drug license numbers. Handwritten on the slip was a sixty-count prescription for oxycodone in eighty-milligram form. For a pill shill or a user it was the Holy Grail. For Bosch it was pay dirt. Not only did he have the makings of a case against the operators of the clinic, he had clearly gotten inside the wire.

'What's this?' he asked. 'You put me through all of this, punch me in the gut, and then just give me the scrip?'

The driver snatched the prescription back out of Bosch's hand.

'You don't want it, fine, we give it somebody else,' he said.

'Look, I want it, okay?' Bosch said. 'I just want to know what the fuck is going on here.'

'We have business,' the driver said. 'You want pills, you work. We share.'

'Share what?'

'Share pills. One for you, two for me, like that.'

'That doesn't sound like a good deal for me. I think I'll just—'

'Unlimited supply. We handle scrips, you pick up pills. Easy. We pay you one dollar for each. So, pills and money, do you say yes?'

'One dollar? I know a place I can get twenty.'

'We offer quantity. We have protection. We have beds.'

'Beds where?'

'You join, you see.'

Bosch looked at the man still leaning on the back wall. The message was clear. Join up or get beat down. Bosch put a look of resignation on his face.

'How long I gotta work?' he asked.

The driver shrugged.

'Nobody quits,' he said. 'Money and pills too good.'

'Yeah, but what if I want to?'

'You want to quit, you quit. That's it.'

Bosch nodded.

'Okay,' he said.

The driver walked out of the room. The counterman came over and handed Bosch his ID and Medicare card.

'You go now,' he said.

'Go where?' Bosch asked.

'The van. Out front.'

'Okay.'

The counterman pointed toward the door. Bosch grabbed his backpack and cane from the floor and moved toward the door. He walked normally. He had the brace down below his knee.

Bosch went back through the clinic and out the front door, with the counterman behind him. The van was parked in front and the shills were climbing in through the side door. Bosch could see the driver behind the wheel, turned and staring at him through the door. He and Bosch both knew that this would be the moment he would bolt if he was going to. He looked around and then off across San Fernando Road toward the tower at Whiteman. He knew he was being watched from there and the ghost team was also stashed somewhere nearby. One quick fist pump into the air was the signal. If Bosch did that, they would come charging in to get him. And it would be the end of the whole operation.

He looked back at the driver. The last shill was climbing in and then it was Bosch's turn. He shook his head like a man with no choice and climbed into the van. He pushed in on the bench seat behind the driver and sat next to a woman with a shaved head. He put his backpack in the space between the driver's seat and the front passenger seat, which was empty.

The counterman slid the door shut with a bang and slapped the roof twice. The van pulled away from the curb. Everyone was silent, even the driver. Bosch leaned forward to get the best angle on the driver's face.

'Where are we going?' he asked.

'To the next location,' the driver said.

'Where?'

'Don't speak. Just do what you are told, old man.'

'Where's my phone? I have a daughter I need to call.'

'No. Not anymore.'

The woman with the shaved head pushed her elbow into Bosch's ribs. He turned to look at her. She just shook her head. Her dark eyes told him that there would be consequences for all of them if he continued to speak.

Bosch leaned back in the seat and stopped talking. He first made a quick look around the van. He counted eleven other people in the seats behind the driver. Many of them he recognized from the surveillance on Tuesday. Men and women: older, haggard, defeated. He lowered his chin to now mind his own business. He saw the hands of the woman next to him clasped tightly together on her lap. In the webbing between her left thumb and forefinger he saw a small tattoo of three stars by what looked like an amateur hand. The ink was dark, the points of the stars sharp, the tattoo not old like his own.

The van took the same route Bosch and Lourdes had watched it take earlier in the week. It drove through the gate into Whiteman and to the hangar where the jump plane waited. The van unloaded and the group started to board the plane through the jump door. Bosch held back, letting the woman climb past him to get out of the van.

'Whoa, wait a minute,' he yelled at the driver. 'What the fuck is this?'

'This is the plane,' the driver said. 'You get on.'

'Where the hell are we going? I didn't sign up for this. Give me my scrip. I'm out of here.'

'No, you get on. Now.'

He reached down under his seat, and Bosch saw his arm muscles flex as he grasped something. He turned to look back at Bosch without revealing what it was. The message, though, was clear.

'Okay, okay,' Bosch said. 'I'm getting on.'

He was the last one to board the plane. There were benches running lengthwise down both sides of the interior, with seat belts hanging loose. People were buckling in. Bosch saw an open space next to the woman with the stars and took it, this time on her left side.

Behind the noise of the plane's engine she leaned into him and spoke into his ear.

'Welcome to hell.'

Bosch pulled back and looked at her. He could see that she had once been a beauty, but her eyes were dead now. He guessed that she was at least fifty years old, maybe a few years younger. Maybe a lot of years younger, depending on how long she'd been ravaged by addiction. He picked up an earthy smell about her. She reminded him of someone – the angle of her cheekbones. She looked like she had Indian blood. He wondered if her shaved head was part of the sell, like his cane and knee brace. She presented as someone who was sick, maybe going through radiation.

Who knew? Maybe it was all legit. He didn't respond. He didn't know what to say to her.

Bosch looked around the plane and noticed that in getting on, he had passed by a man sitting at the front who was obviously part of the operation. He was young and muscular and had an Eastern European look to him. His back was to a makeshift aluminum wall that separated the cockpit from the passenger hold. There was a small sliding window but the opening was closed and Bosch could not see the pilot.

The man at the front reached back and knocked on the separation panel. Immediately, the plane started moving out to the airfield. Once on the runway, the aircraft picked up speed and seemed to effortlessly take off and climb into the sky. The steep incline and gravity pulled the woman sliding into Bosch and he put a hand on her shoulder to steady her. It was as though she had been touched with dry ice. She violently jerked away from him and he raised his arm in a hands-off gesture.

While still climbing, the plane began to bank right in a southerly direction. Bosch leaned toward the woman without touching her and spoke as low as he could while still being heard.

'Where are we going?'

'Where we always go. Don't talk to me.'

'You talked to me.'

'A mistake. Please stop talking.'

The plane hit an air pocket and was buffeted. She was thrown toward him again but she managed to steady herself by gripping an overhead handle once used by skydivers to approach the jump platform.

'Okay?' he tried.

'Yes,' she said. 'Fuck off.'

Bosch made a hand gesture signaling he was finished. He had wanted to ask about the tattoo but he could see fear in her eyes. He looked toward the front of the plane and saw the reason. His efforts to communicate with her had caught the eye of the muscleman at the front. Bosch made a hands-off gesture to assure him that he was finished trying to communicate.

He turned to the window that was behind him and tried to lift the shade, but it appeared to be permanently closed. Only the jump-door window was uncovered, but it was too far forward for Bosch to check the geography passing below. All he could see from his angle was blue, cloudless sky.

He wondered if Hovan and the DEA were tracking the plane, as had been promised. They had already checked and knew the Cessna's transponder had been disabled. They would need to rely on visual tracking from the air. The device hidden in Bosch's wallet was for short-range ground-level tracking.

He looked at the faces of the people lined along both sides of the plane. Eleven men and women who looked as gaunt and hapless as the people in Dust Bowl photos of a century before. People with no hope in their eyes, no place to call home, trapped by addiction. People who couldn't fit in before and never would now, all herded like cattle at the low edge of a national crisis.

He leaned back and did the math. With twelve of them on the plane, if they were each producing a hundred pills a day for the Santos operation, that was twelve hundred pills going for a minimum of thirty bucks a pop on the street. That added up to $36,000 a day coming out of this one crew. More than thirteen million a year. Bosch knew there were other crews and other operations too.

The money and numbers were staggering. It was a giant corporation feeding a demand that infiltrated every state, city, and town. He began to see why the woman with the stars had welcomed him to hell.

24

While in the air Bosch could feel the plane going through maneuvers, making wide circles and changing altitude, going up and then down. He guessed these were efforts to determine if there was any aerial surveillance. What he didn't know was whether this was routine or because of him. He thought about the man Jerry Edgar had mentioned. The shill who had been flipped by the DEA, who had gone up in a plane but had not been aboard when it landed.

Eventually, the plane went into a gradual descent and landed hard, almost two hours after takeoff. That was just a guess on Bosch's part. He was not wearing a watch, part of the pose of a drifter who had checked out of society.

Everyone climbed out of the plane in a quiet and orderly fashion. Bosch saw that they were on a desert runway, a range of brown mountains ringing the sun-torched flats. For all he knew they might be in Mexico, but as he followed the others to a waiting van, he looked around. The dense odor and white, salty crust of the land told him that they were likely close to the Salton Sea. The intel from Jerry Edgar had helped.

Bosch got a window seat in the van and was able to further observe his position. He saw two other jump planes parked further down the strip, and beyond them the sun hung low in the sky. It oriented him and soon he knew the van was moving south from the airstrip.

Bosch looked around for the woman with stars on her hand and saw her sitting two benches ahead of him. He watched her lean forward and tighten her shoulders as she crossed her arms in front of her chest. He recognized the behavior, and it was a reminder that he was only posing as an addict. Everybody else on the van was the real thing.

After a thirty-minute drive, the van pulled into what looked like the kind of shantytown Bosch had seen when he had followed cases into the barrios in Mexicali and other places across the border. There was a collection of RVs, buses, tents, and shacks made of aluminum sheeting, canvas tarps, and other construction debris.

Before the van came to a stop, people were up from their seats and crowding toward the side door as if they couldn't wait for the next leg of the journey. Bosch stayed seated and watched as the shills that had been sitting so quietly and peacefully moments before now pushed and shoved for position. He saw the woman with stars on her hand grabbing at a man's arm to pull him away from the scrum so she could improve her position.

The door slid open and people nearly fell out of the van. Through a side window Bosch saw why. The man who had come out from the encampment to open the door was giving each of the van riders their nightly dosage. He put pills into the outstretched hands of the shills as they came through the van door.

Realizing he had to act to support his cover, Bosch got up, slung his backpack over one shoulder, and slid out of his bench seat. He moved up behind the last man in the line to get out, put his free hand on his shoulder and yanked him backward so that he could move up into the open slot.

'Hey, motherfucker!' the man yelped.

Bosch felt him coming back for his place. He turned, raised the cane up, and held it crosswise in his hands. The man coming at him was much younger but was weak from addiction. Bosch easily deflected his efforts with the cane and the man fell backward into the open channel next to the bench seats. Bosch kept his eyes on him as he inched toward the door.

Bosch was the second to last out of the van, and the man waiting put a pale green pill into his raised palm. Bosch looked at it as he stepped away from the van and saw the 80 stamped on it. The man he had struggled with came out next, and he got one pill as well.

'No, no, no, wait a minute,' he said. 'I need more. I need the two. Give me the two.'

'No, one,' said the distributor. 'You fight, you get one, that's it. Keep moving now.'

His accent was slightly different from that of the men at the clinic back in Pacoima but he was still, Bosch believed, from an Eastern Bloc country.

The addict Bosch had struggled with studied the single pill in his hand with the same look of anguish that Bosch had seen on the faces of the most desperate – refugees he had seen decades earlier in Vietnam, drug addicts he had seen in squats in Hollywood. The look always said the same thing: *What am I going to do?*

'Please,' he said.

'You keep moving, Brody, or you're gone,' said the distributor.

'Okay, okay,' said the addict.

They followed the others, forming a line that led into the encampment. Bosch took the last position in line so he could keep an eye on the man called Brody. As he walked, he noticed the woman with stars, who was several spots ahead, pull something out of her pocket. She then put her hands down in front of her body, and Bosch could tell by the way she was working her shoulders that she was turning something in her unseen hands. He knew it was a crusher. She either needed a hit so badly she couldn't wait or she feared one of the men, maybe Brody, would take her pills away.

Bosch watched as she brought her hands up to her face and cupped her mouth and nose as if she were going to sneeze. She snuffed the powdered pill as she walked.

Brody turned his head as he walked to give Bosch the evil eye. Bosch reached out and pushed him in the center of his back with the rubber-capped tip of his cane, a firm shove.

'Keep going,' Bosch said.

'You owe me an eighty, old man,' Brody said.

'Yeah, come and get it. Anytime.'

'Yeah, we'll see. We'll see.'

Brody had the sleeves of a windbreaker tied around his waist and a yellowed T-shirt clinging to his bony shoulders. From his rear vantage point Bosch could see tattoos running down both of his triceps but they were blurred and unreadable, made with cell-mixed ink in prison.

The man from the plane as well as the greeter and drug distributor walked them into an open area that appeared to be the center of the encampment. Triangular canvas sails were strung overhead to offer shade during the day, but the sun was now behind the mountains on the horizon and it was starting to cool. There was concrete underfoot and Bosch assumed it was one of the slabs that gave the area its unofficial name.

There was a man sitting at a table beneath one of the shade triangles. The group was followed into the space by the van's driver. They looked at the man at the table, who gave them a nod. Bosch saw a badge pinned to the seated man's red shirt. It looked like a tin private security badge. But it apparently made him the sheriff of Slab City. There were two cardboard boxes on the table.

During an intel meeting that morning before the UC operation began, Bosch had viewed the few photos that the DEA had of Santos, and while they were all a minimum of three years old, he was sure that the man at the table was not him. The sheriff stood and looked at the sunken eyes of all those standing in front of him.

'Food is here,' he said. 'One each. Take it with you.'

He started opening the boxes on the table. There was no rush from the group as there had been when pills were being distributed. Food was clearly not the most sustaining part of their lives. Bosch moved forward without pushing and when he got to the table, he saw that one box contained power bars and the other contained foil-wrapped burritos. He took a power bar and turned away.

The group started to break up, with people going in different directions. It was clear to Bosch that everybody had a destination but him. Brody threw him another look and then headed toward the open flap of a large yellow-and-black tent that looked like it had been made with tarps previously used for tenting houses for termite treatment.

Using the cover of people moving in different directions, Bosch dropped to one knee, put the cane down and the power bar next to it, and then started retying his work boot. While the hem of the right leg of his jeans contained the doses of Narcan, the left leg had an open slot in the inside hem. It was a place to stash any pills given to him so he could avoid ingesting but still keep them to be used as evidence in an eventual prosecution. He had practiced the boot-tying maneuver several times during the previous day's training. When he hiked the bottom of his pant leg up to reach the high-top boot's laces, he slipped the pill through the hole in the inside hem.

As he stood up, the woman with the stars brushed by him and whispered, 'Be ready. Brody will come for you tonight.'

And then she was gone, heading to the tent where Brody had gone. Bosch watched her go without saying anything.

'You.'

Bosch turned and looked at the man at the table. He pointed behind Bosch.

'You're in there,' he said. 'Take the open bed and put your shit underneath it. You don't take that pack with you tomorrow.'

Bosch checked behind him while he finished tying his boot. The sheriff was pointing to the back of an old school bus that looked like it had followed its career in student transport with a decade or two spent moving field-workers. It was painted green back then and now was in shambles. Its paint had long been faded and had oxidized. The windows were either painted over or covered with aluminum foil from the inside.

'It's got all my stuff,' Bosch said. 'I need it.'

'There is no room for it,' the sheriff said. 'You leave it here. No one will touch it. You try to take it and it gets tossed outta the fucking plane. You understand?'

'Yeah, I understand.'

Bosch climbed to his feet and walked toward the bus. There were two steps up to the back door and he was in. It was dark inside and the air was dead and sour. It was sweltering. The beds the sheriff was talking about were Army Surplus cots and they were lined end to end down both sides with a narrow aisle in between. Starting to slowly make his way down the aisle, he quickly realized that the cleaner air was near the door he had just entered through and that those cots were already occupied by men who were sleeping or lying there watching Bosch with dead eyes.

The last cot on the right was open and appeared to be unused. Bosch dropped his backpack to the floor and used his foot to push it underneath. He then sat down and looked about. The air was putrid, a combination of body odor, bad breath, and the smell of the Salton Sea, and Bosch remembered something Jerry Edgar had told him years ago, after they had attended an autopsy: that all odors were particulate. Bosch sat there realizing he was breathing in microscopic particles from the drug-addicted men on the bus.

He reached down and pulled the backpack out from under his cot. He unzipped it and dug around in the clothing until he found a bandanna that had been

237

shoved in by one of the DEA undercover tutors. He folded it into a triangle and tied it around his head and across his mouth and nose like a train robber from the Old West.

'Doesn't do any good.'

Bosch looked around. Because the ceiling of the bus had only rounded corners, the voice could have come from anywhere. Everyone appeared to be asleep or uninterested in Bosch.

'Here.'

Bosch turned and looked the other way. There was a man sitting in the driver's seat, looking at Bosch through a mirror on the dusty dashboard. Bosch had not noticed him before.

'Why not?' he asked.

'Because this place is like cancer,' said the man. 'Nothing stops it.'

Bosch nodded. The man was probably right. But still he kept the mask on.

'Is that where you sleep?' he asked.

'Yeah,' the man said. 'Can't lie down. Get vertigo.'

'How long you been here?'

'Long enough.'

'How many people they got here?'

'You ask too many questions.'

'Sorry, just making conversation.'

'They don't like conversation here.'

'So I heard.'

Bosch put his hands back into his pack. He took out one of the T-shirts and rolled it up to serve as a pillow. He lay down with his feet toward the rear of the bus so he could watch the door. He looked at the power bar. It was a brand he had never seen before. He wasn't hungry but he wondered if he should eat it to keep his energy up.

'So what's your name?' he whispered.

'What's it matter?' said the man in the driver's seat. 'It's Ted.'

'I'm Nick. What's the deal here?'

'There you go with the questions again.'

'Just wondering what I've gotten into. It feels like a labor camp or something.'

'It is.'

'And you can't leave?'

'You can leave. But you need a plan. We're in the middle of nowhere out here. You wait till you're in the city. You just better be sure you're clear, because they'll be watching you. Every one of us is worth a lot of money to them. They ain't going to just let that go.'

'I knew I should've said no.'

'Ain't really that bad. They keep you in food and pills. You just gotta follow their rules.'

'Right.'

Bosch let his eyes wander down the center aisle to the open back door of the bus. He pulled the bandanna down below his chin and started opening the power bar. He hoped it would keep him awake and on edge.

The natural light was almost gone now. For the first time, Bosch began to feel the tension of fear in his chest. He knew that there was great danger here – from all directions. He knew he couldn't risk sleeping for five minutes, let alone through the night.

25

Brody came at him in the dead of night. But Bosch was ready for him. Moonlight revealed him as a silhouette in the back doorway of the bus and then as he made his way stealthily down the aisle between the cots where the others slept. Bosch could see an object gripped in one hand. Something small like a knife. Bosch was lying on his right side, the corresponding arm bent at the elbow and seemingly cradling his head. But back behind the end of the cot he gripped the cane tightly.

Bosch didn't wait to determine if Brody had come to rob or assault him. Before the shadowed figure could make any kind of close-in move, Bosch swung the cane viciously and caught Brody flush at an angle that extended the impact up his jawline and across his ear. The noise was so loud that he thought he might have broken the cane. Brody immediately dropped onto the cot behind him, awakening a sleeping man who groaned and shoved him off. His weapon, a screwdriver, clattered on the floor. Bosch was immediately off the cot and on top of him in the aisle between the cots, straddling him and holding the cane like a crossbar on his neck. Brody put both hands on the cane to try to keep it from crushing his throat.

Bosch held the pressure steady. Enough to seriously impede Brody's breathing but not cutting it off all the way. He leaned down and spoke in a hard whisper.

'You come at me again and I'm going to kill you. I've done it before and I'll do it again. Do you understand me?'

Brody couldn't talk but he nodded as best as he could.

'Now I'm going to let you go and you're going to go back to your hole, and you're not going to give me any more problems. Got it?'

Brody nodded again.

'Good.'

Bosch released the pressure but hesitated a moment before getting off the man. He wanted to be ready for the double-cross. Instead, Brody released his grip on the cane and held his hands open, fingers splayed.

Bosch started to get up.

'All right, get out of here.'

Without a word, Brody gathered himself and stood up. He hurried down the aisle to the rear exit of the bus. Bosch didn't think for one moment that he would hesitate if he got another shot at Bosch.

He picked up the screwdriver and pulled the backpack out from under his cot. While he hid the screwdriver at the bottom of the main compartment, he heard a whisper from the front seat of the bus.

'Nice stick work,' said Ted.

'It's a cane,' Bosch said.

He waited and listened to hear whether Brody was confronted outside the bus by the sheriff or anyone else who might have heard their struggle. But there was only silence from out there. Bosch crouched down and went into his backpack, quickly changing into a black T-shirt with the Los Angeles Lakers logo on it. He then stuffed the bottle of laxatives into one of his pockets, stood up, and turned toward the exit at the back of the bus.

'Where are you going?' Ted whispered. 'Don't go out there.'

'Where do people go to the bathroom around here?' Bosch said.

'Just follow your nose, man. It's on the south side of the camp.'

'Got it.'

He moved down the aisle, careful not to run into the human limbs that were extending from some of the cots. When he got to the door, he stayed back in shadow and looked out into the open space where the sheriff had sat upon his arrival. It was empty. Even the table was gone.

Bosch stepped down from the bus and then stood still. The air still carried the odor of the Salton Sea but it was cooler and fresher than any breath taken inside the bus. Bosch pulled the bandanna down over his chin and left it hanging loose around his neck. He listened. The night was cool and quiet, the stars brilliant in the black sky above. He thought he could hear the low hum of an engine coming from somewhere in or near the camp. He just couldn't place the direction it was coming from.

Asking Ted where he could go to relieve himself had been a front. He had no plan other than to scope out the camp so he could learn its landmarks and dimensions and could later be helpful in drawing up search warrants should that be part of any follow-up to the Dirty Denim operation.

He moved away from the bus and randomly chose a path between the tent where he knew Brody was assigned and a row of shanty structures. He walked quickly and quietly and soon realized he was moving away from the engine sound. He followed the pathway to the southern terminus of the camp, and here the air was fouled by a lineup of four portable toilets on a flatbed trailer. They smelled like they had not been serviced by the clean-out pump in weeks, if not months.

Bosch kept moving, following the circumference of the camp in a clockwise manner. From the outside it looked no different from the homeless encampments that had sprung up in the past few years in almost every empty lot and park in Los Angeles.

As he walked toward the north side of the camp, the low hum of the engine got steadily louder, and soon he was approaching a double-wide trailer with a light on inside and an air conditioner powered by an electric generator placed fifty yards out in the scrub behind it.

Bosch guessed that he was looking at the staff quarters. The sheriff and the distributor, maybe even the pilots of the planes he had seen, were housed in air-conditioned comfort.

His guess was confirmed as he cautiously approached at a passing angle and soon saw two vans parked side by side behind the trailer. He also saw a shadow pass behind the curtain of the one window that was lit. Somebody was moving about inside.

Bosch quickly moved toward the vans so he could use them as cover. Once there, he pressed himself against the back corner of one of them and studied the upper edges of the structure, looking for cameras.

He saw no evidence of cameras but knew it was too dark to be sure. He also knew that there were all kinds of other electronic measures that might be taken to guard against intrusion. Nevertheless, he decided to risk it in order to get an inside look at the double-wide.

He moved in toward the lighted window. The door next to it had a large NO ADMITTANCE sign posted, with a threatening kicker: 'Violators Will Be Shot.'

Bosch proceeded undaunted. The curtain had not been closed all the way. There was a two-inch gap that allowed Bosch to visually sweep the room by shifting to his right or left outside.

There were two men in the room. They were white and both wore wifebeaters that revealed heavily tattooed arms and shoulders. They were at a table, playing cards and drinking a clear liquid directly from a bottle with no label. In the center of the table was a pile of pale-colored pills, and Bosch realized that the dosage levels of oxycodone pills made up the betting scheme of the game.

One of the men apparently lost a bet, and while his opponent gleefully used his hand to pull the pot to his side, the other angrily swiped some of the cards off the table and to the floor. The arm movement made Bosch's eyes follow, and it was then that he saw a third person in the room.

There was a nude woman lying on a threadbare couch to the left side. Her face and body were turned in toward the rear cushions and she appeared to be asleep or unconscious. Bosch could not see her face, but it didn't take a genius to figure out what was going on. He leaned his head down for a moment as he filled with revulsion. He had avoided undercover work for all his years in law enforcement for this very reason. As a homicide investigator he had seen the worst of what humans can do to one another. But by the time Bosch was a witness, the crime had been committed and the suffering was over. Every case left its psychological mark but it was balanced by the fulfillment of justice. Bosch didn't solve every case, but there was still accomplishment in giving every case his best work.

But when you went undercover, you moved from the safe confines of justice done and entered the world of the depraved. You saw how humans preyed on one another, and there was nothing you could do about it without blowing cover. You had to take it in and live with it to see the case through. Bosch wanted to charge into the trailer and save that woman from another minute of abuse, but he couldn't. Not now. There was a greater justice he was looking for.

Bosch turned his eyes from the woman and looked at the two men. It seemed clear to him that they were speaking Russian, and the words inked on their arms appeared to be Russian as well. Both men had what cops called convict bodies: outsize upper torsos heavily muscled by years of prison workouts – push-ups, sit-ups, chin-ups – and legs neglected in the process. One was clearly older. He was midthirties, with a soldier's short haircut. Bosch placed the other man at about thirty, with dyed blond hair.

He studied their body sizes and movements and compared them to what he recalled of the videos from the pharmacy shooting and the drop-off and pickup at Whiteman. Could these two be the shooters? It was impossible to know for sure, but Bosch believed that there was a clue in the apparent casualness with which the men in the room had abused the woman. They had most likely drugged her, raped her, and left her unclothed on the couch. Bosch believed any man who did that was capable of the same casualness when it came to murder. His gut told him these were the two men who had gunned down José Esquivel and his son.

And they would lead him to Santos.

Bosch saw a reflection of light on the aluminum skin of the mobile home and turned to see a man with a flashlight approaching. He quickly ducked down and then moved back toward the vans and slipped into the channel between them.

'Hey!'

He had been spotted. He moved to the rear of the vehicles and had to make a decision.

He quickly dropped below the window level of the vans and moved back up on the outside of the van farthest from the mobile home. The man with the flashlight came running up and proceeded down the passage between the vans, the last place he had seen the intruder.

Bosch waited a second and broke for the corner of the trailer. He knew if he could get there, he could use the structure as a blind between him and the flashlight. As he ran, he heard the man talking feverishly and realized he must have a radio. That meant there might be at least one other person in the camp on security patrol.

Bosch made it to the corner of the trailer without drawing another shout. He pressed hard against the wall and looked around the edge. He located the flashlight out near the generator. That gave him an almost fifty-yard lead. He was about to break for the encampment when he saw another flashlight moving down a pathway in his direction. Bosch had no choice. He charged to his left, hoping to get to the cover of an old RV before the second searcher spotted him.

Lungs burning, he passed the back end of the RV before being hit with light. He heard more voices and shouting and realized the commotion had drawn the Russians out of the mobile home to see what was going on.

Bosch kept moving, even as fatigue from the exertion started to grip him. He followed the edge of the camp all the way around until he reached the portable toilets. He thought about hiding inside one but decided against it. He turned and entered the camp and started following the pathway back to the bus. He walked casually after using his shirt to wipe the sweat off his face.

He didn't make it. In the clearing behind the bus, they were waiting. Bosch was hit with the lights first and then shoved to the ground from behind.

'What the fuck you think you are doing?' a voice said.

Bosch held his hands up off the dirt and sand and splayed his fingers.

'I was just using the toilet,' he called out. 'I thought that was okay. Nobody told me I couldn't leave the—'

'Get him up,' said a Russian.

Bosch was roughly pulled up off the ground and held by both arms by the sheriff and a man he assumed was his deputy.

The two men Bosch had seen playing cards were standing in front of him. The older one came in close enough for Bosch to smell the vodka on his breath.

'You like a Peeping Tom?' he asked.

'What?' Bosch exclaimed. 'No, I had to use the shitter.'

'No, you Peeping Tom. Sneaking around, peeping in the window.'

'It wasn't me.'

'Who else, then? You see any Peeping Tom? No, just you.'

'I don't know but it wasn't me.'

'Yah, we see about dat. Search him. Who is this guy?'

The sheriff and deputy started going through Bosch's pockets.

'He's new,' said the sheriff. 'He's the one who had the gun.'

He pulled Bosch's wallet out of his pocket and was about to yank it off its chain.

'Wait a minute, wait a minute,' Bosch said.

He unsnapped the belt loop so the wallet and chain came free. The sheriff threw it to the Russian.

'Gimme the light,' he said.

The deputy held his light out while the Russian looked through the wallet.

'Reilly,' he said.

He pronounced it *really*.

The sheriff found the bottle of laxatives and held it up for the Russian to see. The blond Russian said something in their native tongue but the one holding Bosch's wallet seemed to ignore it.

'Why do you sweat, Reilly?' he asked instead.

'Because I need a hit,' Bosch said. 'They only gave me one.'

'He was fighting on the van,' the sheriff said.

'There was no fight,' Bosch said. 'Just some pushing. It wasn't fair. I need the hit.'

The Russian slapped the wallet against his other

hand as he contemplated the situation. He then handed it back to Bosch.

Bosch thought he had made it. Returning the wallet meant the Russian would let his trespass go.

But he was wrong.

'On his knees,' the Russian said.

Strong hands gripped Bosch's shoulders simultaneously and he was pushed down to his knees. The Russian reached behind his back and produced a gun. Bosch immediately recognized it as the one taken from his backpack.

'Is this your piece-of-shit gun, Reilly?'

'Yes. They took it from me at the clinic.'

'Well, it is mine now.'

'Fine. Whatever.'

'You know I am Russian, yes?'

'Yes.'

'Then how about we play a Russian game and you tell me what you were doing tonight peeping in my window.'

'I told you, I wasn't. I was taking a shit. I'm old. It takes me a long time.'

The deputy laughed but then cut it off when he was hit by a grim stare from the sheriff. The Russian opened the gun's cylinder and dumped the six bullets into his palm. He then held one bullet up into the light and made a show of loading it into the cylinder, snapping it closed and spinning it.

'Now we play Russian roulette, yes?'

He held the gun out and pressed the barrel against Bosch's left temple.

Bosch had confidence in the DEA's saying they had

tricked the weapon, but there was nothing like the barrel of a gun being pressed against the temple to make one contemplate fate. Bosch closed his eyes.

The Russian pulled the trigger and Bosch jerked at the sound of the metal snap. In that moment he knew the two Russians were the pharmacy killers. He opened his eyes and looked directly at the man in front of him.

'Ah, you are lucky man,' said the Russian.

He spun the gun's cylinder again and laughed.

'We try for two now, lucky man? Why were you looking in my window tonight?'

'No, please, it wasn't me. I don't even know where your window is. I just got here. I even had to ask where the bathrooms were.'

This time the Russian pressed the gun's muzzle to Bosch's forehead. His partner spoke to him in an urgent tone. Bosch guessed that he was reminding the man with the gun of what the impact would be on pill production if Bosch was killed.

The Russian withdrew the gun without pulling the trigger. He started reloading it. When he was finished, he snapped the barrel closed and pointed to the spot where the missing grip should be.

'I will fix your gun and keep it,' he said. 'I want your luck. Do you agree, Reilly?'

'Sure,' Bosch said. 'Keep it.'

The Russian reached behind his back and tucked the gun into his pants.

'Thank you, Reilly,' he said. 'You go back to sleep now. No more Peeping Tom shit.'

26

The Santos air fleet left the ground early Saturday after a morning distribution of pills, power bars, and burritos. Bosch was in a group on the same plane he had come in on, but this time the passenger count was higher and there were more than a few new faces, men and women, on the plane's benches. He did see Brody, a stripe of purple bruising on the right side of his face, and the woman with the stars on her hand. They were both on the bench opposite him. Maybe it was the shaved head, which gave the false impression that she was ill from something other than addiction, but Bosch felt a sympathetic need to watch over her. At the same time, he knew never to turn his back on Brody.

This time Bosch was smart enough to muscle his way to a seat at the end of the bench near the jump door and the uncovered window. He'd now have a shot at tracking where the plane was going.

They took off in a northerly direction and stayed on that course, the plane maintaining an altitude of only a few thousand feet. Looking over his shoulder and down through the glass, he could see the Salton Sea below. And then he saw the bright colors painted on the man-made monument known as Salvation Mountain. From high above he saw the warning: JESUS IS THE WAY.

Next it was Joshua Tree National Park and then the Mojave, the land below beautiful in its untouched starkness.

They were in the air almost two hours before the plane landed hard on a strip used by crop dusters. As it made its final descent, Bosch had seen a wind farm in the distance set against hills dotted with cattle, and he knew where they were. In the Central Valley, near Modesto, where Bosch had worked a case a few years before and had seen a helicopter hit one of the wind-mills and go down.

There were two vans waiting, and the group was split up seven and seven. Bosch was separated from both Brody and the woman with the stars. His van had two men from the organization in the front seats, a driver and a handler, both with Russian accents. They stopped first in Tulare, where they started working a series of mom-and-pop pharmacies for pills. At each stop, the handler gave each of the shills, including Bosch, a new ID – driver's license and Medicare card – as well as a prescription and cash for the co-pay. The ID cards were crudely manufactured fakes that any bouncer in his first week on the job would've alerted to in any club in L.A. But that didn't matter. The pharmacists – like José Esquivel Sr. – were part of the game, profiting from the seemingly legitimate fulfillment of seemingly valid pre-scriptions. The ripple effects of the Santos corruption went on endlessly from there to the halls of government and industry.

Despite there seemingly being no need for him to pose as an injured man, Bosch kept up the pretense of wearing the knee brace and carrying the cane. He did it because he did not want to be separated from the cane, his only weapon.

At each stop, the group spent close to an hour, the handler usually breaking the shills into singles and couples at each pharmacy so that seven bedraggled addicts standing in line together would not cause concern among the legitimate customers in the store. From Tulare they moved up into Modesto and then Fresno, a steady supply of amber vials of pills going into the handler's backpack.

The plane had moved and was waiting at another unrestricted airstrip outside a pecan farm in Fresno. The other van was already there, and when Bosch climbed on board, the spots on the benches in front of the windows were already taken. He did get a seat next to the woman with the stars. As previously instructed, he said nothing to her.

Before the plane took off, Bosch saw the capper from his van hand his backpack through the cockpit window to the pilot. The pilot actually signed some sort of receipt or accounting statement on a clipboard and handed it to the capper. The plane then rumbled down the unpaved strip and took off to the south. They stayed on course without banking or taking any antisurveillance measures.

Bosch kept his counsel for a half hour before finally leaning toward the woman next to him and speaking in a voice just loud enough to be heard over the engine noise.

'You were right,' he said. 'He came last night. I was ready.'

'I can tell,' she said, referring to the bruise running the length of Brody's face.

'Thank you.'

'Forget it.'

'How long have you been trapped in this?'

She turned her body on the bench to literally give him the cold shoulder. Then, as if thinking better of it, she turned her head back to him and spoke.

'Just leave me alone.'

'I thought maybe we could help each other out, that's all.'

'What are you talking about? You just got here. You're not a woman, you don't know what it's like.'

Bosch flashed on the image of the woman lying discarded on the couch while the Russians gambled for the pills that were the source of all this degradation and disaster.

'I know,' he said. 'But I've seen enough to know this is like being a slave.'

She didn't respond and kept her shoulder turned to Bosch.

'When I make a move, I'll let you know,' he tried.

'Don't,' she said. 'You're just going to get yourself killed. I want nothing to do with it. I don't want to be saved, okay? Like I said from the beginning, leave me alone.'

'Why'd you warn me about Brody if you want to be left alone?'

'Because he's an animal, and one doesn't have anything to do with the other.'

'Got it.'

She tried to turn even further away from Bosch, but the lower edge of the pale yellow jacket she wore was trapped under his leg. The move pulled the jacket down over her shoulder, exposing the tank top below it and part of a tattoo.

ISY
—2009

She angrily jerked her jacket out from under his leg and back into place, but Bosch had seen enough to know it was part of an RIP tattoo on the back of her shoulder. She had lost someone important eight years before. Important enough to always carry the reminder. He wondered if it was that loss that ultimately put her on the plane.

Bosch leaned away from her and caught Brody watching them from the bench on the other side of the plane. He gave Bosch a knowing smile and Bosch realized he had made a mistake. Brody had recognized Bosch's attempt to connect to the woman. He would now realize that he could get to him through her.

The plane landed an hour later with an easier glide pattern and touchdown. Bosch couldn't tell where they were until he climbed out the jump door and recognized that he was inside the hangar at Whiteman. There were two vans waiting and this time he tried to stick close to the woman with the stars. When the group was split, he ended up in a van with her as well as Brody.

From Whiteman the van turned right on San Fernando Road but then took Van Nuys Boulevard to the first pharmacy stop. They were in Pacoima and apparently staying clear of San Fernando.

The driver, who was the same Russian who had punched Bosch while in the clinic the day before, broke his seven shills into two groups and sent Bosch and two others into the pharmacy first. Brody and the woman with the stars were left in the second group. Bosch went through the process of providing a prescription and bogus ID to the pharmacist and then waited for the pills to be put into the bottle. In most of the previous stops, the pills were already bottled and ready, the pharmacists wanting to limit the time the shills spent in the drugstore. But in this store Bosch was told to either wait outside or come back in thirty minutes.

Bosch went outside and told the Russian. He was not happy. He told Bosch and the two other shills to go back and wait inside the drugstore in order to hurry the pharmacist along. Bosch did as instructed and was milling about in the foot-care aisle, within full view of the pharmacist, when he turned around and saw another shopper looking at the Dr. Scholl's insole cushions. It was Bella Lourdes. She spoke in a low voice without looking at Bosch.

'How are you doing, Harry?'

Bosch checked the location of the other two shills before responding. They had separated and one was looking in the Mexican apothecary aisle and the other was maintaining a vigil at the prescription counter.

'I'm good. What are you doing in here?'

'Needed to check. We lost contact with you last night. Didn't pick you up till you landed at Whiteman.'

'Are you shitting me? Hovan said they were the eye in the sky. They lost the plane?'

'They did. Hovan claimed upper atmospheric interference. Valdez hit the ceiling about it. Where'd they take you?'

'Jerry Edgar's intel was on the button. It's an encampment near Slab City, southeast of the Salton Sea.'

'And you're okay?'

'I am but I almost wasn't. I think I met the two shooters. One of them played Russian roulette on me with that revolver the DEA gave me.'

'Jesus.'

'Yeah. Lucky it was tricked out.'

'I'm sorry. Do you want out? I give the word and we'll swarm this place and pull you out, make it look like a bust.'

'No, but I want you to do something else. Where's Jerry?'

'He's out there watching. We obviously freaked last night when they lost you, but now we're on you and won't drop the ball.'

Bosch checked the shills again. They were not paying attention to him. He checked the front door of the drugstore and saw no sign of the Russian driver.

'Okay, as soon as we get our scrips filled and are out of here, they're going to send in four more. A woman and three men.'

'Okay.'

'Have Jerry swing in on random enforcement and bust them for fraudulent IDs, prescriptions, the whole works.'

'All right, we can do that. Why?'

'The guy named Brody is causing me a problem. I need him gone. He's got a line of purple down the right side of his face.'

Bosch proffered the cane in explanation.

'And the woman, I want to get her into detox and rehab.'

For the first time, Lourdes looked up from her shelf-shopping and tried to get a read on him.

'You sound sympathetic. Is this getting personal? You heard what the DEA undercover trainer said about that.'

'I've only been under twenty-four hours, and I don't even know her name. It's not personal. I just saw some stuff down there in Slab City and I want her pulled out. Besides, the more people they're down, the more important I become. Maybe they'll think twice about playing Russian roulette with me again.'

'Okay, we'll do it. But that will pull a lot of us off the surveillance. I'll make sure at least one car stays with you.'

'Doesn't matter. You can wait for us at Whiteman. We'll be going back for the plane.'

Bosch heard the name that was on his phony ID called out by the pharmacist.

'Gotta go.'

'What about tomorrow?'

'What about it?'

'It's Sunday. These mom-and-pop places are usually closed Sundays.'

'Then I guess I get a day off in Slab City. Tell them not to lose me this time.'

'You better believe I will. Take care of yourself.'

Bosch pointed the cane toward the ceiling and twirled it like a musketeer brandishing a sword. He then limped toward the counter to get his pills.

Twenty minutes later he was sitting in the back of the

van, waiting for the second crew of shills to complete their pharmacy run. He watched Edgar and Hovan enter the pharmacy, and fifteen minutes after that, with the van's driver getting restless and talking to himself in Russian, a pair of LAPD cruisers pulled up.

The Russian cursed.

'*Tvoyu mat'!*'

He turned around in his seat and looked at the three men sitting in the back. He pointed at Bosch.

'You. You go in and see. Find out what is going on in there.'

Bosch slid off his seat and moved to the side door. He got out and crossed the parking lot to the pharmacy. He guessed he had been chosen by the driver because he had the cleanest clothes of those in the van. He walked in, saw the four shills lined up and in handcuffs by the pharmacy counter. The uniformed officers were checking their pockets.

Bosch's entering had rung an overhead bell. The woman with the stars on her hand looked over her shoulder and saw Bosch. She widened her eyes and jutted her chin in the direction of the door. Bosch turned around and walked back out.

Acting as though he had just seen a ghost, Bosch quickly legged it back to the van, dropping any gentleness about his knee. He jumped in through the side door.

'The cops got them! They're all in handcuffs.'

'Close the door! Close the door!'

The van was moving before Bosch could pull the sliding door closed. The driver took an exit onto Van Nuys Boulevard and headed back toward Whiteman. He hit a speed dial on his phone and soon was yelling in Russian at someone at the other end of the line.

Bosch looked through the back windows at the plaza shopping center as it retreated in the distance. For all her fuck-offs and leave-me-alones, the woman with the stars on her hand had warned him about Brody and then about the bust going down. It made him believe that there was still something inside her worth salvaging.

27

There was no calamitous wakeup call on Sunday morning. No one walked down the side of the bus, hitting it with a broomstick and yelling for everyone in the camp to get up. On Sunday the camp slept late. Having not been able to sleep at all his first night in the camp, Bosch had succumbed to his exhaustion Saturday night and slept deeply, moving through murky dreams of tunnels. When he was roused by the Russian with the dyed-blond hair shaking his cot, he was completely disoriented and at first unsure of where he was and who the man looking down at him was.

'Come,' the Russian said. 'Now.'

Bosch finally came to and realized that the guy was the one who spoke the least English and had hung back on Friday night when his partner had put a gun against Harry's head and pulled the trigger.

In his mind, Bosch had labeled them Ivan and Igor, and this was Igor, the one who didn't normally speak.

Bosch swung his legs off the cot and sat up. He rubbed his eyes, got his bearings, and started pulling on his work boots, wondering if they were going to fly off to hit pharmacies again, even though most of the non-chain stores were likely to be closed on Sunday, especially those in low-income Latino neighborhoods,

261

where a reverence for the day of rest and religious reflection was strong.

Igor was waiting for him, holding the front of his T-shirt up over his mouth and nose because of the stench in the bus. He pointed to the door.

'Come. Hurry.'

At first Bosch panicked, because he thought Igor had called him Harry and that his cover had somehow been blown. But then he understood what had been said in the Russian's thick accent.

'Okay, okay,' he said.

Bosch looked around and saw that he was the only one Igor had rousted. Everybody else in the bus was still dead to the world.

'Where are we going?' he asked.

Igor didn't respond. Before pulling on his left boot, Bosch reached to the floor and grabbed the knee brace. He pulled it up over his left calf for use later and then put the other boot on. He tied his laces, grabbed his cane, and stood up, ready to go fill prescriptions, though he had a growing suspicion that wasn't the plan for the day.

Igor pointed to the floor.

'Backpack.'

'What?'

'Bring backpack.'

'Why?'

Igor turned and headed out of the bus without another word. Bosch grabbed the backpack and followed, stepping out of the bus into blinding sunlight. He kept asking questions, hoping for some hint of what awaited him.

'Hey, what's going on?' he asked.

There was no answer.

'Hey, where's your pal with the English?' Bosch tried. 'I want to talk to somebody.'

The Russian continued to ignore Bosch's words and just used his hands to signal him to keep following. They walked through the camp to the clearing where the vans had picked up the shill groups the morning before. There was a van waiting with an open side door. Igor pointed to the opening.

'You go.'

'Yeah, I get it. Go where?'

No answer. Bosch came to a stop and looked at him.

'You go.'

'I need to hit the head first.'

Bosch could tell the Russian didn't understand the slang. He pointed the cane toward the south side of the encampment and started walking that way. Igor grabbed him by the shoulders and roughly redirected him to the van.

'No. You go!'

Igor shoved him hard toward the van and Bosch almost dropped the cane while grabbing for the doorframe.

'Okay, okay. I'm going.'

He climbed onto the bench seat behind the driver. The Russian then climbed in, slid the door closed behind him, and took the bench behind Bosch.

The van started moving, and soon enough Bosch could tell they were heading to the airstrip. He knew the man behind him did not have the language skills to answer questions, but Bosch's growing concern over what was happening left him unable to stop asking. He leaned forward to catch the driver's peripheral vision.

'Hey, driver? What are we doing? Why am I the only one going to the plane?'

The driver acted like he neither saw nor heard him.

In less than ten minutes they were at the airstrip. The van pulled up to a plane with an already spinning prop. It wasn't the 'minivan' Bosch had taken all of his previous flights on but still clearly a jump plane that could carry several passengers. The other Russian, Ivan, was standing next to the open jump door, using the overhead wing to shade his face from the sun.

Igor got up and opened the van door. He grabbed a handful of Bosch's shirt and yanked him toward the opening.

'You go. Plane.'

'Yeah, I figured.'

Bosch nearly tumbled out of the van, but used his cane to keep upright. He immediately started walking toward Ivan. He carried the cane by the barrel rather than walking as if he needed it. He wanted to dispense with any sign of weakness in front of the man he was about to confront.

'What's going on?' he demanded. 'Why am I the only one going?'

'Because you go home,' Ivan said. 'Now.'

'What are you talking about? What home?'

'We take you back. We don't want you here.'

'What? Why?'

'Just get on plane.'

'Does your boss know this? I got you four hundred

pills yesterday. That's a lot of money. He's not going to like losing that.'

'What boss? Get on plane.'

'All you guys do is say the same thing. Why? Why should I get on the plane?'

'Because we take you back. We don't want you.'

Bosch shook his head like he didn't get it.

'I heard people talking. His name is Santos. Santos is not going to like it.'

Ivan smirked.

'Santos long gone. I am boss. Get on plane.'

Bosch stared at him for a moment, trying to get a read for a sign of truth.

'Whatever. Then I want my money and pills. We had a deal.'

Ivan nodded and pulled a plastic bag from his pocket. It contained pills and currency, the outside bill a hundred. He shook it and handed it to Bosch.

'There. You good. Get on plane.'

Bosch climbed through the jump door and went to the back of the plane, as far from the door as he could get. He sat down on the bench that ran along the rear bulkhead and looked back. Both Ivan and Igor climbed on board and took seats on benches on either side of the plane at the front. They looked like they were guarding the exit.

Bosch knew he was in trouble. Giving him the money was the tell. They could easily have gotten away with stiffing him. But giving him what he had earned was a move designed to put him at ease, to make him believe they were actually taking him home.

Ivan knocked a fist on a small aluminum door that

separated the cockpit from the passenger compartment, and the plane started to taxi to the head of the airstrip. Bosch thought of what Ivan had said about Santos and saw where it made sense. The DEA had no current intel on the man who had set up this operation. Hovan said the last known photo they had was almost a year old. Santos and those loyal to him could have been taken out by the Russians, especially if they had gotten wind of the indictment and warrant for his arrest, making him a liability to the operation. This would also help explain why the operation seemed to be short on manpower and why the two apparent bosses were doing the wet work.

Bosch realized that if Ivan and Igor were indeed the killers who had wiped out the pharmacy in San Fernando, then they had made the call themselves. The end of the case was right in front of him.

The plane turned and positioned for a run down the airstrip. Bosch felt he knew how this ride was supposed to end for him. He put the cane across his thighs and pulled out his wallet, yanking it off the chain seemingly by accident. He hoped the pulse alert was delivered to the DEA team that supposedly was watching over him.

Bosch made a show of taking the currency from the plastic bag and putting it into his wallet. He then put the wallet and the bag of pills into his pockets.

The plane started moving down the runway, gathering momentum. Wind started blasting through the compartment. The Russians hadn't closed the jump door. Bosch pointed at the opening and yelled.

'You going to close that?'

Ivan shook his head and gestured toward the opening.

'No door!' he yelled back.

Bosch hadn't noticed that before.

The plane took off. It rose steeply and Bosch was pushed back against the rear wall of the passenger compartment. Almost immediately, the craft started to bank left while still in its climb. It then leveled and was on a course west.

Bosch knew that would take them over the center of the Salton Sea.

28

The unseen pilot throttled back once the plane leveled off. The engine whine lowered significantly and that served as a signal to Ivan. He got up and started moving toward Bosch at the back of the plane. He had to hunch down to keep his head from hitting the curved ceiling. As he came forward, he reached into a front pocket and pulled out a phone. When he got to Bosch, he crouched on his haunches like a baseball catcher. He looked at Bosch, then at the screen of his phone, and then back at Bosch.

'You cop,' he said.

It wasn't a question. It was a statement.

'What?' Bosch said. 'What are you talking about?'

Ivan referred to his phone again. Over his shoulder Bosch could see Igor still in his seat watching.

'Har-ree Boosh,' Ivan said. 'You cop.'

'I don't know what you're talking about,' Bosch said. 'I'm not—'

'San Fernando PD! It say so.'

'What says so?'

Ivan turned the phone so Bosch could see the screen. On it was a photo of a folded section of a newspaper. There was a photo of him that he could tell had been taken last week outside La Farmacia Familia on the day of the murders. It was the continuation page of a story, but not a story on the pharmacy murders. The headline across the body of the story continuation and his photo told Bosch all he needed to know.

DNA CLEARS DEATH ROW INMATE; D.A. MOVES TO VACATE CONVICTION

Somebody had leaked the story to the *Times*. Kennedy. He had gotten word that Bosch and Haller were going to make a move in the Borders hearing and had acted to push Haller back on his heels and vilify Bosch. The story had included his current employment, and the photo of him outside the pharmacy had been a big glaring tip-off to the Russians.

Ivan lowered the phone and put it in his back pocket. A crooked smile formed on his lips as he grabbed hold of the barrel of Bosch's cane and they struggled for control of it. Ivan reached his free hand behind him and pulled a gun from under his shirt. With his other hand he pushed the barrel of the cane in on Bosch and leaned into him.

'Get up, cop,' he said. 'You're going to jump now. Maybe you find your friend Santos, yah?'

Bosch checked the gun. It was a chrome-plated automatic, not the disabled revolver the DEA had planted in Bosch's backpack and that Ivan had brandished on Friday night.

He riffed off of the Russian's last words, hoping to distract him.

'You killed Santos, didn't you? You killed him and took over. And that boy in the pharmacy. You killed him and his father.'

'That boy was punk. He did not listen to his father

and the father could not control the son. They got what they deserved.'

Ivan tilted his head back toward Igor as if to acknowledge their work on eliminating the problem of José Esquivel Jr. For a split second his attention was divided, and that was all the time Bosch needed. He twisted his wrist and turned the curved handle of the cane. He heard the release *snick* and in one quick motion pulled the handle and stiletto free, then drove the point into Ivan's right side with an upward thrust. The thin, sharp blade punctured the skin and went through the ribs and deep into the Russian's chest.

Ivan's eyes widened and his mouth formed a silent O. The two men stared at each other for a second that seemed to last a minute. Then Ivan dropped the gun to clutch at the stiletto's handle. But blood had already spilled over the weapon and Bosch's hand. The surfaces were too slippery for Ivan to find purchase. He brought his left hand up and grabbed Bosch's throat. But he was weakening and it was the desperate move of a dying man.

Bosch looked past Ivan to Igor, who was still seated at the front. He was smiling because he had not seen the blood yet and thought that his partner was sadistically choking Bosch out before throwing him from the plane.

Bosch had killed men face-to-face before – as a young man in the tunnels back in Vietnam. He knew what he needed to do to finish the job. He pulled back on the stiletto and went in again, two quick thrusts up into the neck and near the armpit, where he knew major arteries waited. He then pushed the Russian back. As Ivan fell to the floor, dying, Bosch grabbed the gun.

He stood up, the stiletto dripping blood in his left

hand, the gun in his right. He started moving up the plane toward Igor.

Igor rose from his seat, ready for battle. Then his eyes fell to the pistol. He made a stutter move, first to one side, then the other, as if his body were moving ahead of his mind and seeking escape. Then, inexplicably, he lunged to his left and went through the jump door.

Bosch held still for a moment, stunned by the move, then quickly went up to the door, dropping the stiletto and grabbing the steel handle that skydivers hold before stepping out onto the jump platform. He leaned out. They were flying over the Salton Sea at about two hundred feet. Bosch guessed that they had flown low to cut down on the chance that someone might witness Bosch's drop from the plane.

Bosch leaned further out to look down on the water behind the plane. The sun's reflection off the surface was almost blinding and he could see no sign of Igor. If he had survived the jump, he was miles from shore.

Bosch went to the cockpit door and rapped hard on it with the pistol. He figured the pilot took it as a signal that the disposal of Bosch had been completed. The plane throttled up and started to climb.

He then tried the door and found it locked. He grabbed on to overhead handles for leverage and kicked his heel into the door, bending it on its frame enough that the lock snapped loose. He quickly flung the door open and thrust himself through the narrow opening, leading with the gun.

'What the fuck?' the pilot yelled.

He then did a double-take when he saw that it was Bosch and not one of the Russians.

'Oh, hey, wait, what's going on?' he yelped.

Bosch dropped into the empty copilot's seat. He reached over and put the muzzle of the gun against the pilot's temple.

'What's going on is I'm a police officer and you are going to do exactly what I tell you to do,' he said. 'You understand me?'

The pilot was late sixties and white, with gin blossoms across his nose. A pilot no one else would hire.

'Yes, sir, no problem,' he said. 'Whatever you say.'

His English was unaccented. He was likely native-born American. Bosch took a chance, noting the man's age and the blurred tattoos on his arms.

'You remember the A-six from Vietnam?' he asked.

'I sure do,' the pilot said. 'The Intruder, great plane.'

'I flew 'em back then and haven't flown since. But you make one wrong move and I'll put a bullet in your head and have to learn to fly all over again.'

Bosch had never flown a plane before, let alone an Intruder. But he needed a believable threat to keep the pilot in line.

'No problem, sir,' the pilot said. 'Just tell me where you want to go. I don't have any idea what was going on back there. I just fly the plane. They tell me where.'

'Save it,' Bosch said. 'How much fuel do we have?'

'I tapped it this morning. We're full.'

'What's the range?'

'Three hundred miles easy.'

'Okay, take me back to L.A. Up to Whiteman.'

'Not a problem.'

The pilot started going through maneuvers to change

course. Bosch saw the radio mic hooked to the instrument panel. He grabbed it.

'This on?'

'Yes, press the button on the side to transmit.'

Bosch found the transmit button and then hesitated, unsure what to say.

'Hello, any airport tower that can read this. Come back.'

Bosch looked at the pilot, wondering if he had just revealed that he had never flown a plane before. The radio saved him.

'This is Imperial County Airport, go ahead.'

'My name is Harry Bosch. I'm a detective with the San Fernando Police Department. I am flying in a plane after an in-air event leaving one passenger dead and one missing over the Salton Sea. Requesting radio contact be made with Agent Hovan of the DEA. I can give a number when you are ready to copy.'

Bosch clicked off and waited for the response. He felt the tensions that had gripped him for nearly forty-eight hours start to slacken off as the plane headed north toward safety and home.

From two thousand feet up, the land below looked beautiful to Bosch and nothing like the badlands he knew it to be.

29

Bosch got a crowded reception from state, local, and federal authorities when the plane landed under DEA air escort at Whiteman Airport. There were DEA agents, Jerry Edgar with a team from the state medical board, and Chief Valdez and the investigators from San Fernando standing front and center. There was also a coroner's van and death team, a pair of LAPD detectives from Foothill Division, their own forensic tech, and a pair of paramedics just in case Bosch required medical attention.

The plane was directed into an empty hangar so that it could be processed as a crime scene without media or public scrutiny. Bosch squeezed through the cockpit door and into the passenger section and the pilot followed. He told the pilot to climb through the jump door with his hands up. As he did so, Bosch stepped to the back of the compartment. He took a long look at the man he had killed, his body lying still on the floor of the plane. Blood had run from the body in crisscross patterns as the plane had banked and changed altitude during the flight. Bosch moved back up to the jump door and exited the plane.

Two men in black tactical pants and shirts, their sidearms held down by their sides, helped him off the jump platform.

'DEA?' Bosch asked.

'Yes, sir,' said one agent. 'We are going to go in and clear the plane now. Is there anyone else inside?'

'Nobody alive.'

'Okay, sir. There are some people here who want to talk to you now.'

'And I want to talk to them.'

Bosch stepped away from the plane's wing, and Bella Lourdes was there waiting for him.

'Harry, you all right?'

'Better than the guy in the plane. How are we handling the debrief?'

'The DEA has a mobile command post. You're supposed to go in there with us, the LAPD, Edgar, and Hovan. You ready, or you want to—'

'I'm ready. Let's get this over with. But I want to see the *L.A. Times* first. That story today almost got me killed.'

'We have it for you.'

'Talk about bad timing.'

She led him to a huddle with Valdez, Sisto, Luzon, and Trevino. The chief clapped him on the upper arm and said he had done good. There was an awkwardness about the greeting, considering what Bosch had been through, and it was the first indication that the *Times* story was going to be difficult to deal with.

Bosch pressed on with the case at hand.

'Our case is closed,' he said. 'The dead guy in the plane was one of the shooters. The other one jumped out. I don't think he made it.'

'The fricking guy just jumped out of the plane?' Sisto said.

He said it in a tone that implied he thought otherwise, like maybe the Russian had help jumping.

Bosch held his eyes with a stare.

'Crazy Russians,' Sisto said. 'Just saying.'

'Let's wait on all of that until we sit down with everybody,' Valdez said. 'Bella, you take Harry to the debriefing, I'll get the paper. Harry, you hungry?'

'Starving.'

'I'll have somebody get you something and bring it in.'

Bella had walked Bosch halfway through the hangar when they encountered Edgar. He smiled at Bosch as he approached.

'Partner, you made it,' he said. 'Can't wait to hear the rundown. Sounds like a close fucking call.'

Bosch nodded.

'You know what?' he said. 'If you hadn't told me that rumor about people going up in the plane and not coming back, I might not be here right now, partner. That gave me the edge on these guys.'

'Well, I'm glad I did something,' Edgar said.

The mobile command post was an unmarked RV that had probably been seized in a drug case, then gutted on the inside and reequipped. Bosch and Lourdes stepped into what looked like a mini board of directors' meeting room. There was a separation wall with a door that led to an electronics nest. Agent Hovan stepped out of the nest, shook Bosch's hand, and welcomed him back.

'Anything on the second Russian?' Bosch asked.

Bosch had reported on Igor's jump without a parachute while on the plane flying toward Whiteman. The DEA had dispatched a rescue effort.

'Nothing,' Hovan said. 'It's a long shot.'

Hovan instructed Bosch to sit at one end of the table so he would be visible to all who would gather for the briefing. Lourdes took the seat to his right, and the rest of the SFPD team took the chairs down that side of the table. Valdez came in and dropped the A section of the *Times* on the table in front of Bosch and then sat down.

The story had been a front-page lead, its headline a kick to Bosch's gut. He tried to read it as agents and officers started to file into the command post and take seats.

D.A. Cites DNA, Police Misconduct; Will Vacate Death Penalty

By David Ramsey, *Times* Staff Writer

A man sentenced to death for a 1987 rape and murder of a Toluca Lake actress may walk free as early as Wednesday when prosecutors cite new DNA evidence and misconduct on the part of the Los Angeles police and ask a judge to vacate the conviction.

The Los Angeles County District Attorney's Office has requested the Superior Court hearing in the case of Preston Borders, who has been imprisoned since his arrest almost 30 years ago. Borders had exhausted all appeals in the case and was languishing on death row at San Quentin until the D.A.'s newly created Conviction Integrity Unit decided to review his claims that he was framed for the murder of Danielle Skyler.

Skyler was found raped and murdered in her apartment in Toluca Lake. Borders was an acquaintance who had previously dated her and was tied to the crime when jewelry allegedly taken from the victim during the assault was found hidden in his apartment. In a case built entirely on circumstantial evidence, Borders was convicted after a one-week trial and later sentenced to death.

Deputy DA Alex Kennedy said that recently completed DNA analysis on the victim's clothing revealed a match between a small amount of bodily fluid found on the clothing and a serial rapist named Lucas John Olmer, who was known to be operating in Los Angeles at the time. Olmer was later convicted of sexual assault in several other unrelated cases and died in prison in 2015.

Kennedy said investigators now believe that it was Olmer who murdered Skyler and may also have been responsible for two other murders of young women that police initially suspected Borders of but never filed charges on.

'We think it was Olmer who stalked and murdered her, entering through a balcony door that had been left unlocked,' Kennedy said. 'He was a serial offender who stalked victims in that area.'

Court documents obtained by the *Times* reveal that Borders and his attorney Lance Cronyn have claimed that the jewelry found in Borders's apartment was planted there by a detective who was the lead investigator on the case.

'This has been a gross miscarriage of justice,'

Cronyn said. 'Mr. Borders has lost more than half of his life because of this.'

Cronyn and court documents identify the two detectives who conducted the search of the apartment and reported finding the piece of jewelry in a secret compartment as Hieronymus 'Harry' Bosch and Francis Sheehan. The *Times* has learned that Sheehan is deceased and Bosch retired from the LAPD three years ago.

Bosch testified during the trial in 1988 that he found the jewelry – described as a sea-horse pendant – hidden in the false bottom of a bookshelf during the search of Borders's apartment. Borders, an actor who knew Skyler from auditions and workshops, was arrested shortly after the discovery.

Bosch could not be reached for comment for this story. He was well known as an LAPD detective for more than three decades and was involved in many high-profile investigations. He now works as a volunteer detective for the San Fernando Police Department. Last week he was involved in the investigation of two pharmacists who were murdered during a suspected robbery at a drugstore in the main shopping area of the small town in the San Fernando Valley.

The story jumped inside from there, but Bosch had read enough and was not inclined to unfold the section to the page with his photograph. He was aware that everyone crowded into the room now was watching him and knew what the newspaper report said about him.

He put the paper down on the floor next to his chair.

It had no doubt been a hit piece orchestrated by either Cronyn or Kennedy. There was no mention, before the jump at least, of an opposing view of Borders's innocence. No mention that Mickey Haller had by now hopefully filed a motion seeking to stop the D.A.'s action.

Bosch looked up at the faces lining both sides of the table. Opposite him at the other end was Hovan. And next to him was Joe Smith, his UC trainer.

'Okay, two things before we start,' Bosch said. 'I haven't had a shower since Wednesday and I apologize for that. If you think it's funky from where you're sitting, just be glad you're not where I am. The other thing is that the story today in the *Times* is complete bullshit. I planted no evidence in that or any other case and Preston Borders will never walk free. You can check back after the hearing Wednesday, and the *Times* will be running a story that says so.'

Bosch checked the faces in the room. There were a few nods of approval, but for the most part the investigators in the room gave no indication whether they believed him or not. It was what he had expected.

'Okay, then,' he said. 'The sooner we get to this, the sooner I get to a shower. How do you want to start?'

He looked down the length of the table to Hovan. It was his agency's RV. Bosch figured that made him the man in charge.

'We'll have questions, but I think you can start anywhere you want,' Hovan said. 'Why don't you give us the headlines and go from there?'

Bosch nodded.

'Well, the big headline is that there is no Santos

anymore,' he said. 'The Russians threw him out of a plane into the Salton Sea. One of them told me that right before they were going to do the same to me.'

'Why would he tell you that?' asked an agent Bosch didn't know. 'Russians don't usually break so easy.'

'He didn't break,' Bosch said. 'He was about to kill me. He had the upper hand and wanted to gloat, I guess. He also indicated that he and his partner, the one who jumped, killed the father and son in the pharmacy Monday.'

'Indicated?' Lourdes said.

'Yes, indicated,' Bosch said. 'I asked him straight out if they had killed the father and son. He didn't deny it. He said that they got what they deserved. He was smiling when he said it. But soon after that, things changed and I got the upper hand. That's when I killed him.'

30

They kept him for three hours in the mobile command post, at least half of that time spent going into great detail about what had happened that morning on the plane. All parties except for Edgar, the medical board investigator, had stakes in the death investigation and had questions to cover. Because the actual killing of the Russian occurred in the air over the Salton Sea, it became a jurisdictional dilemma. It was agreed that the National Transportation Safety Board would be apprised of the death, but the LAPD would handle the lead because the plane with the body on board touched land at Whiteman Airport in the city of Los Angeles.

The session in the command post was followed by a two-hour walk-through in the constricted confines of the plane, during which Bosch tried to show the investigators what he had been talking about for the previous three hours. It was agreed at the end that Bosch would make himself available later in the week for follow-up questions from all agencies. He was released at about the same time as the body of the Russian he had referred to as Ivan was removed from the plane and transported to the Medical Examiner's Office for autopsy.

Meanwhile, he was told, the DEA was putting together a raid team to hit the encampment near Slab City and gather up the remaining players in the drug operation. It was decided that a media blackout would be kept tight on the case until that raid had concluded.

Bosch was given a ride back to the SFPD station by Lourdes. He had left his Jeep there as well as his real ID and cell phone. She also had to collect his bloody clothes as evidence in the use of the deadly force investigation. He lowered the window as they drove because he couldn't stand his own stink.

'You going to talk to Mrs. Esquivel about all of this?' he asked.

'I think we should wait until we get the all clear from the DEA,' Lourdes said. 'You want to go with me?'

'Nah. She'll be more comfortable with you and speaking Spanish. It's your case.'

'Yeah, but you cleared it.'

'I won't feel certain of that until they find Igor.'

'Right, well, more salt, more buoyancy. They'll find him one way or the other.'

She knew who both Ivan and Igor were from the debriefing. Assigning names to the various principals had made it easier to tell the story, but the truth was, no one knew the real names of any of the individuals. Bosch thought about that and remembered the woman with the stars on her hand, another person he didn't have a real name for.

'What happened with the woman Edgar and Hovan popped at the pharmacy on Saturday?'

'She got booked and sent to Van Nuys.'

The SFPD's jail was not used for holding female arrestees. They were transported to the Van Nuys jail, which was operated by the LAPD and had a female ward as well as a detox center.

'Did you happen to get her name?'

'Uh, yeah, I did. It was . . . what was it? . . . Elizabeth something. Clayburgh or Clayton, one of those. I'll remember in a sec.'

'Was she cooperative?'

'You mean like was she thanking us for pulling her out of the virtual slavery you described in the debrief? No, Harry, she didn't mention it. She was pretty pissed off, in fact, that she was under arrest and not going to be able to get her next fix in jail.'

'You don't sound like you have a lot of sympathy.'

'I do to an extent. I've dealt with addicts all my life, including in my own family, and it's hard to balance sympathy for them with the damage they do to their families and others.'

Bosch nodded. She had a point. But he could tell she was also upset about something else.

'You think I planted evidence in that case thirty years ago?'

'What? Why are you bringing that up?'

''Cause I can tell I've got people upset all around me. If it's that case, then you don't have to worry. The paper makes it look bad, I know, but it's not going to stick. It's a frame.'

'You're being framed?'

The skepticism in her voice began to offend Bosch but he tried to keep it in check.

'That's right and it will all come out at the hearing,' he said.

'Good. I hope so.'

They got to the station and parked in the side lot. Bosch went into the new jail, where he took off his clothes in front of the duty officer and dropped them all into a cardboard box. While the officer took the box out to Lourdes to process, Bosch went into the jail shower and stood under the lukewarm spray for twenty-five minutes, repeatedly using the jail's industrial-strength antibacterial soap on every part of his body.

When he was clean and dry, he was given a pair of jail pants and a golf shirt left over from the department's annual fund-raiser tournament. There had been blood on his shoes, so they had gone into the box as well and were replaced with a pair of paper jail slippers.

Bosch didn't care how he looked. He was clean and felt human again. He went to the detective bureau to get the key to his office in the old jail – he had left his car keys, phone, and real ID there. Lourdes was in the war room. She had spread butcher paper on the meeting-and-eating table and was taking photos of the individual pieces of Bosch's clothing before bagging each item individually in a plastic evidence bag.

'You cleaned up nice,' she said.

'Yeah, ready to take up golf for the cause,' he said. 'I'm sorry you got stuck with the nasty job.'

'Lot of blood.'

'Yeah, I went for his bleeders.'

She looked up at him. Her face told him that she understood how close he had come to being killed.

'So you still have the key I gave you to the old jail.'

'Yeah, in my top drawer. You taking off?'

'Yeah, I want to call my lawyer and my daughter and then I want to sleep for about twenty hours.'

'We have follow-up on all of this tomorrow.'

'Yeah, I was just kidding about the twenty hours. I just need to get some sleep.'

'Okay, then I'll see you tomorrow, Harry.'

'Right, see you.'

'I'm glad you're okay.'

'Thanks, Bella.'

Bosch crossed the street, ducked through the Public Works yard, and entered the old jail. When he got to his makeshift desk, he saw that someone – probably Lourdes – had used the key to enter the cell and drop off a stamped letter addressed to him at the police department. Bosch decided to get to it later. He folded it and was about to put it in his back pocket when he realized that his jail pants had no pockets. He tucked it into the waistband, then gathered his things and headed back out, locking the doors behind him.

His phone screen said he had seventeen messages. He waited until he got on the freeway heading south and then played them over the phone's speaker as he drove.

Friday, 1:38 p.m.: Just wanted you to know that we are locked and loaded. Request-to-be-heard motion filed, salvos fired. And word to the wise, my brother? Be prepared; there could be some major pushback on this. Okay, later, talk next week. Oh, and by the way, this is your attorney and it's Friday afternoon. I know you are off doin' secret cop stuff somewhere. Give a call if you need to over the weekend.

Friday, 3:16 p.m.: Harry, it's Lucy, call me back. It's important.

Friday, 4:22 p.m.: Detective Bosch, Alex Kennedy. I need you to give me a call as soon as possible. Thank you.

Friday, 4:38 p.m.: Harry, Lucy again, what the fuck did you do? I was trying to watch out for you and now you do this? You just – Kennedy is out for blood now. Call me back.

Friday, 5:51 p.m.: Shit, Harry, this is your old partner, remember me? I had your back and you had mine. Kennedy wants to blow you out of the water. I'm trying to contain this but I'm not sure he's listening to me. You gotta call me back and you have to tell me what you have. I want the truth just as much as you do.

Friday, 7:02 p.m.: Hello, Detective Bosch, this is David Ramsey at the *Los Angeles Times.* Sorry to call you on your personal line but I am working on a story for this weekend about the Preston Borders case. I would love to have your response to some of the things that have come up in court documents. I'll be at this number all night. Thank you.

Saturday, 8:01 a.m.: You don't miss a trick, do you? I thought if I called from a strange number, you might pick up and talk to your old partner. I don't understand you, Harry. But my hands are tied now. The *Times* is running with this. Supposedly it's hitting the website today and in the paper tomorrow. I didn't want this and if you had just talked to me, I think it could have been avoided. Just remember, I tried.

Saturday, 10:04 a.m.: Detective Bosch, this is David Ramsey from the *Times* again. I really want to get your side of things on this story. Court documents allege that you planted key evidence that tied Preston Borders to the murder of Danielle Skyler in nineteen eighty-seven. I really need you to respond to that. It's in documents filed by the D.A.'s Office so it's fair game to report but I would want your side of it. I'm at this number all day.

Saturday, 11:35 a.m.: Hey, Dad, just wanted to say hi and see what you're up to this weekend. I was thinking of coming up today. Okay, love you.

Saturday, 2:12 p.m.: Dad, oh Dad, hello, this is your daughter. Remember me? Are you there? My window for coming up is closing. Call me back.

Saturday, 3:00 p.m.: David Ramsey again. We aren't holding the story any longer, Detective Bosch. I've been to your house, I've called all your numbers. No response. It's been almost twenty-four hours. If I don't hear back from you in the next couple of hours, then my editors say we go with the story without your response. We will, however, out of fairness, document our many efforts to reach you. Thank you. I hope you will call back.

Saturday, 7:49 p.m.: Haller here. Have you seen the fucking *Times* online? I knew there would be pushback but this is beyond the pale. They didn't even call me. They make no mention of our petition or our side of it. This is what you call a hit job. This asshole Kennedy is trying to stack the deck. Well, he just poked the wrong fucking beehive. I'm going to eat his lunch. Call me, bro, so we can put our heads together on this.

Saturday, 9:58 p.m.: Dad, now I'm getting worried. You're not answering either phone and I'm getting scared. I called Uncle Mickey and Lucy and both said they've been trying to get you, too. Mickey said you told him you were going off the grid. I don't know what's going on but call me back. Please, Dad.

Sunday, 9:16 a.m.: Dad, I'm really scared. I'm coming up there.

Sunday, 11:11 a.m.: Call me as soon as you get this, my brudder. We need an attorney—client meeting. I have a few ideas about how to bolster our case and go right at these fucks. Call me.

Sunday, 12:42 p.m.: Dad, I saw the paper and I know what's going on. Nothing is that bad. It doesn't mean a thing. You have to come home. Right now. I'm here. Come home.

Sunday, 2:13 p.m.: Call your attorney. I'm waiting.

Bosch was overcome by the emotion he heard in his daughter's voice. She was holding back tears, being strong for him. She thought the worst. That the professional humiliation and suspicion promulgated by the *Times* story had caused him to disappear or worse. In that moment, he vowed to make those behind the story pay for their crime against his daughter.

289

His first call was to her.

'Dad! Where are you?'

'I'm so sorry, baby. I haven't had my phone. I've been working and—'

'How could you not get all those messages? Oh my god, I thought you were – I don't know, I thought you did something.'

'No, they're wrong. The paper's wrong and the D.A.'s wrong and your uncle and I are going to show it in court this week. I promise you I did nothing wrong, and no matter what, I would not do anything to myself. I wouldn't do that to you.'

'I know, I know. I'm sorry. My mind just went crazy when I couldn't reach you.'

'I went undercover for a couple days on a case and I—'

'What? You went undercover? That's crazy.'

'I didn't want to tell you ahead of time because you'd worry. But I didn't have my phone. I couldn't carry it. Anyway, where are you? Are you still at the house?'

'Yes, I'm here. There was a business card in the door from the reporter who wrote that story.'

'Yeah, he was trying to call me too. He got used. I'll deal with that later. I'm on my way home. Will you wait for me?'

'Of course. I'm here.'

'Okay. I gotta go and make some other calls. I'll be there in less than thirty.'

'Okay, Dad. Love you.'

'Love you too.'

Bosch disconnected. He took a deep breath and then hit the heel of his palm hard on the steering wheel. *The sins of the father*, he thought. His life and his world had once again clobbered his daughter. If he vowed to make those who did this pay, didn't that include himself?

He called Haller back next.

'Bosch! Where you been, man?'

'Out of the loop, obviously. I was without a phone. And of course the shit hit the fan.'

'I'll say. I think the whole thing is actionable. Careless, reckless, you name it.'

'You talking about the newspaper?'

'Yeah, the *Times*. Let's go at them. Defamation of character.'

'Forget it. That guy Ramsey was used. I want Kennedy and Cronyn. Maddie couldn't reach me either. She thought I rolled up in a ball somewhere and killed myself.'

'I know. She called me. I didn't know what to tell her. You didn't tell *me*.'

'Cronyn and Kennedy are going to pay for this. Somehow, some way.'

'Wednesday, baby. We take them down Wednesday.'

'I'm not so sure about relying on a judge to do the right thing.'

'Well, we gotta meet. What are you doing right now?'

'I'm heading home and I have to spend some time with my daughter.'

'Okay, call me. I'm free tonight if you want to get together. Otherwise, what's your schedule tomorrow?'

'I can meet in the morning.'

'Why don't we just do that? You take Maddie to dinner and we meet tomorrow. Du-par's at eight?'

'Which one?'

'You pick.'

Haller lived just off the edge of Laurel Canyon, which put him within striking distance of the Du-par's locations in Studio City and the farmers' market in Hollywood.

'Let's do Studio City in case they need me up at the PD tomorrow morning for follow-ups.'

'I'll be there.'

'Listen, before you go. I got calls from you, Maddie, Kennedy, and the reporter. I also heard from Lucy Soto. Sounded to me like she saw the bullshit in what Kennedy was doing and isn't happy about it. I think she could be on our side on this. If we show her what we've got, we could have somebody on the inside working for us.'

There was silence.

'You there, Haller?'

'I'm here. I'm just thinking. Let's wait on that till tomorrow. We'll figure it out over pancakes.'

'All right.'

Bosch disconnected. He started to even out, now that he had spoken to his daughter and his lawyer. There was a good short-term plan in place. He thought about Lucy Soto and whether he should reach out to her on his own and under the radar. They had only been partners for a brief period during his last year on the job for the LAPD, but unlike in his partnership with Edgar, they had gotten to the point of deep trust. He could blow through an intersection on her 'clear' without hesitation. Any day.

His gut told him that hadn't changed.

31

Maddie came charging out of her room as soon as she heard the front door close. She grabbed Bosch in a desperate embrace that made him feel like he was on top and at the bottom of the world at the same time.

'Everything's all right,' he said.

He held her head against his heart, then he let her go. She stepped back and appraised him while he did the same to her. He could see dried tracks from tears on her face. She also somehow seemed more grown-up since the last time he had seen her. Bosch didn't know if that had come in the past twenty-four hours or was just the natural course of things. It had been a month since they had been together and she looked taller and thinner and had changed her sandy-blond hair into a shorter, layered cut. There was something professional about it.

'OMG, what are you wearing?' she exclaimed.

Bosch looked down at himself. The jail pants and paper slippers were indeed shocking.

'Uh, yeah, well, it's a long story,' he said. 'They had to take my clothes for evidence and this is all they had.'

'Why would your clothes be evidence?' she asked.

'Well, that's the part that's a long story. What are you doing about dinner? You staying up here or do you have to go back? I know you've got your trip to IB, right?'

'We're not leaving till tomorrow but it's my Sunday to cook.'

Bosch knew that his daughter and her three roommates had a Sunday-evening tradition of rotating cooking duties – the only night of the week they had promised to always eat together. Maddie was up and couldn't let the others down.

'But I want to hear the story, Dad,' she said. 'I've been waiting here all day and deserve to hear it.'

Bosch nodded. She was right.

'Okay, give me five minutes to change into my own stuff,' he said. 'I don't like looking like a prisoner.'

He headed down the hall to his room, calling back to her a request that she water the plants. Throughout her high school years, she had insisted on buying several potted plants for the back deck. She had dutifully maintained them with a watering cycle but then went off to college, and Bosch was left holding the responsibility, which proved difficult for a man with his schedule.

'Already did,' she called back down the hall to him. 'I was so nervous I did it twice!'

'Good!' he called down the hall. 'I won't have to worry about it for a week.'

It felt good to get out of the jail pants and slippers. As he did so, the envelope that had been mailed to him at the police station fell to the floor. Bosch put it on the bed table to open and read later. Before putting on his own clothes, he slipped into the bathroom and shaved five days of stubble off his face. He pulled on blue jeans, a white button-down shirt, and a pair of black running shoes. On his way back up the hall, he stopped in the kitchen to put the jail pants and slippers in the trash can under the sink.

He then went to the refrigerator for a beer. But there was none and his leaning down to look into the far recesses of the box didn't change that.

He straightened up and looked at the bottle of bourbon on top of the refrigerator. He decided against it, even though he could have used something to help chill things out. Seeing the bottle, however, made him think that he should give what remained of the precious brand to Edgar to thank him for his warning about the plane ride over the Salton Sea.

'Dad?'

'Yeah. Sorry.'

He went out to the living room to tell the story. There was no one in the world Bosch trusted more than his daughter. He told her everything, more detail than he had even told the collective in the mobile command post. He felt the details would mean more to her, and at the same time, he knew he was telling her about the dark side of the world. It was a place she had to know about, he believed, no matter where she went with her life. He ended the story with an apology.

'Sorry,' he said. 'Maybe you didn't need to know all of that.'

'No, I did,' she said. 'I can't believe you volunteered for it. You were so lucky. What if you had gotten killed by those guys? I would have been all alone.'

'I'm sorry. I guess I figured you'd be all right. You're strong. You're on your own now. I know you have roommates but you're independent. I thought . . .'

'Thanks a lot, Dad.'

'Look, I'm sorry. But I wanted to catch these guys. What that kid did, the son, it was noble. When this all comes out, people will probably say he was stupid and naive and didn't know what he was doing. But they won't know the truth. He was being noble. And there isn't a lot of that out there in the world anymore. People lie, the president lies, corporations lie and cheat. . . . The world is ugly and not many people are willing to stand up to it anymore. I didn't want what this kid did to go by without . . . I didn't want them to get away with it, I guess.'

'I understand. Just think of me next time, okay? You're all I have.'

'Right. I will. You're all I have too.'

'So now tell me the other story. About what's in the paper today.'

She held up the business card from David Ramsey she had found left at the front door. It reminded Bosch that he had not read the full *Times* story. He now told her about the Danielle Skyler case and the move by Preston Borders to get off death row and frame Bosch for planting evidence in the process. This story ran right up until she felt pressed for time, having to drive all the way back to Orange County. She had already decided to pick up dinner on the way instead of cooking it late.

She gave Bosch another long embrace and he walked her out to her car.

'Dad, I want to come up for the hearing on Wednesday,' she said.

Normally Bosch didn't like her to go to hearings on his cases. But this one would be different because it would feel like he was on trial. He could use all the moral support he could get.

'What about Imperial Beach?' he asked.

'I'll just come back early,' she said. 'I'll take the train up.'

She pulled her phone out of her back pocket and opened an app.

'What are you doing?'

'It's the Metrolink app. You keep saying you're going to take the train down to see me. You gotta get the app. There's a six thirty I could take up, gets to Union Station at eight twenty.'

'You sure?'

'Yeah, it says it right—'

'No, I mean about you coming up.'

'Of course. I want to be there for you.'

Bosch hugged her again.

'Okay, I'll text you the details. I don't think court starts till about ten. Maybe we do breakfast before-unless I have to meet with your uncle.'

'Okay. Whatever.'

'What are you going to pick up for dinner?'

'I want to get Zankou and bring it down, but then my car will smell like garlic for about a month.'

'That might be worth it.'

Zankou Chicken was a local chain of Armenian fast-food restaurants that had been a favorite takeout source for them over the years.

'Bye, Dad.'

He stayed on the curb until he watched her car make the turn and disappear down the hill. Back in the house, he looked at the business card she'd left on the table and thought about calling Ramsey to set him straight. He decided against it. Ramsey wasn't his opponent and it would be better not to use the newspaper to let his real opponents know what was coming. The *Times* reporter would undoubtedly be in court Wednesday and would get the full story then. Bosch just had to nut it out for three days under the shadow the newspaper story had shrouded his life in.

Bosch opened his phone and, after doing some research online to get the number, called the Van Nuys jail and asked for the control officer. He identified himself and said he wanted to set up an interview with a custody on the female tier.

'Can it wait?' the officer asked. 'It's Sunday night and I don't have people to sit on an interview room.'

'It's a double homicide,' Bosch said. 'I need to talk to her.'

'Okay, what's the name?'

'Elizabeth Clayburgh.'

Bosch heard him type it into his computer.

'Nope,' the officer said. 'We don't have her.'

'Sorry, I meant Clayton,' Bosch said. 'Elizabeth Clayton.'

More typing.

'We don't have her either,' the officer said. 'She R-O-R'ed a couple hours ago.'

Bosch knew that meant she was released on her own recognizance.

'Wait a minute,' he said. 'You let her go?'

'No choice,' the officer said. 'Capacity protocol. Nonviolent offense.'

Countywide, the jail system was overcrowded, and nonviolent offenders were regularly released early from minor sentences or released without having to post bail.

Elizabeth Clayton had apparently fallen into the latter category and was released after one day and before she could be placed in a drug rehabilitation unit.

'Wait a minute, wasn't she in detox?' Bosch asked. 'You release early from detox now?'

'I don't have her on the box as having been in detox,' the officer said. 'They have a waiting list in detox, anyway. Sorry, Detective.'

Bosch held his frustration in check and was about to thank the officer and hang up. Then he thought about something else.

'Can you put another name in, just to see if you have him?'

'Give it to me.'

'Male, white, last name Brody. I don't have a first handy.'

'Well, that might be a – no, I found him. James Brody, also arrested Saturday, same charge-prescription fraud. Yeah, he got kicked too.'

'Same time as Clayton?'

'No, earlier. By a couple hours. Most violent offenders are male and that's who we need to make room for. So the male NVs get out sooner than the ladies.'

Bosch thanked the officer and disconnected. Five minutes later he was in his Jeep, following the winding road down to the 101. He took the freeway north, back into the Valley, and over to Van Nuys. He made a call along the way to Cisco, attempting to make arrangements for Elizabeth Clayton, if he could find her.

The jail from which Clayton and Brody had been released was located on the top floor of the LAPD's Valley Bureau Headquarters, which anchored a mini-civic center, where local courthouses, a library, and satellite city hall and federal buildings were located at the edges of a public plaza.

Bosch parked on Van Nuys Boulevard at the western end of the plaza and started walking toward the Valley Bureau at the far end of the concrete-and-tree-lined concourse. It was a Sunday evening and the plaza was largely deserted except for the homeless strays who inhabited every parcel of public property in the city. Bosch could not remember the last time he had been in the plaza but thought it had been at least a couple of years. The bushes and shade trees around the contours of the buildings had all been cut back. Many had been replaced with palm trees that offered no cover. He knew this was a disguised effort to keep to a minimum the homeless population who were living in the plaza.

He checked every corner he passed and every homeless face that looked at him. He did not see Clayton or Brody. The library – usually a bastion for those with nowhere to go – was closed. Bosch covered one side of the plaza, until he got to the Valley Bureau building and then turned back and went down the other side. His search turned up nothing and he returned to his car.

Sitting behind the wheel, he thought about things and then called the number Jerry Edgar had given him when Bosch and Lourdes had visited his office. Edgar answered and it sounded like he had been asleep.

'Jerry, it's Harry. You up?'

'Just taking a nap. I bet you took a long one.'

'Yeah, sort of, but I have a question.'

'Shoot.'

'The woman you and Hovan arrested at the pharmacy

yesterday with the others?'

'Yeah, with the shaved head.'

'Exactly. I wanted to talk to her. Bella said she got booked into Van Nuys. I just went there and they kicked her loose a couple hours ago.'

'Like I told you, Harry, this is not a high-priority crime. I don't know what it will take. Maybe if a million people die from this, people will wake up and pay attention.'

'Right, I know. I got a question. Where would she go? She's put out on the street in Van Nuys, needs a hit pretty bad by now, and she's on foot.'

'Shit, man, I have no idea where she—'

'Did you book her?'

'Yeah, I did. Me and Hovan booked them all.'

'Did you go through her stuff? What did she have?'

'She had a fake ID, Harry. There was nothing there.'

'Right, right, I forgot. Shit.'

There was a pause before Edgar finally spoke.

'What do you need her for? She's a lifer, man, I could tell.'

'It's not like that. One of the guys you busted her with, Brody – he was kicked too.'

'He's the guy you wanted out of the picture.'

'Yeah, because he had it in for me and for her. Now today I find out he got released a couple hours ahead of her from the same jail. If she runs into him on the street, he's gonna either hurt her because of me or find a way to use her to get his next hit. Either way, I can't let that happen.'

Bosch knew that it was not unusual in the drug underworld for a male user to connect with a female in an alliance where one could provide protection while the other procured drugs through sexual barter. Sometimes the alliance wasn't voluntary on the woman's part.

'Fuck, Harry, I don't know,' Edgar said. 'Where are you?'

'The Van Nuys jail,' Bosch said. 'I looked around, she's not here.'

There was a longer pause this time before Edgar broke the silence.

'Harry, what's going on? I mean, it's been a while, but I remember Eleanor.'

Bosch's ex-wife and the mother of his daughter. Now deceased. Bosch had forgotten that he and Edgar were partners when he met her and later when he married her. Edgar had picked up on the resemblance in Elizabeth Clayton.

'Look, it's not that,' Bosch said. 'She did me a solid when I was under. I owe her and now she's out here somewhere on the street. And that guy Brody is too.'

Edgar said nothing, his silence making it clear he was not convinced.

'I gotta go,' Bosch said. 'If you think of something, call me back, partner.'

Bosch disconnected.

32

Bosch started driving north on Van Nuys Boulevard, looking at every pedestrian and in every recess behind the facade of every store and business. He knew it was a needle-in-a-haystack proposition but he had no other ideas. He considered calling the Van Nuys Division watch office to ask the lieutenant to put a flag out to all patrol units, but he knew that on a Sunday evening the number of cars on the street would be low and the request from the SFPD would not be treated with any kind of enthusiasm. It could also blow back on him with Chief Valdez asking the same sort of questions Edgar had asked.

So he continued the solo search, turning around at Roscoe and making his way south. He was twenty minutes into it when he got a call back from Edgar.

'Harry, you still up there looking for her?'

'Yeah, you got something?'

'Look, man, I'm sorry about my assumptions from before, okay? I'm sure you have good reason to—'

'Jerry, you have something for me, or are you just calling to shoot the breeze? Because I don't—'

'I have something, okay? I have something.'

'Then give it to me.'

Bosch pulled to the curb to listen and possibly take notes.

'We have something at the office we call the hot one hundred,' Edgar said. 'These are doctors who are on our radar as likely being involved with cappers and shady scrip writing. Doctors we're building cases on.'

'Was Efram Herrera on there?'

'Not yet, because I hadn't taken up that complaint, remember?'

'Right.'

'Anyway, I just called one of my colleagues and asked about Van Nuys. She told me there's a hot one hundred guy up there who runs a clinic on Sherman Way. It's supposedly seven days a week and some of the intel on him is that if you're a woman and need a scrip, he is more than likely going to offer a discount for special favors, if you know what I mean. This doctor's in his seventies, but—'

'What's the name of the clinic?'

'Sherman Health and Med, at Sherman Way and Kester. The doctor's name is Ali Rohat. People call him Chemical Ali because he comes through with the meds – the chems – and he's one-stop shopping. Known to prescribe and fill. If your girl is plugged into the scene up there at all, she'd know about him.'

'She's not my girl, but I appreciate it, Jerry.'

'I was joking, man. Jesus. Still Hard-Ass Harry, after all these years.'

'That's right. This guy Chemical Ali, how come he wasn't shut down with all that you're saying?'

'Like I told you before, Harry, these things are tough. Medical bureaucracy, Sacramento bureaucracy ... We'll shut him down eventually.'

'Okay, thanks for your help. Anything else comes to mind, hit me back.'

Bosch disconnected and pulled away from the curb. He made a U-turn and took Van Nuys back up to Sherman Way, where he turned west. He drove through the intersection at Kester without seeing the clinic. He continued a few blocks and then turned around.

On the second go-by he saw the clinic in the inside corner of the small shopping plaza. A liquor store and a pizza shop were open as well, and the parking lot was half-filled with cars. Bosch pulled down the sun visor to give him a bit of a visual blind and pulled in. He cruised through the lot, keeping an eye on the clinic. There was a pass-through to either a rear alley or another parking lot. The clinic's entrance was in this passage, which gave it visual protection. At a quick glance, he saw people milling about outside the door to the clinic but he could not identify anyone.

He turned out of the lot and went down a block before finding an alley that would take him to the rear of the shopping plaza. He cruised by and saw a line of head-in parking spaces behind the plaza's stores. Parked first in line by the pass-through was a Mercedes-Benz coupe with a vanity plate that said DR ALI. As he went by, he got a better look at the people congregating by the clinic door. Three men, none of whom Bosch recognized, other than that they had the haggard and desperate look of addicts. He almost smiled when he saw one of them was wearing a knee brace similar to the one he had employed.

At Sherman Way he turned right and entered the front lot of the plaza again. He went down the first lane and took a parking place that would allow him to see into the pass-through. The clients were mostly just in silhouette, but he was confident that he would be able to identify a female figure if a woman left the clinic.

Bosch pulled his phone, Googled the name of the clinic, and got a phone number. He called and asked the woman who answered how long the clinic would be open.

'We are closing soon,' she said. 'The doctor must leave at eight.'

Bosch thanked her and disconnected. He checked his wrist and realized he had forgotten to put his watch back on after coming in from undercover. He looked at the dash and saw he had twenty minutes until closing time. He settled in and kept his eyes on the clinic's entrance.

Ten minutes into the surveillance, Bosch's attention was drawn to his right, to the pizza shop. It appeared to be largely a takeout-and-delivery operation, but two tables were set up on the sidewalk out front. Bosch noticed a man wearing an apron leaning through the front door, gesturing and talking to a man sitting by himself at one of the tables. The seated man was partially hidden from Bosch's view by a row of potted plants. He would not have even noticed him if the man with the apron had not come to the door.

It looked to Bosch like the aproned man was telling the other man to leave. He was pointing toward the parking lot. Bosch lowered his windows so he might be able to hear the confrontation, but it ended abruptly with the man behind the plants standing up and cursing the pizza man. He then walked out from the seating area and headed down the line of shops toward Sherman Way.

Bosch immediately recognized him. It was Brody.

All at once Bosch felt a charge and a sense of dread. He thought he understood things. Brody knew about Chemical Ali but had no money upon his release from jail and nothing to offer. Brody had followed Elizabeth Clayton from the jail and was watching and waiting for her to emerge with pills in her possession so he could take them and then exact his misguided revenge.

He knew the situation could also be that Clayton and Brody had come to the clinic together and he was simply waiting for her to come out, but from what Bosch knew of her leave-me-alone personality, he didn't see her as a team player.

Bosch got out of the Jeep, quickly went to the back, and raised the tailgate. Because he was not assigned a vehicle at SFPD, he carried his work kit in the back of his own car. This was a duffel bag filled with personal equipment he might need in any circumstance that might come up during an investigation. He looked back over his shoulder and caught sight of Brody making it to the end of the plaza and turning the corner heading west. Bosch knew that would take him to the back alley and possibly down to the pass-through, where Clayton would emerge if she was in the clinic.

Bosch quickly unzipped the go bag and rummaged through it. He found a Dodgers baseball hat and, putting it on, pulled the brim down over his forehead. Then he found the plastic zip ties and took two. He coiled them so they would fit in the back pocket of his jeans. He zipped the bag closed and dropped the tailgate. He was ready.

After checking the corner of the plaza for any sign of Clayton, Bosch headed to the end of the plaza where he had last seen Brody. He quickly covered the distance and turned onto the sidewalk fronting Sherman Way. There was no sign of Brody, and that confirmed for Bosch that he had slipped down the alley behind the plaza. He moved quickly to the alley entrance and made the turn as well.

Again, there was no sign of the man. The alley was much darker than when Bosch had driven through earlier. The dimming light of dusk was reduced to shadow because of the structures on either side of the alley. Bosch proceeded cautiously, trying to hold to the shadows himself as he moved along.

'Where's your cane now, shitbird?'

Bosch turned at the sound of the voice in time to see Brody stepping out from between two Dumpsters and swinging a broomstick. Bosch was able to cock his left arm like a chicken wing, raise it, and take the main force of the blow across the forearm.

The impact sent a jolt of pain shooting up Bosch's arm. But it only served to sharpen his response. Rather than step back, Bosch stepped into Brody, whose momentum was carrying him forward. He brought his knee up hard into Brody's crotch and heard the air blast out of him. The broomstick clattered to the asphalt and Brody doubled over. Bosch grabbed the back of his shirt, pulled it up over his head and shoulders, and swung him around 180 degrees before releasing him headfirst into the side of one of the Dumpsters. Brody hit and went down with a groan.

Bosch moved in. Because Brody's arms and wrists were tangled in the shirt, Bosch went to his ankles.

'Nice move,' Bosch said. 'Warning me like that. Smart.'

Bosch pulled the zip ties out of his back pocket and secured Brody's ankles tightly, using both plastic strips to double down on the bindings. Of course, Brody could easily work his hands free of the shirt, Bosch knew, but then he would be faced with the dilemma of how to free his feet. He would have to pogo out of the alley and find someone willing to cut him loose. It would slow him down long enough for Bosch to do what he needed to do.

The quickest way to the clinic was to continue down the alley. As Bosch went along, he noticed two figures moving away in the darkness from the pass-through. It was too dark for him to determine their gender, so he picked up his pace to a trot and soon he got close enough to see they were men.

Bosch moved by the Mercedes, cut into the pass-through, and went to the clinic door. It was locked. He rapped hard on the glass with his fist. He noticed an intercom box mounted on the door's frame and pushed the button three times.

A few moments later, a woman's voice sounded from the box. Bosch recognized it from the call he had made to the clinic earlier.

'We're closed. I'm sorry.'

Bosch pushed the button to respond.

'Police. Open the door.'

There was no response. Then a man's voice with a Middle Eastern accent came from the box.

'Do you have a warrant?'

'I just want to talk, Doctor. Open up.'

'Not without a warrant. You need a warrant.'

'Okay, Doc. Then what I'm going to do is wait for you at your Mercedes in the alley. I've got all night.'

Bosch waited. Ten seconds went by while the doctor apparently considered his options. The door was then opened by a woman wearing nursing scrubs. Behind her stood a man with white hair who Bosch assumed was Dr. Rohat.

The woman pushed her way through the door and past Bosch.

'Wait a minute,' he said.

'I'm going home,' the woman said.

She kept going toward the alley.

'We are closed,' the man said. 'Her work is done today.'

Bosch looked at him.

'You're Chemical Ali?'

'What?' the man exclaimed indignantly. 'I am Dr. Rohat.'

He gestured toward a wall behind a reception counter, where there were several framed diplomas with writing too small to read.

Bosch couldn't be one hundred percent sure that Clayton was in the clinic. Brody could have been waiting and watching for any frail-looking patient to rip off. But the intel from Edgar about Rohat's proclivities made him feel like he was on firm ground.

'Elizabeth Clayton, where is she?' Bosch asked.

Rohat shook his head.

'I do not know that name,' he said.

'Sure you do,' Bosch said. 'Is she in there?'

'There is no one here. We are closed.'

'Bullshit. You would've walked out with the nurse if you were done here. Do I have to go through this whole place? Where is she?'

'We are closed.'

The sound of something clattering to the floor came from behind the closed door behind the reception counter. Bosch immediately pushed by Rohat and headed toward the door, assuming it led to the rear offices and exam rooms.

'All right!' Rohat exclaimed. 'I have a patient in room three. She is resting and should not be disturbed. She is sick.'

Bosch didn't break stride. He went through the door, Rohat calling after him.

'Wait! You can't go in there.'

There were no markings on any of the doors that lined the rear hallway. Bosch went to the third door on the left and flung it open. It was a storage room that looked like it was managed by a hoarder. There was junk piled upon junk. Bicycles, TVs, computer equipment. Bosch assumed these were the things Rohat took in trade for prescriptions and drugs. He left the door open and went across the hall to the door directly opposite.

Elizabeth Clayton was in the room. She was sitting on an examination table, a paper drape sheet wrapped around her shoulders and covering most of her body, her bare legs dangling off the table. On the floor was the source of the sound Bosch had heard. A stainless-steel cup lying in a pool of spilled water.

Clayton was naked beneath the drape sheet and one of her breasts was exposed, though she seemed unaware of it. The skin of her breast was a shocking white against her chest and neck, which had been burned dark brown by so many days spent in the desert sun. She was in a daze and did not even look up as Bosch entered. She was staring at the tattoo of the stars on her hand.

'Elizabeth!'

She slowly raised her chin as Bosch came to her. She dropped her hand into her lap, and her eyes held on his. He saw recognition in them but no understanding of where she knew him from.

'I'm going to take care of you. How much did he give you?'

He started to pull the sheet around her to cover her nakedness. Her body was emaciated and he wanted to look away but didn't. She held one of her hands between her legs, not in a show of modesty but in what Bosch interpreted was a meager protective gesture.

'I'm not going to hurt you,' he said. 'You remember me? I'm here to help.'

He got no response.

'Can you get up? Can you get dressed?'

Rohat came into the room behind him.

'You are not allowed in here! She is a patient and what you—'

'What did you give her?'

Bosch turned on him.

'I don't discuss patient care with—'

Bosch lunged at him and drove him backward into

312

the wall. Ali's head banged against a print showing the vital organs of the human body. Bosch gripped the lapels of his white lab coat and pushed hard against him.

'You're not a doctor, you're a monster. And I don't care how old you are, I will beat you to death in this room if you don't answer my questions. How much did you give her?'

Bosch could see real fear in Rohat's eyes now.

'I prescribed two eighty-milligram oxycodone pills for pain. It is time-release and to be taken separately, but when I was not in the room, she crushed and snorted them both. This tripped her into an overdose. It is not my fault.'

'Bullshit, not your fault. How long ago?'

'Two hours. I am treating her with naloxone and she'll be fine, as you can see by her sitting up.'

'And what did you do to her while she was out? You fuck her, you piece of shit?'

'I did not.'

'Yeah, well, we'll see about that when I take her to the rape center.'

'We had sex before, yes. She agreed. It was completely consensual.'

'Fuck you, consensual. You're going to go to jail.'

Bosch's anger overcame him, and he swung Rohat away from the wall so that when he punched him he'd have the satisfaction of seeing Rohat's head snap back before he dropped like a wet blanket. Bosch pulled his left arm back to deliver the blow. But before he brought his fist forward, there was a loud beep from the intercom box on the wall next to the door.

Bosch hesitated. That gave Rohat time to bring his

hands up to block or at least slow down the coming impact.

'Please,' the doctor begged.

'Hey, I know you,' Elizabeth said.

Bosch dropped his left and used his right to shove Rohat toward the intercom.

'Tell them to get lost.'

Rohat pushed the intercom button.

'We are closed, sorry.'

He looked back at Bosch for approval. Then a voice Bosch recognized came through the intercom.

'Jerry Edgar, Medical Board of California. Open up.'

Bosch nodded. His old partner had come through.

'Go let him in,' he said.

33

Edgar came into the examination room as Bosch was helping Elizabeth get dressed.

'Harry, I saw your car out there. I thought maybe you needed help.'

'I do, partner. Help me get her dressed. I have to get her out of here.'

'We should call an ambulance or something. This is crazy.'

'Just hold her up. She's coming out of it.'

Bosch was trying to pull her blue jeans up her rail-thin legs. He coaxed her into a standing position and then Edgar held her steady as Bosch brought the pants up over the bony points of her hips.

'I wanna leave,' she said.

'That's exactly what we're doing, Elizabeth,' Bosch said.

'He's a mean motherfucker,' she said.

Bosch was about to agree and looked around the room.

'Hey, where's Rohat?'

Edgar did the same quick survey. Rohat wasn't in the room.

'I don't—'

'I've got her. Go check.'

Edgar left the room. Bosch turned Elizabeth so her

back was to him. He quickly reached down to the pale yellow jacket that was in the pile of her clothes on the floor. He held it around in front of her.

'Can you put this on? We'll take the rest of your clothes with us.'

She took the jacket and slowly started to put one of her arms into a sleeve. Bosch gently pulled the paper sheet off her shoulders and dropped it to the floor. He saw the full RIP tattoo on the back of her shoulder.

DAISY
1994–2009

A fifteen-year-old girl, Bosch thought. That gave him a clue and an understanding that made him all the more resolved to stay on this path with Elizabeth.

Operating mechanically, Elizabeth managed to pull the jacket on but fumbled with the zipper. Bosch turned her around and zipped it up. He then gently pushed her back onto the exam table so he could put on her socks and shoes.

Edgar returned from his search for Rohat.

'He's gone. He must've slipped out after he let me in.'

He looked relieved and Bosch realized it had nothing to do with Rohat. It was because Elizabeth was now fully dressed.

'Probably because I told him he was going to jail. Doesn't matter. We can hook him up later. Let's get her out of here.'

'To where? No shelter's going to take her in this condition. We have to go to a hospital, Harry.'

'No, no hospital, and I'm not talking about a shelter. Hold her steady.'

'You can't be serious, Harry. You're not taking her home.'

'I'm not taking her home. Let's get her to the door and then I'll pull my car up.'

It took almost ten minutes to move Elizabeth through the clinic and out the exit to the passage connecting the front and back of the plaza.

'This way,' Bosch said.

He led her toward the front parking area. Once there, he left her leaning against Edgar and ran across the asphalt to his Jeep. He scanned his surroundings as he went and saw no sign of Brody.

Bosch brought the Jeep up to Edgar and Elizabeth and then hopped out to help get her into the front passenger seat and secure her with the seat belt.

'Harry, where are you going?'

'A treatment center.'

'Which one?'

'It doesn't have a name.'

'Harry, what the fuck?'

'Jerry, you gotta trust me. I'm doing what's best for her, and it doesn't have anything to do with what the rules are. I am past all of that, okay? What you need to worry about is how to secure these premises now that Chemical Ali is on the run. There are probably enough pills in that clinic to create an army of zombies like her.'

Bosch stepped back, closed the door to the Jeep, and moved around to the driver's side.

'And that army's going to be here by sunup.'

As Bosch slipped into the Jeep, he saw Edgar glance

back at the entrance to the unlocked clinic. Once inside the car, he checked Elizabeth and saw that she was leaning her head against the window of the passenger-side door and already nodding off.

Bosch pulled away and headed for the parking lot exit. He checked Edgar in the rearview. His former partner was just standing there, watching Bosch drive away.

The good news was that they didn't have far to go. He got back over to Van Nuys Boulevard and took it north to Roscoe. He turned west at that point and took Roscoe under the 405 freeway and into an industrial neighborhood dominated by the size and smell of the giant Anheuser-Busch brewery, its stacks billowing beer smoke into the night.

Bosch made two wrong turns in the neighborhood before finally finding the place he was looking for. The entrance gate in the metal and barbed-wire fence that surrounded the property was open. There was no sign on the building, not even an address, but the row of six Harleys parked out front was the dead giveaway.

Bosch parked as close as he could to the black door at the center of the structure's facade. He got out and went around to help Elizabeth. He put his arm across her back and half held her up as they approached the door.

'Come on, Elizabeth, help me here. Walk. You gotta walk.'

The door opened before they got to it.

Cisco stood there.

'How is she?' he asked.

'She was able to get a heavy hit before I could find her,' Bosch said. 'She OD'd and then was given Narcan and is coming out of it. Are you ready for her?'

'We're ready. Let me take her.'

Cisco bent down and simply picked Elizabeth up and carried her inside. Bosch followed and, once past the threshold, saw what was not revealed on the outside-a clubhouse. There were two pool tables in a large room, as well as an unmanned bar, couches, tables, and chairs. Neon signs depicted skulls and motorcycle wheels with halos – the symbols of the Road Saints. A couple of large men with long beards watched Cisco and company parade through.

Bosch followed Cisco down a dimly lit hallway and into a small room that was equally dim and contained only an army cot like the one Bosch had spent the past two nights on in the migrant bus in the desert.

Cisco put Elizabeth down gently on the cot and then took a step back and looked at her skeptically.

'You sure you shouldn't have taken her to the hospital?' he asked. 'We can't have her croak in here. If she does, she disappears. They aren't going to call in the coroner, you know what I mean.'

'I know,' Bosch said. 'But she's coming out of it. I think she'll be okay. The doctor said so.'

'The quack doctor, you mean?'

'He wouldn't have wanted her dying in his place either.'

'How much did she take?'

'She crushed two eighties.'

Cisco whistled.

'Sounds like she maybe kinda wanted to end things, you know?'

'Maybe, maybe not. So . . . this is where you did it? This room?'

'Different room, same place. I was nailed in. This one's got locks on the outside of the door.'

'And she's safe here?'

'I guarantee it.'

'Okay. I'm going to leave and come back in the morning. Early. I'll talk to her then. And you're all set?'

'We're set. I'll wait on the Suboxone until you come back and she can decide. Remember, she's gotta make the call or we're done here.'

'I know. Just keep an eye on her and I'll be back.'

'Will do.'

'And thanks.'

'Pay it forward, isn't that what they say? This is me paying it forward.'

'That's good.'

Bosch stepped close to the cot and bent over to look down at Elizabeth. She was already asleep but seemed to be breathing normally. He then straightened up and turned toward the door.

'Need me to bring anything when I come back?' he asked.

'Nope,' Cisco said. 'Unless you want to bring me back my cane and knee brace, if you're done with them.'

'Uh, yeah, that might be a problem. Both were seized as evidence in the case.'

'Evidence of what?'

'That's a long story. But I may have to replace those for you.'

'Forget it. In a way, they were a temptation. Good to be rid of them, I guess.'

'I get that.'

Bosch got back into the Jeep and considered the trek

home – at least forty minutes in Sunday-night traffic – and felt so besieged and tired that he knew he could not make it. He thought about how easily Elizabeth had fallen asleep with her head against the glass. He reached down to the seat's side lever and popped the back rest to its farthest recline angle.

He closed his eyes and was soon dead to the world in a deep sleep.

Eight hours later the unfiltered light of dawn snuck in under Bosch's eyelids and woke him. He looked around and saw that there was only one motorcycle parked next to the Jeep. The others had somehow left in the night without their pipes penetrating his sleep. It was a testament to his exhaustion.

The one remaining bike had a black fuel tank with orange flames painted on it. Bosch recognized a match to the paint job of the cane Cisco had lent him. It told him that Cisco was still on duty.

After getting his bearings, Bosch unlocked the glove compartment and checked to make sure his gun and badge were still there.

Nothing had been taken. He relocked the compartment, climbed out of the Jeep, and went inside. He saw no one in the front room and proceeded down the hallway toward the rear of the structure. He found Cisco sitting on a cot that had been set up across the door to the room where Bosch had left Elizabeth Clayton almost eight hours before.

Next to the cot there was a short stool used for sitting on while working on a motorcycle engine.

'You're back.'

'Technically, I never left. How is she?'

'It was a good night – no bumps. She's been awake now for about an hour and is starting to hit the wall. So you should go in the room and talk to her before she starts chewing her fingernails off.'

'Right.'

Cisco got up to move the cot out of the way.

'Take the stool. Be on her level when you talk.'

Bosch grabbed the stool, turned the lock on the door, and entered the room.

Elizabeth was in a sitting position on her cot, leaning back against the wall, arms folded in front of her chest, showing the early stages of need. She leaned forward when she saw Bosch enter.

'You,' she said. 'I thought it was you last night.'

'Yeah, me,' he said.

He put the stool down four feet from the cot and sat down.

'Elizabeth, my name's Harry. My real name, that is.'

'What the fuck is this? Am I in jail again? Are you a narc?'

'No, you're not in jail and I'm not a narc. But you can't leave yet.'

'What are you talking about? I need to go.'

She made a move to get up but Bosch shot up off the stool and put his hands out, ready to push her back down on the cot. She stopped.

'What are you doing to me?'

'I'm trying to help you. You remember what you said to me when I got on the plane the first time? You said, "Welcome to hell." Well, all of that is gone now. The Russians, the camp down there, the planes, everything.

All shut down, the Russians are dead. But you're still in hell, Elizabeth.'

'I really need to go now.'

'Where? Chemical Ali's gone. He was shut down last night. There's nowhere to go. But we can help you here.'

'What do you have? I need it.'

'No, not like that. I mean, really help you. Get you off this addiction and out of this life.'

She shrieked with laughter, a short staccato burst.

'You think you can save me? You think you're the only one who's ever tried? Forget it. Fuck you. I can't be saved. I told you before. I don't want to be saved.'

'I think you do. Deep down, everybody does.'

'No, please. Just let me go.'

'I know it's going to be rough. A week in this room, it will probably feel like a year. I'm not going to lie to you about anything.'

Elizabeth raised her hands to her face and started crying. Bosch couldn't tell whether it was a last-ditch effort to use his sympathy to get out of the room or whether the tears were truly for herself and what she knew lay ahead. Bosch didn't want her to leave the room but he needed to get her to acknowledge and approve of what was happening.

'There's a guy sitting outside the door who is here for you. His name's Cisco. He's been where you are.'

'Please, I can't.'

'Yes, you can. But you've got to want it. Deep down. You have to know that you are in the abyss and that you want to climb out.'

'No,' she moaned.

Bosch now knew the tears were real. Between her fingers he could see true fear in her eyes.

'Has any doctor ever put you on Suboxone? It helps. You still carry the weight of withdrawal, but it helps.'

She shook her head and was back to holding her arms tightly across her chest.

'It will help you. But you have to gut it out and you've got to want to.'

'I'm telling you, nothing works. I can't be saved.'

'Look, I know you lost somebody. You've got it written on your skin. I know it can drive you down into a hole. But think of Daisy. Is this the end she would want for you?'

Elizabeth didn't answer. She brought a hand up to cover her eyes again while she cried.

'Of course it's not,' Bosch said. 'It's not what she would want.'

'Please,' Elizabeth said. 'I want to go now.'

'Elizabeth, just tell me you want this to end. Give me the nod and we'll get through it.'

'I don't even know you!' she screamed.

'You're right,' Bosch said, his voice remaining calm. 'But I know there is something better than this for you. Tell me you want it. For Daisy.'

'I want to go.'

'There's nowhere to go. This is it.'

'Fuck.'

'Stay here, Elizabeth. Say you want to try.'

She stopped hiding behind her hand and dropped it lifelessly into her lap. She looked away from him to her right.

'Come on,' Bosch said. 'For Daisy. It's time.'

Clayton closed her eyes and held them closed as she spoke.

'Okay,' she said. 'I'll try.'

34

Bosch got to his breakfast meeting fifteen minutes late. Haller was in a booth near the back of the restaurant. Bosch slid in across from him, wondering if he could stomach any food. He decided not.

'You're late and you look like shit,' Haller said.

'Thanks,' Bosch said. 'Let's just say the past seventy-two hours haven't been the best of my life.'

'Then, good news, my brother. We're here to plot your rise from the ashes.'

'Sounds good to me.'

'You know, a lot has happened in the past seventy-two hours. I wish I had Cisco here to talk about his end of it, but he seems to be off the grid.'

'You can't fill me in?'

'Of course I can. The main thing is, we have a strong lineup of testimony for Wednesday, as long as we can get our foot in the door. That'll be the key. The D.A. and Cronyn are going to argue like hell to exclude us from the hearing, but I think we have a strong argument for standing. So I need you to practice your outrage.'

'I don't need to practice it. And Borders will be there?'

'The judge issued a transfer order. He's probably coming down in a van as we sit here.'

'Yeah, well, if he's there and that close to freedom, then I'll have all the outrage you need.'

Haller nodded. That's what he wanted to hear.

'Now, as upsetting as that article in the *Times* was, it's going to work in our favor,' the lawyer said. 'Because that kicks this thing out into the open, and the state's not going to be able to argue that your professional reputation hasn't taken a big hit. It's clear as day, right there in black and white.'

'Good,' Bosch said. 'I'm glad that's backfiring on that asshole Kennedy.'

'Right. Now, we have to be ready for all eventualities. After I make my argument, the judge might want to question you back in chambers. The story yesterday guarantees full media coverage of this, so the judge may want to take you back and hear your side of it before he puts it out in front of the media. You have a problem with that?'

'No, none.'

The waitress came to the table and Bosch ordered coffee. Haller ordered a short stack of pancakes and the waitress left them alone.

'You don't want to eat?' Haller asked.

'No, not now,' Bosch said. 'So what about Spencer, the counter guy? Where's that gone since I've been out of the loop?'

'We put a solid buzz in his ear last night.'

'What's that mean?'

'I had him hit with a subpoena. It freaked him the fuck out because he didn't know we were onto where they were hiding his ass.'

'Okay, back up. I've been out of the loop since Thursday, you remember? Last I heard, Cisco was on him and saw him meet with Cronyn's wife in the bookstore parking lot. What happened after that?'

'The next morning, I put Cisco back on him. Cronyn and Cronyn obviously suspected you were up to something and not going to take this lying down. So they tried to stash Spencer until after the hearing so we wouldn't have him. But fuck that, Cisco and his guys already had him and followed him to the stash house they set up down in Laguna. It was their own weekend house. You should've seen the look on Spencer's face when he got the subpoena.'

'You were there?'

'No, that would have been against the rules, me delivering a subpoena. But I've got the next best thing to being there.'

Haller pulled out his phone and continued as he set up the playback of a video.

'I issued a subpoena and faxed it to a P.I. I know down in OC. Lauren Sachs, ex-Orange County sheriff and a real looker. People call her Sexy Sachsy. She does a lot of matrimonial work now – you know, going into bars to see if the husband's got the wandering eye, that sort of thing. She's got these glasses with the hidden camera she wears on those jobs, and I told her I wanted a video record of service on this thing. This is what she got.'

Haller turned his phone so Bosch could see it. Harry leaned across the table so he could pick up the audio. On the screen was a door. It was shot through the point of view of Sachs's video glasses. Bosch saw her arm reach out as she knocked on the door. There was silence but then a shadow could be seen through an ornamental stained-glass square set in the center of the door.

Someone was standing silently on the other side.

'Mr. Spencer,' Sachs said. 'I need you to open the door, please.'

Her stern tone was met with a long silence.

'Mr. Spencer, I can see you,' Sachs said. 'Please open the door.'

'Who are you?' said a voice. 'What do you want?'

'I have legal documents for you to sign. From Los Angeles.'

'I don't know what you're talking about.'

'Your law firm is Cronyn and Cronyn, right? Then these are for you.'

No response. Then a lock could be heard turning, and the door opened three inches. A man looked out with one eye. But enough of his face appeared in the opening for Bosch and anyone else to confirm it was Spencer. Sachs quickly shoved a folded white document through the door. Spencer tried to close it but, unseen in the video, Sachs had put her foot over the threshold. The document got through and Spencer let it fall to the floor in the hallway behind him.

'That is a subpoena demanding your appearance in court this coming Wednesday morning,' Sachs said. 'It is all clear in the document you have been served with. If you do not appear, you will be subject to warrant and arrest by the Los Angeles County Sheriff's Department. I'd be there if I were you.'

Spencer's eyes widened as he realized that his worst nightmare was about to unfold. When he spoke, he stuttered.

'I – I – I'm not Terry Spencer.'

'Well, sir, I never used the name Terry here and the

subpoena says "Terrence." If I were you, I would not try that tack to avoid appearance in court. You have been duly and legally served, sir. I have documented service. To not show up or to claim you have not been served will only anger a Superior Court judge and probably your employer, the Los Angeles Police Department.'

Sachs removed her foot and Spencer closed the door. His shadow remained behind the stained-glass panel. Sachs held at the door for a moment, then reached out and knocked again, this time employing a gentle, almost sympathetic tap.

'A piece of advice, Mr. Spencer? Come with a lawyer. And you should know that using Kathy Cronyn would be a conflict of interest. Her firm represents the interests of Preston Borders, not yours. Have a good day, sir.'

The POV of the video swung 180 degrees as Sachs turned and walked down a stone pathway to a waiting car. The location was clearly the hills of Laguna, and Bosch could see the cobalt blue ocean over the roofline of the house across the street.

The video ended and Haller took his phone back. He looked at Bosch with a smile.

'Pretty neat, huh?' he said. 'I think we teed up Mr. Spencer pretty good.'

'What do you think he'll do?'

'I'm hoping he shows up. I told her to say that part about angering the judge and his employer. Maybe that will make him show.'

'Did you tell her to suggest he bring a lawyer? A lawyer might tell him to take the fifth.'

'Maybe. But I thought it was worth the risk. We need

him to cut the Cronyns loose. The hope is he won't let them know what's going on.'

'I get that, but if he takes the fifth, we'll never know how he played the evidence and got into that box.'

'Some secrets you live with if you win your case. Know what I mean?'

'I guess. What else have we got?'

'Well, that's where I need you, broheim. Cisco is at large – I hope he hasn't slipped up – and I need an investigator. I want to locate—'

'Just so you know, Cisco's been working for me. Since yesterday afternoon. Not on this. On a personal matter.'

Haller laughed, thinking it was a joke.

'I'm serious,' Bosch said.

'A personal matter,' Haller said. 'What personal matter?'

'He's helping a friend of mine and it's confidential. It's got nothing to do with this.'

'It has everything to do with this if I don't have my investigator. What the fuck is going on?'

'Look, it was an emergency and I needed him. He'll be clear later on and I'll be able to tell you all about it then. But you've got me. You said you want to locate something or somebody. What? Who?'

Haller stared at him for a long moment before answering.

'It's a who,' he finally said. 'I pulled the court file on the original trial and have been reading the transcription. I want to locate Dina Skyler.'

Bosch didn't need long to place the name. Dina was Danielle Skyler's sister. She was the one who had been scheduled to visit Danielle through the holidays.

The visit never happened but Dina did come out from Hollywood, Florida, during the trial to testify about the plans the sisters had for living together and taking Hollywood, California, by storm. Dina was younger and Danielle had been protective of her. While testifying, she spoke of their loving the movie *White Christmas* – because it was a show business story about two sisters. She told the jury that every holiday season, they would put on a rendition of the song 'Sisters' for their parents.

Dina was a powerful witness during the penalty stage of the trial. Bosch had always felt that her hour of tearful testimony was what swayed both the jury and then the judge toward the death penalty.

'I'm thinking we might need her for the emotional pull,' Haller said. 'I want the judge to know the family still cares, that the victim's sister is right there in the courtroom, and he had better get this thing right.'

'She was a strong presence at the trial.'

'Did she ever move out here, like she and her sister planned?'

'Yeah, she did. I stayed in touch with her at the beginning and then it kind of tapered off. I think I was a reminder of what had happened to Dani. I got the message and stopped checking on her.'

'Dani?'

'Danielle. People who knew her called her Dani.'

'If you are allowed to testify Wednesday – and I will go apeshit crazy if you're not – make sure you call her that.'

Bosch didn't respond. These kind of subtle manipulations were part of Haller's daily life but they always bothered Bosch, even if they were done in his favor.

He felt that if he didn't condone them from attorneys working against him, he shouldn't accept them from one working for him.

Haller moved on.

'So, did she make it?' he asked. 'I looked her up on IMDB and there was nothing. Did she change her name or something?'

'Uh, I didn't really track that. I don't know whether she stayed in the business.'

'Do you think you can find her?'

'If she's alive, I'll find her. But if she's not in L.A., I don't know about getting her here by Wednesday morning.'

'Right. Just see what you can do. Maybe we get lucky.'

'Maybe. What else?'

'For you, that's it. I'm going to work here this morning and figure out a case path.'

'What's that?'

'The one thing we can count on is that our request to intervene on the motion to vacate will draw heavy fire from both the D.A. and Borders. I'll make an argument and I'll offer a proffer to the judge – sort of an unofficial look at what we'll present if granted standing. I'll run down our witness list and say what each of them is willing to testify to. If we convince the judge, then we're in and then we kick their asses.'

'Got it. Do you mind if I split? I gotta go in for some follow-up stuff this morning and I want to go to work on finding Dina.'

'No problem, Harry. Go get 'em. But between now and Wednesday get some sleep. I don't want you coming into that courtroom looking like you're guilty.'

Taking a last gulp of coffee, Bosch pointed a finger at Haller like a gun and then slid out of the booth. Haller spoke again before he could walk away.

'Hey, Harry, one last thing? You are a damn fine detective, brother, but I want my man Cisco back.'

'Right. I'll tell him.'

35

Bosch saw a TV truck from one of the Spanish-language stations parked in front of the SFPD headquarters when he drove in. He assumed it was there because of the *farmacia* murders, but he didn't think that what had happened over the weekend could be contained for very long, and the Spanish-language media was often ahead of the game when it came to the news in San Fernando.

Before going to his office in the jail across the street, Bosch went in the side door of the station to get more coffee and check on things in the detective bureau. It was a full house this time, with all three detectives in their work pods and even Captain Trevino visible behind his desk through the open door of his office.

Only Bella Lourdes looked up at Bosch's entrance, and she immediately signaled him over to her cubicle.

He held up a finger, telling her to hold a moment. He turned to the nearby coffee station and quickly poured his second jolt of the day into a cup. He then worked his way around the three-desk module to get to Bella's spot in the back.

'Morning, Harry.'

'Morning, Bella. What's up?'

She pointed to her computer screen, where a video was playing. It was obviously taken from a helicopter and shot downward at a water recovery of a body. Two divers were wrestling with the body of a man floating facedown. He was clothed but the T-shirt he wore was torn off and held to his body by the collar only. The rest of it waved in the water like a white flag of surrender. The divers were struggling as they tried to roll the body onto a rescue stretcher attached to a cable extending down from the chopper.

'Salton Sea,' Lourdes said. 'This was two hours ago. They spotted the body on a flyover at dawn.'

Bosch leaned down, careful not to spill his coffee, to look more closely at the screen and the body.

'That the second Russian?' Lourdes asked.

Before Bosch could answer, he noticed that they had been joined by Sisto, who was looking over Bella's other shoulder.

'Clothes look the same,' Bosch said. 'From what I can remember. Gotta be him.'

'I asked them to send us a close-up of the face once they have the body at the coroner's,' Lourdes said.

'That would wrap things up nice,' Sisto said. 'On our case at least.'

'Sure would,' Lourdes added. 'Why don't we all go into the war room for updates and to figure out who's doing what on this today?'

'Sounds like a plan,' Sisto said.

Lourdes got up and called to Trevino and Luzon.

Bosch could still smell the breakfast he had missed lingering in the air of the war room. The four detectives took seats around the table and Trevino joined as well. Bosch spoke first.

'Uh, before we start divvying up paperwork and stuff, I'm here to do what I need to do and be available

336

for any follow-ups with other agencies. But as you all know, I have a thing in court Wednesday morning with my reputation and possible future with this department on the line. So I need some prep time for that today. There are some things I have to do, and they can't wait.'

'Understood, Harry,' Trevino said. 'And if there's anything we can do here to help with that, you let me know. I've talked to the chief and, speaking for him and everybody in this room, we are behind you one hundred percent. We know what kind of detective and person you are.'

Bosch could feel his face turning red with embarrassment. In all his years in law enforcement, he had never heard such accolades from a supervisor.

'Thanks, Cap,' he managed to say.

They settled down and got to the business at hand, starting with Lourdes summarizing a report she had gotten that morning from Agent Hovan on the DEA's activities since the previous afternoon. She reported that the encampment down near Slab City had been raided and shut down. The addicted inhabitants were evacuated to the naval base in San Diego, where they were being medically evaluated before being offered placement in pro bono rehab programs.

Lourdes reported that the DEA had also shut down the clinic in Pacoima and arrested the men operating it, along with the physician of record, Efram Herrera. Among those arrested was the driver of the van. Though he was suspected of being the getaway driver in the *farmacia* murders, he had so far been charged under federal law only for taking part in a continuing criminal organization.

From there, report writing, follow-up inquiries, and notifications were distributed among the detectives, with Bosch getting a full pass. Lourdes and Luzon were assigned to go to the federal detention facility downtown and take a shot at interviewing the driver about the *farmacia* shootings, a task all of those in the room predicted would be fruitless. Fifteen minutes later Bosch was crossing the street to the old jail, carrying his third cup of coffee of the day. He noticed that the TV truck was now gone and he guessed that the reporter and crew had been shined on by Chief Valdez. A joint press conference on the case would be held at three p.m. at the station with DEA and state medical board officials. It would be announced that the double murder at La Farmacia Familia had been solved and that the suspects were dead, provided that Bosch was able later to identify the body recovered that morning from the Salton Sea as the second Russian.

Because Bosch had worked undercover on the case, he had an out and would not be required to appear at the press conference.

Besides his coffee, Bosch carried a file containing copies of documents that had been pulled together overnight on the case. The one he was most interested in studying was the Interpol report on the man he had killed on the plane. Once in his cell in the old jail, he sat down behind his makeshift desk and opened the file.

It turned out that the man he killed was not technically Russian, though it was clear from the Interpol data that he grew up speaking the language. Fingerprints had identified him as Dmitri Sluchek, born in 1980 in Minsk, Belarus. He had served time in two different Russian prisons for theft and assault. The Interpol file tracked him until 2008, when he slipped into the United States illegally and never returned. It described him at that time as a 'six' who was associated with a Minsk-based subset of the Russian *Bratva* – meaning 'brotherhood,' a general word encompassing all of Russian organized crime. The report stated that a six was a low-level mob associate used on the front line of criminal enterprises. The reference came from the lowest rank in a deck of cards used in a Russian game called The Sixes. Such associates were often used as enforcers until they showed leadership skills and were moved up to the position of *bratok*, or soldier.

It appeared to Bosch that once he was in the United States, Sluchek started showing leadership skills and had moved Santos out of the picture in the California operation. He assumed that if the man pulled that morning from the Salton Sea was identified, he would have a history similar to Sluchek's.

The report concluded that Sluchek was most likely still connected to the *Bratva* and reported to and contributed profits from the California operation to a *pakhan*, or boss, back in Minsk who had been identified as Oleg Novaschenko.

Bosch closed the file and thought about the chain of events that resulted in the Esquivels' being executed in their place of business and people like Elizabeth Clayton being literally enslaved in the desert. The seeds were planted thousands of miles away by faceless men of greed and violence. Bosch knew that people like Novaschenko and the men between him and Sluchek would never pay for their crimes here, and that their operation, though down now, would rise again in another spot with other sixes stepping up and showing their leadership skills. The men who fired bullets into José Esquivel Jr. and his father were dead, but the justice gained was small. Bosch could not bring himself to take part in a press conference to laud the quick closing of the case. Some cases were never closed.

Bosch put the file on a shelf behind his chair, where he put the cases he believed he had worked to the extent of his ability and reach.

He turned back to the desk and went to work on the computer, attempting to locate Dina Skyler. Using the department computer to further his own private investigations had been forbidden when he had first come to work in San Fernando. But once he built an impressive record of closing cases, that rule was treated with a wink and a nod. Valdez and Trevino wanted to keep him happy and in the office as often as possible.

The search didn't take long. Dina was still alive and still in L.A. She had gotten married and her last name was now Rousseau. The address on her current driver's license placed her on Queens Road above the Sunset Strip.

Bosch decided to go knock on her door.

PART THREE
The Intervention

36

Bosch got to Union Station by 8:15 Wednesday morning. He parked in the short-term lot in front and went inside to wait for his daughter. Her train was only ten minutes behind schedule, and when they connected in the vast central waiting area, she had no baggage with her and only carried a book. She explained that her plan was to take a train back down to San Diego after the court hearing-unless Bosch needed her to stay. They ate crepes – her choice – at the station for breakfast before crossing Alameda and walking through the plaza by the El Pueblo de Los Ãngeles on their way into the civic center. There, the monolithic Criminal Courts Building stood like a tombstone at the top of a rise.

They split up at the main entrance so Bosch could enter through the law enforcement pass-through because of his weapon. He showed his badge and made it through a solid ten minutes ahead of Maddie, who had to inch her way through the metal detector at the public entrance in a long line. They made up for the lost time by hopping onto an employees-only elevator and riding up to the ninth floor and Department 107, the courtroom at the end of the hallway, where Judge John Houghton presided.

The Preston Borders case was not scheduled to be called until ten a.m. but Mickey Haller had told Bosch

343

to get to court early so they could discuss last-minute details and maneuvers. Bosch appeared to be the first person on his team to arrive. He sat in the back row of the gallery with his daughter and watched the proceedings. Houghton, a veteran jurist with a shock of silver hair, was on the bench, going through a calendar call of other cases on his docket, getting updates and scheduling further hearings. There was also a video crew setting up a pool camera in the jury box. Haller had told Bosch that so many local news stations had requested access to the hearing following the *Times* story that Houghton had specified that one randomly chosen crew could record the hearing and then share the video feed with the others.

'Is he going to be here?' Maddie whispered.

'Who?' Bosch asked.

'Preston Borders.'

'Yes, he'll be here.'

He pointed to the metal door behind the desk where the courtroom deputy sat.

'He's probably in a holding cell back there now.'

Bosch realized by her first question that she might have a fascination with Borders, the unrepentant death row killer. He second-guessed his allowing his daughter to come.

Bosch looked around. While Houghton was not the original judge on the Borders case, Department 107 was the original courtroom, and it looked to Bosch like it hadn't been updated in the intervening thirty years. It was 1960s contemporary design, like most of the courthouses in the county. Light wood paneling covered the walls, with the judge's bench, witness stand, and clerk's corral all part of one module of sharp lines and faux wood. The great seal of the State of California was affixed to the wall at the front of the courtroom, three feet above the judge's head.

The courtroom was cool, but Bosch felt hot under the collar of his suit. He tried to calm himself and be ready for the hearing. The truth was, he felt powerless. His career and reputation were essentially going to be in Mickey Haller's hands and their fate possibly determined over the next few hours. As much as he trusted his half brother, passing the responsibility to someone else left him sweating in a cold room.

The first familiar face to enter the courtroom belonged to Cisco Wojciechowski. Bosch and his daughter slid down the bench and the big man sat down. He was as dressed up as Bosch had ever seen him, in clean black jeans and matching boots, an untucked white collared shirt, and a black vest with stylized swirls of silver thread. Bosch introduced his daughter and then she went back to reading her book, a collection of essays by a writer named B. J. Novak.

'How you feeling?' Cisco asked.

'One way or another, it will all be over in a few hours,' Bosch said. 'How's Elizabeth?'

'She had a rough night, but she's getting there. I got one of my guys watching her. Maybe if you can, you could come by and see her. Encourage her. Might help.'

'Sure. But when I was there yesterday, it looked like she wanted to use my head as a battering ram on the door.'

'You go through big changes in the first week. It will be different today. I think she's about to crest. It's an uphill battle and then there's a point where you're suddenly going down the other side of the mountain.'

Bosch nodded.

'The question is, what happens at the end of the week?' Cisco said. 'Do we just cut her loose, drop her off somewhere? She needs a long-range plan or she won't make it.'

'I'll think of something,' Bosch said. 'You just get her through the week and I'll take it from there.'

'You sure?'

'I'm sure.'

'Did you ever find anything out about the daughter? She still doesn't want to talk about it.'

'Yeah, I found out. Daisy. She was a runaway. Got into drugs in junior high, ran away from home. Was living on the street down in Hollywood and one night she got in the wrong car with somebody.'

'Shit.'

'She was . . .'

Bosch turned his body casually as if he were reaching down with his left hand to adjust the cuff of his right pant leg. His back to his daughter, he continued.

'Tortured – to put it politely – and left in a Dumpster in an alley off of Cahuenga.'

Cisco shook his head.

'I guess if anybody ever had a reason . . .'

'Right.'

'Did they at least catch the bastard?'

'Nope. Not yet.'

Cisco laughed without humor.

'Not yet?' he said. 'Like it's going to get solved ten years later?'

Bosch looked at him for a long moment without replying.

'You never know,' he said.

Haller entered the courtroom then, saw his investigator and client sitting together, and pointed in the direction of the hallway outside. He hadn't noticed Maddie because the two bigger men had eclipsed her from the doorway angle. Bosch whispered to Maddie to stay where she was, and started to get up. Maddie put her hand on his arm to stop him.

'Who were you just talking about?'

'Uh, a woman from a case. She needed help and I asked Cisco to get involved.'

'What kind of help? Who's Daisy?'

'We can talk about it later. I need to go out and talk to my – your uncle – about the hearing. Stay here and I'll be back.'

Bosch got up and followed Cisco out. Most people in the long hallway congregated down in the middle near the snack bar, restrooms, and elevators. Team Bosch found an open bench with some privacy by the door to Department 107 and sat down, Haller in the middle.

'Okay, boys, are we ready to rock?' the lawyer said. 'How are my witnesses? Where are my witnesses?'

'Locked and loaded, I think,' Cisco said.

'Tell me about Spencer,' Haller said. 'You guys stayed with him, right?'

'All night,' Cisco said. 'As of twenty minutes ago, he was still at his new lawyer's office in the Bradbury.'

Bosch knew that meant Spencer was only two blocks away. Haller turned on the bench and looked at him eye to eye.

'And you, I told you to get some sleep,' he said. 'But you still look like shit, and there's dust on the shoulders of that suit, man.'

Haller reached out and roughly slapped off the dust that had settled on the suit during the two or more years it had been on a hanger in Bosch's closet.

'I don't have to remind you, this is probably all going to come down to you,' Haller said. 'Be sharp. Be forthright. These people are fucking with everything that is important to you.'

'I know that,' Bosch said.

As if on cue, the CIU team came out of the stairwell down the hall, having taken the steps down from the D.A.'s Office. It was Kennedy, Soto, and Tapscott. They were heading to Department 107. Another woman, who was carrying a cardboard file box with two hands, followed. She was most likely Kennedy's assistant.

Further behind them, coming from the elevator alcove at the same time, walked Cronyn and Cronyn. Lance Cronyn wore steel-rimmed glasses and had slicked-back jet-black hair that was obviously dyed. His suit was black with pinstripes and his tie a loud aqua. He looked like he went to great lengths to appear young, and the reason was right next to him, matching him stride for stride. Katherine Cronyn was at least twenty years his junior. She had flowing red hair and a voluptuous figure clad in a blue calf-length skirt and matching jacket over a chiffon blouse.

'Here they all come,' Bosch said.

Haller looked up from a yellow legal pad he was referring to and saw the opposition approaching.

'Like lambs to slaughter,' he said, his voice brimming with bravado and confidence.

Team Bosch remained seated as the others made the turn toward the courtroom door. Kennedy kept his eyes averted, as though there was no one sitting on the bench fifteen feet away. But Soto locked eyes with Bosch and peeled off from her team to approach him. She was unhesitant about speaking in front of Haller and Wojciechowski.

'Harry, why didn't you call me back?' she asked. 'I left you several messages.'

'Because there was nothing to say, Lucia,' Bosch said. 'You guys believe Borders over me and there's nothing else to say.'

'I believe the forensic evidence, Harry. It doesn't mean I believe you planted the other evidence. The stuff in the paper didn't come from me.'

'Then how did the evidence I found get there, Lucia? How did Dani Skyler's pendant get into the suspect's apartment?'

'I don't know, but you weren't in there alone.'

'So you're still willing to pass the buck to a dead guy.'

'I didn't say that. What I'm saying is that I don't need to know the answer to that.'

Bosch stood up so he could speak to her face-to-face.

'Yeah, well, see, that doesn't work for me, Lucia. You can't believe in the forensic evidence without believing that the other evidence was planted in the apartment. And that's why I didn't call you back.'

She shook her head sadly and then turned away. Tapscott was holding the courtroom door open for her. He gave Bosch the deadeye stare as Soto went by him.

Bosch watched the door silently close behind them.

'Look at this,' Haller said.

Bosch looked down the hall and saw two women approaching. They were dressed for a night of clubbing, with black skirts cut to midthigh and patterned black stockings, one with skulls on them, the other crucifixes.

'Groupies,' Cisco said. 'If Borders walks out of here today, he'll probably be banging a different broad every night for a year.'

The first two were followed by three more, dressed similarly and with tattoos and piercings to the max. Then from the elevator alcove came a woman in a pale yellow dress appropriate for court. Her blond hair was tied back and she walked with a hesitancy that suggested she had not been in a courthouse since the first trial thirty years before.

'Is this Dina?' Haller asked.

'That's her,' Bosch said.

When Bosch had visited her Monday night, he thought Dina Rousseau was beautiful and the image of what her sister might have grown to be. She had given up on acting when she got married to a studio executive and started a family. She told Bosch she had no doubt that Preston Borders had been her sister's killer and would not hesitate to tell a judge so or to appear in court simply as moral support.

Haller and Cisco joined Bosch in standing as she approached, and Bosch introduced her.

'We certainly appreciate your willingness to come here today and to testify if necessary,' Haller said.

'I couldn't live with myself if I didn't,' she said.

'I don't know if Detective Bosch told you this, Ms.

Rousseau, but Borders will be in the courtroom today. He's been transported down from San Quentin for the hearing. I hope that is not going to cause you any undue emotional distress.'

'Of course it will. But Harry told me that he would be here, and I'm ready. Just point me to where I need to go.'

'Cisco, why don't you take Ms. Rousseau into the courtroom and sit with her. We still have a few minutes and we're going to wait for our last witness.'

Cisco did as instructed, and that left Bosch and Haller standing in the hallway. Bosch pulled his phone and checked the time. They had ten minutes until the hearing was scheduled to start.

'Come on, Spencer, where are you?' Haller said.

They both stared down the long hallway. Because the top of the hour was approaching, the crowds were thinning as people went into the various courtrooms for the start of hearings and trials. It left the space outside of court wide open.

Five minutes went by. No Spencer.

'Okay,' Haller said. 'We don't need him. We'll work his absence to our advantage – he defied a valid subpoena. Let's go in and do this.'

He headed toward the courtroom door and Bosch followed, taking one last glance toward the elevator alcove before disappearing inside.

Bosch saw that a number of reporters had slipped into the courtroom and were in the front row. He also saw that Cisco and Dina were in the last row, next to his daughter. Dina was staring toward the front of the courtroom, a growing look of horror on her face. Bosch followed the line of her vision and saw that Preston Borders was being led into the courtroom through the metal door that accessed the courthouse jail.

Courtroom deputies were on either side of and behind him. He walked slowly toward the defense table. He was in leg and wrist shackles, with a heavy chain running up between his legs and connecting the bindings. He was wearing orange jail scrubs – the color given to jailhouse VIPs.

Bosch had not seen Borders in person in nearly thirty years. Back then he had been a young man with a tan and 1980s actor hair – big, full, and wavy. Now he had a curved back and his hair was gray and thin, matching papery skin that received sunlight only one hour a week.

But he still had the flinty deadeye stare of a psychopath. As he entered, he glanced out into the courtroom gallery and smiled at the groupies who longed to be held by those eyes. They were standing in a middle row, bouncing on their heels and trying to hold themselves back from squealing.

Then his eyes went beyond them, and he found Bosch standing with Haller at the back. They were dark, sunken eyes, glowing like trash-can fires in an alley at night.

Glowing with hate.

37

Once Borders was seated at the defense table between Lance and Katherine Cronyn, the court clerk alerted Judge Houghton and he emerged from his chambers and retook his seat on the bench. He scanned the courtroom, eyeing those at the front tables as well as those in the gallery. His eyes seemed to hold on Haller as a recognizable face. He then got down to work.

'Next on the docket, California versus Borders, a habeas matter and motion to vacate set for evidentiary hearing,' Houghton said. 'Before proceeding I want to make clear that the Court expects the rules of decorum to be followed at all times. Any outburst from the gallery will result in the quick removal of the offending party.'

As he spoke, Houghton was looking directly at the group of young women who had come to get a look at Borders. He then continued with the business at hand.

'We also have a motion to be heard that was filed on Friday by Mr. Haller, who I see in the back of the courtroom. Why don't you come up, Mr. Haller. Your client can take a seat in the gallery.'

While Bosch slid into the row next to Cisco, his lawyer started up the center aisle toward the well of the courtroom. Before he even got to the gate, Kennedy was on his feet, objecting to Haller's motion on technical terms. He argued that the motion was filed too late in the game and was without merit. Lance Cronyn stood and offered support to Kennedy's argument, adding his own description of Haller's motion.

'Your Honor, this is just a stunt by Mr. Haller to curry favor with the media,' Cronyn said. 'As Mr. Kennedy aptly put it, this motion has no merit. Mr. Haller is simply looking for some free advertising at the expense of my client, who has suffered and waited for this day for thirty years.'

Haller had pushed through the gate and moved to a lectern located between the two tables at the head of the room.

'Mr. Haller, I'm assuming you have a response to that,' Houghton said.

'Indeed, I do, Your Honor,' Haller said. 'For the record, I am Michael Haller, representing Detective Hieronymus Bosch in this matter. May it please the Court, my client has become aware of the petition for habeas corpus filed by Mr. Cronyn and supported by the District Attorney's Office alleging that Mr. Bosch falsified material evidence used to convict Mr. Borders some twenty-nine years ago. Inexplicably, he was not subpoenaed for this hearing or otherwise invited to attend and testify in answer to these allegations. And I note here for the record that these unfounded allegations made their way into the *Los Angeles Times* and were reported as fact, and therefore have irrevocably damaged his professional and personal reputation, as well as his livelihood.'

'Mr. Haller, we don't have all day,' Houghton said. 'Make your argument.'

'Of course, Your Honor. My client fervently denies the allegations, which impugn his integrity, good name, and reputation. He has testimony and evidence he wants to present that is relevant and material to the resolution of these issues. In short, this whole thing is a scam, Your Honor, and we can prove it, if given the opportunity. Hence, I have filed on my client's behalf a motion for leave to intervene, as well as a complaint answering the allegations against him. I have served notice to all parties, and it was most likely that service that resulted in the newspaper article mentioned earlier that trashed Mr. Bosch's good reputation and standing in the law enforcement community.'

'Your Honor!' Kennedy cried. 'The state objects to the malicious allegation made by Mr. Haller. The source of the newspaper story was certainly not my office or investigative team, as we attempted diligently to handle this in a manner least impactful to Mr. Bosch. The story came from somewhere else, and the state asks for sanctions against Mr. Haller.'

'Your Honor,' Haller said calmly. 'I am willing to show Clerk of the Court records, and my client is willing to show his phone records, which together make it clear that within two hours of my filing motions Friday, the reporter for the *Los Angeles Times* was calling Mr. Bosch and asking for comment. My motions were filed under seal and therefore copied only to the parties opposing Mr. Bosch right here, right now. You can draw your own conclusions, Judge. I have drawn mine.'

Houghton swiveled in his high-backed leather chair for a moment before responding.

'I think we've batted that back and forth enough,'

he said. 'There won't be any sanctions. Let's move this along. Mr. Haller, both Mr. Kennedy and Mr. Cronyn object to your client's standing in this matter. How do you respond to that?'

Haller banged a fist down on the lectern for emphasis before wading into the fray again.

'How do I respond?' he asked. 'I'm incredulous, Your Honor. Sunday's newspaper dragged my client through the mud. It clearly implied that he planted evidence that sent a man away to death row. And here we are, and he was not even invited to the party? Given that the newspaper account and the allegations contained in the state's petition implicate my client's property rights in reputation and good name, I believe he has standing to intervene and defend those rights. If that is not the correct vehicle, then I would suggest the alternative, that he be viewed as a friend of the court and be permitted to testify and adduce evidence relevant to the issues the Court must weigh.'

Houghton solicited responses from Kennedy and Cronyn, but it became clear to Bosch that the judge found it difficult not to give him his day in court after his name and reputation were called into question by the *Times* and by the details of the original petitions, which the D.A.'s Office did not seek to seal from public view. Kennedy became frustrated when he made the same read on the judge's words and demeanor as Bosch had.

'Your Honor, the state can't be held responsible for an article in the newspaper,' he said. 'I – we – were not the source of the story. If we made a mistake in not asking for our motion to be sealed, then okay, that is on us, but it's surely not enough of an infraction to warrant this intervention by Bosch. There is a man sitting in this courtroom who has been on death row for more than ten thousand days – yes, I did the math – and it is our duty as officers of the court to make that injustice our priority today.'

'That is, if it's an injustice,' Haller said quickly. 'The evidence we seek to present tells a different story, Your Honor. It's the story of a scam carried out by cunning minds and perpetrated on the citizenry as well as on Mr. Kennedy and his office.'

'I'm going to take ten minutes to refer to the code and then we'll reconvene,' Houghton said. 'Nobody go far. Ten minutes.'

The judge was up and off the bench quickly and he disappeared into the hallway behind the clerk's corral that led to his chambers. Bosch liked that about Houghton. He had been in trials with the judge in the past and knew he was very assured as a courtroom referee. But he wasn't conceited enough to assume he knew every nuance of the law as written. He was willing to call a quick time-out to check the code books so that when he made a ruling, it had the solid backing of the law.

Haller turned around and looked at Bosch. He pointed toward the rear door of the courtroom and Bosch understood that he was still wondering about Spencer. It was a sign that Haller was confident that the judge's ruling was going to go his way.

Bosch got up and walked out of the courtroom to check on Spencer. The hallway was practically deserted now and there was no sign of him.

Bosch went back into the courtroom. The sound of the door drew Haller's attention and Bosch shook his head.

The judge returned to the bench a minute early and immediately shot down a request from Kennedy to provide further argument. He then proceeded with his ruling.

'Although the statute and rules governing habeas procedure are within the penal code, it's axiomatic that such a petition is in the nature of a civil action. Hence, an intervenor under civil rules would seem to be appropriate. Detective Bosch's property right in his good name and reputation is an interest that he is entitled and permitted to protect and that is, to the Court's observation and research, not being protected by the existing parties to this action. So I grant the motion for leave to intervene. Mr. Haller, you can call your first witness.'

Kennedy, who had inexplicably remained standing after his last objection was denied, quickly objected again.

'Your Honor, this is unfair,' he said. 'We are not prepared for witnesses. The state requests that we carry this over thirty days in order to seek depositions and prepare for a hearing.'

Cronyn stood as well. Bosch expected him to protest any postponement but instead he seconded the request. Bosch thought he saw Kennedy wince. It was probably at that moment that the prosecutor knew he had somehow been played by Cronyn or Borders or both.

'What happened to the ten thousand days Mr. Kennedy mentioned earlier?' Houghton said. 'The travesty of justice? Now you want to send the man whom your petition exonerates back to death row for another thirty days? We all know that with court calendars being what they are, there is no thirty-day delay. Putting this off for thirty days might as well be ninety, because my calendar is that far out. I'm not seeing a reason to delay these proceedings, gentlemen.'

Houghton swiveled in his chair again and looked down from the bench at Borders.

'Mr. Borders, are you willing to go back up to San Quentin for another three months while the attorneys get into this?'

There was a long moment before Borders responded and Bosch savored every second of it. There was no good answer for Borders. To accept the delay would be to reveal, as his attorney just had, that there was something wrong here. To say he did not accept his own attorney's wish for a delay would be to invite Haller to trot his witnesses to the stand and risk the whole scam being exposed.

'I just want to get it right,' Borders finally said. 'I've been up there a long time. I don't suppose a little more time matters if it means they get it right.'

'That's exactly what the Court is trying to do here,' Houghton said. 'Get it right.'

Bosch caught movement in his peripheral vision and turned to see the courtroom door opening. A man in a suit who he presumed was a lawyer entered and he was followed by Terry Spencer.

They stepped in and surveyed the courtroom, and the soft bang of the door closing behind them drew the rest of the eyes in the room to them. Bosch turned to check that Haller saw that their witness had arrived. Then he looked at the faces at the defense table. Borders showed minimal interest in the new arrivals because he didn't know Spencer by sight. But the reactions of the Cronyn legal team were telling. Lance Cronyn pursed his lips and blinked. He looked like a chess player who knew three moves out that he had lost. Katherine Cronyn's reaction went beyond surprise. She looked like she was seeing a ghost. Her jaw went slack and her eyes turned from the man standing at the back of the courtroom to her husband, sitting on the other side of their client. Bosch read fear in them.

Bosch's eyes then hunted through the rows of benches in the gallery for Lucia Soto. He found her in the front row by the courtroom deputy's desk. It was clear that she recognized Spencer, but she had a puzzled look on her face. She genuinely wasn't sure why the man from property control was in the courtroom.

'May I make a suggestion to the Court?'

The words came from Haller and they drew all attention away from Spencer.

'Go ahead, Mr. Haller,' Houghton said.

'What if all the lawyers and principals continue the hearing in camera?' Haller said. 'I will give Mr. Kennedy and Mr. Cronyn a verbal proffer for each witness I intend to call and for each document and video I plan to introduce. They will then be better informed on whether to seek a delay or not. The reason I ask to move to chambers is that I would want to be shielded from the media should I not be one hundred percent accurate in my proffers.'

'How long will this take, Mr. Haller?' the judge asked.

'I'll be quick. I think I can do it in fifteen minutes or less.'

'I like your idea, Mr. Haller, but we have a problem. I'm not sure I have room in chambers for all attorneys and their clients as well as Mr. Kennedy and his investigators. Additionally, we have a security issue with Mr. Borders, and I don't think our courthouse deputies want him moved around the building. So, what I am going to do is use the courtroom for a closed in camera conference and ask that witnesses, members of the media, and all other observers leave for fifteen minutes so we can hear your proffers, Mr. Haller.'

'Thank you, Your Honor.'

'The pool camera can stay but it needs to be turned off. Deputy Garza, please call for an additional deputy who can stand outside the door in the hallway until we are ready to invite the public back in.'

There was a commotion as several people stood at once to leave the courtroom. Bosch sat still at first, just admiring the genius of Haller's move. Because he was giving the judge a summary of what would be shown and testified to, there would be no oaths taken and therefore no consequences for any exaggerations or untruths that might be exposed later.

Haller was about to get a free swing at the case against Bosch, and there was nothing Kennedy and the Cronyns could do about it.

38

Haller signaled Bosch to the front. He went through the gate and took a seat against the railing. He looked around and saw he was only about six feet from where Borders sat shackled between Cronyn and Cronyn. Two deputies were in chairs directly behind him.

He looked to the rear of the courtroom and saw people still bunched at the door and moving out. His daughter was last in line and looking back at him. She gave him a nod of confidence and he returned it. After she moved through the doorway, he returned his attention to Borders. He made a low whistle sound and it caught Borders's ear. The man in orange turned and looked directly at Bosch.

Bosch winked.

Borders looked away. Haller stepped over and blocked Bosch's view of him.

'Don't worry about him,' he said. 'Stay focused on what's important.'

He took the empty seat next to Bosch and leaned in to him to whisper.

'I'm going to try to get you on the record,' he said. 'No proffer from me. You. So, remember, be forthright, act outraged.'

'I told you, not a problem,' Bosch said.

Haller turned to check the back of the room.

'Did you talk to Spencer or Daly before they left?'

'No. Is Daly the lawyer?'

'Yeah, Dan Daly. He's usually a federal court guy. Must be slumming today. Or he previously knew Spencer. I'll put Cisco on it.'

Haller took out his phone and started typing a text to his investigator, who had been among those invited by the judge to leave the courtroom. Bosch stood up so he'd have an angle on the screen. Haller was telling Cisco to see if Daly would reveal what Spencer was willing to testify to. He told Cisco to text him back. Just as he sent the message off, Houghton called the courtroom back to order.

'Okay, we're going to be on the record here, but this is a case management conference of the related parties present. Not part of the official hearing record. What is said here is not to go outside the courtroom. Mr. Haller, why don't you walk us through what you plan to do with your witnesses and documents if your motion is granted. And let's be brief.'

Haller stood up and went to the lectern, placing a legal pad down. Bosch could see that the top page was covered in notes, several of which were circled with arrows pointing to other circles. It was a schematic of the frame against Bosch. Beneath the pad he had a file containing the documents he would put before the judge.

'Thank you for this opportunity, Your Honor,' he began. 'You won't regret it. Because Mr. Cronyn and Mr. Kennedy are correct, there has been a miscarriage of justice here. Just not the one most people think has occurred.'

'Your Honor?' Kennedy said, holding his hands palms out and up in a what-is-going-on? gesture.

'Mr. Haller,' Houghton said. 'If I may draw your eyes to the jury box to your left, you will see it is empty. I said be brief. I didn't say make a statement to a non-existent jury.'

'Yes, Your Honor,' Haller said. 'Thank you. Moving on, then. The District Attorney's Conviction Integrity Unit took on this case and in a forensic review of the evidence found DNA on the clothing of Danielle Skyler that did not come from her convicted killer, Preston Borders. Instead, it came from a now-deceased serial rapist named Lucas John Olmer.'

'Mr. Haller,' Houghton interrupted again. 'You are reciting the known facts of the matter before the Court. I granted you entrance to the case as an intervenor. An intervention requires something new, a change in direction. Do you have that or not?'

'I do,' Haller said.

'Then get to it. Don't tell the Court what it already knows.'

'What I have that's new is this: Detective Bosch can show through documentation and sworn testimony that Lucas John Olmer's DNA was planted in the evidence box in LAPD property control as part of an elaborate scheme to set Preston Borders free and realize millions of dollars in damages from a false conviction.'

Houghton held a hand out to stay Kennedy from an obvious objection.

'A scheme by whom, Mr. Haller?' Houghton asked. 'Are you saying that Preston Borders on death row at San Quentin orchestrated this?'

'No, Your Honor,' Haller said. 'I'm saying Preston Borders bought into it because he had no other shot left at freedom. But the scheme was orchestrated right here in Los Angeles by the law firm of Cronyn and Cronyn.'

Immediately Lance Cronyn was on his feet.

'I strenuously object to this charade!' he said. 'Mr. Haller is besmirching my good reputation with this insidious accusation, when it is his client who—'

'Noted, Mr. Cronyn,' Houghton said, cutting off Cronyn in mid-paroxysm. 'But let me remind you that we are in closed session here and nothing offered by counsel will reach the ears of the public.'

But then the judge turned his attention to Haller.

'You are making a very strong allegation, Mr. Haller,' he said. 'You need to put up or shut up.'

'I'll be putting up,' Haller said. 'Right now.'

Haller briefly outlined the essential contradiction of the case as Bosch had expressed to Soto in the hallway. If the DNA found in evidence was legit, then the sea horse found during the search of Preston Borders's apartment was not. It was an either/or proposition.

'Our position is that the sea-horse pendant was and always has been the true evidence of the case,' Haller said. 'It is the DNA from Lucas John Olmer that was planted. And before outlining how that occurred, I would ask the Court to indulge me and allow my client to speak to this matter of planting evidence. He has spent more than forty years in law enforcement and it is his good name and reputation that are at stake here.'

Both Kennedy and Cronyn stood and objected to Bosch's being allowed to enter testimony without cross-examination. Houghton quickly made a decision.

'We are not going to go down that road in this conference,' he said. 'If we get back in open court and on the record, the Court will entertain that. I will say this, however. Detective Bosch has appeared in this courtroom many times over the years while I've had the honor to serve on the bench, and his integrity has never been called into question until now.'

Bosch nodded his thanks for the slim measure of support from the judge.

'Proceed, Mr. Haller,' Houghton said.

'Moving on, then,' Haller said as he opened the file he had on the lectern. 'It is known to the Court and all parties here that Mr. Cronyn represented Lucas John Olmer in the case that resulted in his imprisonment until the time of his death sixteen months ago. Key evidence in that case was DNA evidence connecting Olmer to a series of sexual assaults for which he was charged. I submit to the Court now a copy of a court order taken from the record of that case requiring prosecutors to split DNA evidence with the defense for private testing.'

Kennedy stood to object.

'Your Honor, if counsel is trying to insinuate that Olmer's DNA was handed to Cronyn so that he could secrete some of it for himself to use years later in a scheme to free a man from death row, then that is ridiculously offensive. As Mr. Haller certainly knows, Mr. Cronyn would not have come near that material. Chain-of-evidence protocol would require a secure lab-to-lab transfer. Mr. Haller is blowing smoke and wasting the Court's time.'

Haller shook his head and smiled before defending himself.

'Blowing smoke, Your Honor? We will see who is blowing smoke. I am not suggesting that there was anything untoward in the lab-to-lab transfer before Olmer's trial. But at trial the DNA was not ultimately challenged, as the defense chose to claim that the sex acts were consensual. The DNA matching was even stipulated to by the defense. The evidentiary record, however, is not complete post trial. According to Mr. Kennedy's vaunted protocol, all genetic materials not used in the private lab's analysis were to be returned after trial to the custody of the LAPD lab. There is no record of any material being returned. It's missing, Your Honor, and was last in the hands of a lab working for Mr. Cronyn.'

Now it was Cronyn's turn to stand up and protest.

'This is ridiculous, Judge. I never had that material and I wouldn't know if the lab returned it or not. To have to sit here and have this sort of allegation—'

'Again, we are in closed session here,' Houghton said. 'Let's stay on point. Mr. Haller, what else do you have?'

'I have a couple more documents here I would like to tender to the Court,' Haller said. 'The first is a letter from deputy city attorney Cecil French that confirms that the city has received a complaint for damages from Preston Borders regarding what he says is his false imprisonment for murder following a corrupt investigation by the LAPD. The complaint was filed by Lance Cronyn, attorney at law. The amount of damages being sought is not listed because they never are this early in the game, but common sense dictates that a man allegedly framed for murder by a city employee and sent to death row for almost three decades would be seeking millions of dollars in damages.'

Cronyn started to stand again but Houghton held up a hand like a traffic cop and the lawyer slowly sank back down to his seat. Haller continued.

'Additionally,' he said, 'we have here a copy of the visitor log from San Quentin that shows Lance Cronyn has made regular visits to Preston Borders beginning in January of last year.'

'He is his attorney,' Houghton said. 'Is there something sinister about an attorney visiting a client in prison, Mr. Haller?'

'Not at all, Your Honor. But in order to visit a death row inmate, you must be his attorney of record. Mr. Cronyn became that as of January of last year, several months before he sent the letter to the Conviction Integrity Unit allegedly clearing his conscience about Olmer's confession to him.'

Bosch almost smiled. The timing of Cronyn's beginnings with Borders was proof of nothing, but it certainly smacked of collusion, and the way Haller had walked the judge right into it was perfect. Bosch put his arm up on the empty chair next to him so he could casually glance to his right at Soto and Tapscott. They looked like they were seriously tracking the story Haller was spinning.

'Additionally,' Haller said, 'if the motion to intervene is granted, Detective Bosch is prepared to present witnesses who contradict the key elements of the petitioner's habeas motion. To wit, the petitioner throws the reputation of his trial attorney, Mr. David Siegel, to the wolves, saying that the late Mr. Siegel suborned Mr.

Borders's perjury at trial by telling him to testify that the key piece of evidence found in his apartment – the sea-horse pendant – was not the victim's but a facsimile he bought on the Santa Monica pier.'

'And you have a witness who contradicts that testimony?' Houghton asked.

'I do, Your Honor,' Haller said. 'I have Mr. David Siegel himself, who is willing to contradict the report of his own death as well as the contention that he suborned perjury from his client at the trial in nineteen eighty-eight. He is willing to testify that the entire testimony given by Mr. Borders was concocted by Mr. Borders himself in an attempt to explain away the damning evidence that he was in possession of the victim's jewelry.'

Kennedy and Cronyn were both quickly to their feet, but Cronyn spoke first.

'Your Honor, this is absurd,' he said. 'Even if it is proven that David Siegel is alive, his testimony would be a flagrant violation of attorney—client privilege and completely inadmissible.'

'Judge, I beg to differ with Mr. Cronyn,' Haller said. 'Attorney—client privilege was wholly shattered by Mr. Borders when he revealed the inner workings of his trial strategy and sought to impugn the good name and reputation of his attorney in his petition – much as he maligned my client, Detective Bosch. I have in my possession a video proffer – an interview with Mr. Siegel seven days ago that shows him to be alive and sound of mind and defending himself against the slander perpetrated by Mr. Borders and his attorney.'

Haller reached into his pocket and produced a digital-storage stick containing the video in question.

He held it up above his head, drawing all eyes in the courtroom to it.

The judge hesitated and then pulled the stemmed microphone closer. Cronyn and Kennedy sat back down.

'Mr. Haller,' Houghton said. 'We're going to hold off on your video for the time being. The Court finds it intriguing, but your fifteen minutes are just about up and this matter comes down to one thing. Olmer's DNA was found on the victim's clothing, and there seems to be no dispute about that. That clothing had been sealed in evidence archives for years – years before Mr. Olmer went to trial and Mr. Cronyn may or may not have come into possession of his genetic material, years before Mr. Cronyn ever met Mr. Borders, and years before Mr. Olmer died in prison. Do you have an answer for that? Because if you don't, then it's time to move on to a ruling on this matter.'

Haller nodded and looked down at his legal pad. Bosch caught a glimpse of Kennedy in profile and thought that he was smirking, no doubt because he believed Haller had no answer for the DNA's being in the archive box.

'The Court is correct,' Haller then began. 'We do not dispute the finding of DNA on the victim's clothing. Detective Bosch – and I also – have the utmost belief in the integrity of the LAPD lab. We do not suggest that the results of the analysis are to be doubted. It is our belief that the DNA from Olmer was planted on the clothing prior to its being turned over to the lab.'

Kennedy jumped up again and hotly objected to the implication that there was corruption in either the

property control section of the LAPD or the two detectives who reworked the case for the CIU.

'The moves by detectives Soto and Tapscott were well
documented and aboveboard,' Kennedy said. 'Knowing
that desperate people sometimes make desperate claims,
they went so far as to video their unsealing of the evidence box themselves in order to document that no
tampering had taken place.'

Haller jumped in before the judge could respond.

'Exactly,' he said. 'They videoed the whole thing, and
if it may please the Court, I would like to play that video
as part of my proffer. I have it cued up and ready to go
on my laptop, Your Honor. I ask for the Court's indul-
gence in extending my time. I can hook up my computer
to the screen very quickly.'

He gestured toward the video screen on the wall opposite the jury box. There was a silence as Houghton
considered the request, even as others in the courtroom
were probably considering how Haller got a copy of the
video. Bosch saw Soto sneak a sideways glance at him.
He knew he was breaking their unspoken rule of confi-
dentiality. She had not shared the video with him so he
could use it in court.

'Set it up, Mr. Haller,' Houghton said. 'I'll consider it
part of the proffer.'

Haller turned from the lectern and grabbed his briefcase, which was on the floor in front of the chair next
to Bosch. As he opened the briefcase on the chair and
retrieved his laptop, he spoke under his breath to Bosch.

'This is it,' he said.

'Like lambs to slaughter, right?' Bosch whispered.

Five minutes later Haller had the video playing on the

wall screen. Everyone in the courtroom, including those who had already seen the video multiple times, watched with rapt attention. It ended without reaction from the judge or anyone else.

Haller then passed out copies of an 8×10 screen grab from the video to all the parties and the judge, then returned to the lectern.

'I'm going to play the video again but what you have in front of you is a screen grab from the one minute, eleven second mark,' he said.

He started replaying the video and then stopped it, freezing the screen on the moment that Terrence Spencer could be seen watching the two detectives from the next room.

Haller now pulled a pen-size laser pointer from the inside pocket of his suit jacket and circled the image of Spencer with a glowing red dot.

'This man, what is he doing? Just watching? Or does he have an interest that goes beyond curiosity?'

Kennedy stood once again.

'Your Honor, counsel's flights of fancy are getting ridiculous. The video clearly shows the box was not tampered with. So what does he do? He tries to draw the eye away from what is obvious to something and someone who clearly works in the property control unit and would have a vested interest in monitoring the unsealing of evidence. Can we please move on from this charade and get to the sad business of correcting a severe miscarriage of justice?'

'Mr. Haller,' Houghton said. 'My patience is also wearing thin.'

'Your Honor, if allowed to continue, my proffer will

be completed in the next five minutes,' Haller said.

'Very well,' Houghton said. 'Continue. With speed.'

'Thank you. As I was asking before being interrupted, what is this man doing? Well, we got curious and tried to find out. As it happens, Detective Bosch recognized this man as a longtime employee of the Property Control Unit. His name is Terrence Spencer. We decided to look into Mr. Spencer and what we found may startle the Court.'

Haller took another document from his file and glanced over at Lance Cronyn as he delivered it to the clerk, who in turn delivered it to the judge. While the judge was looking at it, Bosch saw Haller step back behind the lectern and use it as a blind as he pulled his phone from his pocket, held it down by his hip, and read a text message that was on the screen.

Bosch knew it was most likely the message from Cisco about Spencer that Haller had been waiting for.

Haller dropped the phone back into his pocket and continued to address the judge.

'What we found was that seven years ago Terrence Spencer almost lost his house in a foreclosure. It was a bad time in this country and a lot of people were in the same boat. Spencer got upside down, couldn't make double mortgage payments, and the banks had lost patience. And he would have lost his house if it had not been for the efforts of his foreclosure attorney, Kathy Zelden, whom many of us in this courtroom now know as Kathy Cronyn.'

Bosch could literally feel the air in the courtroom go still. Houghton went from slouching in his luxurious leather chair to coming forward and leaning intently over the bench. He was holding up the document Haller had provided and intently scanning it as Haller continued.

'Zelden, now Cronyn, saved Spencer's house at the time,' he said. 'But all she really did was put off the inevitable. She put Spencer into a hard-money refi that carried a massive, half-million-dollar balloon payment due in seven years. Due, I should say, to a privately held investment fund that controlled whether or not Spencer could sell his property in an effort to get out from beneath the balloon. They chose to prevent the house's sale because they knew it would come to them in foreclosure this summer.

'Well, poor Terry Spencer had no way out. He didn't have half a million dollars and had no way to get it. He couldn't even sell his house, because the mortgage holder wouldn't allow it. So what does he do? He calls up his old lawyer, now a full partner in Cronyn and Cronyn, and says, What am I going to do? And Your Honor, from that point on, a conspiracy began. A conspiracy to defraud the District Attorney's Office and frame my client for planting evidence. All in an effort to free Preston Borders and collect a multimillion-dollar settlement from the city of Los Angeles.'

Lance Cronyn stood up, ready to argue. Kennedy was hesitantly rising. But the judge held up his hand to stop all from speaking and looked squarely at Haller.

'Mr. Haller,' he intoned. 'Those are very significant allegations. Do you plan to offer any evidence to go with them if I allow you to present this in open court?'

'Yes, Your Honor,' Haller said. 'The last witness I would present is Terrence Spencer himself. We were able to locate him over the weekend, hiding out at a home down in Laguna Beach that happens to be owned by the Cronyns. I had him served with a subpoena, and at this moment he's out in the hallway with my investigator and ready to take the stand.'

39

The threat of Terrence Spencer's testimony seemed to momentarily freeze things in the courtroom. Then it was Preston Borders who broke the silence with laughter. It started low and soon became a head-back, full-throated burst of mirthless irony. He then cut it off as if with the blade of a knife and spoke to his lawyer with a deadly snarl in his voice.

'You fucking moron. You said this would work. You said it was foolproof.'

Borders tried to stand but forgot that the lead chain between his legs had been clamped to his seat. He rose with the seat still awkwardly attached to him and then dropped back down.

'Get me out of here. Just take me back.'

Cronyn tried to huddle in close in order to silence his client.

'Get the fuck away from me, asshole. I'm going to tell them everything. Your whole fucking plan.'

Kennedy rose then, seeing the only path he could take. There was a stunned look on his face.

'Your Honor, at this time, the state wishes to withdraw its motions in this matter,' he said. 'The state now opposes the habeas petition.'

'I'm sure it does,' the judge said. 'But you can take your seat for the moment, Mr. Kennedy.'

Houghton turned his attention to the other table, specifically to Borders instead of the two lawyers who flanked him.

'Mr. Borders,' he said. 'As you have seen, your petition for habeas corpus is no longer uncontested. It is opposed now by the District Attorney and the lead detective on the case. Furthermore, you have just expressed what I take as a desire to discharge your lawyer and abandon these proceedings. Is it in fact your desire to withdraw your petition?'

'Might as well,' Borders said. 'It ain't fucking going anywhere.'

'Very well,' the judge said. 'The matter before the Court is withdrawn. Deputy Garza, you can take Mr. Borders out of here. But keep him in holding. I believe the detectives here may want to talk to him.'

The judge gestured toward Soto and Tapscott.

Garza nodded to the two deputies seated behind Borders and they moved in on the convict to unlock the lead chain and remove him. As he was stood up, Borders took a last look down at Lance Cronyn.

'Thanks for the road trip,' he said. 'Better than three days in the cage.'

'Get him out,' Houghton ordered loudly.

'Fuck you all very much,' Borders called out as he was half walked, half carried through the door into the courthouse holding area. 'And please tell my girls to stay in touch.'

The door banged closed and the sharp metal-on-metal reverb rolled through the courtroom like an earthquake.

Cronyn stood slowly to address the Court, but Houghton cut him off as well.

'Counselor, I advise you not to speak,' he said. 'Anything you say here could be used against you later in another court of law.'

'But, Your Honor, if I may,' Cronyn insisted, 'I need to put on the record how my client threatened me and my family and—'

'Enough, Mr. Cronyn. Enough. I've heard more than I need in order to know that you, your co-counsel, and your client came into this courtroom today with the clear intent of manipulating the court for financial gain, not to mention gaining the release into society of what appears to have been a rightfully convicted murderer, and tarnishing the reputation of a veteran police detective.'

'Your—'

'I'm not speaking to hear myself talk, Mr. Cronyn. I told you to be quiet. One more interruption and I will have you silenced.'

Houghton surveyed the entire court before bringing his eyes back to Cronyn and continuing.

'Now, I am assuming that the Los Angeles Police Department will have an interest in talking to you as well as to Terrence Spencer. Criminal charges may arise from that. I don't know. I can't control that. But what I can control is what happens in this courtroom, and I have to say that never in my twenty-one years on the bench have I seen such a concerted effort to undermine the rule of law by attorneys appearing before me. Therefore, I find Lance Cronyn and Katherine Cronyn in criminal contempt of this Court and order them taken into custody forthwith. Deputy Garza, you need to call a female court deputy in here as soon as possible to take custody of Ms. Cronyn.'

Katherine Cronyn immediately collapsed onto her husband's shoulder in tears. As Bosch watched, her emotions shifted, and soon she was pounding a fist into her husband's chest. He corralled her with his arms and pulled her into an embrace that stopped the pummeling and left only the tears. Deputy Garza walked up behind him, handcuffs dangling from one hand, ready to take him back into the jail.

'Now, Mr. Kennedy,' Houghton said, 'I don't know what you plan to do with the information Mr. Haller has brought to light, but I know what I'm going to do. I'm going to call members of the media and the public back into the courtroom and tell them exactly what happened in here today. You're not going to like it because you and your agency are not going to come off too well, considering it was a defense lawyer and his investigators who put this together under the nose of the LAPD and assorted other agencies.

'But I'll say this. Your office owes Detective Bosch a big fat apology and I will be watching to make sure you give it on a big stage, in a timely manner, and without any "buts" or "becauses" or asterisks attached. Nothing short of full exoneration of the suspicions and allegations that were published in Sunday's newspaper will suffice. Do I make myself clear on that, Mr. Kennedy?'

'Yes, Your Honor,' Kennedy said. 'We would be doing that even if you had not ordered it.'

Houghton frowned.

'Knowing what I know about politics and the justice system, I find that highly unlikely.'

The judge scanned the room again, found Bosch, and asked him to stand.

'Detective, I imagine you have been put through the wringer in recent days,' he said. 'I want to apologize on behalf of the Court for this needless torment. I wish you the best of luck, sir, and you are welcome in my courtroom anytime.'

'Thank you, Your Honor,' Bosch said.

Two deputies, including a female, entered through the holding area door and joined Garza in taking the Cronyns into custody. The judge instructed his clerk to go out into the hallway to tell those waiting that they could return to the courtroom.

An hour later Houghton adjourned his court for the day, and Kennedy was left to wade through the gaggle of reporters who demanded his comments and reaction to what the judge had just announced.

Out in the hallway, Bosch watched Soto and Tapscott approach Terrence Spencer and take him into custody. Cisco came up next to Bosch and they watched the detectives lead Spencer down the hall.

'I hope he tells them how he rigged the box,' Bosch said. 'I really want to know.'

'Not going to happen,' Cisco said. 'He's taking the fifth.'

'But you said he was going to testify.'

'What are you talking about?'

'Your text to Haller in the courtroom. You said he was ready to testify.'

'No, I said you can put him on the stand but he'll

take the nickel. Why, what did Mick say?'

Bosch stared across the hallway at Haller, who was talking one-on-one with a reporter writing in a notebook. There was no camera, so Bosch assumed it was a print reporter – which most likely meant he was from the *Times*.

'Son of a gun,' he said.

'What?' Cisco asked.

'I saw him read your text, and then he told the judge that Spencer was ready to go on the stand. He didn't exactly say he would testify, only that he'd go on the stand. He tipped the whole thing with that bluff. Borders took the bait and blew a gasket. That was it.'

'Smooth move.'

'Dangerous move.'

Bosch continued to stare at Haller and he started to put things into place.

40

After all the interviews were over, Team Bosch decided to get out of the courthouse and walk over to Traxx in Union Station to celebrate the across-the-board victory. While Haller and Cisco went into the restaurant to get a table, Bosch walked his daughter down to the ramp to the Metrolink train she was due to board. She had bought a return ticket on her app.

'I'm so glad I was here, Dad,' Maddie said.

'I'm glad you were here too,' Bosch said.

'And I'm so sorry if it sounded like I ever doubted you.'

'Nothing to be sorry about, Mads. You didn't.'

He pulled her into a long embrace and looked up the tunnel to the sunlight waiting at the boarding platform. He kissed the top of her head and let her go.

'I still want to come down for dinner when you get back to your house. I'll get the app and take the train.'

'Definitely. Bye, Dad.'

'Bye, sweetie.'

He watched her walk up the ramp to the light. She knew he would and she turned at the top to wave. She was entirely in silhouette and then she was gone.

Bosch joined his lawyer and his investigator in a booth next to a window that looked out on the train station's waiting area of mixed Art Deco and Moorish designs. Haller had already ordered martinis all around. They clinked glasses and toasted. The three musketeers, all for one and one for all. Bosch caught Haller's eyes and nodded. His attorney apparently didn't interpret it as the thank-you he felt he deserved.

'What?' Haller asked.

'Nothing,' Bosch said.

'No, what? What was that look you gave me?'

'What look?'

'Don't bullshit me.'

Cisco watched them silently, knowing better than to get in the middle.

'All right,' Bosch said. 'I saw you talking to that reporter in the hallway. After court. He was from the *Times*, wasn't he?'

'Yeah, that's right,' Haller said. 'They have a major skinback to write. That's what he called it when they have to set the record straight. It's not a correction, because what they went with Sunday came out of court documents. But it was one-sided. It will be the full story tomorrow.'

'What was his name?'

'You know, I didn't catch his name. All those guys, they're the same.'

'Was it David Ramsey?'

'I just told you I didn't get the guy's name.'

Bosch just nodded and Haller once again saw judgment.

'If you have something to say, then say it,' he said. 'And stop with the know-it-all judgmental looks.'

'I don't have anything to say,' Bosch said. 'And I don't know it all but I know what you did.'

'For chrissakes, what are you talking about?'

'I know what you did.'

'Oh, here we go. What did I do, Bosch? Would you just tell me what the fuck you're talking about?'

'You're the leak. You gave the story to the *Times* on Friday. You're the one who gave it to Ramsey.'

Cisco was in the middle of a second sip from his martini, the fragile stemmed glass held by his thick fingers. He almost spilled it all over his nice dress vest.

'No fucking way,' he said. 'Mick would never do—'

'Yeah, he did,' Bosch said. 'He sold me out to the *Times* for a headline.'

'Whoa, whoa, whoa,' Haller said. 'Are you fucking forgetting something? We won the case, man, and you had a Superior Court judge apologizing to you and demanding that the D.A.'s Office and the LAPD do the same thing. And you're going to complain about my strategy?'

'So, you're saying it was you,' Bosch said. 'You admit it. You and Ramsey.'

'I'm saying that in order to win the day, we had to raise the stakes,' Haller said. 'We needed to kick this thing out into the streets so that it would become public and it would be something that was talked about and would then draw every goddamn news channel in the city to that courtroom today. I knew if we did that, then the judge would have no choice but to give us standing and allow us to intervene.'

'And you would get, what, about a million dollars' worth of free publicity out of it?'

'Jesus Christ, Bosch. You're like a feral cat. You don't

trust anybody. I did it for you, not me, and look at what happened.'

Haller pointed out of the booth in the direction of the courthouse.

'The judge let us in over the objections of everybody in that courtroom,' he said. 'And then we fucking won. Borders goes back up to death row for the rest of his sorry existence and every one of those bastards who tried to set you up and frame you is going to end up disbarred, fired, and probably in jail. Cronyn and Cronyn *are* already in jail, while you're sitting here drinking a martini. You think the judge would have given us standing if the media wasn't all over this?'

'I don't know,' Bosch said. 'But my daughter read that shit Sunday and has had to wonder for three days if her father is the kind of guy who would plant evidence and send an innocent man to death row. On top of that, that story almost got me killed. If that had happened, I'd be dead and Borders would be walking the earth as a free man, to kill again.'

'Look, I'm sorry about that. I truly am. I didn't want that to happen and I didn't know you were working undercover, because you didn't fucking tell me. But this is one of those rare times where the end justifies the means. Okay? We got the result we wanted, your reputation came out intact, and your daughter is riding that train, knowing her dad is a hero, not a criminal.'

Bosch nodded as though in agreement. But he wasn't.

'You should've told me,' he said. 'I'm the client. I should have been informed and given the choice.'

'And what would your choice have been?' Haller asked.

'We'll never know now because you didn't give it to me.'

'I know what it would've been, and that's why I didn't. End of fucking story.'

They stared at each other for a long, hard moment. Cisco hesitantly raised his glass over the middle of the table.

'Come on, water under the bridge, fellas,' he said. 'We won. Let's toast again. I can't wait to read the paper tomorrow.'

As if each was waiting for the other to make the first move, Haller and Bosch continued their stare-down.

Haller broke first. He grabbed his glass by the stem and raised it up, sloshing vodka over the brim and down over his fingers. Bosch finally did the same.

The three musketeers clinked glasses like swords again, but it no longer seemed much like all for one and one for all.

41

As Bosch rounded the last curve on Woodrow Wilson Drive, he saw the city ride parked in front of his house. Someone was waiting for him. He turned the sound down on Kamasi Washington's 'Change of the Guard.' It was nearly five, and his plan was to get out of the suit and shower and change into street clothes before heading up to the Valley to visit Elizabeth Clayton in the dungeon where she was taking the cure.

As he pulled into the side carport, he saw who it was. Lucia Soto was sitting on the house's front step, looking at her phone. Bosch parked and walked around to the front rather than avoiding her and going through the side door. She stood up, put the phone away, and wiped dust from the step off the back of her pants. She was still in the dark blue suit she had worn in court that morning.

'Been waiting long?' Bosch asked by way of a greeting.

'No,' she said. 'I had some e-mailing to do. You should sweep your steps every now and then, Harry. Dusty.'

'Keep forgetting. How'd they take things today down at RHD?'

'Oh, you know, in stride. They always take things, good and bad, in stride.'

'And was it a good or bad thing?'

'I think good. Whenever a former detective is cleared of wrongdoing, that's a good thing. Even if it is Harry Bosch.'

She smiled. He frowned and unlocked the door. He pushed it open for her.

'Enter,' he said. 'I'm out of beer but I have some pretty good bourbon.'

'That sounds right,' she said.

Bosch entered behind her and then moved by so he could get to the living room first and make it a little more hospitable for a visitor. The past two nights he had fallen asleep on the couch, watching television and trying to clear his mind of all things related to his cases.

He squared up the couch pillows and grabbed the shirt draped over the arm. He headed back toward the kitchen with it.

'Have a seat and I'll get the glasses.'

'Can we go out on the deck? I like it out there and it's been a while.'

'Sure. There's a broomstick in the slider track.'

'That's new.'

He put the shirt in the washer, which was located by the kitchen's side door to the carport. He grabbed the bottle off the top of the refrigerator and took two glasses down from a shelf before joining Soto on the deck.

'Yeah, there've been a couple break-ins in the neighborhood lately,' he said. 'Both times the guy climbed up a tree to get on the roof and then came down on the back deck, where people sometimes don't lock their doors.'

He gestured with the bottle toward the house next

door, which was cantilevered like Bosch's. The rear deck hung out over the canyon and seemed impossible to get to other than from inside. But it was clear the roof gave access.

Soto nodded. Bosch could tell she wasn't really interested. She wasn't visiting as part of the Neighborhood Watch committee.

He opened the bottle and poured a healthy slug into each of the glasses. He handed one to Soto but they didn't toast. Considering everything between them at the moment, it would not have felt right.

'So did he tell you how he did it?' Bosch asked.

'Who?' Soto said. 'How who did what?'

'Come on. Spencer. How'd he rig the evidence box?'

'Spencer hasn't told us jack shit, Harry. His lawyer won't let him talk to us and he said he wasn't going to testify either. Your lawyer lied to the judge during the proffer.'

'No, he didn't lie. Not to the judge, at least. Check the record. He said Spencer was in the hallway and was ready to take the stand. That wasn't a lie. Whether he was going to testify once he got up there or take the fifth was another matter.'

'Semantics, Harry. I never knew you to hide behind words.'

'It was a bluff and it worked. If it makes you feel any better, I didn't know about it. But it got the truth out, didn't it?'

'It did, and it got us a search warrant. We didn't need Spencer to talk.'

Bosch looked sharply at her. She had solved the mystery.

'Tell me.'

'We opened his locker. He had a stack of the twenty-year-old evidence stickers they put on the boxes back then. They were supposed to be destroyed when we went to the red crackle tape. But somehow he got a leftover stack and kept it.'

'So he opened the box, planted Olmer's DNA, and put new labels on it.'

'He opened the bottom seam, because your signature was on the labels on top. And because his labels were old and yellow, the box looked totally legit. The thing is, we don't think it was the only time. We got a search warrant for his house too, and we found some receipts from a pawn shop in Glendale. We checked there and he's a regular customer, selling jewelry mostly. We think he might have been raiding boxes from closed cases, looking for valuables to pawn. He probably thought since the cases were old and closed, nobody would ever look.'

'So when Cronyn asked Spencer if he could get something *into* a box, he said no problem.'

'Exactly.'

Bosch nodded. The mystery was solved.

'What about the Cronyns?' he asked. 'I assume they're going for a one-for-one deal, right?'

'Probably,' she said. 'She walks and he takes the hit. He'll get disbarred but then he'll just prop her up. Everyone will know that if you hire her, you hire him.'

'And that's it? No jail time? The guy used the law to try to break a killer out of prison. Death row, no less. He gets a slap on the wrist?'

'Well, last I heard, they were still in jail because

Houghton won't set bail till tomorrow. Anyway, it's early in negotiations, Harry. But Spencer still isn't talking, and the only one who is talking is Borders. When your one and only witness is a murderer on death row, you don't have a case you want to take to a jury. This is going to come down to plea agreements all around, and maybe Cronyn goes to jail, maybe not. Truth is, they're more interested in nailing Spencer because he was inside the wire. He betrayed the department.'

Bosch nodded. He understood the thinking on Spencer.

'The department's management team has already moved in,' Soto said. 'They're revamping the whole booking-and-retrieving process so that something like this can never happen again.'

Bosch moved to the wooden railing and leaned his elbows down. It was still at least an hour from sundown. The 101 freeway down in the pass was clogged in both directions. But there were very few sounds of horns. Drivers in L.A. seemed resigned to a fate of waiting in traffic without the kind of impotent cacophony of horns that Bosch always seemed to hear in other cities he'd visited. He always thought his deck gave him a unique angle on that distinctive L.A. trait.

Soto joined him at the railing and leaned down next to him.

'I didn't really come up here to talk about the case,' she said.

'I know,' Bosch said.

She nodded. It was time to get to it.

'A really good detective who used to mentor me taught me to always follow the evidence. That's what

I thought I was doing with this thing. But somewhere I got manipulated or I took a wrong turn and I ended up where the evidence told me something my heart should have known was flat-out wrong. For that I'm truly sorry, Harry. And I always will be.'

'Thank you, Lucia.'

Bosch nodded. He knew she could have easily blamed it all on Tapscott. He was the senior detective in the partnership and he called the final shots on case decisions. Instead, she put it all on herself. She took the weight. That took guts and that took a true detective. Bosch had to admire her for it.

Besides, how could he hold anything against Soto when he had heard in his own daughter's voice a worry that it all might be true, that Harry had fixed a case against an innocent man?

'So', Lucia asked. 'Are we good again, Harry?'

'We're good,' Bosch said. 'But I sure hope people read the paper tomorrow.'

'Fuck anybody who still has a doubt after today.'

'I'll go with that.'

Soto straightened up. She had said what she'd come to say and was ready to go home. Soon she would be in the iron ribbon of traffic he was staring down at.

She poured the remainder of her bourbon into Bosch's glass.

'I gotta go.'

'Okay. Thanks for coming here to talk. Means a lot, Lucia.'

'Harry, if you need anything or there's anything I can do for you, I owe you. Thanks for the booze.'

She headed for the open slider. Bosch turned and leaned back against the railing.

'There is, actually,' he said. 'Something you could do.'

She stopped and turned around.

'Daisy Clayton,' he said.

She shook her head, not getting it.

'Am I supposed to know that name?'

Bosch shook his head and stood straight.

'No. She was a murder victim from before you ever made it to homicide. But you're on cold cases. I want you to pull the file and work it.'

'Who was she?'

'She was a nobody, and nobody cared. That's why her case is still open.'

'I mean who was she to you?'

'I never knew her. She was only fifteen years old. But there's somebody out there who took her and used her and then threw her away like trash. Somebody evil. I can't work the case because it's Hollywood. Not my turf anymore. But it is yours.'

'You know what year?'

'Oh-nine.'

Soto nodded. She had what she needed, at least to pull the case and review it.

'Okay, Harry, I'm on it.'

'Thank you.'

'I'll tell you what I know when I know it.'

'Good.'

'See you, Harry.'

'See you, Lucia.'

42

After showering and changing into street clothes, Bosch
went to the closet next to the front door and pulled the
fireproof box off the shelf. He used a key to open it.
It contained old legal documents, including birth cer-
tificates and his discharge papers from the U.S. Army.
Bosch kept his wedding ring in the box as well as his
two Purple Hearts, and the two life-insurance policies
that listed his daughter as beneficiary.

There was also a faded color photo of Bosch and his
mother. It was the only photograph of her he had, so he
had always wanted to keep it safe rather than display
it. He looked at it now for a few moments, this time his
eyes drawn to his own image at eight years old rather
than to his mother's. He studied the hopefulness in the
boy's face and wondered where it had gone.

He put the photo to the side and dug further into the
strongbox until he found what he was looking for.

It was an old sock stuffed with a rubber-banded roll
of money. Without pulling it out of the sock now or
counting it, Bosch shoved it into the side pocket of his
jacket. The roll of money was the earthquake fund,
mostly large bills he had been accumulating slowly – a
twenty here and a fifty there-since the last big earthquake in 1994. In L.A., nobody wanted to be stuck
without cash when the big one hit. ATMs would be

knocked off-line and banks would be closed in a time of civic catastrophe. Cash would be king and Bosch had been planning accordingly for over twenty years. By his estimate, there was close to ten thousand dollars in the sock.

He put the other items back into the box, taking one last look at the mother-and-son photo. He had no recollection of posing for the shot or where it had been taken. It was a professional shot with a white – now yellowed – background. Maybe young Harry had tagged along with her when she had gotten head shots for her efforts to be cast as a movie extra. Maybe she then paid the photographer a little more for a quick photo with her son.

Bosch drove up the hill to Mulholland and then followed the snake to Laurel Canyon Boulevard, which dropped him down the north side into the Valley. As soon as he got bars on his phone, he called Bella Lourdes on her cell. He expected that she would be off duty and home by now. Still, she answered right away.

'Harry, I was going to call you, but I thought maybe you'd be out celebrating.'

'Oh, you mean the case? No, no celebration. Just glad it's over.'

'I'll say. Well, I was also going to call to tell you they ID'd the other Russian off his prints. You know how you were calling him Igor for the sake of keeping all the parties straight when you were telling the story?'

'Yeah.'

'Well, the guy's name actually was Igor. I mean, what are the chances?'

'Probably pretty good if you're Russian.'

'Anyway, Igor Golz – G-O-L-Z – age thirty-one. Interpol had him as another member of the *Bratva* and longtime associate of Sluchek's. They met in a Russian prison and probably came over here together.'

'Well, I guess that wraps things up on the *farmacia* case, huh?'

'I was nailing down the paperwork today. You back in tomorrow, now that your court thingy is over?'

'Yeah, my thingy's over and I'll be in tomorrow.'

'Sorry, you know what I mean. It'll be nice to have you back around.'

'Listen, I was calling to ask you something. The other day you mentioned that you had been around addicts, including someone in your own family. Do you mind if I ask who that was?'

'Yeah, my sister. Why do you want to know?'

'Is she all right now? I mean, not addicted?'

'As far as we know. We don't see her that much. Once she got clean, she didn't really want to be around the people who saw her at the low points, you know what I mean?'

'I think so.'

'She stole like crazy from my parents. Me too.'

'That's what happens.'

'So we saved her but consequently we lost her. At least in a good way. She lives up in the Bay Area, and like I said, she's supposedly four years sober and clean.'

'That part's great. How did you get her clean?'

'Well, we didn't actually do it. It was rehab.'

'Which one did you use? That's why I'm calling. I need to get somebody into a place and I don't know where to start.'

'Well, there's the fancy ones that cost a fortune and those that don't. You get what you pay for as far as creature comforts, but my sister was basically on the streets. So the place we got her into was like heaven. A room and a bed, you know? It was a mixture of circle jerks and private sessions with the shrinks. A piss test every day.'

'Where was it? What was it called?'

'It was called the Start. It was over there in Canoga Park. Four years ago it was like twelve hundred a week. There was no insurance, so we all chipped in. It's gotta be more now. The opioid thing has made it hard to find a bed in some of these places.'

'Thanks, Bella. I'm going to check it out.'

'See you tomorrow at the station?'

'I'll be there.'

Bosch was on the 101, transitioning north to the 405. He could see the plume of smoke from the brewery up ahead.

He called directory assistance and was connected to the Start. After being put on hold twice he was finally speaking to someone called the director of placement. She explained that the facility specialized in treating opioid addiction and that they did not reserve beds, choosing to work strictly on a first-come, first-served basis. At the moment, there were three beds open in the forty-two-bed facility.

Bosch asked about pricing and learned that the weekly all-inclusive fee had jumped more than fifty percent in four years to $1,880, paid in advance with a recommended four-week minimum of treatment. Bosch was reminded of Jerry Edgar's sermon about the crisis being too big to shut down because everybody was making money on it.

Bosch thanked the director of placement and disconnected. Five minutes later he was pulling into the Road Saints compound. This time there were several motorcycles parked about the front yard and he wondered if he had stumbled into the monthly membership meeting. Before getting out of the Jeep, he called Cisco to see if he had arrived at the wrong time.

'No, man, I'll come out and bring you in. Wednesdays are always big here for some reason. I don't even know why.'

Bosch was leaning against the Jeep when Cisco came out.

'So how's she doing?' he asked.

'Uh, resentful as ever,' Cisco said. 'But I think that's a good sign. I remember Mick Haller came by to visit me when I was in day four or five. I told him through the door that he could take his job and shove it up his ass. 'Course, a week later I had to ask him to pull it out of his ass and give it back to me.'

Bosch laughed.

'So have you heard about this place over in Canoga Park called the Start?' he asked.

'Yeah, the rehab,' Cisco said. 'I've heard of it. But I don't really know anything about it.'

'I heard from somebody that it was good. It got results for them. It costs about two grand a week, so it better.'

'That's a lot of bread.'

'When Elizabeth is finished here, I want you to take

her there, try to get her in. It's first come, first served, but there are beds open now.'

'I think she's going to need at least another day here, maybe two, before she gets cleaned up and can take that next step.'

'That's fine. Whenever she's ready.'

Bosch reached into the pocket of his jacket and pulled out the sock containing the cash roll. He handed it to Cisco.

'Use this. It should get a month at that place. Maybe longer if she needs it.'

Cisco reluctantly took it.

'This is cash? You just want to give it to me?'

Cisco looked around the yard and through the fencing to the outside streets. Bosch realized how it might look to anyone watching.

'Shit, I'm sorry. I wasn't thinking.'

Now Bosch looked around. He saw no sign of surveillance, but he probably wouldn't have.

'No worries,' Cisco said. 'For a good cause.'

'So, you'll handle that?' Bosch asked. 'You've been paying forward, backward, and sideways with this.'

'I don't mind. We're doing a good thing. You want to go in now?'

'You know what? I was thinking maybe I shouldn't. If she's going to get agitated, then she doesn't need to see me. I don't want to set her off.'

'You sure?'

'Yeah, if she's doing good, keep her doing good. I'm happy with that.'

Cisco tossed the sock up and then caught it.

'Let me guess,' he said. 'Earthquake money?'

'Yeah,' Bosch said. 'I thought, what the hell, put it to good use.'

'Yeah, but you know you just jinxed the whole city. As soon as you spend the earthquake money, the big one hits. Everybody knows that.'

'Yeah, well, we'll just have to see. I'll let you get back to it. Thanks, Cisco.'

'No, thank you. And someday I think she'll be doing the thanking.'

'Not necessary now, not necessary then. Let me know how it goes with that other place if you get her in.'

'Will do.'

After driving away, Bosch cut west and went by the Start after Googling its location on his phone. He could tell it had once been a Holiday Inn or some other midrange hotel. It was now painted stark white. It looked clean and cared for – at least on the outside. He was happy with that.

He kept driving and started heading home. Almost the whole way he thought about his decision not to go in and visit Elizabeth Clayton. He wasn't sure what that meant or what he was doing. She had tapped into a need he had to reach out and help someone, whether they welcomed his help or not. He was sure that if he sat down with a shrink for an hour – maybe his longtime LAPD counselor Carmen Hinojos – there would be a whole raft of psychological underpinnings to his actions. And the money. He had very specifically committed funds that would not upset any financial aspect of his life. So was there a sacrifice in that?

There had been a time when Bosch as a boy, obviously wanting to escape his life in youth halls and foster homes, had become fascinated with the great explorers who had discovered new lands and cultures. Men who had left their places and stations in life to find something new or to stand against something old, like slavery. As he traveled from one bed to another, the one thing he carried from place to place was a book about the Scottish missionary and explorer David Livingstone, who had done both. Bosch didn't remember the title of the book anymore but he remembered many of the ideas the man espoused. Over time he had cemented them like a mason into his own belief system and they formed the brick foundation of who he was as both a detective and a man.

Livingstone had said sympathy was no substitute for action. That was an essential brick in Bosch's wall. He had built himself as a man of action and, at the moment when the integrity of his life's work had been called into question by a man on death row, he had chosen to turn his sympathy for Elizabeth Clayton into action. He understood that but was unsure if anyone else would. They would see other motives. Elizabeth would as well, and that was why he had chosen not to see her.

He knew he had done what he needed to do and that he would probably never see her again.

It was only nine when he reached home, but Bosch was exhausted and looking forward to crashing into his bed for the first time in almost a week. He got in, checked the locks, and put the broomstick back into the track of the deck slider. He then walked down the hall, dropping his jacket and shirt on the floor as he went.

He finished getting undressed and crawled onto the bed, ready to completely succumb to sleep's rehab and restoration. When he reached over to the clock so he could push the daily six a.m. alarm back a couple hours, he saw a folded envelope on the bed table. He unfolded it to find that it was addressed to him at the SFPD station.

He suddenly thought someone had been in the house and put the envelope there for him to find. Then his weary mind focused and he remembered placing the letter there three nights earlier. He had completely forgotten about it and had not slept in the bed since.

He decided the letter could wait until morning. He adjusted the alarm, turned off the light, and put his head between two pillows.

He lasted no more than thirty seconds. He pulled the top pillow away, reached up, and turned the light back on. He opened the envelope.

It contained a folded newspaper clip. It was a *San Fernando Valley Sun* story from almost a year earlier, reporting on the department's renewed effort to find out what had happened to Esmerelda Tavares. Bosch had given the interview to a reporter for the local weekly, hoping to spawn feedback and possible information from the public. A few tips had come in but nothing of merit, nothing that panned out. And now a year later, this letter.

The clip was accompanied by a piece of white paper folded three times. In a handwritten scrawl it said,

I know what happened to Esme Tavares.

The note included the name Angela and a phone number with an 818 area code.

The Valley.

Bosch got up and reached for his phone.

43

Angela Martinez, the author of the note to Bosch, turned out to know exactly what had happened to Esmerelda Tavares because she was Esmerelda Tavares.

On Wednesday night, Bosch had called the number on the letter he had received, and the woman who identified herself as Angela said she would meet him at nine the next morning at her home in Woodland Hills.

The woman who answered the door of the condo on Topanga Canyon Boulevard was blond and in her midthirties. Bosch had spent a lot of time over the previous two years looking at photographs of the dark-haired, dark-eyed Esme Tavares of fifteen years before. He had one shot of her, her lips pursed in a pout, posted in the cell so that he would always be reminded of the case. He had chosen the pout photo out of all the rest because he knew the set of a person's closed mouth changed little over time. The woman who called herself Angela wasn't smiling when she answered the door, and he knew right away that she was Esme.

And she recognized that he knew.

'You have to stop looking for me,' she said.

They sat in her living room and she told him her story. Once she got going, he could have filled in the details ahead of her, but he let her tell it just the same. Young woman caught in a bad marriage to an older, dominating man; physically abused regularly and tied to a baby she never wanted to have – that her husband wanted only as a means of controlling her. She made the hard choice to leave everything behind, including the child, and disappear.

She had help, and when Bosch probed deeper with his questions, it became clear that help came from a lover she had had on the side at the time and had now lived with for fifteen years. They had first moved away and lived in Salt Lake City together. They came back ten years later because both missed the city where they had grown up.

Her story had more holes in it than a San Pedro fishing net but Bosch thought the omissions and incongruities were designed to cast her in the best light in a place of deep shadows. She seemed to show no guilt about the daughter she had left in a crib or about the efforts of the community to find her. She professed to be unaware of all of that because she was then living in Salt Lake City.

She also claimed that her disappearance was not an effort in any way to cast suspicion on the husband she left behind. She said she had no alternative but to run.

'If I had tried to just leave him, he would have killed me,' she said. 'Admit it, you thought he had killed me.'

'That might be true,' Bosch said. 'But that was at least in part dictated by the circumstances of you disappearing with the baby left in the crib.'

In the end, Angela Martinez née Esmerelda Tavares was singularly unapologetic for what she had done. Not to Bosch, the police, or the community. And most of all not to her baby daughter, whom her husband gave up for adoption a year after his wife was gone.

'Do you even know where she is?' Bosch asked, the dispassionate detective pose not working at the moment.

'Wherever it is, I'm sure she's in a better place than if I had stayed in that house of horrors,' Martinez said. 'She might not have survived it. I know I wouldn't have.'

'But how did you know he would give her up once you were gone? She could still be in that house of horrors as far as you knew back then.'

'No, I knew he would give her up. He only wanted her so I would be tied to him. I proved him very wrong.'

Bosch thought about the intervening years and all the efforts to find her. He thought about Detective Valdez, now the chief of police, haunted by the case for so long. Bosch knew that on one level it was a good outcome. The mystery was solved and Esme was alive. But Bosch didn't feel good about it.

'Why now?' Bosch said. 'Why'd you reach out now?'

'Albert and I want to get married,' she said. 'It's time. My husband never divorced me – that's how controlling he was. He never had me declared dead. But I hired a lawyer and he'll handle it now. The first step was to solve the mystery that everybody's been so worked up about for so long.'

She smiled as though she was proud of her actions, energized by knowing she had kept the secret for so long.

'Aren't you still afraid of him, your husband?' Bosch asked.

'Not anymore,' she said. 'I was just a girl then. He doesn't scare me now.'

Her smile had now turned into the pout from the photo Bosch had hung in the cell where he worked.

He stood up.

'I think I have what I need to close this out,' he said.

'That's all you need to know?' she asked.

She seemed surprised.

'For now,' Bosch said. 'I'll get back to you if there's anything else.'

'Well, you know where to find me,' she said. 'Finally.'

Bosch headed to the station after that. He was morose. He was coming in with another case closed but there was nothing to feel good about. A lot of people had spent time, money, and emotions on Esme Tavares. As had always been suspected, Esme Tavares was dead. But Angela Martinez was alive.

After parking at SFPD, he made a swing through the detective bureau on his way to the main interior hallway of the station. The pods were empty and Bosch heard voices from the war room. He suspected the detectives were taking a joint lunch break.

The chief of police's office was located at the center of the station and across a hallway from the watch lieutenant's office. Bosch stuck his head in the door and asked Valdez's secretary if the boss had a free five minutes. He knew that once he got in the room with the man, the conversation would likely last a lot longer. The secretary called back to the room behind her desk and got an approval. Bosch stepped in.

Valdez was in uniform as usual and seated behind his desk. He held up the A section of the *Times*.

'Just reading about you, Harry,' he said. 'They exonerated you pretty good here. Congratulations.'

Bosch sat down across the desk from him.

'Thanks,' he said.

Bosch had read the story that morning before heading off to his appointment and was satisfied with it. However, he knew that more people read the Sunday edition of the *Times* than the Thursday paper. There was always going to be a gulf between those who had read that he was a crooked cop and those who read the never-mind-he's-straight story.

It didn't bother him too much. The one person he wanted most to read the latest story had already seen it online and had texted him, saying again that she was very proud of him and happy with the outcome of the Borders case.

'So,' he said. 'I'm not sure how to tell you this, so I'll just tell you. I just met Esme Tavares. She's alive and well and living in Woodland Hills.'

Valdez almost came out of his seat. He leaned violently forward across the desk, his face showing his surprise.

'What?'

Bosch ran down the story, beginning with him opening the letter the night before.

'Mother of God,' Valdez said. 'I've had her as dead for fifteen years. Let me tell you, many was the night I wanted to go to that house and drag that asshole husband of hers behind the back of my car until he told me where she was buried.'

'I know. Me too.'

'I mean, Christ, I fell in love with her. You know how you do with victims sometimes?'

'Yeah, I had a little bit of that too. Until today.'

'So did she tell you why?'

Bosch recounted the conversation he'd had that

morning with Angela Martinez. As he told it, Valdez's face grew increasingly dark with anger. He shook his head several times and wrote some notes down on a scratch pad on his desk.

When Bosch was finished, the chief checked his notes before speaking.

'Did you advise her?' he asked.

Bosch knew he was asking if Bosch had informed Martinez of her constitutional rights to an attorney and to avoid self-incrimination.

'No,' Bosch said. 'I didn't think I had to. She called me to her place and we sat in her living room. I identified myself and she obviously knew who I was. But it doesn't matter, Chief. I know what you're thinking, and those things never work out.'

'This is a fraud,' Valdez said. 'Over the years, we've spent probably close to half a million dollars looking for her. I remember when she was first reported missing, the overtime was flowing like an open fire hydrant. It was all hands on deck. And then we've never let up, right on up to you taking the case and running with it.'

'Look, I hate to come off as defending her, but she committed a moral crime, not a crime that the D.A. will find prosecutable. She was escaping from what she considered a dangerous situation. She was long gone before the overtime and everything else started flowing. She can claim she didn't know or that it was too dangerous to call in and say she was okay. She's got a lot of defenses. The D.A. won't touch it.'

The chief didn't respond. He leaned back in his chair and stared at a toy police helicopter hanging on a string from the ceiling. He liked to say it was the tiny department's air squadron.

'Shit,' he finally said. 'I wish there was something we could do about it.'

'We just have to live with it,' Bosch said. 'She was in a bad situation back then. She made the wrong choice, but people are flawed. They're selfish. All this time we thought she was dead, she was pure and innocent to us. Now we find out she was the kind that would leave a baby in a crib to save herself.'

Bosch thought about Jose Esquivel Jr. dying with his cheek on the linoleum in the back hallway of his father's business. He wondered if anybody was pure and innocent.

Valdez got up from his desk and went to the bulletin board over the low row of filing cabinets against the right wall. He flipped back some deployment sheets, then weeded through a stack of Wanted flyers until he found the MISSING leaflet with the photo of Esme Tavares on it circa 2002. He tore it off the board and crumpled it between his hands, crushing the ball as small as he could. He then fired a shot at a trash can at the end of the file cabinets.

He missed.

'What's this world about, Harry?' he asked.

'I don't know,' Bosch said. 'This week I closed out a double murder and a fifteen-year-old missing-persons case. And I don't feel good about any of it.'

Valdez dropped back into his seat.

'You gotta feel good about the *farmacia* caper,' he said. 'You took two pieces of shit off the board.'

Bosch nodded. But the truth was, it felt to him like he

was walking in circles. True justice was the brass ring just out of reach.

Bosch stood up.

'You going to call up Carlos and tell him he's off the hook?' he asked.

Carlos Tavares was Esmerelda's husband, fifteen years a suspect.

'Fuck him,' Valdez said. 'He's still an asshole. He can read about it in the paper.'

Bosch went to the door and then looked back at his boss.

'I'll have the report on this finished today,' he said.

'Good,' Valdez said. 'Then we go drinking.'

'That sounds right.'

44

Bosch wanted to avoid the detective bureau. He didn't want to talk anymore. Bella Lourdes and the others would find out soon enough about Esme Tavares being alive and well, and it would be the talk of the department and then the whole town. But Bosch had talked about it enough for the time being.

He walked out the front door of the station and then crossed the street. He went through the Public Works yard and into the jail. After unlocking his cell, he slid the heavy steel door open and it banged hard against its frame. Like the police chief, Bosch went to the photo of Esme Tavares to yank it down. But then he stopped. He decided to leave it in place so he would always see it and it would remind him about how wrong he had been about the case.

It was the child in the crib that had misled him. He knew this. It seemed against all laws of nature, and so it had led him and many others before him down the wrong path.

He stood there looking at the photo and considered the irony of the week. Elizabeth Clayton couldn't recover from the loss of a child and wandered the earth as a zombie, not caring what was done to her or what depravity she had willingly sunk to. Esme Tavares left a child in a crib and apparently never looked back.

The reality of the world was dark and horrifying. Bosch sat down behind his makeshift desk to do the paperwork that would document the grim reality of it. But he found that he couldn't even begin.

He contemplated this for a long moment and then stood back up. There was a bench that ran down the center of the cell perpendicular to his desk. He used it mostly to spread out photos and files so that he could review stubborn cases from a fresh angle, often looking at the crime scene photos placed side by side down the length of the scarred wooden bench. He had been told that the bench had been nicknamed 'the diving board' back in the day because it had been the jumping-off point to oblivion for a handful of inmates over time. They would step up on the bench, wrap one leg from their jail pants through the bars guarding the overhead air vent, then wrap the other around their neck.

They'd jump off the end of the bench into the dark pool of emptiness, and their misery would be over.

Bosch stepped up onto the bench now. He reached above his head to grasp one of the overhead bars for support.

He dug into his pocket and pulled out his phone. Checking the screen, he held the phone up, turning on the bench, moving his arm until he saw one service bar finally appear in the corner. With his thumb, he went to his contact list and scrolled until almost the end and hit the number he was looking for.

Lucia Soto answered right away.

'Harry, what's up?'

'Did you pull that case I told you about?'

'Daisy Clayton? Yes, first thing this morning.'

'And?'

'You were right, gathering dust. Nobody's worked it in three, four, years except for the annual due diligence reports, which are word-for-word copies of the year before. You know how it goes: "No viable leads at this time" because they didn't really look for viable leads.'

'And?'

'And I think they were wrong. I saw some stuff. There are workable angles. It was pretty much written off as a serial. Somebody who moved through Hollywood, did his thing, and moved on. But I'm not so sure about that. I looked at the photos. There was a familiarity with her and the place she was left. He knew the area. I'm going to—'

'Lucia.'

'What, Harry?'

'Cut me in.'

'What do you mean?'

'You know what I mean. I want in. Let's go get him.'

Acknowledgments

Many people contributed their time, experience, and expertise to the author in the research and writing of this novel. On the research side of things they include Rick Jackson, Tim Marcia, Mitzi Roberts, David Lambkin, Dennis Wojciechowski, Irwin Rosenberg, Anthony Vairo, Lynn Smith, Adam Frisch, Henrik Bastin, and Daniel Daly. On the writing side, there was Asya Muchnick, Bill Massey, Harriet Bourton, Emad Akhtar, Pamela Marshall, Terrill Lee Lankford, Jane Davis, Heather Rizzo, John Houghton, and Linda Connelly. Many of those named here had their feet firmly planted in both sides of the equation.

To those listed and those left off inadvertently or by choice to remain anonymous, the author is deeply grateful.

At the end of a long night, Detectives Renée Ballard and Harry Bosch cross paths for the first time in

DARK SACRED NIGHT

Detective Renée Ballard is working the graveyard shift, and returns to Hollywood Station in the early hours to find that an older man has snuck in and is rifling through past crime files.

The intruder is none other than legendary LAPD detective Harry Bosch, working a cold case that has gotten under his skin. Bosch is investigating the death of fifteen-year-old Daisy Clayton, a runaway who was brutally murdered.

Ballard, Bosch, and his former partner Lucia Soto, will soon become dangerously obsessed with finding out what happened to Daisy and trying to finally bring her killer to justice.

Turn the page for an exclusive early look at the new blockbuster thriller from the crime writing genius that is Michael Connelly . . .

Ballard

1

The patrol officers had left the front door open. They thought they were doing her a favor, airing the place out. But that was a violation of crime scene protocol regarding evidence containment. Bugs could go in and out. There were extenuating circumstances, though. The report that Ballard had gotten from the watch lieutenant was that the body was two to three days old in a closed house with no air conditioning and, in his words, ripe as a bag of skunks.

There were two black-and-whites parked along the curb in front of Ballard. Three blue suits were standing between them, waiting for her. Ballard didn't really expect them to have stayed inside with the body.

Up above, an airship circled at three hundred feet, holding its beam on the street. It looked like a leash of light, tethering the circling craft, keeping it from flying away.

Ballard killed the engine but sat in her city ride for a moment. She had parked in front of the gap between two houses and could look out at the lights of the city spreading in a vast carpet below. Not many people realized that Hollywood Boulevard wound up into the mountains, narrow and tight, to where it was strictly residential and far in all ways from the glitz and grime of the Hollywood Boulevard tourist mecca, where visitors posed with costumed superheroes and sidewalk stars. Up here it was money and power and Ballard knew that a murder in the hills always brought out the department's big guns. She was just babysitting. She would not have this case for long. It would go to West Bureau or possibly even Robbery-Homicide Division downtown.

She looked away from the view and tapped the overhead light so she could see her notebook. She had just come from her day's first call out, a routine break-in off Melrose, and had her notes for the report she would write once she got back to Hollywood Division. She flipped to a fresh page and wrote the time—1:47 a.m.—and the address. She then turned the light off and got out, leaving the blue flashers on. She went to the trunk, where she kept her crime scene kit.

It was a Tuesday morning, her third shift of a week running solo, and Ballard knew she would need to get at least one more wear out of her suit. That meant not fouling it with the stink of decomp. At the open trunk she slipped off her jacket, folded it carefully, and placed it in one of the empty cardboard evidence boxes. She then removed her crime scene overalls from a plastic bag and pulled them on over her boots, slacks, and blouse. She zipped them up to her chin and then, placing one boot and then the other up on the bumper, tightened the Velcro cuffs around her ankles. After she did the same around her wrists, her clothes were hermetically sealed.

She got gloves and a breathing mask out of the kit and, leaving the trunk open, walked up to join the three uniformed officers. As she approached, she recognized Sergeant Stan Dvorek, the area boss, and two officers whose longevity on the graveyard shift got them the cushy and slow Hollywood Hills beat.

Dvorek was leaning against one of the car's trunk with his arms folded in front of his chest. He was known as the Relic. Anybody who actually liked being on the midnight shift and lasted significant years on it ended up with a nickname. Dvorek was the current record holder, celebrating his tenth year on the late show just a month before. The officers with him, Anthony Anzelone and Dwight Doucette, were Caspar and Deuce. Ballard, with little more than two years on graveyard, had no nickname bestowed upon her yet. At least none that she knew about.

'Fellas,' Ballard said.

'Whoa, Sally Ride,' Dvorek said. 'When's the shuttle taking off?'

Ballard spread her arms to display herself. She knew the overalls were baggy and looked like a space suit. She thought maybe she had just been christened with a nickname.

'That would be never,' she said. 'So whadda we got that chased you out of the house?'

'It's bad in there,' said Anzelone.

'It's been cooking,' Doucette added.

The Relic pushed off the trunk of his car and got serious.

'Female white, fifties, looks like blunt-force trauma and facial lacerations,' he said. 'Looks like somebody worked her over pretty good. Domicile in disarray. Could've been a break-in.'

'Sexual assault?' Ballard asked.

'Her nightgown's pulled up. She's exposed.'

'Okay, I'm going in. Which one of you brave lads wants to walk me through it?'

There were no immediate volunteers.

'Deuce, you're low man,' Dvorek said.

'Shit,' said Doucette.

He pulled a blue bandanna up from around his neck and over his mouth and nose.

'You look like a fucking Crip,' Anzelone said.

'Why, because I'm black?' Doucette asked.

'Because you're wearing a fucking blue bandanna,' Anzelone said. 'If it was red, I'd say you look like a fucking Blood.'

'Just show her,' Dvorek said. 'I really don't want to be here all night.'

Doucette broke off the banter and headed toward the open door of the house. Ballard followed.

'How'd we get this thing so late, anyway?' she asked.

'Next-door neighbor got a call from the victim's niece back in New York,' Doucette said. 'Neighbor has a key and the niece asked him to check because the lady wasn't responding to social media or cell calls for a few days. The neighbor opens the door, gets hit with the funk, and calls us.'

'At one o'clock in the morning?'

'No, much earlier. But see, he reported it as a suspicious odor but didn't go in and confirm the DB. So we are not talking about a hot shot. PM watch was cranking last night, so it got put on the back burner and then passed on to us. We got it in roll call and came by here as soon as we could.'

Ballard nodded. The buck had been passed shift to shift because nobody wants to work a possible body

424

case that has been cooking in a closed house.

'Where's the neighbor now?' Ballard asked.

'Back home,' Doucette said. 'Probably taking a shower and sticking Vicks Vapo up his nose. He's never going to be the same again.'

'We gotta get his prints to exclude him, even if he says he didn't go in.'

'Roger that. I'll get the print car up here.'

Ballard followed Doucette over the threshold and into the house. The breathing mask was almost useless. The putrid odor of death hit her strongly, even though she was breathing through her mouth.

She looked around. The house was cantilevered out over the hillside, making the view through the floor-to-ceiling glass wall a stunning sheath of twinkling lights. Even at this hour the city seemed alive and pulsing with light and grand possibilities.

'What about lights?' Ballard asked.

'Nothing was on in here when we came in,' said Doucette.

Ballard noted the answer. No lights on could mean that the intrusion occurred during the daytime or late at night, after the homeowner had shut things down for the night. She knew that most home invasions were nighttime capers.

Doucette, who was also wearing gloves, hit a wall switch by the door and turned on a line of ceiling lights. The interior was an open-loft design, taking advantage of the view from any spot in the living room, dining room, kitchen. The staggering view was counterbalanced on the rear wall by three large paintings that were part of a series depicting a woman's red lips.

Ballard noticed broken glass on the floor near the kitchen island but she saw no shattered windows.

'Any sign of a break-in?' she asked.

'Not that we saw,' Doucette said. 'There's broken shit all over the place but no broken windows, no obvious point of entry that we found.'

'Okay.'

'The body's down here.'

He moved into a hallway off the living room and held his hand over the bandanna and his mouth as a second brace of protection against the intensifying odor.

Ballard followed. The house was a single-level contemporary. She guessed it was built in the fifties, when one level was enough. Nowadays anything built in the hills was multilevel and built to the maximum extent of code.

They passed open doorways to a bedroom and a bathroom, then entered a master bedroom that was in disarray with a lamp on the floor, its shade dented and bulb shattered. Clothes were strewn haphazardly over the bed, and a long-stemmed glass that had contained what looked like red wine was snapped in two on the white rug, its contents spread in a splash stain.

'Here you go,' Doucette said.

He pointed through the open door of the bathroom and then stepped back to allow Ballard in first.

Ballard stood in the doorway but did not enter the bathroom. The victim was faceup on the floor. She was a large woman with her arms and legs spread wide. Her eyes were open, her lower lip torn, and her upper right cheek gashed open, exposing grayish pink tissue. A halo of dried blood from an unseen scalp wound surrounded her head on the white tile squares.

A flannel nightgown with hummingbirds on it was pulled up over the hips and bunched above the abdomen and around the breasts. Her feet were bare and spread three feet apart. There was no visual injury to the genitalia.

Ballard could see herself in a floor-to-ceiling mirror on the opposite wall of the room. She squatted down in the doorway and kept her hands on her thighs. She studied the tiled floor for footprints, blood, and other evidence. Besides the blood that had pooled and dried around the dead woman's head, she noted an intermittent ribbon of small blood smears on the floor between the body and the bedroom.

'Deuce, go close the front door,' she said.

'Uh, okay,' Doucette said. 'Any reason?'

'Just do it. Then check the kitchen.'

'For what?'

'A water bowl on the floor. Go.'

Doucette left and Ballard heard his heavy footsteps move back up the hallway. She stood and entered the room, came up close on the body, and squatted again. She leaned down, putting a hand on the floor for balance, in an attempt to see the scalp wound. The dead woman's hair was too thick and curly for her to locate it.

Ballard looked around the room. The bathtub was surrounded by a marble sill holding multiple jars of various bath salts and candles burned down to nothing. There was a folded towel on the sill as well. Ballard shifted so she could see into the tub. It was empty but the drain stopper was down. It was the kind with a rubber lip that creates a seal. Ballard reached over, turned on the cold water for a few seconds and then turned it off.

She stood up and stepped over to the edge of the tub. She had put in enough water to surround the drain. She waited and watched.

'There's a water bowl.'

Ballard turned. Doucette was back.

'Did you close the front door?' she asked.

'It's closed,' Doucette said.

'Okay, look around. I think it's a cat. Something small. You'll have to call animal control.'

'What?'

Ballard pointed down at the dead woman.

'An animal did that. A hungry one. They start with the soft tissue.'

'Are you fucking kidding me?'

Ballard looked back into the tub. Half of the water she had put into the tub was gone. The drain's rubber seal had a slow leak.

'There's no bleeding with the facial injuries,' she said. 'That happened postmortem. The head wound on the back of the head is what killed her.'

Doucette nodded.

'Someone came up and cracked her head from behind,' he said.

'No,' Ballard said. 'It's an accidental death.'

'How?' Doucette asked.

Ballard pointed to the array of items on the bathtub sill.

'Based on decomp, I'd say it happened three nights ago,' she said. 'She turns out the lights in the house to get ready for bed. Probably that lamp on the floor in the bedroom was the one she left on. She comes in here, fills the tub, lights her candles, gets her towel ready. The hot water steams the tiles and she slips, maybe when she remembered she left her glass of wine on the bed table. Or when she started pulling up the nightgown so she could get in the tub.'

'What about the lamp and the spilled wine?' Doucette asked.

'The cat.'

'So, you just stood here and figured all this out?'

Ballard ignored the question.

'She was carrying a lot of weight,' she said. 'Maybe a sudden redirection as she was getting undressed—'Oh, I forgot my wine'—causes her to slip and she cracks her skull on the lip of the tub. She's dead, the candles burn out, the water slowly leaks down the drain.'

This explanation only brought silence from Doucette. Ballard looked down at the dead woman's ravaged face.

'The second day or so, the cat got hungry,' Ballard concluded. 'It went a little nuts, then it found her.'

'Jesus,' Doucette said.

'Get your partner in here, Deuce. Find the cat.'

'But wait a minute. If she was about to take a bath, why's she already in a nightgown?'

Ballard gestured to the mirror.

'She was obese,' Ballard said. 'She probably didn't like looking at herself naked in the mirror. So she comes home from work or her day, gets into nightclothes, gets her wine, maybe watches TV, who knows? She stayed dressed until it was time to get in the tub.'

Ballard turned to go past Doucette and step out of the room.

'Find the cat,' she said.

2

By three a.m. Ballard had cleared the scene of the death investigation and was back at Hollywood Division, working in a cubicle in the detective bureau. That vast room, which housed the workstations of forty-eight detectives by day, was deserted after midnight and Ballard always had her pick of the place. She chose a desk in the far corner, away from spillover noise and radio chatter from the watch commander's office down the front hallway. At five-seven she could sit down and disappear behind the computer screen and the half walls of the workstation like a soldier in a foxhole. She could focus and get her report writing done.

She had already completed the report on the home break-in that she had rolled on earlier in the night and was now ready to type up the accidental death report on the bathtub case. She was working alone, her partner, John Jenkins, on bereavement leave. There were no replacements for detectives who worked the late show. Ballard was halfway through a Tuesday night of at least a week going solo. It all depended on when Jenkins came back. His wife had endured a long, painful death from cancer. It tore him up and Ballard told him to take all the time he needed.

She opened her notebook to the page containing the details she had written about the second investigation and then opened up a blank incident report on her screen. Before beginning she dipped her chin and pulled the collar of her blouse up to her nose. She thought she picked up the slight odor of decomposition and death but couldn't be sure if it had permeated her clothes or was simply an olfactory memory.

While her head was down, she heard the metal-on-metal bang of a file drawer being closed. She looked up over the workstation divider to the far side of the bureau, where four-drawer file cabinets ran the length of the room. Every pair of detectives was assigned a four-drawer stack for storage.

But the man Ballard saw now opening another drawer to check its contents was not a detective she recognized, and she knew them all from once-a-month squad meetings that drew her to the station during daylight hours. The man who was seemingly checking file drawers at random had gray hair and a mustache. Ballard instinctively knew he didn't belong. She scanned the entire squad room to see if there was anybody else. The rest of the place was deserted.

The man opened and closed yet another drawer. Ballard used the sound to cover getting up from her chair. She squatted down and used the row of work cubicles as a blind as she moved to the central aisle, which would allow her to come up behind the intruder without being seen.

She had left her suit jacket in the cardboard box in the trunk of her car. This gave her unfettered access to the Glock holstered on her hip. She put her hand on the grips of the weapon and came to a stop ten feet behind the man.

'Hey, what's up?' she asked.

The man froze. He slowly raised his hands out of the open file drawer he was looking through and held them so she could see them.

'That's good,' Ballard said. 'Now, you mind telling me who you are and what you're doing?'

'Name's Bosch,' he said. 'I came in to see somebody.'

'What, somebody hiding in the files?'

'No, I used to work here. I know Money up front. He told me I could wait in the break room while they called the guy in. I sort of started wandering. My bad.'

Ballard came down from high alert and took her hand off her gun. She knew the name Bosch, and the fact that he knew the watch commander's nickname gave her some ease as well. But she still was suspicious.

'You kept a key to your old cabinet?' she asked.

'No,' Bosch said. 'It was unlocked.'

Ballard could see the push-in lock at the top of the cabinet was indeed extended in unlocked position. Most detectives kept their files locked.

'You got some ID?' she asked.

'Sure,' Bosch said. 'But just so you know, I'm a police officer. I have a gun on my left hip and you're going to see it when I reach back for my ID. Okay?'

Ballard brought her hand back up to her hip.

'Thanks for the heads-up,' she said. 'Tell you what, forget the ID for now. Why don't we secure the weapon first? Then we'll—'

'There you are, Harry.'

Ballard looked to her right and saw Lieutenant Munroe, the watch commander, entering the squad room. He saw Ballard and read her stance.

'Ballard, what's going on?' he asked.

'He came in here and was going through the files,' Ballard said. 'I didn't know who he was.'

'You can stand down,' Munroe said. 'He's good people—used to work homicide here. Back when we had a homicide table.'

Munroe turned his gaze to Bosch.

'Harry, what the hell were you doing?' he asked.

Bosch shrugged.

'Just checking my old drawers,' he said. 'Sort of got tired of waiting.'

'Well, Dvorek's in the house and waiting in the writing room,' Munroe said. 'And I need you to talk to him now. I don't like taking him off the street. He's one of my best guys and I want him back out there.'

'Got it,' Bosch said.

Bosch followed Munroe to the front hallway, which led to the watch office and the report-writing room, where Dvorek was waiting. Bosch looked back at Ballard as he went and nodded. Ballard just watched him go.

After they were gone, Ballard stepped over to the file drawer Bosch had last been looking in. There was a business card taped to it. That's what everybody did to mark their drawers.

DETECTIVE CESAR RIVERA
HOLLYWOOD SEX CRIMES UNIT

She checked the contents of the drawer. It was only half full and the files had fallen forward, probably while Bosch was leafing through them. She pushed them back up so they were standing and looked at what Rivera had written on the tabs. They were mostly victim names and case numbers. Others were marked with the main streets in Hollywood Division, probably containing miscellaneous reports of suspicious activities or persons.

She closed the drawer and checked the two above it, remembering that she had initially heard Bosch open at least three drawers.

These drawers were like the first, containing case files primarily listed by victim name, specific sex crime, and case number. At the front of the top drawer she noticed a paper clip that had been bent and twisted. She studied the push-button lock on the top corner of the cabinet. It was a basic lock and she knew it could easily have been picked with a paper clip. Security of the files themselves were not a priority because they were contained in a high-security police station.

Ballard closed the drawers and locked the cabinet and went back to the desk she had been using. She remained intrigued by Bosch's middle-of-the-night visit. She knew he had used the paper clip to unlock the file cabinet and that indicated he had more than a casual interest in the contents of its drawers. His nostalgic story about checking out his old file drawers had been a lie.

She picked up the coffee cup on the desk and walked down the hall to the first-floor break room to replenish it. The room was empty as usual. She refilled and carried the cup down the hallway to the watch office. Lieutenant Munroe was at his desk, looking at a deployment screen that showed a map of the division and the GPS markers for the patrol units out there. He didn't hear Ballard until she came up behind him.

'Quiet?' she asked.

'For the moment,' Munroe said.

Ballard pointed to a cluster of three GPS locators in the same spot.

'What's happening there?'

'That's the Mariscos Reyes truck. I've got three units ten-seven there.'

It was a lunch break at a food truck at Sunset and Western. It made Ballard realize she had not taken a food break and was getting hungry. She wasn't sure she wanted seafood, however.

'So, what did Bosch want?'

'He wanted to talk to the Relic about a body he found nine years ago. I take it Bosch is looking into it.'

'He said he's still a cop. Not for us, right?'

'Nah, he's a reserve up in the Valley for San Fernando PD.'

'What's San Fernando got to do with a murder down here?'

'I don't know, Ballard. You shoulda asked him while he was here. He's gone now.'

'That was quick.'

'Because the Relic couldn't remember shit.'

'Is Dvorek back out there?'

Munroe pointed to the three-car cluster on the screen.

'He's back out, but code seven at the moment.'

'I was thinking about going over there, getting a couple shrimp tacos. You want me to bring you back something?'

'No, I'm good. Take a rover with you.'

'Roger that.'

On the way back to the D bureau she stopped in the break room and dumped the coffee in the sink, rinsed out the cup, and put it on the drying rack. She then pulled a rover out of the charging rack in the bureau and headed out the back door of the station to her city car. The middle-watch chill had set in and she got her suit jacket out of the trunk and put it on before driving out of the lot.

The Relic was still parked at the food truck when Ballard arrived. As a sergeant, Dvorek rode in a solo car, so he had a tendency to hang with other officers on break for the company.

'Sally Ride,' he said, when he noticed Ballard studying the chalkboard menu.

'What's up, Sarge?' she said.

'Halfway through another night in paradise.'

'Yeah.'

Ballard ordered one shrimp taco and doused it liberally with one of the hot sauces from the condiment table. She took it over to Dvorek's black-and-white, where he was leaning against the front fender and finishing his own meal. Two other patrol officers were eating inside their car parked in front of his.

Ballard leaned against the fender next to him.

'Whatcha get?' Dvorek asked.

'Shrimp,' Ballard said. 'I only order off the blackboard. Means it's fresh, right? They don't know what they'll have until they buy it at the docks. Then they write it down.'

'If you think so.'

'I need to think so.'

She took her first bite. It was good and there was no fishy taste. She inspected the shrimp inside the taco and it looked like it had been cleaned.

'Not bad,' she said.

'I had the fish special,' Dvorek said. 'It's probably going to take me off the street as soon as it gets down into the lower track.'

'TMI, Sergeant. But speaking of coming in off the street, what did that guy Bosch want with you?'

'You saw him?'

'I caught him snooping in the files in the D bureau.'

'Yeah, he's kind of desperate. Looking for any angle on a case he's working.'

'In Hollywood? I thought he worked for San Fernando PD these days.'

'He does. But this is a private thing he's working. A girl who got killed here about nine years ago. I was the one who found the body, but damn if I could remember much that helped him.'

Ballard took another bite and started nodding. She asked the next question with her mouth full of shrimp and tortilla.

'Who was the girl?' she asked.

'A runaway. Name was Daisy. She was fifteen and putting it out on the street. Sad case. One night she got in the wrong car. I found her body in an alley behind the Pantages. Came in on an anonymous call—I do remember that.'

'Was that a street name?'

'No, the real thing. Daisy Clayton.'

'Was Cesar Rivera working the sex table back then?'

'Cesar? I'm not sure. We're talking nine years ago. He coulda been on sex then.'

'Well, did you remember Cesar having anything to do with the case back then? Bosch picked his file cabinet.'

Dvorek shrugged.

'I found the body and called it in, Renée—that's it,' he said. 'I had no part in it after that. I remember they sent me down to the end of the alley to string tape and keep people out. I was a slick sleeve back then.'

Uniformed cops got a hash mark on their sleeves for every five years of service. Back then, the Relic was a near-rookie. Ballard nodded and asked her last question.

'Did Bosch ask you anything I didn't just ask?'

'Yeah, but it wasn't about her. He asked about Daisy's boyfriend and whether I ever saw him on the street again after the murder.'

'Who was the boyfriend?'

'Just another runaway. I knew him as Speedy. Bosch said his name was Adam something. I forget. But the answer was no, I never saw that one after that.'

'What was their relationship?'

'They ran in a group. You know, for protection. Girl like that, she needed a guy out there. Like a pimp. She worked the street, he watched out for her, and they split the profits. Except that night, he dropped the ball. Too bad for her.'

Ballard nodded. She guessed that Bosch wanted to talk to Adam/Speedy as the person who would know the most about who Daisy Clayton knew and interacted with, and where she went on the last night of her life.

He could also have been a suspect.

'You know about Bosch, right?' Dvorek asked.

'Yeah,' Ballard said. 'He worked in the division way back when.'

'You know the stars out on the front sidewalk?'

''Course.'

There were memorial stars on the sidewalk in front of Hollywood Station honoring officers from the division who were killed in the line of duty.

'Well, there's one out there,' Dvorek said. 'Lieutenant Harvey Pounds. The story on him was he was Bosch's L-T when he worked here, and he got abducted and died of a heart attack when he was being tortured on a case Bosch was working.'

Ballard had never heard the story before.

'Anybody ever go down for it?' she asked.

'Depends on who you talk to,' Dvorek said. 'It's supposedly cleared-other, but it's another mystery in the big bad city. The word was that something Bosch did got the guy killed.'

'Cleared-other' was a designation for a case that was officially closed but without an arrest or prosecution.

'Supposedly the file on it is sealed. High Jingo.'

'High Jingo' was LAPD-speak for when a case involved department politics. The kind of case where a career could be diverted by a wrong move.

The information on Bosch was interesting but not on point. Before Ballard could think of a question that would steer Dvorek back toward the Daisy Clayton case, his rover squawked and he took a call from the watch office. Ballard listened as Lieutenant Munroe dispatched him to a Beachwood Canyon address to supervise a team responding to a domestic dispute.

'Gotta go,' he said as he balled up the foil his tacos had come in. 'Unless you want to ride along and back me up.'

It was said in jest, Ballard knew. The Relic didn't need backup from the late show detective.

'I'll see you back at the barn,' she said. 'Unless that goes sideways and you need a detective.'

'Roger that,' he said.

3

Dayside detectives were all about traffic patterns. Most days the majority of daysiders got to the bureau before six a.m. so they could split by midafternoon, missing the traffic swell both coming and going. Ballard counted on this when she decided she was going to ask Cesar Rivera about the Daisy Clayton case. She spent the remainder of her shift waiting on his arrival by pulling up and studying the electronic records available on the murder of Daisy Clayton.

The murder book, a blue binder full of printed reports and photos, was still the bible of a homicide investigation in the Los Angeles Police Department, but as the world turned digital, so did the department. Using her detective services password, Ballard was able to access many of the reports and photos from the case that had been scanned into the department's digital archives. Most important, she was able to view the chronological record, which was always the spine of the case, a narrative of all moves made by investigators assigned to the case.

Ballard determined immediately that the nine-year-old murder was officially classified as a cold case and assigned to the Open-Unsolved Unit, which was part of the elite Robbery-Homicide Division working out of headquarters downtown. Ballard had once been assigned to the RHD and knew many of the detectives and associated players. Included in that number was her former lieutenant, who pushed her up against a wall and tried to force himself on her in a bathroom at a squad Christmas party three years earlier. Her rejection of him and subsequent complaint and internal investigation was what landed her on the night shift at Hollywood Division. The complaint was determined to be unfounded because her own partner at the time did not back her up, even though he had witnessed the altercation. Department administrators determined that it would be for the good of all involved to separate Ballard and Lieutenant Robert Olivas. He stayed put in RHD and Ballard was moved out, the message to her clear. Olivas got by unscathed, while she went from an elite unit to a posting no one ever applied or volunteered for, a slot normally reserved for the department's freaks and fuckups.

In recent months, the irony of this was not lost on Ballard as the country and the Hollywood entertainment industry in particular were awash in scandals involving sexual harassment and worse. The chief of police even instituted a task force to handle all the claims pouring in from Hollywood, many of them decades old. Of course, the chief's task force was composed of RHD detectives, and Olivas was one of its supervisors.

The history with Olivas was not far from Ballard's mind as her curiosity about Bosch and the case he was working sent her into the department's digital channels. She knew that her snooping around on the Daisy Clayton case could come to the attention of her nemesis and he might attempt to do something about it.

The threat was there but it wasn't enough to stop her. She wasn't afraid of Olivas when he followed her into the bathroom at the Christmas party three years ago; she shoved him back and he fell into a bathtub. She wasn't afraid of him now.

She scrolled to the end of the chrono first in order to see the latest moves on the case, if any. She quickly learned that outside of annual due diligence checks, the investigation had largely been dormant for eight years, until it was assigned six months earlier to a cold case detective named Lucia Soto. Ballard didn't know Soto but she knew of her. She was the youngest female detective ever assigned to RHD, beating the record Ballard had previously held by being eight months younger when appointed.

'Lucky Lucy,' Ballard said out loud.

Ballard also knew that Soto was currently assigned to the Hollywood Sex Harassment task force because the powers that be in the department—mostly white men—knew that putting as many women on the task force as possible was a prudent move. Soto, who already had a media profile and nickname because of an act of heroism that led to her RHD posting, was often used as the face of the task force when it came to press conferences and other media interactions.

This knowledge now gave Ballard pause. She put together a quick chronology. Six months earlier, Soto either requested or was assigned to the unsolved Daisy Clayton case. Shortly after, she was reassigned from the Open-Unsolved Unit to the harassment task force. Then Bosch shows up at Hollywood Station to ask questions about the case and attempt to get a look at the files of a sex crimes detective.

There was a connection there that Ballard didn't yet have. She quickly found it and started to understand things better when she conducted a new search of the department database and called up all cases in which Bosch was listed as having been a lead investigator. She zeroed in on the last case he handled before leaving the department. It was a multiple-victim murder involving an arson of an apartment building in which several victims, including children, died of smoke inhalation. On several of the reports associated with the case Bosch's partner was listed as Lucia Soto.

Ballard now had the connection—Soto took the Clayton case on and then somehow drew her former partner Bosch into it, even though he was no longer with the department. But Ballard didn't have the cause, meaning there was no explanation as to why Soto would go outside the department for help with the investigation, especially when she was moved out of Open-Unsolved for the task force.

Unable to answer that question for the moment, Ballard went back to the case files and started reviewing the investigation from the start. Daisy Clayton was deemed a chronic runaway who repeatedly left her own home as well as the temporary group homes and shelters she was placed in by the Department of Children and Family Services. Each time she ran, she ended up on the streets of Hollywood, joining other runaways and throwaways in homeless camps and squats in abandoned structures. She abused alcohol and drugs and sold herself on the streets.

The first record of a police interaction with Daisy was nineteen months before her death. It was the first of several arrests for drugs, loitering, and solicitation for prostitution. Because of her age, the early arrests only resulted in her being returned to her single mother, Elizabeth, or to DCF authorities. But nothing seemed to stop the cycle of her returning to the streets and of being under the influence of Adam Sands, a nineteen-year-old former runaway with his own history of drugs and crime.

Sands was interviewed at length by the original investigators on the case and was eliminated as a potential suspect through confirmation of an alibi. He was being held in the Hollywood Division jail at the time of Daisy Clayton's murder.

Cleared as a suspect, Sands was questioned extensively about the victim's routines and relationships. He claimed to have no information on who she had met with on the night of her murder. He revealed that her routine was to loiter near a shopping plaza on Hollywood Boulevard near Western Avenue that included a mini-market and a liquor store. She would solicit men as they were leaving the stores and then have sex with them in their cars after they drove into one of the many nearby alleys for privacy. Sands said he often stood lookout for her during the transactions but on the night in question he had been grabbed by police on a warrant for not appearing in court on a misdemeanor drug charge.

Daisy was left on her own at the shopping plaza and her body was found the next night in one of the alleys she used for her tricks. The body was found nude and had been cleaned with bleach. None of the victim's clothes were ever found. Detectives determined that as many as twenty hours passed between the time she was last seen at the shopping plaza soliciting johns and when police received an anonymous call about a body being seen in an alley and Officer Dvorek was dispatched to roll on the call. The missing hours were never accounted for but it was clear from the bleaching of the body that Daisy had been taken somewhere and then used and murdered, and her body was carefully cleaned of any evidence that might lead to her killer.

The one clue that the original detectives puzzled over throughout the investigation was a bruise on the body that they were convinced was a mark left by the killer. It was a circle two inches in diameter on the upper right hip of the body. Within the circle was a crossword with the letters A-S-P arranged horizontally and vertically with the S in common.

The circle around the crossword appeared to possibly be a snake eating itself but the blurring of the bruising in the tissue made this impossible to confirm. Detectives believed the mark might have come from some sort of stamp or weapon. Many hours of investigative work were expended on its meaning and application but no definitive conclusion was reached. The case was originally investigated by two homicide detectives assigned to the Hollywood Division and then reassigned to Wilshire Division when the regional homicide teams were consolidated and Hollywood lost its fabled murder unit.

The investigators' names were King and Carswell, and Ballard knew neither of them.

Time of death was established during the autopsy at ten hours after the victim was last seen and ten hours before the body was found.

The coroner's report listed the cause of death as manual strangulation. It further defined this conclusion by stating that marks left on the victim's neck by the killer's hands indicated that she was strangled from behind, possibly while being sexually assaulted. Tissue damage in both the vagina and anus was listed as both pre- and postmortem. The victim's fingernails were also removed postmortem, a move by the killer viewed as an attempt to make sure no biological evidence was left behind.

The body also showed postmortem abrasions and scratches that investigators believed occurred during an effort to clean the victim with a stiff brush and bleach, which was found in all orifices as well as the mouth and throat and ear canals of the victim. This led the medical examiner to conclude that the body had been submerged in bleach during this cleaning process.

This finding coupled with the time of death led investigators to conclude that Daisy had been taken off the street and to a hotel room or other location by the killer where a bleach bath could be prepared for cleaning the body.

'He's a planner,' Ballard said out loud.

The conclusions about the bleach led the original investigators to spend much of their time during the initial days of the investigation on a thorough canvas of every motel and hotel in the Hollywood area that offered

448

direct access to rooms off the parking lot. Photos of Daisy were shown to employees on all shifts, house-keepers were quizzed with regard to any reports of a strong odor of bleach, trash dumpsters were searched for bleach containers. Nothing came of the effort. The location of the murder was never determined, and with-out a crime scene, the case was handicapped from the start. Six months into the investigation the case went cold with no new leads and no suspects.

Ballard saved the crime scene photos for last because she knew they would be difficult to view. She wasn't wrong. The victim's age, the marks on her body and neck showing the overwhelming strength of her killer, her final naked repose on a spread of trash on the dirty asphalt . . . it all drew a sense of horror in Ballard, a sad empathy for this girl and what she had been through. Ballard had never been a detective who could leave the work in a drawer at the end of her shift. She carried it with her and it was her empathy that fueled her.

Before being assigned to the night beat, Ballard had been working toward a specialization in sexually motivated homicide at RHD. Her then-partner, Ken Chastain, was one of the premier investigators of sex killings in the department. Both had taken classes from and been mentored by Detective David Lambkin, long considered the department expert, until he pulled the pin and left the city for the Pacific Northwest.

That pursuit was largely sidelined by her transfer to the late show, but now as she reviewed the Clayton files, she saw a sexual predator hiding behind the words and reports, a predator unidentified for nine years now, and she felt a deep tug inside. It was the thing that went way back to her first thoughts of being a cop and a hunter of men who hurt women and leave them like trash in the alley. In her mind, she already gave this one a name— the Bleacher—and she wanted in on whatever it was that Harry Bosch was doing.

Ballard was pulled out of these thoughts when she heard voices. She looked up from the screen and over the workstation wall. She saw two detectives taking off their suit jackets and draping them over their chairs, readying themselves for a new day of work.

One of them was Cesar Rivera.

4

Ballard packed up her things and left her borrowed workstation. She first went into the print room to gather the reports she had fed into the communal printer after she had typed them up earlier. The detective squad lieutenant was old school and still liked hard-copy reports from her in the morning, even though she also filed them digitally. She separated the reports on the death investigation and the earlier burglary call, stapled them, and then walked them to the in-box on the desk of the lieutenant's adjutant so they were ready for his arrival. She then sauntered over to the sex crimes section and came up behind Rivera as he was sitting at his station and preparing for the day by dumping an airline-size bottle of whiskey into a mug of coffee. She didn't let on that she had seen this when she spoke.

'Hail, Cesar.'

Rivera jolted a bit in his seat, afraid his morning routine had been seen. He swiveled his chair around but relaxed when he saw it was Ballard. He knew she would not make any waves.

'Renée,' he said. 'What's up, girl? You got something for me?'

Ballard let the *girl* go. It was the least of the infractions that occurred around the department.

'No, nothing,' she said. 'Quiet night.'

She came around and leaned an elbow on the cubicle partition.

'So what's up?' Rivera asked.

'About to leave,' Ballard said. 'I was wondering, though. You know a guy who used to work out of here named Harry Bosch? He worked homicide.'

She pointed to the corner of the room where the homicide squad was once located. It was now the Crimes Against Persons section.

'Before my time,' Rivera said. 'I mean, I know who he is—everybody does, I think. But no, I never dealt with the guy. Why?'

'He was in the station this morning,' Ballard said.

'You mean on graveyard?'

'Yeah, he said he came in to talk to Dvorek about an old homicide. But I found him looking through your cabinets.'

She pointed toward the long row of file cabinets running along the wall. Rivera shook his head in confusion.

'My cabinets?' Rivera said. 'What the fuck?'

'How long have you been at Hollywood Division, Cesar?' Ballard asked.

'Seven years, what's that got to—'

'You know the name Daisy Clayton? She was murdered in '09. Classified as sexually motivated.'

Rivera shook his head.

'That was before my time here,' he said. 'I was at Hollenbeck then.'

He got up and walked over to the row of file cabinets. He pulled a set of keys out of his pocket and opened the top drawer of his four-drawer stack.

'Locked now,' he said. 'Was locked when I left last night.'

'I locked it after he left,' Ballard said.

She said nothing about finding the bent paper clip in the drawer.

'Isn't Bosch retired?' Rivera said. 'How'd he get in here?'

'He used his friendship with Lieutenant Munroe to get in and waited for Dvorek to come in off patrol,' Ballard said. 'He wandered, and that's when I saw him looking in the files. I was working over in the corner and he didn't see me.'

'He's the one who mentioned the Daisy case?'

'Daisy Clayton. No, actually I talked to Dvorek about what Bosch wanted to talk to him about and he told me about Clayton. Dvorek was first officer on scene with her. Bosch wanted to talk about the case.'

'I take it it's still open.'

'Yes. Hollywood had it initially, now it's assigned to Open-Unsolved downtown.'

Rivera walked back to his desk but stayed standing while he grabbed his coffee cup and took a long drink out of it. He then abruptly pulled the cup away from his mouth.

'Shit, I know what he was doing,' he said.

'What?' Ballard asked.

There was a sense of urgency in her voice.

'I got here just as they were reorganizing and moving homicide over to Wilshire Division,' Rivera said. 'The sex table was expanding and they brought me in. Me and Sandoval were add-ons, not replacements. We both came from Hollenbeck, see.'

'Okay,' Ballard said.

'So the lieutenant assigned me that cabinet, all four drawers, and gave me the key. But when I opened the top drawer to put stuff in there, it was full. All four drawers were full. Same with Sandoval—his four were filled up as well.'

'Filled with what? You mean with files?'

'No, every drawer was filled with shake cards. Stacks and stacks of them crammed in there. The homicide guys and the other detectives had decided to keep the old cards after the department went digital. They stuck them in the file drawers.'

Ballard knew that Rivera was talking about what were officially called field interview cards. They were 3x5 cards that were filled out by officers when they encountered people on the streets and while they were on patrol. The front of each card was a form with specific identifiers regarding the person interviewed, such as name, date of birth, address, gang affiliation, tattoos, and known associates. The back of each card was blank and that was where the officer could write any ancillary information about the person being interviewed.

Officers carried stacks of blank FI cards on their person or in their patrol cars—Ballard had always kept hers under the sun visor in her car when she had worked patrol in Pacific Division. At the end of shift, the cards were turned in to the divisional watch commander and the information on them was entered by clerical staff into a searchable database. Should a name that was run through the database produce a match, the inquiring officer or detective would have a ready set of facts, addresses, and known associates to start with.

The American Civil Liberties Union had long protested the department's use of the cards and the collection of information from citizens who had not committed crimes, calling the practice unlawful search and seizure and routinely referring to the unwarranted Q&As as shakedowns. The department had fended off all legal attempts to stop the practice, and many of the rank and file referred to the 3x5 cards as shake cards, a not-so-subtle dig at the ACLU.

'Why were they keeping them?' Ballard asked. 'Everything was put into the database and would be easier to find there.'

'I don't know,' Rivera said. 'They didn't do it that way at Hollenbeck.'

'So, what did you do, clear them out?'

'Yeah, me and Sandy emptied the drawers.'

'You threw them all out?'

'No, if I've learned anything in this department, it's not to be the guy who fucks up. We boxed them and took them to storage, let it be somebody else's problem.'

'What storage?'

'Across the lot.'

Ballard nodded. She knew he meant the structure at the south end of the station's parking lot. It was a single-level building that had once been a city utilities office but had been turned over to the station when more space was needed. The building was largely unused now. A gym for officers' use and a padded martial arts room had been set up in two of the larger rooms but the smaller offices were empty or used for nonevidentiary storage.

'So, this was seven years ago?' she asked.

'More or less,' Rivera said. 'We didn't move it all at once. I cleared one drawer out and when it got filled and I had to go down to the next, I'd clear that one. It went like that. Took about a year.'

'So, what makes you think that Bosch was looking for shake cards last night?'

Rivera shrugged.

'There would have been shake cards in there from the time of the murder you're talking about, right?'

'But the info on the shake cards is in the database?'

'Supposedly. But what do you put in the search window? See what I mean? There's a flaw. If he wanted to see who was hanging around Hollywood at the time of the murder, how do you search the database for that?'

Ballard nodded in agreement but knew that there were many ways to search the database to pull up info on field interviews by geography and timeframe. She thought Rivera was wrong about that but probably right about Bosch. He was looking for the shake cards but he probably had a different purpose in mind.

'Well,' she said. 'I'm out of here. Have a good one. Stay safe.'

'Yeah, you too, Ballard,' Rivera said.

Ballard left the detective bureau and went up to the women's locker room on the second floor. She changed out of her suit and into her sweats. Her plan was to head out to Venice, pick up her dog, and then carry her tent and a paddleboard out to the beach. In the afternoon, after she had rested and considered her approach, she'd deal with Bosch.

The morning sun blistered her eyes as she crossed the parking lot behind the station. She walked past her van and continued on to the old utilities building. She entered and found a couple other denizens of the late show working out before heading home after the morning rush hour.

She threw a mock salute at them and went down a hallway that led to former city offices now used for indiscriminate storage. The first room she checked contained items recovered in one of her own cases. The year before, she had taken down a burglar who had filled a motel room with property either stolen from the homes he broke into or bought with the money and credit cards he had stolen. Now a year later, much of it had still not been claimed and would remain in storage until the division organized an open house for victims as a last chance for them to claim their property.

The next room down was stacked with cardboard boxes containing old case files that for various reasons had to be kept. Ballard looked around here and moved several boxes in order to get to others. Soon enough, she opened a dusty box that was filled with FI cards. She had hit pay dirt.

Twenty minutes later she had culled twelve boxes of FI cards and lined them along the wall in the hallway. By individually sampling cards from each of the boxes she was able to determine that the cards spanned the years from 2006, when the digitizing initiative began, to 2010, when the homicide section was moved out of Hollywood Division. With the homicide detectives gone, there was no one in the bureau who felt the need to keep the original cards.

Ballard estimated that each of the boxes held up to a thousand cards. It would take several hours to comb through them all thoroughly. She wondered if that was what Bosch was expecting to do, or if he was planning a more precise search for one card or one night in particular. Perhaps the night Daisy Clayton was taken off the street.

Ballard knew she wouldn't know the answer until she asked Bosch.

She left a note on the row of boxes in the hallway, saying that the boxes were on hold for her. She returned to the parking lot and got into her van after checking the straps holding her boards to the roof racks. Shortly after she had been assigned to Hollywood Division and word leaked that she was involved in an internal harassment investigation, there were some in the division who attempted to retaliate against her. Sometimes it was basic bullying, sometimes it went deeper. One morning at the end of her shift, when she stopped her van at the station lot's electric gate, her paddleboard slid forward off the roof and crashed against the gate, splintering the nose's fiberglass. She repaired the board herself and started checking the rack straps every morning after her shift.

She took La Brea down to the 10 freeway and headed west toward the beach. She waited until a few minutes after eight o'clock to call the number for RHD that she still had programmed in her phone. A clerk answered and Ballard asked for Lucy Soto. She said the name with a clipped familiarity that imparted the idea that this was a cop-to-cop call. The transfer was made without question.

'This is Detective Soto.'

'This is Detective Ballard, Hollywood Division.'

There was a pause before Soto responded.

'I know who you are,' she said. 'How can I help you, Detective Ballard?'

Ballard was used to detectives she didn't know personally knowing about her. With female detectives, there was always an awkward moment. They either admired Ballard for her perseverance in the department or believed her actions had made their own jobs more difficult. Ballard always had to find out which it was, and Soto's opener gave no hint as to which camp she was in. Her repeating Ballard's name out loud might have been a move to let someone like a partner or supervisor on the task force know who she was talking to.

Not being able to read Soto yet, Ballard just pressed on.

'I work the late show here,' she said. 'Some nights it keeps me running, some night's not so much. My L-T likes me to have a hobby case to kind of keep me busy.'

'I don't understand,' Soto said. 'What's this have to do with me? I'm sort of in the middle of—'

'Yeah, I know you're busy. You're on the harassment task force. That's why I'm calling. One of your cold cases—that you're not working because of the task force—I was wondering if I could take a whack at it.'

'Which case, Ballard?'

'Daisy Clayton. Fifteen-year-old murdered up here in—'

'I know the case. What makes you so interested?'

'It was a big case here at the time. I heard some blue suiters talking about it, pulled up what I could on the box, and got interested. It looked like with this task force thing you weren't doing much with it at the moment.'

'And you want to give it a shot.'

'I make no promises but, yeah, I'd like to do some work on it. I would keep you fully in the loop. It's still your case. I'd just do some street work.'

Ballard was on the freeway but not moving. Her weeding through the boxes in the storage room had pushed her into the heart of rush hour. She knew the morning breeze would also be in full effect on the coast and she'd be paddling against it and the chop it would kick up. She was missing her window.

'It's nine years later,' Soto said. 'I'm not sure the street's going to produce anything. Especially on grave-yard. You'll be spinning your wheels.'

'Well, maybe,' Ballard said. 'But they're my wheels to spin. You okay with this or not?'

There was another long pause. Enough time for Ballard to move the van about five feet.

'There's something you should know,' Soto said. 'There's somebody else looking into it. Somebody outside the department.'

'Oh, yeah?' Ballard said. 'Who's that?'

'My old partner. His name's Harry Bosch. He's retired now but he . . . he needs the work.'

'Okay. Anything else I should know? Was this one of his cases?'

'No. But he knows the victim's mother. He's doing it for her.'

'Good to know.'

Ballard was now getting a better sense of the lay of the land. It was the true purpose of her call. Permission to work the case was the least of her concerns.

It was now time to end the call.

'If I come up with anything, I'll feed it to you,' Ballard

said. 'And I'll let you get back to the reckoning.'

Ballard thought she heard a muffled laugh.

'Hey, Ballard?' Soto then added quietly. 'I said I knew who you were. I also know who Olivas is. I mean, I work with him. I want you to know I appreciate what you did and I know you paid a price. I just wanted to say that.'

Ballard nodded to herself.

'That's good to know,' she said. 'I'll be in touch.'

Bosch

5

From the San Fernando Courthouse it was only a block's walk back to the old jail where Bosch did his file work. He covered the distance quickly, a spring in his step caused by the search warrant in his hand. Judge Atticus Finch Landry had read it and signed it while Bosch had waited outside his chambers in the courtroom. Bosch now had forty-eight hours to execute the warrant and hopefully find the bullet that would lead to a match that would lead to an arrest and the closing of another case.

He took the shortcut through the city's Public Works yard to the back door of the old jail. He pulled the key to the padlock as he moved toward the former drunk tank, where the open-case files were kept on steel shelves. He found that he had left the lock open and silently chastised himself. It was breach of his own as well as departmental protocol. The files were to be kept locked up at all times. And Bosch liked to keep the matters on his desk secure at all times too, even during a forty-minute search-warrant run to the courthouse next door.

He moved behind his makeshift desk—an old wooden door set across two stacks of file boxes—and sat down. Immediately, he saw the twisted paper clip sitting there on top of his closed laptop.

He stared at it. He had not put it there.

'You forgot that.'

Bosch looked up. The woman—the detective—from the night before at Hollywood Station was straddling the old bench that ran between the freestanding shelves full of case files. He could not have seen her coming into the cell. He looked over at the open door where the padlock dangled from its chain.

'Ballard, right?' he said. 'Good to know I'm not going crazy—I thought I had locked up.'

'I let myself in,' Ballard said. 'Lock picking one-oh-one.'

'It's a good skill to have. Meantime, I'm kind of busy here. Just got a search warrant I need to figure out how to execute without my suspect finding out. What do you want, Detective Ballard?'

'I want in.'

'In?'

'Daisy Clayton.'

Bosch considered her for a moment. She was attractive, maybe midthirties, and was wearing off-duty clothes. The night before, she was in a sharp-cut suit that made her seem more formidable—a must in the LAPD, where Bosch knew female detectives were often treated like office secretaries.

Ballard also had a deep tan, which to Bosch was at odds with the idea that someone who worked graveyard would need to sleep during the day and avoid the sun. But most of all he was impressed that it had been only twelve hours since she had surprised him at the file cabinets in the Hollywood detective bureau and she already appeared to have caught up to him and what he was doing.

'I talked to your old partner, Lucy,' Ballard said.

'She gave me her blessing. It is a Hollywood case, after all.'

'Was—till RHD took it,' Bosch said. 'They have standing now, not Hollywood.'

'And what's your standing? You're out of the LAPD. Doesn't seem to be any link to the town of San Fernando that I could see in the book.'

In his capacity as an SFPD reserve officer for the past three years, Bosch had largely been working on a backlog of cold cases of all kinds—murders, rapes, assaults. But the work was part time.

'They give me a lot of freedom up here,' Bosch said. 'I work these cases and I also work my own. Daisy Clayton's one of my own. You could say I have a vested interest. That's my standing.'

'And I have twelve boxes of shake cards at Hollywood Station,' Ballard said.

Bosch nodded. He was even more impressed. She had somehow figured out exactly what he had gone to Hollywood for. As he studied her, he decided it wasn't all tan. She had a mix of races in her skin. He guessed that she was probably Polynesian.

'I figure between the two of us, we could get through them in a couple nights,' Ballard said.

There was the offer. She wanted in and would give Bosch what he was looking for in trade.

'The shake cards are a long shot,' he said. 'Truth is, I've run the string out on the case. I was hoping there might be something there.'

'That's surprising,' Ballard said. 'I heard you're the kind of guy who never lets the string run out.'

Bosch didn't know what to say to that. He shrugged.

Ballard got up and walked toward him down the aisle between the shelves.

'Sometimes it's slow, sometimes it isn't,' she said. 'I'm going to start looking through the cards tonight. Between calls. Anything in particular I should look for?'

Bosch paused but knew he needed to make a decision. Trust her or keep her on the outside.

'Vans,' he said. 'Look for work vans, guys who carry chemicals maybe.'

'For transporting her,' she said.

'For the whole thing.'

'It said in the book the guy took her home or to a motel. Some place with a bathtub. For the bleaching.'

Bosch shook his head.

'No, he didn't use a bathtub,' he said.

She stared at him, waiting, not asking the obvious question of how he knew there was no bathtub used.

'All right, come with me,' he finally said.

He got up and led her out of the cell and back to the door to the Public Works yard.

'You looked at the book and the photos, right?' he said.

'Yes,' she said. 'Everything that was digitized.'

They walked into the yard, which was a large open-air square surrounded by walls. There were four bays, where equipment was stored and repaired. Bosch led Ballard into one of these.

'You saw the mark on the body?'

'The A-S-P?'

'Right. But they got the meaning of it wrong. The

original detectives. They went down a spiral with it and it was all wrong.'

He went to a workbench and reached up to a large translucent plastic tub with a blue snap on top. He brought it down and held it out to her.

'Twenty-five-gallon container,' Bosch said. 'Daisy was five-two, a hundred and five pounds. Small. He put her in one of these, then put in the bleach as needed. He didn't use a bathtub.'

Ballard studied the container. Bosch's explanation was plausible but not conclusive.

'That's a theory,' she said.

'No theory,' he said.

He put the container down on the floor so he could unsnap the top. He then lifted the tub up and angled it so she could see into it. He reached inside and pointed to a manufacturer's seal stamped into the plastic at the bottom. It was a two-inch circle with the A-S-P reading horizontally and vertically in the center.

'A-S-P,' he said. 'American Storage Products or American Soft Plastics. Same company, two names. The killer put her in one of these. He didn't need a bathtub or a motel. One of these and a van.'

Ballard reached into the container and ran a finger over the manufacturer's seal. Bosch knew she was drawing the same conclusion he had. The logo was stamped into the plastic on the underside of the tub, creating a ridged impression on the inside. If Daisy's skin was pressed against the ridges, the logo would have left its mark.

Ballard pulled her arm out and looked up from the tub to Bosch.

'How'd you figure this out?' she asked.

'I thought like he did,' Bosch said.

'Let me guess, these are untraceable.'

'They make them in Gardena, ship them everywhere, sell them online. No trace possible.'

'That would be too easy.'

'Yeah.'

Bosch snapped the top back on the tub and was about to put it back up on the high shelf.

'Can I take it?' Ballard asked.

Bosch turned to her. He knew he could replace it and knew she could easily get her own. He guessed it was a move to draw him further into a partnership. If he gave her something, then it meant they were working together.

He handed the tub over.

'It's yours,' he said.

'Thank you,' she said.

She looked at the open gate to the Public Works yard.

'Okay, so I start tonight on shakes,' she said.

Bosch nodded.

'Where were they?' he asked.

'In storage,' Ballard said. 'Nobody wanted to throw them out.'

'I figured. It was smart.'

'Right. Well, I'm gonna go. Might even go in early to get started.'

'Happy hunting. If I can get by, I will. But I have this search warrant and forty-eight hours to execute.'

'Right.'

'Otherwise, call me if you find something.'

He reached into a pocket and produced a business card with his cell number on it.

'Copy that,' she said.

Ballard walked off, carrying the container in front of her by holding it by indented grips on either side. As Bosch watched, she made a smooth U-turn and came back to him.

'Lucy Soto said you know Daisy's mother,' she said. 'Is that the standing you said you had?'

'I guess you could say that,' Bosch said. 'When did you talk to Soto?'

Ballard realized that she had made a mistake revealing her conversation with Soto. She quickly tried to cover.

'Oh, I just called her to get permission to pull files on the case,' she said. 'Where's the mother—if I want to talk to her?'

'My house. I can arrange it.'

'You live with her?'

'She's staying with me. It's temporary.'

'Okay. Got it.'

Ballard turned again and walked off. Bosch watched her go. She made no further U-turns.

Don't miss out – order your copy now.

ENJOYED TWO KINDS OF TRUTH?

Tweet him @ConnellyBooks

Follow him on facebook/MichaelConnellyBooks

Keep up to date with the latest news by visiting www.michaelconnelly.com